LESSONS IN LOVE:1989

SJ Michael

Copyright © 2024 SJ Michael
All rights reserved.

AUTHOR'S NOTE

As you progress through this novel, you will encounter attitudes, language, and scenarios that reflect the social norms and cultural context of the late 1980s. Some of this content may jar with modern sensibilities, as it represents a time when specific perspectives and behaviours were commonplace but are now viewed differently.

I have strived to portray this era authentically, with the confidence that you, the reader, will understand the importance of historical context in storytelling. My aim is not to offend but to depict the challenges and triumphs the characters face honestly in their pursuit of identity, love, and acceptance.

Thank you for your understanding and for joining me on this nostalgic journey through the highs and lows of adolescence in 1989.

PART 1

Make it Big!

WEDNESDAY 4TH JANUARY

This isn't a diary; it's a document. I tried keeping one of the former in early 1988, and when it came to reading it over, I began to loathe myself after only the third page. If the universe is indifferent to you, it won't change its mind just because you spend every evening moaning about life in barely legible scribble.

The start of the year seems to be the ideal time to adopt a new approach, and as such, starting tomorrow, I'm going to give this one existence everything that I've got and record what happens here. This process will be more straightforward thanks to the new, albeit cheap, computer waiting for me under the Christmas tree last week.

I'm some way into my seventeenth year, and it seems such a long time since the puberty fairy paid me her night-time visit, waved her magic wand, and flicked the switch on my dormant love organs to active. Since then, in the game of love, I've yet to leave the sub's bench. There was one night of kissing, but the memory can make me ache with embarrassment, so let's not go there, OK?

I'm starting to feel a little overwhelmed by it all; however, if I've learned just one thing in this short life, it's this: Mother Nature makes the rules, not us. As such, there's only one way to deal with this problem–head-on. Besides, it's not that *it* isn't happening out there, as my school is awash with sex; it's just not happening to me. Aside from the s-word from the first bell to the last, I hear about little else.

So debauched was the year four Christmas disco that an outright ban has been imposed on any such future event. Sorry, just for clarification, *for some*, the event was debauched; however, *for me*, the evening involved nothing more exciting than drinking two cans of weak lager behind the school gym with my friend Drake. The modest effects of which wore off soon enough, and the evening rapidly descended into tedium thereafter.

In short, it's time to get in the game. As such, I have devised a four-point action plan for the year:

Get the look! I've been told I have a handsome face but still carry some puppy fat. Judging by the coupling habits I've observed in my year group, the search for the ideal mate starts with an assessment from the neck down. I haven't got a specific diet plan - I'm just limiting myself to no more than 1500 calories a day, and I won't stop until my body looks like Prince's does on the *Lovesexy* cover. In addition, I'm going to do a lot more exercise. I invested £20 of Christmas money in a second-hand racing bike, which I took out for the first time earlier today. So far, so good, as I'm 2 lbs lighter than I was on New Year's Day.

Get rich! I'll be honest; I'm writing this in a household, which is the textbook definition of modest circumstances. My allowance is OK, but that's all spent on music, library fines, and, when the occasion permits, alcohol. Girls are attracted to guys who wear cool clothes and have the funds to take them out. Jobs for 16-year-olds are thin on the ground around here. Scratch that; *jobs* are thin on the ground in the Northeast of England, so I'm starting a business as paid employment is an unlikely prospect.

Raise my profile! It's not like I'm a ghost at school; people know who I am, but I'm rarely headline news. I'm captain of a sports team that generates near-zero interest, and even my frequent run-ins with the school authorities somehow seem to fail to register as noteworthy with the kids in my year. Things will change this year, and I'm auditioning for the leading part.

Be cool! I am a smart mouth, the archetypal classroom clown; however, if amusing your schoolmates brought genuine female attention, then I'd be our school's very own Casanova, but if you've been paying attention so far, you'll know that's not the case. Also, I'm hopelessly out of step with the fashions of the age. House music is all the rage, but I listen to Prince and Frank Sinatra, neither of whom the other kids consider even remotely hip. The fashion for boys is to let your hair grow long, but I style mine like Eddie Cochran on the recommendation of my ex-Teddy Boy barber, Ray. *Christ*, I even still watch *Dr Who*. In short, I am as far from being cool as it's possible to get. However, I'm reliably informed, even by teachers who hate my guts, that I'm a bright kid and, as such, I'm sure I'll figure something out.

Now, this plan is undeniably self-centred. However, I have it on reliable account that this *is* the age of the individual.

School starts tomorrow, so I'm heading to bed early. I go by the name X, by the way. I'd tell you how I got it, but it's a long story. Actually, that's not true; it's a short story- it's just *really* underwhelming.

THURSDAY 5TH JANUARY

The school day began as usual when I called for Drake at 8.30 this morning. With an ever-expanding collection of blackheads and hair that errs towards greasy, he's not exactly the best-looking of kids. However, he's enviably slim—a miracle because the boy never stops eating.

I hadn't seen him since we'd spent a particularly drunken New Year's Eve at our friend JG's house. JG is the only one of the three of us with a girlfriend. Although most of the evening remains an indistinct blur, I do retain one clear memory of Drake, for reasons best known to himself, exposing himself to JG's love, Clare, or as she will be referred to hereafter, Clare, Who Has Seen Drake's Phallus- this naming process will prove invaluable as the year proceeds as there is an overabundance of girls at school named Clare, Lisa, and Helen.

As Drake can be moody at the best times, I decided not to mention this unsavoury incident. Instead, we walked to school silently, but just before we got to the gates, I said, "Listen, Drake, come over tonight. I've got a business proposition for you."

After mulling my invite over momentarily, he shrugged in acceptance, and we headed in separate directions to our respective form groups.

Our school is divided into the old school and the new school. The old school is a stately Victorian building, formerly Marketon Grammar School, and is generally considered the place to be by pupils and teachers alike. The new school is a modern, cheaply built, former comprehensive, where the school's headmaster, Dr Harris, has exiled all his least favourite academic departments. Sixteen years ago, the Church of England united both schools under their banner. My form group is in the new school.

Form group only lasts from 8.50 to 9.10, but it can be a painfully slow 20 minutes. This is mainly due to the relatively uninspired selection of students it is comprised of

At Luther Parkinson, there are two coveted top 10 lists: one for the most attractive girls and another for the most gorgeous boys. These rankings are in constant flux, and a simple change in appearance- a bad haircut, an eruption of acne, or sudden, dramatic weight loss- can significantly impact your positioning.

Unfortunately, my name doesn't grace these lists, but I'm sure you already guessed that. Only one person in my form group, Lisa Mead, is featured in these charts.

Lisa is an over-talkative, arch-contrarian who is prone to telling me the same gossip multiple times—we'll call her Lisa the Repeater, shall we?—and the person I talk to most. She has bleached blonde hair, wears a near-constant scowl and seemingly conducts her morning makeup using a bricklayer's trowel.

In addition to Lisa, there's Stuart Moor, the school thug, who is, in my humble opinion, pound for pound, the stupidest boy in the school. Aside from these two, the only other person of interest is Driffid; he's a mungo- that's what we call goths, and, at our school, they're considered the lowest of the low- and he sits by himself most of the time, nodding his head gently whilst lost in, what I imagine to be dark thoughts.

With little else to distract me, most of my exertions during this relatively short period are put into upsetting my form tutor, Mr Crackett, who hates me. This is for a variety of reasons. Firstly, he doesn't think I'm getting the grades a 'bright kid' like me should be attaining. Secondly, on principle, I stopped playing for his school cricket team last summer. During my heated resignation speech, I *may* have told him to go and do something unspeakable with a small, domesticated mammal. Finally, and most importantly, the man can't stand the sight of me because *I know* that he's having an extra-marital affair with Miss Jacobs, the textiles teacher.

This revelation occurred last year when I dragged Drake and JG to watch *Wall Street*. The not-so-subtle illicit couple were kissing in the queue ten yards in front of us, and so, when we got into the theatre, I insisted, despite Drake and JG's protestations, that we take the seats directly behind them. Every fifteen minutes, I leant forward and politely asked Mr Crackett to explain what one of the immeasurable financial terms being used on screen meant. Eventually, with over half of the movie still to go, they got up and left, which I thought was a shame as the ending really gave the film its moral bearings.

He's a large-framed, stocky man with a balding head and a ginger beard, and yes, Miss Jacobs *is* a little on the long-sighted side.

I drew a rude sketch on the blackboard to amuse my classmates as we awaited Mr Crackett's predictably tardy arrival. The rest of the form group had just ceased sniggering at my artwork when he entered.

"Good morning, 4F," he said brightly.

Everyone ignored him.

"I trust you all had a good Christmas break?"

Everyone continued to ignore him.

"A year four-only assembly has been called this morning at nine, and so, as soon as I've finished taking the register, you are to make your way to the old school hall," he said, as he briefly scanned us, his charges.

There was a murmur of interest.

"Are we to expect an announcement of import, sir?" I asked. Admittedly, it's an archaic term, but I believe certain words and phrases should be preserved.

"As a matter of fact, X, you are." As he answered my question, his eyes caught sight of my drawing. Despite glowering slightly, though, he did not comment on it.

Mr Crackett's insistence on dutifully calling the register daily would make for a dry experience if it weren't for the fact that, ever since his conversion to mungoism a year ago, Driffid refuses to answer to anything other than his adopted nickname. Mr Crackett, meanwhile, refuses to address him by anything other than his real name. We watch a war of attrition fought out every day of the week between them.

"Martin Peters?" My form tutor said, staring directly at Driffid, "Martin Peters?"

"Sir," I chimed in. "He's made it clear that he likes to be called Driffid, and he's sat right there; please mark him as present—some of us have an assembly to get to. Besides, you don't call me by my real name."

"Stay out of it, X," he said, pointing at me with the eraser end of his pencil.

"Martin Peters? Martin Peters?" Eventually, he ceased and reluctantly placed one final tick in the register. "I don't know," he said, looking at Driffid in disgust. "You're named after a goal scorer in the '66 World Cup Final, yet you refuse to answer. If I had my way, you'd be hung for treason."

Driffid's ghostly white face stared blankly back at Mr Crackett before he flicked his long, dyed-black hair nonchalantly to celebrate his first victory of the new year.

"Right, everyone except X, off you get to assembly," Mr Crackett said dispassionately.

The rest of the form shuffled out while I remained seated. When the door finally closed, Mr C said, "Take the board rubber and wipe it off, X." and indicated my biologically inaccurate sketch on the blackboard.

With mock outrage, I replied, "I sincerely hope you don't think *I'm* responsible for that obscenity, sir."

"Please don't waste both of our time, X," Mr Crackett said disdainfully.

"I wouldn't dream of it, sir."

Mr Crackett studied the drawing on the board and then returned his attention to me. "Ironic, isn't it?" he said, grinning inanely.

"What's that, sir?" I asked with feigned curiosity.

"A big fat penis drawn by a... " he patted his stomach, "big fat penis."

"Actually, sir, it may interest you that I'm presently on a diet."

"Oh, really?" he asked with genuine curiosity. "Which one?"

Proudly, I replied, "It's not a specific diet plan as such. I'm just limiting myself to 1500 calories a day, and I'm not going to stop until my body looks like Prince's does on the *Lovesexy* cover."

Mr Crackett sneered, "*Dickhead*," and I'm 85% certain that the insult was aimed at Prince and not at me. "Anyway, *imbecile*," he continued, and that one *was* meant for me: "are you going to wipe it off the board or are we going to stay here all day?"

Starting to tire of our first clash of the year, I sighed and said, "You know, sir, it's a shame you didn't catch the last part of

Wall Street as *I* think the ending really gives the film its moral bearings,"

Mr Crackett's face reddened, and his teeth were clenched.

"May I join the others in assembly?" I asked smugly, as he appeared to have no reply.

Rather meekly, he indicated to the door with his finger.

When I reached the old school hall, the assembly had begun, and Dr Harris, the school's headmaster, was already in full flow.

As I entered, he said brightly, "Ah, good to see you, X; take a seat quickly, my boy."

Unlike most of the school's teaching staff, Dr Harris is fond of me. Our relationship started in my first year when he taught me history and classics, and I was briefly an academic prodigy. I changed tack in the second year, and we became even closer as, ultimately, he was responsible for discipline, and I was never out of trouble.

These days, we're as friendly as ever for two main reasons. Firstly, I'm among the few students who opted to sit the classics GCSE. Secondly, I'm now the captain of the school tennis team, and that's his sport of choice.

Despite being in his early sixties, Dr Wilberforce H. Harris J.P., has kept himself from going to seed. He is tall and sleek, and his hair firmly resists greying. As always, he addressed the school in his graduation cap and gown this morning. His assemblies are usually something to look forward to, as he can always be guaranteed to say something improper. Today, however, the man was in blistering form.

"Now, as I was saying, year four," he continued, "when old school and *new school*," he always pronounces 'new school' with disdain, "were first incorporated under the Church's banner, there were high hopes that the Luther Parkinson Church of England School would prove to be a shining beacon amongst Marketon's, otherwise barely adequate, educational institutions. However, grade averages don't lie, I'm afraid, and we now find ourselves poised precariously on the slippery slope to academic oblivion. Some of this is beyond our control. The *radicals* who run the local authority have made us subject to the same rules of… " He paused to take a sip of water from the glass on his lectern, "*catchment* as the… " another sip, "*comprehensives*. This means we are no longer free to shop around for the best of the best and have to take, in certain cases especially," he paused and glared at Stuart Moor in utter disgust, "whatever comes rolling off the back of the wagon."

Dr Harris surveyed his audience and continued, "What is to be done then? Well, I'm not the type who cancels his morning paper because the news is bad; trust in that. And so, I turn to you, year four; you have been identified as *the* year group that will stop the rot. It's too late for those above you—your so-called seniors in year five are, without doubt, without question, the single most uninspired, insipid bunch of ne'er do wells ever to cast a shadow over the glorious name of our founder. We will undoubtedly slide further into the educational abyss when the GCSE results are announced in August. However, what's done is done. You are the future, year four, and you will turn this ship around. To aid you in this service to your school, I have appointed a head of year four who will guide you in this holiest of missions."

There was a murmur of interest from the assembled students.

"So, after leading you in a short prayer, I will introduce you to *Ms* James." He pronounced 'Ms' slightly resentfully and then looked to his left, and, for the first time, I noticed the attractive, stylishly coiffured and smart-suited woman who was keenly scanning the faces of her new students. "Year four, please bow your heads in prayer," Dr Harris said solemnly.

I'm a non-believer. In fact, I scored myself as a 9 on my 10-grade atheism scale. To become a grade 10, you would need to travel all of space and time and find no evidence of an interventionist, omnipresent being whatsoever. Therefore, the only person who could score a full house is Dr Who; unfortunately, he isn't real. So, when prayer is called at school, I do not close my eyes or clasp my hands, but I do bow my head, as this was the agreement reached with Dr Harris back in my second year after an afternoon of intense negotiation.

"Lord, we ask you to deliver us from mediocrity.

And please, oh Lord, spare us from yet *another* unannounced visit from the bishop.

Lord, bless the year fives with more sense than they possess presently.

And Lord, get behind the year fours, *our* chosen ones.

Please grant us good favour on the sporting field.

And more favourable LBW decisions than we got last year.

But most of all, oh Lord,

grant us your divine grace on the holy court of tennis

and allow *the* miracle to take place this year.

Amen."

As I said, *it's* his sport of choice.

The 'miracle' to which he referred is the one thing Dr Harris longs for even more than a good set of GCSE results; just once, he wants his beloved school tennis team to take to the courts and win a match.

Following the prayer, Ms James walked delicately to join Dr Harris. They whispered a few words to one another, and then the headmaster shuffled to the side of the hall.

"Good morning, year four. As Dr Harris said, my name is *Ms* James," she emphasised the word 'Ms' and gave Dr Harris a sharp, sideways glance as she did. "I am your new head of year. As you are probably aware, there have already been heads put in place for years one and three, and there is a vacancy for the year two equivalent. Having spoken to my new colleagues, I understand that they operate an 'Open door, let's sit down and talk this through, bounce a few ideas off one another, two heads are better than one' approach. I, however, will be taking a different tack, and my door is *never* to be considered open. If you wish to book an appointment to see me, then please follow *pro-to-col*," she pronounced the word slowly and deliberately, "and read the detailed instructions I have attached to the clipboard outside my office in new school. Should there be repeated violations of this procedure, then I will, soon enough, commence the operation of a *locked* door policy." She paused for a moment to allow the murmuring in the hall to subside. "Now, if I have one mantra, it is this, year four: personal choice, personal responsibility."

There was another buzz of excitement, and as I looked over at him, I saw Dr Harris roll his eyes in dismay.

Ms James continued, "What do I mean by this? Well, I encourage you *all* to make the decisions *you* feel are right. However, I would also like to state further that the consequences of these decisions are wholly *your* responsibility to resolve. Suffice to say, if I'd wished to work for a counselling service, then I'd have joined the Samaritans."

The murmuring was reaching a fever pitch now.

"Now, there are just a few more business items before I send you on your way to classes, year four. Firstly, there is a new woodwork teacher named Mr Shaver. Most of you, I imagine, have not opted to study for the woodwork GCSE; however, those of you who are... ", she smiled slightly, "—good with your hands… can look forward to meeting Mr Shaver very soon. Finally, we have a new girl in year four." The hall, particularly the male contingent, became highly animated, "named Rachael Williams. She has just relocated to Marketon from the south of England." Excited chatter was replaced by moans and jeers. "Oh, come now, year four, please don't believe everything you read in the papers; they're really not as bad as they're made out to be," Ms James said reasonably.

Her comment did little to quell the noise. Finally, she resorted to raising her voice. "Year four, *please!*"

The room fell silent again.

"Please do all you can to make your new classmate feel as welcome as possible. Finally," her face had turned severe, "is Alan Ball here?" The assembled students turned their heads towards a small mungo sitting in the front row. "Alan Ball?" she asked firmly.

Eventually, he meekly raised his arm.

"You, young man, are to report to my office immediately after this assembly… No appointment is necessary," she said, glaring at him intently. Softening her facial expression, she turned back to face her audience and said, "Right, off to classes, year four, and remember, personal choice, personal responsibility."

Maths was the day's first lesson, and we were a little taken aback when we entered the classroom. Mr Griffiths, our teacher, had rearranged the desks from ragbag pods of four, five, and six into perfectly symmetrical rows of two. I sat at the back of the class, and Rich Wilson, all-round nice guy, sat beside me.

Mr Griffith started the lesson by briefly explaining the new seating arrangement: "You are more likely to absorb mathematical information efficiently if you are positioned with geometric grace," he said before launching a piece of chalk at Mark James's head for talking in class.

At break time, I caught up with JG. My friend has cultivated a look best described as preppy. His fringe is intentionally overgrown, and he spends at least half of his waking life sweeping it from his eyes. He is pleasingly plump, mainly due to his strong opposition to all forms of physical exercise. His well-fed face can still be described accurately as cherubic, despite his ongoing journey into maturity. Today, he was concerned that Claire, Who Has Seen Drake's Phallus, had ignored him. I wasn't sure whether he was aware of Drake's deeply unpleasant stunt on New Year's Eve and, keen not to drive a wedge between my two best friends, so I said, "I wouldn't worry about it, JG. It's the first day of term, and she's probably just catching up with people. Besides, you know what women are like."

JG looked at me in bemusement and said bluntly, "X, thanks, but you know *absolutely nothing* about girls and, therefore, have no frame of reference for this situation."

You get used to this with JG, as he's very matter-of-fact and a stickler for detail.

Next, it was English, my favourite lesson for three reasons: One of my greatest passions is reading. Secondly, I sit next to Jack Parker, and we make each other laugh a lot. Finally, and most significantly, it's because of my teacher, Mrs Simpson. She is an attractive, mousy-haired late twenty-something with a penchant for the hippy style. When I hang back after lessons to discuss whatever I am reading that week, she always takes an ardent interest and is one of the few teachers in school who talks to you like an adult rather than a child.

Jack wasn't in today; he'd been lucky enough to contract a flu bug just as the holidays ended. As such, I was expecting a lesson without the usual conversational distraction when, as I looked up towards the front, I saw a new girl—scratch that, *the* new girl—looking uncertainly at the spare desk next to me.

"Just take a seat next to X, Rachael," Mrs Simpson kindly advised her and pointed towards me. "Don't worry, though, we won't make you sit next to him twice." As she said this, Mrs S gave me a wink.

The new girl smiled brightly, marched smartly to the desk beside me, and promptly sat down. We don't have many Rachaels at school. However, as the year is new and she is too, we'll call her Rachael1989.

"Hey," she said, smiling brightly at me.

Hey?

"Hello," I replied carefully.

"Why do they call you X?" she asked genuinely.

"It's a long story," I said. "Actually, that's not true; it's a short story; it's just *really* underwhelming."

Sincerely, she replied, "Oh, I like it, though. It really suits you."

Rachael Williams is pretty; there's no denying it. Top 10 pretty. However, there's something different about her. Most of the girls I fancy wear as much make-up as they can get away with, skirts that seem to get shorter as the day goes on, and, for every year they progress in school, they appear to undo another button on their blouses. Rachael, meanwhile, had her brunette locks fixed back in a tight ponytail; her petite features bore no trace of make-up, and she was the only girl I'd seen that day who was dressed in line with official school policy. What really got me about Luther Parkinson's latest addition, though, were her eyes— big, brown, and distractingly beautiful.

"How's the first day treating you?" I asked, attempting to have a polite conversation.

She sighed deeply and replied, "Oh, my God, I'm *so* stressed!"

I nodded in understanding. "I'm not surprised; through no fault of your own, you've been uprooted from your previous place of study and thrust into a new and, no doubt, intimidating environment where you have yet to find your feet. In addition, you are from down south, we are up north, and there's naturally going to be mutual suspicions on either side,"

Rachael1989 studied me intently. "That's very empathetic of you, X."

I was unsure what empathy meant then, so I smiled back at the new girl and resolved to look the word up later. She, however, continued to gaze at me. Eventually, she blinked and asked, "Is it true that Luther Parkinson was the Bishop of Rugham?"

"Oh, yeah," I said. "Old Luther holds the record."

"For what?" she asked curiously.

I promptly replied, "He spent the shortest time on the job; he choked on a pineapple cube just two hours after his confirmation."

Rachael burst out laughing. "That's funny, X!"

My face remained impassive, however.

"Really?" she asked, her look turning grave.

"*Lovebirds*, excuse me, *lovebirds*." It was Mrs Simpson. "Sorry to interrupt, but I have just two words for both of you: *store cupboard*. Twenty-three copies of *Pygmalion*, please."

I dutifully led the new girl to the English cupboard, secluded at the far end of the corridor.

"Mrs Simpson seems nice," Rachael remarked as I searched the shelves for the required texts.

"Favourite teacher, well, her and Dr Harris," I replied distractedly.

"Oh, I've got him for classics," she said enthusiastically.

I was genuinely stunned. "You opted for classics? Wow! That makes… " I counted in my head. "Seven of us."

"Well, it'll be nice to know someone in the class," Rachael said warmly.

I smiled. "Oh yes, you've got the famous Friday afternoon shift to look forward to. A warning in advance, though, if you want to pass the GCSE, you'll need to learn it all yourself, as we rarely cover anything related to the syllabus in class."

"Hey," she said as I found the battered copies of *Pygmalion*, "we better get back, or people might start to talk."

I shook my head and said, "No, they won't; I know nothing about girls, so if you're looking to be gossiped about, I strongly recommend you visit the store cupboard with another boy."

She laughed as I handed her half of the pile of books. "I like you, X; I'm glad we sit together."

I was about to correct her but thought better. "Thanks, but I'm sure it won't last."

And sure enough, *it* didn't.

On the way back to the class, I quizzed her about why she had moved to the town. "So, as *nobody* relocates to Marketon voluntarily, then I'm guessing it had something to do with your father's job?" I asked.

"Actually, X, I don't like talking about my dad," Rachael replied curtly.

We'd reached the door to the classroom, and I dutifully held it open for her. "Why don't you two see eye to eye?"

With that, she threw all the books she was carrying on the floor and screamed, "If you must know, X, *he's dead!*"

"Oh!" began forming on my lips as she shrieked and ran away along the corridor. Mrs Simpson and the rest of the class stared at me as if I'd physically assaulted the girl. All I could think of doing was shrugging my shoulders in astonishment. And there we have it, just three hours into the new school term, and my stock had never traded so cheaply—as I've already said, I've seen *Wall Street*.

Stuart Moor stopped by my table at lunch to congratulate me on making the new girl cry.

"I didn't mean to!" I protested.

However, he patted me on the shoulder and said, "Maybe, but what's a school without traditions, X?"

Just as I was about to enter French, Alan Ball, or Ralek as he prefers to be known, walked up to me, handed me a slip, and said in his only recently broken voice, "Ms James wants to see you, X."

On arriving at the head of year's office, I gave three loud knocks on the door, allowed a polite pause, and entered. Most teachers decorate their offices with pictures of their family; Ms James only has images of herself. There's one of her being awarded her degree, one of her standing atop a snowy mountain peak, and one of her scuba diving in deliciously blue ocean waters somewhere exotic. In addition, I noted that there are only three books on her shelf. The same title in different editions, *Atlas Shrugged* by Ayn Rand. On the wall behind her desk was a plaque.

YOU ARE MOST WELCOME HERE WITH SOLUTIONS, *NOT* PROBLEMS!

She was sitting at her desk, scribbling away in a notebook, and paying me no attention.

I gave a slight cough and said, "Good afternoon, Ms. My name is X; I believe you wanted to see me." Ms. James continued to ignore me. Eventually, I asked, "I can come back at another time if you are busy."

Without looking up, she indicated with her pen the plaque behind her and then returned to scribbling.

I reread the sign and began to understand our game. "Excuse me, Ms. You sent for me because I upset the new girl in English this morning."

"Correct, go on," she said without looking up.

"Though my line of questioning was in no way meant to cause any distress, I was insensitive to a girl who, through no fault of her own, has been uprooted from her previous place of study and thrust into a new and, no doubt, intimidating environment where she has yet to find her feet. In addition, she is from down south; we are up north, and there will naturally be mutual suspicions on either side. Also, it turns out her father recently died, something I was unaware of," I said formally.

"Died three years ago, actually," Ms James said absently.

"Really? Then why... " I began.

Ms James finally ceased writing, put down her pencil ,and gave me her full attention. "If there is but one eternal truth in this godforsaken world, X, it is this: when someone under the age of 18 loses a parent, they will repeatedly pull that ace out of the deck from now until kingdom comes. It's a defence mechanism, a sword, and a shield. Employed in times of high stress."

"Right, Ms," I said, quite uncertain whether and how I should respond.

The head of year continued, "Besides this character flaw, I'm rather fond of the girl; at this very moment, I'd say she is my favourite pupil in the school by some measure." Ms James said it thoughtfully.

Curiously, I felt jealous. "Bit early in the game for that, isn't it, Ms?"

She smiled. "Go in *hard* with the first challenge, X; let them know you mean business. There's no point in hogging the sidelines like a pansy waiting for the ball to break. That's *my* motto."

I laughed. "Very good, Ms; I've had similar thoughts lately."

The new head of year studied me intently. "Have you really?" I nodded enthusiastically. "Hmm," she said, appraising me. Eventually, she added, "Is there anything else you have to say today, X?"

I was a little perplexed, so I punted, "Perhaps you've also been informed that I drew a gigantic cock on the black… "

Ms James' face soured. "*Please* don't use that language in this office, X," she said with disdain.

"I apologise… a large penis on the blackboard in form group this morning," I said, correcting myself quickly.

She waved her hand dismissively. "I have not been informed; therefore, it is not part of my job; *ergo*, I do not care. Though I would here express a mild disappointment that a bright boy like you cannot develop a more imaginative way of tormenting his form tutor."

"Point taken, Ms. I'll give it some thought," I replied.

Smiling politely, she said, "Thank you, X. Now, unless you know any good magic tricks, I would be most pleased if you would leave this office with the maximum possible haste."

"Yes, Ms"

I have to say this new self-disciplinary system is remarkably efficient; a trip to Dr Harris' office can quickly drain an admittedly entertaining hour from your day and much longer should you happen to be summoned there during Wimbledon fortnight.

After much cajoling, Drake is now on board with the painting business; it wasn't, as always with him, a straightforward process, however. I'd carefully laid out everything we'd require in the garage for him; most of it was my dad's, who'd said we could use what we wanted, but I was particularly proud of my first purchases for the enterprise.

"I don't get it, X; why must we wear white dungarees?" Drake said, looking at the crisp new overalls in puzzlement.

Frustrated, I sighed, "Because that's what painters wear, Drake. If we turn up in our school uniform, people will laugh in our faces. Besides, I paid five quid for them, you ungrateful sod."

"What about the other stuff we need?" Drake asked, clearly oblivious to his surroundings.

I waved my arm, indicating the materials I'd laid out. "Take a look around, Drake. Brushes, *check;* rollers, *check;* step ladder, *check;* sheets to stop the paint from going everywhere; *check;* white spirits, *check.* Everything we need is right here."

"I don't know, X; I've only done a little bit of painting before; I'm not sure I'm good enough," Drake said uncertainly.

"*Jesus Christ, Drake*, all *you've* got to do is the walls; *I'll* do the gloss work; that's the difficult part," I implored.

Drake frowned. "And whom the hell is going to pay two kids

to paint their house anyway?"

I smiled. "Fear not, my friend; we have a unique entry to the marketplace."

"Yeah, what's that?"

"We're the cheapest in town!" I said it theatrically. "People around here don't have much cash, so they get their painting done for a bargain, and we get to earn way more money than the average 15-year-old."

His head, finally, was slowly starting to nod with a sense of understanding.

"What's more, Mr Roberts lives four doors down and runs a painting business," I said smugly.

Drake shrugged. "And?"

"*And* every day, he's out there fishing for business. Guess what he does when he catches a big fish?" I said, acting out the scene with an imaginary rod.

"Keeps it?" Drake answered.

"That's right, Drake!" I said dramatically; I was starting to enjoy this now. "Guess what he does with the little fish?"

"Throws 'em back?" he replied.

"He did," my eyes widened, "now he throws them to us."

Drake nodded, and I could tell he was impressed. His face frowned again, though. "Why would he do that?"

Casually, I replied, "Oh, I agreed to babysit for him."

"*What?*" Drake asked incredulously and then laughed. "You don't know the first thing about kids, X."

"Ok," I said defensively, "but I'm bright, and I'll learn as I go." Drake was still laughing, though. "And I'll tell you another thing," I added. "Every hour I do spend looking after the gruesome twosome, counts as painting hours."

Drake rolled his eyes. "*See*, I knew this would happen, X. It starts off sounding OK, but then you come with your conditions."

"All right," I said, interrupting him, "you bloody babysit, and I'll do the painting because he bites that little sod down there, the two-year-old. I've seen him, Drake. The little swine will take a chunk out of your arm when you take your eyes off him."

Drake was suddenly lost in contemplation. "How much then?"

Finally seeing him in my crosshairs, I said concisely, "Minimum of £2.50 an hour, plus a monthly bonus if we make anything on the materials cost."

He was impressed. "OK, I'm in," he said.

"Good man!" I said and seized his hand.

As he was leaving, he asked, "What's got into that girlfriend of JG's? Every time I saw her today, she giggled at me."

"*Oh*, you showed her your cock on New Year's Eve," I advised him casually.

Drake rolled his eyes. "Jesus, X, that's a really sick thing to say. You're *not* funny!"

With Drake on board, the painting business can move to phase two. I slightly regret the incident with Rachael1989, however. When a new person joins the school, they are usually very quickly assimilated into one social grouping or another, and I don't even get a look in. Still, she's a little highly strung, so maybe it's best never to sit next to one another in class again.

One final piece of good news has sent the day into positive territory: I just got off the scales and am another pound lighter.

FRIDAY 6TH JANUARY

Biology is a lesson to look forward to. Firstly, it is a subject that interests me immensely. Secondly, it is the only class I have with Clare Parkin, the second most gorgeous girl in the school—we'll call her Clare Anatomy. I sit at a table with three other boys, but I take the trip over to her table at every opportunity and do my best to amuse her. Our relationship is strictly one of owner and pet, though, and when she tires of me, she soon indicates her displeasure and sends me back to my basket with my tail between my legs.

Having been deprived of the many delights of Clare's company these past two weeks, I was elated at the prospect of spending some precious moments in her magnetic presence. However, my heart sank when I entered the lab this morning and saw Rachael1989 sitting at her table. To make matters worse, Clare and Rachael spent half the lesson gossiping intently while regularly looking in my direction. As a result, I decided to forego my usual pilgrimage.

Fortunately, the new topic, genetics, proved to be a worthy distraction, and I will be reading further on the subject in the coming weeks.

The third lesson of the day was English, and I was relieved to see that Jack was back, even though he was quite repulsively blowing his nose into a snot-logged tissue. As I took my usual seat, in a voice several octaves lower than his norm, he asked, "I hear you made the new girl cry, X?"

"I *didn't* mean to," I replied.

"Maybe, but what's a school without traditions, X?" Jack said and sniffed loudly.

At that moment, Rachael1989 entered the room, looked straight at us, and marched purposely towards our desks. She didn't say a word but stood before Jack, glaring at him with her arms folded tightly across her chest.

"This is my desk; I sit next to X," Jack said defensively after blowing his nose.

Rachael didn't reply; she fixed her gaze on him and commenced tapping her foot impatiently.

"X, tell her this is my desk," he said, looking at me helplessly.

However, wary of Rachael's somewhat uneven temperament and mindful not to cause a repetition of yesterday's drama, I, rather meekly, just shrugged my shoulders in response.

"*Fine*," Jack said to her, "I'll sit by myself at the back, should I? Catch you later, X."

Rachael1989 smiled demurely at Jack's retreat, and as soon as he vacated the chair, she neatly took her place next to me.

"Jack and I sit together; it's one of the reasons English is my favourite class," I said, but Rachael1989 ignored me. "Look, I'm sorry if I upset you yesterday; I didn't mean to, but yesterday's seating arrangement was an interim measure as Jack was off sick, and you were new. Mrs Simpson said as much herself. Can I *please* have my friend back?"

Rachael1989 continued to ignore me.

"Hello," I said in desperation, "can you even hear me?"

Rachael sighed irritably, opened her bag, withdrew a pad of Post-it notes and a pen, and commenced writing. Upon completion, she slapped the notice down upon my desk; it read, "I AM NOT SPEAKING TO YOU!"

"As I've said, I'm sorry if I upset you yesterday; I honestly didn't mean to," I said sincerely.

Rachael ignored me.

Eventually, in frustration, I grabbed the pad of Post-it notes, and wrote, "I AM SORRY!" and stuck the message down in front of her.

Rachael smiled ever so slightly, took the pad back, and wrote again, "APOLOGY ACCEPTED, BUT I AM STILL NOT TALKING TO YOU."

I replied, "WHY DO YOU WANT TO SIT NEXT TO SOMEONE YOU ARE NOT SPEAKING TO?"

She replied, "I SIT HERE. YOU SIT THERE!"

I decided to be clever, "TECHNICALLY, WE ARE SPEAKING, BY THE WAY."

She responded, "WE ARE COMMUNICATING, BUT WE ARE NOT SPEAKING."

Rachael was right, and this irked me somewhat. She wrote another message: "IN FUTURE, PLEASE PROVIDE POST-IT NOTES YOURSELF."

And that was that—we did not speak *or* communicate another word for the rest of the lesson.

I didn't find JG or Drake during lunch and was making my way to French when a year three girl called Mary stepped in front of me, saying, "Hey, X, Dr Harris wants to see you."

Hey?

"I haven't done anything wrong," I said defensively.

Mary smiled pleasantly. "Dr Harris said you'd say that and asked me to relay to you that the invite is entirely social."

"OK, thanks, Mary."

I hate French, and I'm no good at it, so I wasn't exactly put out by the headmaster's summons.

Dr Harris' secretary is well-used to my visits. So frequently do I sit opposite her in the area outside the headmaster's study that I've come to learn the names and ages of all her children, her hobbies and interests, and all the twists and turns of her somewhat precarious marriage. As I entered, I said, "Hi, Rosie."

"Hey, X," she replied.

Blimey, when something spreads around this school, it spreads fast.

"Good Christmas?" I asked.

"Not really," she replied. "He's drinking again."

"I'm sorry to hear that," I said sincerely.

"Yeah, me too, X, but what will I do?"

I was 80% sure that she intended the question to be rhetorical, so I remained silent.

"Just go in, X; he's ready for you," the secretary said politely.

"Thanks, Rosie," I replied as I knocked on the door.

"Come in!" the headmaster barked.

Dr Harris had, as always, racket in hand and was practising a tennis stroke—today, it was the turn of the forehand volley. "Ah, X, good to see you, my boy. Not keeping you from anything; am I?" He asked keenly.

"Only classes, sir," I replied dryly.

Dr Harris failed to recognise my sarcasm, and instead, he fixed me with an eager stare. "Have you met him yet?"

"Met whom, sir?" I inquired.

"Jacobs, the new boy, recruited him just for you," he said

enthusiastically.

I had *no* idea what he was talking about.

The head's face was a mix of frustration and dismay. "Oh, good God, man, I told him to make his introductions to you."

"In that case, sir, I believe he has yet to," I replied.

"Good heavens, if you want something done in this ruddy place, you've got to do it yourself," he said, opening the door. "Rosie, fetch Jacobs in year three, quick as you can now, woman."

I heard Rosie's acknowledgement of the request before Dr Harris closed the door again and returned to practising his tennis. "Matthew Jacobs, fourteen, *damn* good player." Dr Harris paused in his practice momentarily and held up his hand apologetically. "Not as good as you, X, I'll grant you, but a strong signing regardless—he'll be your two."

"What about Wilkins, sir?" Dr Harris always refers to people by their surnames, and so, in his presence, I do too.

"What's that, 'Wilkins', you say? He'll be sitting exams when the season is in full swing—though, to no avail, I imagine, eh, X?" Dr Harris said and sneered. "Besides, we don't want any year fives on the team; they're an unseemly breed for sure, X, and I'll be glad when June rolls around, and they become the rest of the world's problem rather than mine."

"How did you come across... Jacobs, sir?" I asked with interest.

"Oh, good question, X, at the club, obviously. I got on friendly terms with his parents a few months back, and then it came to light that he'd fallen in with the wrong crowd at Marketon High and had been caught taking a ride on the magic roundabout, if you get my meaning, X?" Dr Harris asked with a wink.

I was 90% certain I did, so I allowed him to continue.

"So, his parents were planning to bite the financial bullet, as it were, and ship young Jacobs off to a private school for his last two years when I stepped in."

"Stepped in, sir?" I asked.

Dr Harris smiled. "Stepped in, that's right, X, that's exactly what I did. I told them that the Luther Parkinson Church of England School could offer strong moral guidance, a minimum of four hours of sport a week, and a considerably lower incidence of buggery than your average private school, and guess what, X?"

"He's here, sir?" I asked.

There was a knock at the door.

"He *is* here, X. *Come in!*" Dr Harris yelled.

A handsome, neatly attired, blonde-haired youth entered the office. "You wish to see me, sir?" he politely asked.

"Ah, yes, come in, Jacobs," Dr Harris said as the boy stepped into the office and gently closed the door behind him. "Jacobs, this is X. X, this is Matthew Jacobs." I shook the younger boy's hand firmly. "Now, Jacobs, X is the tennis team captain this year, and so, as far as you're concerned, that puts him two rungs down the ladder from the Lord God Almighty and just one rung down from me, is that clear?" Dr Harris asked intently.

"Crystal, sir," the boy said obediently.

Matthew continued to look at the headmaster as if he expected him to say more, though Dr Harris looked back at him blankly. "Well, Jacobs, get along with you now. Two break periods and a lunch hour are not sufficient, eh?" the head said and smirked again.

"I'll be getting back then, sir. It's good to meet you, Captain." We shook hands again, and Matthew left.

"Good recruit, eh, X?" the headmaster asked after the door had closed.

"Excellent, sir," I replied politely.

"Anyway, speaking of the club, X didn't see you there over Christmas," Dr Harris said suspiciously.

"I did get a couple of games in, sir," I lied.

"Really?" he asked with interest. "How's the form?"

"Not bad for winter," I said after contemplating.

Dr Harris nodded. "Well, we don't want you peaking too soon now, do we?"

"Also, sir, I've taken up cycling and am on a diet," I added.

"Anything that gets you around that court quicker gets my backing, X," Dr Harris said positively. "I'll have a word with the head cook and make sure you don't get charged for anything green you buy from the canteen."

Gratefully, I replied, "Most kind, sir."

I was beginning to think our appointment was coming to an end when Dr Harris ceased his tennis practice and asked carefully, "Day and a half into the new term, X, so I'm guessing, going on your previous form, that you've already paid a visit to the new woman."

"James, sir?" I asked.

"Spot on, X, *James*," Dr Harris said with a wink.

"I have, sir."

With mild concern, he asked, "What did you do, X?"

"Oh, I made the new girl cry on her first day, sir, but I didn't mean to," I said honestly.

He waved his hand dismissively. "Well, X, what's a school without traditions, eh? Anyway, what do you think of her?"

For some reason, I couldn't help but smile. "The new girl? Actually, sir, she's a bit of an enigma—"

The head looked at me in bewilderment. "Not the new girl, man, *James!*"

Holding my hand up in apology for my faux pas, I said, "Ah, I see. Early days, sir, though she certainly has a new approach."

"What's that, 'new approach', you say?" Dr Harris asked with interest.

"Yes, sir,"

The head looked slightly alarmed. "Well, that's rarely a good thing, X. If you ask me, the woman's a nutter, a right-wing ideologue on an atheist recruitment drive. I'm pretty certain she's only here to drive the spirit of Jesus Christ right out of the building," he said disapprovingly.

Curiously, I asked, "May I enquire why she got the job then, sir?"

Dr Harris leant forward. "Of course, *you* can, X. She won the board of governors over with her tricky newspeak, that's how. If you ask me, my boy, there's something of the enchantress about the woman. I see it in her eyes when she's in this office, X; I reckon she's got her heart set on the big one."

Oh, Christ, I hope that wasn't a sex reference.

Perhaps my face *had* registered some alarm, as Dr Harris quickly added, "And when I say big one, I mean big job, *my* job, to be precise. Can you imagine that, my boy?"

In truth, I'd prefer to imagine that rather than the other thing.

"I've set her up in the new school with the rest of the dross, so if she plans a coup, good luck raising an army over there, eh?" Dr Harris added wickedly.

A little dejectedly, I said, "My form group is in new school, sir."

"Is it? Oh well, get me the win this year, and I'll soon despatch the boat service and bring you back to dry land," the head said reassuringly.

I smiled. "Thank you, sir."

"Anyway, X, I would like you to keep an eye on her if you get my meaning," the headmaster said conspiratorially.

"Sir?" I asked, a little taken aback by the request.

Sensing my discomfort, Dr Harris reassured me. "Nothing indiscreet, of course; just let me know if you see anything… improper."

"Improper, sir?" I asked for clarification.

Dr Harris beamed. "*That's* the ticket, X; I knew I could count on you. You see, you're not just my favourite pupil because you're sent to me with the regularity of the local paper, you know? Anyway, I suppose you'll want to be heading off for the weekend?"

"Only ten past two, sir," I said after checking the clock on his wall. "There is another lesson to go yet—your classics lesson, to be precise."

"What's that, 'classics', you say?" he asked, looking somewhat disgruntled. Checking his watch, he said, "No chance of getting a supply teacher on such short notice." I imagine he was thinking aloud. "Well, run along, X, and I'll see you shortly."

As I've already mentioned, classics is far from being an oversubscribed class and, despite lessons taking place in a small room on the second floor of old school, there is still an abundance of spare desks, and we, the class, are in the habit of sitting apart in randomly selected seats. Having failed to return for the end of my French lesson, I arrived first, followed by Rachael1989.

Upon entering, she looked at me, smiled, and said, "Hey, X." The new girl then proceeded to sit three desks from me.

"I thought we weren't talking." I enquired delicately.

Without altering her gaze, Rachael answered with a sigh, "We weren't."

"But now we are?" I asked expectantly.

"Obviously," she replied flatly.

To engage her in further conversation, I said, "Ms James is a big fan of yours."

Without looking at me, Rachael replied, "She said the *new* girls should stick together."

Next to enter was Dr. Harris. "Ah, X. It's good to see you, my boy. And?" He stared at Rachael in consternation.

"Rachael Williams, sir, new girl," she said brightly.

"Well," he said. "I've got just two words for the pair of you: *store cupboard.*"

Dr Harris had sent us on a mission to locate seven copies of an abridged version of *The Odyssey* in the storeroom classics shares with history on the floor below. "Two trips to the store cupboard in two days; people will talk now," Rachael1989 said, smiling as I scanned the shelves for the required texts.

"Not in classics; they won't," I replied with a slight scoff.

"What makes you say that?" Rachael said as she casually started to peruse the shelves.

While continuing to search, I replied, "I'm almost certain our classmates don't concern themselves with such matters. You see, the other kids are not here because they have any deep love of the subject, nor are they there purely to gain the good grace of Dr Harris. Rather, they are there simply because they think it will look good on their university application forms. People like that are so well ordered and so precise in their planning that any thought of underage sex would be a heresy. They will put it off to some more appropriate point in the future, when, no doubt, they will agree to do it with another like-minded individual and only then to ensure that it does not become a gnawing distraction from their academic success."

"Well," Rachael said passionately. "*I* have a deep love of the subject," and I was about to explain my rationale for opting for the school's most undersubscribed GCSE when Rachael added, "You're different, X."

"I have been informed so previously," I assured her. "Anyway," I continued, "you must excuse me as I intend to remain silent for the rest of this exercise."

"Why?" she asked.

I looked at my companion and said, "Because, Rachael, if I manage to get back to the classroom without making you cry, I may be able to count this day as a success."

"*Well*, you could just try saying something nice to me, X," she suggested a little frostily.

Without thinking first, I said, "OK, in that case, you have beautiful eyes."

Did I say that out loud?

Obviously, I had, as Rachael was now smiling at me.

Her smile is out of pure politeness. X, really, she thinks you're a sex maniac now.

"Sorry!" I said. "Sometimes my mouth and brain work independently," and my face reddened rapidly.

"Don't be embarrassed, X; that was a lovely thing to say," Rachael said kindly.

"I...err." The words were refusing to come.

JG's right; I'm hopeless with girls.

There was a somewhat awkward pause, after which, thankfully, Rachael1989 changed the subject. "Is *The Odyssey* even a required text?"

"No, but as I have already warned you, very little we do in classics is related to the syllabus. In that sense, it's a very refreshing class," I said, relieved to be off the subject of my yet-to-be-defined feelings towards the new girl. Rachael was staring at me intently once more, and I continued, "There is a textbook, which, I'm reliably assured, contains everything you need to know to get you through the exam. I have a copy; I can give you the name or—" I didn't get the chance to finish my sentence.

"You could bring it over!" she suggested.

"Pardon me?"

"You could bring it to my house!" she said excitedly.

There is a phrase, 'blowing hot and cold', which, after today, I am more in tune with its meaning than was previously the case.

I proceeded with caution, mindful not to incur a repeat of yesterday's incident. "I *could* bring it over to your house, I *suppose*," I said carefully.

"*When?*" she demanded to know.

"Err... Wednesday?" I suggested it uncertainly.

"Date!" she said enthusiastically, clapping her hands in delight.

I was about to start a hopefully brief, semantic discussion on the word 'date', but I thought better of it and said, "I can't find any copies of *The Odyssey* in here; come on, let's go back."

The rest of the class was seated when we returned, and Dr Harris lectured them on the merits of Boris Becker's tennis service: "—and speaking of the holy game, here's Luther Parkinson's very own miracle man himself. Have you had any luck with the books X and New Girl?"

"Sorry, sir, there are no copies of *The Odyssey* that I could find," I replied.

"Never mind, X; I'm sure you did your best. Right, class, some light-fingered, good-for-nothing has made off with the goods, I'm afraid. However, I'm not the type of man who closes the fishmongers just because the trawler sank; trust in that. We will manage a lesson without it, and you can each buy a copy for next week. I should add that anyone struggling with this provision should request the appropriate form from Rosie. However, before doing so, please remember that the school is bankrupt for all intents and purposes. *Right*, what can any of you tell me about *The Odyssey*? X?" Dr Harris asked and looked at me expectantly.

"One of the major Greek poems, sir, generally attributed to Homer," I said confidently.

Looking at the rest of the class, Dr Harris asked, "Excellent, X, excellent. Is there anyone else?"

Rachael1989 politely raised her hand.

"Yes, New Girl?" he asked enthusiastically.

"It tells the story of Odysseus as he returns from the fall of Troy, sir," she answered.

The headmaster clapped his hands in delight. "Excellent, New Girl, excellent, cross-court forehand, right back at you, X, what are you going to do about that?"

"Odysseus intends to return to his home in Ithaca, sir." I was hoping this wouldn't be a long, drawn-out rally, as my knowledge of the text stretches to a page I've read about it in an encyclopaedia.

Dr Harris turned to Rachael. "Excellent, X, forehand return

to you, New Girl; what's your next shot?"

"The journey takes ten years, sir, and he's presumed dead," Rachael looked over at me and smiled.

Dr Harris beamed delightfully. "Well done, New Girl; tricky backhand slice over to you, X."

"He is protected by the goddess Athena, sir," I answered, and smiled smugly back at Rachael.

"Good, X, good, forehand whip, back to you, New Girl."

Rachael looked very much at ease. "His wife, Penelope, awaits his return in Ithaca and is bombarded with requests by potential suitors."

"Brilliant, lob to the back of the court, X," Dr Harris said gleefully.

"The Lotus Eaters snare him and his men," I replied.

Dr Harris desisted with the commentary, turned sharply to Rachael1989, and looked at her expectantly.

"He is captured by and eventually defeats the Cyclops, sir."

Back to me. "The god Poseidon despises him."

Over to Rachael. "His ship is wrecked when they approach the Island of the Sirens."

Shit! That was my last fact!

Dr Harris looked at me in anticipation. "X, backhand drop shot. Are you brave enough to make it?" He desperately tried to coax an answer from my mouth with his hands.

Humbly, I said, "Sorry, sir, I think I'm out."

"Game to the new girl." Dr Harris looked at Rachael for assistance.

"Williams, sir," Rachael replied smugly. "Rachael Williams."

I spent the rest of the lesson in a deep funk.

As the bell went, I began slowly packing my things away. Before leaving, Rachael smiled and said, "See you next week, X."

Meekly, I smiled back at her.

JG called tonight, heartbroken. Clare, Who Has Seen Drake's Phallus, has dumped him. I offered the rather lame advice "Give her time," before eventually suggesting, "Hey, why don't we go to the arts centre and watch a film on Sunday night. It might help to take your mind off things."

JG accented. I have no idea whether *The Last Temptation of Christ* will prove to be any form of consolation, but I'm not brave enough to go by myself, and he was clearly in too weakened a state to refuse.

Today brought mixed fortunes; being outsmarted by Rachael1989 on two occasions stung. However, I may have a 'date', though whether I actually want to attend is another matter altogether.

SATURDAY 7TH JANUARY

My parents headed off early this morning to visit my aunt. My mother has two sisters who live just four miles apart. However, they rarely speak. One of them, Auntie L, who Dad reliably informs me is a lesbian—my mother prefers the term cat-lover—is my favourite relative. Her generosity is why I am writing this document on a new computer. The other was vile to me when I was younger in too many ways to name. Thankfully, I wasn't invited for the trip, as they planned to see Auntie Violence.

You may have noted that I do not mention my parents much. It's not a conscious omission; it's just that we're not close. Please understand that I'm not neglected, far from it. I'm fed at the established intervals, and my clothes are washed and ironed; it's just that following the events of three years ago, I feel I may have become surplus to requirements. On the odd occasion when this situation lowers my spirits, I cheer myself up by stating that I am a child of nature.

After retrieving some of the cash I had squirrelled away in various receptacles around my bedroom, I headed to town with a small to-do list.

Firstly, the new/old racing bike is far noisier than it should be. I have made friends with Ron, the owner of Ripton Cycles. After giving it the once-over, he advised me that the bike's performance would improve significantly by simply putting the appropriate amount of air in the tyres and oiling the chain. Ron agreed to service the bike at a student discount as, in his words, he had "... fuck-all else to do today." I thanked him heartily and assured him I would recommend his establishment to all my schoolmates.

Next, I went to the bookshop and purchased a copy of *The Odyssey* for classics.

My third call was to my barber, Ray. "What will it be, X?" he asked after I was seated and he had secured the drape around my neck.

"Cochran me up, my friend," I replied.

"You're speaking my language, X," Ray replied brightly. As the barber worked, he made his usual chit-chat. "I see less and less of your age in here, X; what's going on?"

"What can I say, Ray? The fashion for boys is to let your hair grow long," I replied.

Sighing, he said, "That's fucked-up in ways I can't even begin to describe, X."

I nodded in understanding. "I hear you, Ray."

The barber stopped cutting my hair for a moment and, in the mirror, looked at me intently. "Everything you need to know about *the look*, X, you'll find in the fifties—blue jeans, a white T-shirt, and a black leather jacket—the original teenager."

"I'll remember that, Ray," I said.

"Hey, X, did I ever tell you about my theory on things?" he asked.

Only every time I come in here.

"No," I lied.

"Life without hair wax is not *really* living."

My fourth task was the library. Since June, a new librarian has been in place. Her name is Michelle, and she is, as I have discovered, 24 years old, a would-be writer, and incredibly pretty. This recruit is far friendlier than her colleagues. She always takes the time to chat with me and lets me off my late fees if no one else is around.

As I handed her my selections, she asked, "What have you got this time, X?" Reading the cover of the first book, she said, "Richard Dawkins' *The Selfish Gene*. Sounds a bit heavy for me, X."

"Genetics is my new passion, Michelle," I replied.

"Is that so, X? Oh, now this *is* a classic," she said, holding up *Wuthering Heights*. "If you ask me, it's all about *sex*," she whispered the last word.

"*Oh, good*," I responded, probably a little too eagerly.

"'*Healthy Eating Tips*. Are you on a diet, X?" she asked as she studied the cover.

"Yes, I am, Michelle. It's not a specific diet plan as such; I'm just limiting myself to 1500 calories a day, and I'm not going to stop till my body looks like Prince's does on the *Lovesexy* cover," I said proudly.

Smiling, Michelle stamped the book, put it to one side, and leant over the counter towards me. "Tell me something, X. Are you doing that because you want to, or because you think girls will like you more?"

I mirrored her gesture and leaned closer. "Can I be honest with you, Michelle?"

"Of course you can, X," she replied sweetly.

"If it would make me more popular with the girls I like, then I would gladly gift my soul to Satan and commit every evil deed he commanded me to do in his most unholy name," I said honestly.

This made Michelle laugh a lot. "I know how you feel, X—

and trust me—I've been there," she rolled her eyes. "Oh boy, have I been there? However, listen to me—you're a cute kid, X. The right girl will see that straight off."

I nodded my head obediently.

Sorry, did she really call me cute?

"See you next time, X," Michelle said, giving a wink, and I walked out of the library in a dream.

My final call was to the copy shop to invest further in the painting business.

Just as I was about to leave town, I remembered one other item I'd need next week, a pack of Post-it notes, and I duly headed to the stationers.

Later, after a short, cold bike ride, I grabbed the flyers from the copy shop and called around for Drake.

"What are you after, X?" he asked after opening the door to me.

"Grab your coat; we're going to deliver these," I said, waving the bag of flyers. "Come on, we can get these done before it turns dark."

As we walked up the street away from his house, Drake read one of the leaflets intently, an increasing look of consternation crossing his face as he did. "I don't understand, X, exactly who are Pete and Dennis when they're at home?"

"We are, *obviously*," I informed him. "Drake and X, well, they don't sound like any painters I've ever heard of—Pete and Dennis do, though, see?"

"Oh," he said blankly. "So which one am I then?"

It didn't take long to get rid of the flyers, and as I was about to head back home, I told Drake, "JG and I are going to the arts centre to watch *The Last Temptation of Christ* tomorrow night if you want to come?"

"No thanks, X; I made a New Year's resolution that I wouldn't let you drag me to any more of your weird films," Drake said firmly.

"OK, forgive me for attempting to broaden your cultural palate," I said, quickly adding, "There's lots of sex in it, by the way."

Drake raised his eyebrows. "OK, cool, what time?"

As I haven't been raised in the house of love, my bedroom is my sanctuary. It's not untypical for a teenager; a poster of my star of the moment, Michelle Pfeiffer, adorns one wall, and my sporting hero, Boris Becker, stands proudly on another. Aside from that, my books, records, and a dartboard with a picture of a gurning Mr Crackett stuck on it, which I cut out from the local paper. Beside my computer's keyboard sits the obligatory Rubik's Cube; although it looks solved now, I must cheat to get it that way. As I sit here, and document of an evening, I like to toy with it idly. However, every night before I go to sleep, I break it into pieces and put it back together so it looks as it did on the day it was bought for me nine years ago.

SUNDAY 8TH JANUARY

After my breakfast ration, I took my freshly serviced bike out for a bracing ride. Next, I did some reading. I considered Homer, but after losing The Odyssey battle against Rachael1989 on Friday afternoon, the appeal of classics has dimmed somewhat, so I plumped for Dawkins instead, and this is what I learned:

Humans are just giant machines created for one purpose: to carry and then transmit genetic information to a subsequent generation. Once the transmission has taken place, humans provide for and protect the next generation until it becomes self-sufficient and goes off on its transmission mission. Following this, the original machine becomes increasingly irrelevant and eventually shuts down.

Some of you may find this depressing; however, as a Grade 9 atheist, I find this strangely exciting.

This greater understanding of genetics has shone the light of knowledge upon my present mission. I am to become a gloriously lean genetic machine, one invited to transmit his genetic material with an increasingly regular frequency.

Despite the three of us still being under the legal drinking limit, we are always guaranteed to get served alcohol in the bar of the local arts centre. This is not because we look eighteen or make a particular effort to dress up for our visits, and it is certainly not because of our lousy, fake ID. No, we get served because Brian, the barman, doesn't care. We figure he'd serve an eleven-year-old an alcoholic drink if one were bold enough to ask.

Aware that this evening would bring an opportunity for both a pre- and post-film drink, I had dutifully allocated a 400-calorie allowance for this by only having a sandwich for dinner. JG and Drake were more than a little antsy with one another before the movie started. Mindful not to further incite things, I remained silent.

"If I wanted your advice on girls, Drake, then I'd ask," JG said irritably.

Drake smiled smugly. "All I'm saying is, JG, of the three of us, it's only me who's managed to lose his virginity."

I apologise if I haven't made it explicitly clear. Drake is no longer a virgin. Last year, he was holidaying in Spain with his parents in their timeshare apartment. Every morning, a young Spanish girl came to tidy their rooms. As the holiday progressed, Drake noticed that the girl was staring at him more and more intently, mainly when he was shirtless. Anyway, one day, he was alone towards the end of their stay when the girl called in to clean. Though not precisely fluent in each other's languages, Drake managed to get her to understand that his parents would be gone for some time. With that, the girl led him by the hand to his bedroom, took off her dress, and made love to him.

Such a story might, in certain circumstances, have just the faintest whiff of fantasy about it. However, Drake told it in such a matter-of-fact way that I'm 85% certain I believe him.

When I quizzed him further, he said, "It lasted no more than 90 seconds, X, and it's not the big deal it's made out to be."

When my big moment comes, the story resonates with more incredible passion.

Anyway, that's how he got his nickname. No one calls their kid Drake around here; his real name's Timothy.

It was a good film, though the experience was slightly sullied by Drake repeatedly asking, "When does the sex start, X?" throughout and eating endless bags of peanuts. As we were walking out of the theatre, I thought it might be wise to forgo the traditional post-film pint and head straight home when someone called my name, "Hey, X!" I turned around to see Rachael1989 with an older lady who, I was 95% certain on first sight, just had to be her Mum.

"Hey!" I said back brightly.

"Mum, this is X. X, this is my Mum," Rachael said with a smile.

Rachael1989's mother, who is her daughter thirty years from now, held out her hand for me to shake. "Nice to meet you, X. I've heard so much about you," she said genuinely.

I'm sure she was just being polite by saying this, so I just smiled and shook her hand. As I could feel my two friends lurking suspiciously behind me, I said, "Rachael, I don't know if you've met JG and Drake."

Rachael smiled. "Yes, Drake's in my French class, and I've got maths with JG."

"JG and Drake, this is Mrs Williams, Rachael's mum," I said politely.

The older lady smiled. "Actually, I'm Mrs Jackson now, X. However, please *do* call me Alison."

This was indeed odd. We always refer to our friends' parents as Mr and Mrs without exception. Really, life must be *very* different in the South.

"Anyway, boys," Alison continued. "We're just going for a post-film natter in the bar. Would you care to join us?"

The three of us shrugged our shoulders in ascent.

Once in the bar, we took a table by the window. Alison stood up, purse in hand, and asked, "Right, what can I get you boys to drink?"

"Pint of bitter, please," we all replied in unison.

"Right, err," Alison suddenly looked very uncomfortable.

"If it's a problem, Mrs Williams, we're quite happy to buy our own," Drake said, sensing her dilemma.

"Yes," JG said. "We figure Brian would serve an eleven-year-old an alcoholic drink if one were bold enough to ask."

"Right, well," Alison still seemed to be resolving the issue internally. "We *are* in an arts centre, and I suppose—it is Sunday evening—why not? Three pints of bitter it is then—and for you, Rachael?"

"Just a Coke for me, Mum," Rachael replied.

"Darling, if you want something stronger like the boys, it isn't a problem."

Rachael weighed the decision momentarily. "Just a little glass of wine then, please, Mum."

"Right! That's three pints of bitter then and two glasses of wine. Anything else?"

"Bag of nuts," Drake said impolitely.

I kicked him under the table and looked at Rachael's mum. "He really did intend to say please at the end of that sentence, Alison."

"Oh yeah, sorry, I meant to say please, of course," Drake said humbly.

"Not a problem." Alison smiled and added, "Back in a moment, then."

As her mother headed towards the bar, I noticed that

Rachael 1989 was studying me. "What kinds of music do you like, X?" she asked.

"Err... lots," I replied, sounding more than a little uncomfortable.

Drake sniggered gleefully. "X likes Prince and Frank Sinatra."

"Well, *I* can't stand Prince, though I might quite like Frank Sinatra," Rachael said, staring intently at me.

Feeling slightly uncomfortable, I said, "I'll go and help your Mum with the drinks." I shuffled off towards the bar.

Once we had returned with the drinks, the conversation soon settled into an easy groove. Alison and her new husband, Arthur, are academics at the local polytechnic. After the college had won significant funding for Rachael's stepdad's specialist field, they decided to relocate to Marketon from Reading.

Rachael's mother asked us generic questions about school and the local area, which we answered relatively intelligently and as politely as possible. "Anyway, what did you make of the film? Frankly, I don't know why those nutty Americans have gotten their knickers in a twist over it quite the way they have."

The rest of us just stared at her blankly.

"Tell me, X." She turned to me. "Would you describe yourself as spiritual?"

"Alison, I believe human beings are just biological machines whose only purpose is storing and transmitting genetic information," I said frankly.

Alison's eyes widened. "Well, that is profound," she said, laughing. "Tell me, how long have you thought like this?"

"Since approximately 2.30 pm this afternoon," I replied honestly.

Realising that my answer, despite being truthful, may have

sounded ever so slightly odd, I proceeded to explain to Alison about the book I was reading. Coming to the end of a long and particularly cack-handed explanation of the genetics text and my thoughts about it, I finished by saying, "I'm convinced I'm an atheist, and I've scored myself as a Grade 9 on my 10-grade atheism scale."

"What's a Grade 10?" Alison asked with genuine interest.

"You'd need to have travelled all of space and time and found no evidence whatsoever of a divine, omnipresent being," I replied.

Alison was thoughtful momentarily and then asked, "Just Dr Who, then?"

"He's the only one I could think of, too," I said flatly.

I like Alison, like Mrs Simpson; she talks to you like an adult rather than a child.

"Well," she said, turning to the others. "It's nice to see three young men spending the evening in a cultural pursuit rather than getting up to no good hanging around on street corners."

"Oh," JG answered. "I'm only here to distract myself from the fact that my girlfriend has dumped me, and Drake only came because X told him there were sex scenes in the film."

As I've said, he's very matter-of-fact and a real stickler for detail.

"Oh well, still, you've all made an effort, I suppose," Alison said slightly uncomfortably. "Sorry to hear about the girlfriend, JG," she added sincerely.

"Thank you, Alison," JG replied.

"If you want my advice, give her time; that's what we women always seem to need more than you men ever do," Alison added.

JG nodded intently. "It's funny you should say that, Alison, as that's *exactly* what X advised me to do, but I chose to ignore him as he has absolutely no experience with girls whatsoever."

This made Drake burst out laughing, Rachael1989 smile, and my cheeks turn an, no doubt, alarming shade of scarlet.

"Oh, I'm sure that's not true," Alison said kindly, giving me a warm smile.

"Anyway, I might still have a girlfriend if someone hadn't exposed himself to her on New Year's Eve," JG said accusingly, and glared at Drake.

So, *that* was the cause of the earlier disharmony.

"Did I really do that?" Drake asked in alarm.

"Yes, you bloody well did," JG said intently.

"Well," Alison said quickly. "We best be off; besides, it sounds like you boys have much to discuss. Lovely to meet you all. X, I look forward to seeing you on Wednesday evening. Tell me, do you like gnocchi?"

I felt incredibly uncomfortable suddenly. Drake and JG had stopped glaring at one another and were now staring at me intently.

"Have you got a date, X?" JG asked in genuine wonder.

"It's not a date, as such," I said uncertainly.

"Yes, it is!" Rachael1989 corrected me.

"I'm taking a…err…a textbook over and…eating g…" the word had gone.

"Gnocchi," Alison prompted me.

"Gnocchi," I repeated.

"Yes, that's a date," Drake said with a laugh.

Fortunately, Alison and Rachael1989 swiftly departed before my friends could embarrass me further. Leaving an agonisingly slow bus journey home for Drake and JG to interrogate me about how what they termed 'the miracle' had come to pass.

Still, despite the rather embarrassing end, the day has been a success. I've lost another 2 pounds.

MONDAY 9TH JANUARY

Today's big news at school was the party happening this Friday night at Helen Flannigan's house—we'll call her House Party Helen—to which everyone is going. Sorry, just to be precise here, to which everyone is going except me. House Party Helen's oversight is slightly annoying, as I thought we were friends. As she is, by far, the best female tennis player in the school, we frequently find each other's company during the summer term. Also, JG and I sit behind her and her friend Penny in chemistry—Penny Chemistry, naturally—and the four of us are always talking.

Usually, such exclusion would cause a minor bout of teenage melancholy. However, further developments have made the matter seem somewhat trivial now.

We had English today, and Rachael1989 immediately stuck a Post-it note on my desk. At first, I thought I'd upset her in some way at the arts centre last night, but then I realised it was her address.

After reading it, I said, "Thanks. I hope your mum didn't think we were too weird last night."

Rachael turned to me and smiled. "She liked you." Then, she turned her gaze back to the front of the class and ignored me for the rest of the lesson.

I'd been home from school for about an hour when the phone rang. It was Mrs Grifton, who lives twenty doors or so from Drake. She politely asked if I could pop over sometime during the week and give her a quote for the living room, dining room, and ceilings. I was so excited that I said I'd come over immediately, stopping only to get out of my school uniform and don the white dungarees.

On arriving, Mrs Grifton looked at me, sneered, and did her level best to slam the door straight in my face: "Eh, I know you! I'm not having some bloody kids paint my house."

I just managed to get my hand in the way of the door before it closed. "Mrs Grifton," I said calmly. "I appreciate that I am of tender age, but please hear me out."

Her eyes narrowed with suspicion.

"I'm very serious about this business. There are very few opportunities for a young lad to make a few quid around here, and I would love the opportunity to come into your house, make a quick estimate, and give you the quote you've requested. If you would be kind enough to allow me to, that is," I said as politely as possible.

The door slowly opened again. Really, there was no need to make a quote; where Drake and I live, there's nothing but postwar, three-bed, semi-detached housing, and the dimensions of Mrs Grifton's house are no different from mine. However, it was essential to play the part. Once over the threshold, I took out a notepad and started making nonsensical scribbles to look like a professional, "What made you decide to have the place freshened up?" I asked, as chit-chat, as I have been led to believe, is an integral part of the tradesman's art.

"Oh, my nephew's coming home next week. He's been… *away* for a while, so I thought I'd make the place look nice."

Ha! I know Mrs Grifton *and* her nephew, Pete, not personally, but by reputation; he's presently inside Backton prison for nearly beating someone to death. He's more commonly known around here as Psycho Pete.

"How nice of you, Mrs Grifton. I'm sure he'll appreciate your efforts," I said cheerily.

"Is this part of a school project, then?" she asked as I continued to survey her living room.

"Oh, no," I assured her, "I'm doing this entirely off my own back; I just want to earn my own money instead of asking my mum and dad for everything. Drake and I, sorry, *Timothy*, who lives down the road from you…"

"The Adams' boy?"

"Yes," I confirmed. This seemed to please Mrs Grifton, and I could feel the situation starting to go my way. "Anyway, we'll work outside of school hours and on weekends, at times to suit you, obviously, Mrs Grifton."

"Very enterprising of you, I must say. Shame there's not more like you around here," she said sincerely.

"Thank you, that's very kind of you to say."

She studied me momentarily and asked, "Go on then, how much?"

I quoted the price, with the additional cost for materials. Mrs Grifton momentarily considered the offer and said, "Well, I've already got the paint, so don't worry. But, seeing as you're local and you seem like a nice lad… and as you are cheaper than all the others, I'll give you a go… From five till eight tomorrow evening, if you manage not to spill any paint and don't break any of my trinkets, the job's yours."

As soon as I was out of the door, I sprinted down to Drake's to tell him the news.

1989 is a go!

TUESDAY 10TH JANUARY

In religious education today, we discussed miracles—correction, the rest of the class debated the New Testament miracles. However, I was staring absently out the window, watching one of the grounds staff reline the old school football pitch.

"What does our resident atheist think?" Mr Jacobs asked, "X?"

Turning to face the teacher, I said, "Oh, sorry, sir, what was the question?"

Mr Jacobs smiled. "What do you think about miracles, X?"

"Err... they are feats that defy both science and logic. Therefore, I think it's safe to discount them, sir," I said dismissively.

"OK, what would you describe as a miracle, X?" Mr Jacobs asked.

It was an excellent question, so dutifully, I thought about the matter before answering. "A miracle occurs when something improbable takes place, the effect of which is immensely positive."

"Very good, X. Have you got an example?" Mr Jacobs asked with interest.

"Boro winning the FA Cup," I suggested.

This made both Mr Jacobs and the rest of the class laugh.

"Or Helen Wells going out with a boy from this school," I

added.

The laughter continued. Helen Wells is the hottest girl in year four, the hottest girl in the school, and quite possibly the hottest girl in Marketon. Guys at school don't show up on her radar, and all her boyfriends, I believe, are always in their twenties. We'll call her Helen Heaven.

Mr Jacobs looked at the class and said, "So, we have two types of miracles now: the biblical kind and X's type."

After school, I got changed and called for Drake; it was time to go to work. For the first hour, Mrs Grifton watched us like a hawk; however, as soon as she realised we were taking the painting seriously, she left us alone and retired to her bedroom to watch TV. Before we left, she even made us a cup of tea.

The job is ours!

When I returned home, I made something to eat and read for a little while. During said study, I realised that bullying is merely the highlighting of a genetic disadvantage…

"Hey, four eyes," translated into genetic logic, means, "This person has genes that cause poor eyesight; mine is perfect, and therefore, my genetic information is stronger. Let me transmit it to you."

"Hey, fat boy," translates into genetic logic: "This person has genes that allow for weight gain. As I do not. My information is stronger. Let me transmit it to you."

I could go on, but you get the idea. However, the same applies to shortness, tallness, big boobs, small boobs, ginger hair, curly hair, greasy hair, body odour, and, most of all, unattractiveness.

However, my gene-carrying machine is now 8 pounds

lighter. Someone's got to notice sooner or later, surely?"

WEDNESDAY 11TH JANUARY

I skipped school this morning. Mum had a funny turn first thing, and I thought it was best to stay with her. I should explain at this juncture that she is not precisely with us anymore. We lost my younger sister to cancer three years ago, and unfortunately, my mother has never fully recovered. The doctors keep her propped up with pills, but she's the ghost of the woman she used to be. Dad's way of dealing with the grief is simple; he works every hour God sends and, therefore, never has to think about things aside from what's happening at his office. Besides, even before my sister died, he had his problems upstairs, if you catch my drift.

What can I say? There is a strong history of mental illness in my family, and madness is in these genes of mine. What are you going to do?

By lunchtime, she seemed much better, so I headed to school. I was a little 'emoted out' after the morning and in a daze, so when Rachael1989 smiled at me in the corridor and said, "See you later," it didn't register.

Everything felt a little off today, and I was looking forward to focusing on the painting at Mrs Grifton's. She said we could stay if we wanted to, so we worked until nine. At that point, Drake asked, "Hey, X, what happened to your date tonight?"

Fuck!

THURSDAY 12TH JANUARY

Not entirely unexpectedly, a mute Rachael1989 and a Post-it note stuck firmly to my desk were waiting for me in English. The note read, "I AM NOT SPEAKING TO YOU!"

I withdrew my pack of Post-it notes, removed the cellophane wrapper, and wrote, "ARE WE COMMUNICATING?" I placed the note delicately in front of her.

Rachael responded, "OBVIOUSLY!"

I replied, "CAN I EXPLAIN?"

Rachael slapped another note before me. "YOU DON'T NEED TO. SOMETHING ELSE WAS MORE IMPORTANT!"

I sensed futility in my actions. However, I penned one last note. "I AM SORRY, RACHAEL1989."

She studied the note with curiosity, then placed it to one side and ignored me for the rest of the lesson.

After we'd finished painting tonight, I headed over to Rachael1989's with flowers I'd kept fresh in a vase at Mrs G's.

"Oh, I'm sorry, Rachael's already in bed for the night, X," her mother said as she answered the door to me.

"No problem, Alison; I just called to say I'm sorry about last night."

"And you brought flowers? How sweet of you, X," she said

warmly.

"The flowers are for you. Apologies for missing the… " The word had gone again.

"Gnocchi," she said.

"Gnocchi," I repeated.

Alison beamed. "That's most charming of you, X. There really was no need."

"I insist," I replied, handing the flowers over to her.

"I'll let Rachael know you called," she assured me, and I bade her good night.

The Dawkins book unleashed a revelation tonight: memes.

Like genes, memes are strong or weak; some survive and prosper, while others die out. However, unlike genes, memes can be ideas.

Here's an example of how the school meme machine works: Clare Anatomy is a year older than nearly all other kids in our year group. In her third year, she suddenly stopped coming to school, only to return the following September, still a year three student. Initially, the dominant meme suggested that Clare had suffered from a life-threatening illness during her absence. However, this meme soon had a competitor, and this one proposed that Clare had fallen pregnant, given birth, and the child had subsequently been put up for adoption.

I am still determining which is true. However, the latest meme is currently winning the battle for dominance.

As the more sleuth-minded amongst you may have already clocked, it's not just Clare whose age is out of sync with the year four average. Yours truly, too, has a missing 12 months, but, somewhat fortunately, my 'gap year' took place at primary school age and before we even relocated to Marketon.

Therefore, no one beyond the need-to-know bracket at Luther Parkinson and the local authority has even the faintest clue regarding my not-so-sweet little mystery. This is a blessing, as Clare would have needed to have given birth to a minotaur to match the shock value of my dark secret. What can I say? This story is long and overwhelming, so I'll save it for another day, OK?

FRIDAY 13TH JANUARY

I arrived in English to find a Post-it note on my desk, which read, "MY MOTHER THINKS YOU ARE WONDERFUL!" It made me smile until it was followed moments later. "I DO NOT!"

Despite Rachael1989's frostiness, the lesson will still be my favourite of the year by some length.

"X, don't chew gum in class; how many times do I need to tell you?" Mrs Simpson said irritably, pointing to the waste basket beside her desk.

"Sorry, Mrs Simpson," I said, standing up.

I placed the gum in the bin, and as I casually walked back to my desk, my English teacher asked, "Have you lost weight, X?"

"Thank you for noticing, Mrs Simpson," I replied brightly.

As I sat back down, another post-it note arrived. "WHY ARE YOU LOSING WEIGHT?"

I was tired of non-verbal communication with Rachael, so I replied flippantly, "SEX!"

My response elicited a loud groan from the girl next to me.

Dr Harris did not make it to classics this afternoon and sent Mr Shaver, the new woodwork teacher, in his stead. The meme around the school about Mr S is that he had more than a bit of bother with the law last summer after beating up a burglar he'd caught breaking into his house. He does possess a mean stare; it has to be said. The braver kids whisper "Killer" when they pass him in the corridor, only for him to turn sharply to the miscreant and issue them with *the stare*.

His instructions were precise and to the point. "Get on with whatever it is you are reading and keep the noise down." He occasionally looked up from the Tom Clancy novel he was reading to glare at one of the pupils like he wanted to kill them, only to return his attention to the pages of his book a moment later.

A night off from painting tonight as Mrs G has *company*. I could have done with the distraction, as I've just realised that House Party Helen's invite-only spectacular is presently well underway and, right now, schoolmates of mine are taking further, alcohol-fuelled journeys into the sexual heavens, whilst I will have to wait to hear about their brave adventures second-hand on Monday morning.

Yes, the teenage melancholy has descended, and as Mum and Dad are out for the night, I am tempering it with a large glass, potentially two, of white wine stolen from the store in the garage.

Some good news, though, is that another pound has been shed from my gene-carrying machine. However, it's no good losing all this weight if I'm never allowed to mix socially with attractive and, ideally, intoxicated girls of my age. The Valentine's Day disco would have served as the ideal opportunity. Also, with it still being five weeks away, there is every chance that I could have arrived at it looking like a snake-hipped sex-machine. Unfortunately, it would take a miracle for that event to be reinstated in the school calendar, and, just for clarity, that's a biblical miracle, not the X-type. Nothing else is on the horizon until the year four camp, but that's not until the end of the summer term.

Also, Pete & Dennis' Painting Services doubled its job book tonight. Mr Roberts knocked on the door an hour ago, handed me a slip of paper, and said, "Job for you, X."

I read the note. It was a name with a residence address a few streets away. "Thanks, Mr Roberts. What do I have to do?"

"Nothing; the job's yours, just call round, and check what colours she wants," Mr Roberts said. "Also, X, her husband ran off a while back and left her with twins; she's selling up to move nearer her folks. Money's tight, and she's nice, so *be* nice, OK?"

"Thanks, Mr Roberts," I said enthusiastically.

"No problem, X, just do a good job for her, do you hear me?"

I nodded in understanding.

"Oh, and X, you're babysitting next Friday at seven. Bring a girl, will you? It would make the missus a little happier with the arrangement."

"OK," I said uncertainly.

Bring a girl? Oh sure, I'll go and check the Rolodex, should I? Who exactly does he think I am, Patrick fucking Swayze?

SATURDAY 14TH JANUARY

After introducing myself to Mrs Fry, the lady with the painting job, I headed over to Mrs G's, who had allocated us a three-hour slot this afternoon to paint in whilst she took herself off to town for her weekly shop. She returned with bags of food, and when I left, Drake was still sitting happily at her table, his skinny, should be fat, face stuffed with food.

Tonight, I'm going over to JG's. I'm sure he wants to moan about Claire, Who Has Seen Drake's Phallus, but I don't mind. Besides, he has eight cans of strong lager for us to share. He made it quite clear that Drake was not welcome.

Four cans of nuclear lager = 800 calories, so dinner is off the menu tonight.

Later

Jesus, if you want to get drunk on a budget, you only need to skip a meal—I am smashed! JG's place is only a mile from here, but I must have done double that distance on the way home due to my inability to walk straight.

JG came clean on the real reason for the break-up with Clare, Who Has Seen Drake's Phallus. It turns out that Clare is keen to move the relationship forward in ways he is not yet ready to. In their final exchange, JG had asked, "Is this because of what Drake did?"

Clare replied, "Well, I'll say one thing for the boy; at least *he* knows where it is!"

Ouch!

"I just don't see why we can't enjoy each other's company. I'm sure we will get to the physical stuff in good time, X," JG said miserably.

This struck me as a little odd, as even though Clare, Who Has Seen Drake's Phallus, is not the best-looking girl in year four *if* she made a sexual invitation to me, I'd probably burn the carpet in my dash to her bedroom. Still, each to their own, I suppose. I mean, really, what do I know about teenage sex?

"Anyway, enough about my problems; how did the date with Rachael go?" JG asked with interest.

After I had explained, JG buried his head in his hands, and said, "Jesus, X, you are such a loser with girls! I'm being serious; she likes you!" He then proceeded to give me his best 'I know more about women than you do' look.

"She might like me, but she doesn't like me *like that*," I replied. "Besides, Rachael's top 10 material, I'm the sort who enters the chart at thirty-seven, climbs three places the following week, then promptly disappears."

JG thrust his hand towards me. "I'm positive on this, and two quid says she does."

As a working man now, two quid seemed a little thin, so I pushed the bet up to a fiver. After that, the strong lager soon got the better of us, and conversation worthy of repetition ceased.

Anyway, I've got to stop typing; from my vantage point, it looks as if I've written every one of these sentences at least three times.

SUNDAY 15TH JANUARY

I awoke with a hangover this morning. As Mrs G has forbidden work on the Sabbath, I headed to Mrs Fry's to start there. Jenny and her twins are pretty lovely. After I'd finished painting, we chatted for an hour. As I left, she said, "You're a nice lad, X; just make sure you don't have kids too young."

MONDAY 16TH JANUARY

A miracle occurred today; just for clarity, it was the X-type, not the biblical kind.

Only one meme flew around the school when I arrived this morning. House Party Helen's invite-only spectacular had produced the mother of all headlines. Carl Rogers had attempted to suck off David Fairweather. Admittedly, you probably do not see the miraculous element yet, but please bear with me.

This *happening* took place in full view of the other revellers. Carl dropped to his knees, undid his friend's belt and button-fly, and David, thinking his pal was fooling around to get cheap laughs, allowed him to continue—and *continue* Carl indeed did. Only after the act had commenced did David realise that Carl had no intention of stopping. He hastily removed his manhood from his friend's mouth—something, I am reliably informed, he managed to do without sustaining an injury. Meanwhile, Carl, suddenly aware of the awkward position he had placed himself, bolted from House Party Helen's residence with a howling cacophony of laughter and ridicule ringing in his ears.

At this school, the news doesn't get any bigger than this. Firstly, Marketon is not an enlightened town, and devil worshipping would be considered a more respectable lifestyle choice than open homosexuality. Secondly, the nature of the act itself, fellatio, even in my sex-crazed year group, blow jobs, I understand, are not yet on the menu of options.

Naturally, fellow pupils could talk about nothing else, and

upon hearing the same tale told for the fourth time—really, it did sound like *everyone* had been invited to that bloody party—an idea, no, scratch that, *inspiration*, hit me. I decided to book an appointment with Ms James.

Rachael1989 was the only pupil seemingly disinterested in the whole affair, as, when I briefly raised the subject in English, she turned red and said, "X, please do not mention *that* party to me!" That was all she said during the entire lesson. I'm really starting to miss sitting next to Jack.

I was busy reading the detailed instructions Ms James had left outside her office when I heard her voice behind me. "X, to what do I owe the pleasure?"

I turned to face her. "A matter of business, Ms, I was just following *pro-to-col*." I pronounced the word slowly and deliberately, "by learning how to schedule an appointment."

"How very compliant of you, X; I will reward your endeavours by seeing you immediately if you don't mind my eating lunch while we chat." Ms James held a tray containing a small plate of salad and a glass of orange juice; as such, I opened the office door for her. "Oh, thank you, X."

"No problem, Ms, didn't you fancy the canteen today?" I asked.

"X, if I'm forced to watch Mr Crackett dribble food into his beard one more time, I fear I may vomit, and so, instead, I've decided to beat a tactical retreat back here." Ms James then sat down and kindly invited me to do the same.

I waved my hand dismissively. "Thanks, but I find I blag better when standing."

Pointing at me with her fork, she said, "Fair enough, give it to me with both barrels, Top Gun."

"I'm here about the cock-sucking incident, Ms James," I said frankly.

She frowned in distaste. "*Please* don't use that language, X."

I held my hand in apology. "Sorry, Ms, let me rephrase that… the unfinished flute solo."

"Unfinished?"

I smiled. "Indeed, according to eye-witness reports, the act was not seen through to its natural conclusion."

"You weren't there?" she asked in wonder.

Sadly, I shook my head. "No, I wasn't invited. You weren't, were you, Ms?" I asked with genuine interest.

Ms James frowned. "*No*, of course not, X; why would you ask such a ludicrous question?"

"No reason, Ms. *Anyway*, this incident has got me thinking radically."

She smiled with understanding. "Oh, just go with it; I know I did, and I've never regretted it once."

In genuine confusion, I asked, "Sorry, Ms, but what *exactly* are we talking about here?"

Ms James raised her eyebrows. "Same-sex experimentation?"

My face must have been a picture. "No, I came here to discuss a school disco."

"Oh," she said neatly. "In that case, I would kindly ask you to disregard my previous statement."

"Yes, of course," I replied politely, then, with feigned concern, I continued, "*Anyway*, with this *incident*, we don't want to see a repeat occurrence, do we?"

Her expression turned grave. "Absolutely not bad for pupils, bad for teachers; I've had three male staff members in this office already today, all terrified at the thought of being in the same room as Carl."

I nodded sagely. "I can understand that, and I think *I* know the problem."

"What is it, X?" she asked with keen interest.

Confidentially, I said, *"It's* the school disco ban."

"Really?" she asked, sounding surprised.

"Absolutely! That's the place where *it* all happens."

"It?" she asked in wonder.

In a whisper, I replied, "The courting."

Miss James looked at me curiously. "I didn't realise they still referred to it as such."

Shaking my head, I said, "Not many do, but I believe some words and phrases should be preserved."

Sarcastically, she replied, "How kind of you to carry such a burden for humanity, X."

Ignoring her put down, I continued, "Anyway, the school disco is a holy ritual; you haven't extinguished it; you've simply pushed it underground."

"Underground?"

I nodded eagerly. "Yes, *underground.* So instead, parties are thrown like the one on Friday night."

"The one you weren't invited to?" Ms James asked for clarity.

I nodded again. "The very same, except these parties are dangerous, anarchical, and, most worryingly, unsupervised."

"Maybe so, X, but at least they don't take place on the school grounds," Ms James said, pointing at me again with her fork for emphasis.

My face turned serious. "They don't, but they damage the

school regardless. The spirit of *that* party has boldly walked into *this* school this morning and taken a gigantic ghostly piss on…"

Ms James frowned in distaste. "*Please* don't use that language, X."

I held my hand apologetically. "Sorry, Ms… has urinated on the school motto."

"The school motto?" she asked in confusion.

"*The school motto*," I repeated for emphasis.

Ms James continued to look baffled, and I let out a slight sigh. "Out of your door, turn left, plaque on the wall by the secretaries' office, 'Semper ruminat inmunda cibum tuum ante deglutire'."

Smiling gratefully, the head of year said, "Right, thanks, I'd better just take note of that." She scribbled on the pad before returning her attention to me, "So how do we play it? I can't allow another school disco to descend into the last days of Sodom and Gomorrah."

"I concur; things did get a little out of hand with the alcohol," I said, nodding in agreement.

She looked at me accusingly. "Were *you* drunk, X?"

"*No!*" I assured her passionately. "Drake and I did drink two cans of weak lager behind the school gym, the modest effects of which soon wore off, and the evening rapidly descended into tedium after that."

Ms James nodded. "Well, I'm all for moderation… But then there was all that lewd behaviour, X," she added with concern.

I agreed. "There was a lot of lewd behaviour, Ms."

"Did *you* behave lewdly, X?" Ms James asked with what seemed to be genuine curiosity.

"Please refer back to my previous comment, Ms," I said frankly.

She looked slightly embarrassed. "Yes, of course. Sorry, X, that was a foolish question to ask... Still, it sounds like a risk," she added uncertainly.

Boldly, I replied, "*Not* if we institute a door policy, Ms."

"A door policy?" Ms James appeared to be taking an interest suddenly.

"Absolutely! We'll turn away anyone who... "

"Has been drinking!" she said excitedly.

I shook my head gravely. "Not an option."

"Why?"

"We'd have to turn them all away."

Ms James' eyes widened with disbelief. "*Really?*"

"Oh yes, but we *will* turn away anyone who is excessively inebriated or attempts to smuggle alcohol into the building. As you said, Ms, you *do* believe in moderation."

Ms James smiled and tapped the desk. "Yes, I do, I genuinely do. Whom are you going to get to control the door?"

Shrugging my shoulders, I answered, "Frankly, I have no idea now."

Her expression turned serious. "OK, but you'll need to think of something, as you'd have to be higher than a Columbian farmer at harvest time to think a teacher's going to walk that line for you."

"Don't worry about the door. I'll think of something. Also, I was thinking of Valentine's Day; it falls on a Tuesday, and year four discos are always on a Tuesday... Frankly, Ms James, I think it could be a sign," I said raising an awed gaze to the heavens.

Ms James rolled her eyes and sighed. "*It's* not a sign, X; *it's* a coincidence, and if you wish to refrain from being detained in an institute for the mentally unsound, then you would be wise to learn the difference."

Ms James isn't like Dr Harris—you must use logic to get around her. "You're right, Ms. It's a coincidence... and a fortunate one." I momentarily let her consider the idea before asking, "Well, what do you think?"

Ms James seemed genuinely conflicted. "I'm not sure, X. Just mentioning the words 'year four school disco' might be enough to give Dr Harris a heart attack."

"We'll call it something different then!" I suggested enthusiastically.

"Such as?"

"The Year 4 Dance Party," I said boldly.

Smiling knowingly, Ms James said, "I like that, X. How will it be different from a disco exactly?"

"In no way whatsoever, except name, Ms," I replied.

"I like that even more, X; clever, very clever!" she said, genuinely impressed. After some final contemplation, Ms James nodded and said, "OK, we'll give it a whirl. What's the worst that could happen? On second thoughts, keep your own counsel on that question, X."

"No worries, and thank you, Ms," I said sincerely.

I was about to leave when Ms James added, "Just one more thing, X."

"Ms?"

"What's your angle?" Ms James asked, arching an eyebrow.

Innocently, I asked, "Angle, Ms?"

Her eyes narrowed. "Yes, *angle*. Why are *you* doing this?"

Solemnly, with my hand pressed to my heart, I replied, "Everything I do, I do in the name of school spirit, Ms."

Ms James rolled her eyes incredulously and said, "X, if you ever say anything so ludicrous in this office again, I will send you to sit with a year five class for the day."

As I'd been rumbled, I chose to opt for honesty. "Ok, well, *in truth*, I'm trying to raise my profile within the school; I am on a diet now…"

"Oh, really, which one?" she asked with genuine interest.

"It's not a specific diet plan as such. I'm just limiting myself to 1500 calories a day, and I'm not going to stop till my body looks like Prince's does on the *Lovesexy* cover. *Anyway*, by the time mid-February rolls around, I should be considerably thinner and, as a result, more attractive to the girls in my year, so even though I will be engaged primarily with organisation and management on the big night, some journey, no matter how small and brief, into the sexual ether would be most welcome and, in many respects, overdue."

Ms James studied me intently, then smiled warmly. "Thank you, X. Keep hitting me with those honest shots, and there'll always be a warm welcome for you in this office, no matter how many teachers and students you manage to distress. Besides, take away self-interest, and you condemn the species to extinction. *That's* my motto. I will write a letter of commendation to your form tutor right away. Now, you've got some work to do, so please leave this office quicker than a flash."

1989 saw its first miracle.

As I was heading home from school, JG came running over to me and thrust two coins into my hands. "Here you go, X; I'll pay you the rest tomorrow."

He was about to take off when I asked, "What's this for?"

"You won the bet! She snogged Daniel Martin at that party on Friday night. Sorry, mate." And with that, he was gone.

I was most upset upon hearing this bombshell.

Jesus, even the bloody new girl got invited to that party.

This evening, I designed the poster for the Year 4 Dance Party. I used an initial teaser campaign rather than a bland, formal notice.

LESSONS IN LOVE:1989

BE
WHOSE
VALENTINE

?

Year 4 Dance Party

New School

Tuesday 14th February

X

After thinking long and hard about the 'X', I decided to make it far more prominent than it originally was. Well, if profile-raising is the name of your game, then there's no point in being coy, is there?

TUESDAY 17TH JANUARY

I arrived early this morning to put the poster on the year four notice board and headed to new school for my form group.

"Well, what do we have here, a letter of commendation for X from Ms James?" Mr Cracket said, holding a white slip of paper for the rest of the group to see. Smiling sadistically at me, he proceeded to scrunch the note into a tight ball and throw it into the waste bin by the side of his desk without even giving it a cursory glance.

"Thank you, sir," I said sarcastically and turned to Lisa the Repeater, sitting beside me, lost in conversation with another pupil. "Hey, Lisa."

"Hey, X," she said, turning to me and smiling.

"What do you know about babysitting?" I asked.

"Everything there is to know!" she replied confidently. "I do it all the time; a girl has gotta make a living somehow, X."

I explained the arrangement with Mr Roberts to her. Lisa listened intently, paused, and said, "OK, X, here's the deal. I want half of whatever you're making; the video rental is on you—no action films whatsoever—and if you plan on doing anything more than kissing, you'd better bring something strong to drink along. You may have lost some weight, but that's still not a swimming team body you're packing there just yet, Mister. Deal?"

Although I was pleased that Lisa had noted the effects of my dieting, there was something uniquely unappealing about her proposal, and I replied, "I'll let you know tomorrow."

By break time, the word was out about the Year 4 Dance Party; disappointingly, though, the X had failed to hit the spot. Some of the brighter kids had suggested it was the start of a countdown in Roman numerals, though everyone else just assumed it denoted a kiss. I made a mental note to myself not to be so subtle again.

When scanning for a table in the canteen at lunch, I saw Cocksucker Carl sitting alone, staring into space. I like Carl; he's a friend, and I feel genuinely sorry for him, but when your profile-raising campaign has just crashed and burned like mine, taking the seat next to the school leper is not the most brilliant next move, so I elected to sit elsewhere.

Matt Jacobs quickly took the seat opposite me at the table. "Good afternoon, Captain. Is there anything I can do for you today?" He asks this same question daily, and I fear he may be taking Dr Harris' words at the start of the term just a little too seriously.

After three hours of painting at Jenny's, I returned home and began working on the second poster.

DISCO IS DEAD

YEAR 4 DANCE PARTY

Tuesday 14th February 7.30 pm New School

BROUGHT TO YOU BY X!

Sometimes, you've just *got* to spell it out for people.

WEDNESDAY 18TH JANUARY

Drake dropped a bombshell this morning—he's no longer available to work on Wednesday nights. While we were at the arts centre, he picked up a flyer for the Marketon Young Actors Group, and he's already joined. That means we have two outstanding jobs and only one man available. Utilising all my powers of persuasion, I endeavoured to convince him to prioritise the pursuit of wealth above idle distractions. However, it was to no avail. Another painter was urgently required.

When I got to school, I replaced yesterday's Year 4 Dance Party poster with the new one.

In form group, Lisa the Repeater demanded to know whether her services were required for Friday night. I fudged it and said I would let her know by the end of the day. As Driffid wasn't in, I sat next to Stuart Moor, school thug.

I have become partial to adding a splash of aftershave at the start of the day, and as I withdrew the bottle from my rucksack, Stuart sneered, "What *are you* putting aftershave on for, X? No one's going to want to do *it* with you."

Coming from the mouth of an overweight by three stone, pock-marked ignoramus, this was a little hard to take. However, I have learned over the years that you do not bite on Stuart's bait. Instead, you play with his mind.

"I'm not going to wear it, *you idiot*. I'm going to drink it. *The shave* gives you visions, *man!*"

Behind his eyes, I heard Stuart's brain reluctantly begin to function.

By break time, my name was everywhere. Really, I should have been investing time in resolving the babysitting and painting issues; instead, I spent the entire 15 minutes soaking up every bit of praise that came my way. You'd have thought I had performed a biblical miracle rather than the X-type. Even Helen Heaven put her hand on my shoulder as she walked by me and said, "Nice one, X."

I swear, I nearly fainted.

As I paid for my lunch, I saw Cocksucker Carl sitting by himself again, and you know what? When your market value has rocketed up as mine did today, you can sit wherever the fuck you want to.

"Hey, Carl," I said as I sat opposite him.

"Hey, X," he said in surprise.

"Some week, eh?"

He nodded glumly. "You know, X, it's nice of you to sit here, but you don't have to." The guy could barely look me in the eye.

I made a dismissive gesture with my hand. "You know me, Carl. I've never been one to care about popular opinion."

"Well, I appreciate it, and just so you know, I wouldn't have come in this week, but what am I supposed to tell my mum?" he asked.

"*That* is a toughy!" I said, nodding in understanding.

"I'm not gay, you know?"

I waved his comment away. "Carl, I'm not sitting here in judgment. If you want my opinion, the worst thing you could do is spend too much time locked up in your room beating yourself up about this. You need an activity to take your mind off all this, somewhere away from…" I indicated to the rest of the canteen with my fork, "These *vultures*."

"Sounds good; what exactly did you have in mind, X?" Carl asked, brightening suddenly.

I smiled. "Well, Carl, in a word, *painting*."

By the end of the lunch period, three girls had come over to me and said how nice it was of me to sit with him.

Really, it wasn't.

I was spared the start of French by a summons to Ms James' office.

"Ah, X, I saw the poster, perfect!" She said it brightly as I entered.

"Thank you, Ms James," I said sincerely. "I was rather keen on art until my dad made me opt for tech drawing in year three instead."

Ms James rolled her eyes with sardonic relish. "Oh yes, that's right. Lay the tragedy on nice and thick, John Constable. It makes you wonder how they'll keep the National Gallery full without you. Now, *X*, who's on the organising committee?" She asked intently.

Baffled, I enquired, "Organising committee?"

Ms James' face registered disbelief. "Oh, good god, boy, of course, we'll need a committee. *Now!* I want at least three appropriate names from you by tomorrow, a mixed group, please, and I would strongly recommend Rachael Williams as a candidate, X."

"Yes, Ms, I'll certainly bear her in mind," I said with a little nod.

Ms James arched her eyebrows. "No, X, you *will* appoint her to the committee."

"Right, you are, Ms," I said in compliance.

"She's bright, responsible, and trustworthy..." the head of year began.

I had a light bulb moment and interrupted her eulogy, "Actually, Ms, she is. Sorry, you just gave me a great idea."

In a well-practised deadpan, she remarked, "Well, *thank God* you said that, X, because, before you did, I had no idea where my sense of fulfilment was coming from today."

I smiled to recognise her wit and then carefully asked, "Actually, would it be ok if I pulled her from class and appointed her right now?"

Ms James waved her hand irritably. "If you must, X, if you must... oh, and two more names by tomorrow, please."

As I entered Rachael's religious education class, six or seven pupils said, "Hey, X!"

"Rachael Williams to Ms James' office," I announced.

Rachael blushed ever so slightly, stood up, and walked towards the door. As we left the room, six or seven students said, "Bye, X."

"What have I done?" she asked, looking concerned as soon as the door was closed behind us.

"Nothing," I said casually. "She doesn't even want to see you; I do."

"Pulling me from class? People are certainly going to talk now, X." Rachael said coyly.

As we headed towards new school, I said, "I'd like to appoint you to my Year 4 Dance Party Organising Committee."

"Oh yes, I've heard about all of this. You're the flavour of the month suddenly."

I shrugged with false modesty.

Rachael stopped walking. "So, why me, X?"

"In truth, Rachael, Ms James told me I had to."

Rachael considered me intently. "You could have lied to me then, X. I'm glad you didn't."

"OK, so can I count you in?" I asked.

"Yes, of course," she said with a smile.

"OK, I did have something else I wanted to ask you, Rachael." I explained to her my predicament with Mr Rogers.

Suspiciously, she asked, "How many girls did you ask me before me, X?"

I held up one finger.

"What did she say?" Rachael asked.

"Really, Rachael, you don't want to know." However, she did want to, and so I explained.

"And that didn't appeal?"

"Not in the slightest," I assured her.

"OK, then, I'll do it if you agree to answer one question. Why am I Rachael1989?"

I was initially confused, then remembered my apology note last week. "Because you're new, and so is the year."

She nodded, smiled, and clapped, "Date!"

That word again.

Just as she was about to head back to class, Rachael looked at me and said, "Oh, and X, I saw you sitting with Carl at lunch. *That* was a nice thing to do."

Really, it wasn't.

With Drake answering the call of the stage, I headed over to

LESSONS IN LOVE:1989

Mrs G's to paint and found an unwelcome surprise waiting for me there. Psycho Pete, Mrs G's nephew, was home from prison. He's over 6 feet tall, his head is shaved, and he possesses the sort of face that would cause a tree to shed its spring blossom.

As always, Mrs G busied herself while I finished the work. Pete, however, spent the first half-hour standing, watching me silently and intently. At first, it wasn't an entirely comfortable experience. However, it started getting on my nerves after a while.

"Is there something I can help you with, Pete?" I asked, stepping off the stool I'd been standing on.

Pete's eyes shifted to the floor. "Do you know about me?"

I sighed and asked, "Prison?"

He nodded in shame. "I wanna make a fresh start. If I get sent down again, she's not letting me back here, and I got nowhere else to go." His desperate voice made me pity him, so I gently placed the paint tin and brush down and gave him my full attention.

"She's very fond of you, your aunt," I said reassuringly, "*This*," I indicated to the wall I was painting, "is all in your honour, you know?"

This seemed to brighten Pete somewhat. "Well, my aunt said I could learn a thing or two from a kid like you. She says you're proper smart and the problem is I don't read and write too good. I was thinking of getting a job as a bouncer, but that means filling out forms. If I ask my aunt for help, she'll pack me off to classes, and I ain't going back to school."

My mental light bulb illuminated for the second time today, and I held up my hand to silence him. "*Bouncer?* OK, here's the deal, Pete. You get the forms, and I'll help you fill them out, but you've got to do me a favour in return. Have we got a deal?" I asked.

Pete smiled warmly. "You're all right, you are, X," he said, holding his hand out to me.

I've never shaken hands with a criminal before. Really, it was rather dramatic.

When I got home, Mum informed me that Pete and Dennis had another customer—a lady who lives across the street from Jenny. I called her and said I'd be over after school tomorrow.

Three jobs, all unfinished; I'm going to need more staff.

THURSDAY 19TH JANUARY

Drake was a little nonplussed about my recruiting of Cocksucker Carl until I explained that we would earn extra money for every hour Carl worked. To further mollify him, I offered my friend a place on the Year 4 Dance Party Organising Committee. As his mood was once again sweetened, I refrained from telling him whom I was considering making Pete & Dennis' next recruit.

In form group, I finally told Lisa the Repeater, that her services would no longer be required this Friday night.

"You're getting very fussy suddenly, aren't you, X?" she said coldly. "Don't come crying back to me when you realise that's the best offer you're going to get all year!"

Christ, I hope that's not the case. Anyway, to be safe, I think I'll sit next to Driffid for the next few days.

When I got into English, Rachael1989 was in fine spirits. "Is there anything you want me to get for Friday? I could ask Mum if bringing a bottle of wine is OK."

"Lovebirds," it was Mrs Simpson, "I've just two words for the pair of you: *store cupboard*. Phillip Larkin, 23 copies, please."

"Rachael, you're doing me a favour, so *I'll* bring the wine," I said as Rachael scanned the shelves of the English store cupboard.

She took the required texts from the shelf and replied, "OK, I could call at the video store on the way over. Hey, what would you like to watch?"

"Well, there's a film called *Angel Heart* I'd like to see…" I started.

"With Mickey Rourke?" she asked with genuine interest.

"Yes and… "

She smiled. "Mickey Rourke is all I need to know, X. You've got a deal."

At lunch, I sat with Cocksucker Carl again, and as soon as I did, the table filled up with other year fours. He'd dutifully purchased a pair of white overalls and was ready to work. I told him he would be painting at Mrs G's tonight with Drake while I hopefully lined up the next job and continued at Jenny's.

After the rest of the table had cleared off, I was left sitting by myself when JG took the seat opposite me. "Hey, X," he said brightly.

"Hey, JG," I replied absently.

"Here!" he said, neatly putting three coins before me. That's the rest of the money I owe you."

"Cheers!" I replied and pocketed the coins. It did cross my mind that, at this point, I should perhaps declare the babysitting 'date' on Friday night. However, in a court of law, I'm 51% sure that would be classified as inconclusive evidence, and therefore, I refrained from doing so.

Judging by the way he was tapping his fingers on the table, JG had something he wanted to say, but he was struggling to find the words for once. Finally, he came out with it. "Hey, X, I heard about your committee for the dance party, and I was wondering…"

I looked at him in disbelief for a moment, and, seeing in his eyes how important this was to him, I said, "Of course, JG, if you want in, you're in."

JG smiled brightly. "Cheers, X. I won't forget it." He offered his hand to me over the table, which I took and shook while he told me what a remarkable friend I was.

This experience was a first for me. Having spent three and a half years at Luther Parkinson as wallpaper in a scene being acted out by others, being someone of note suddenly felt good.

After school, I secured the third job for Pete & Dennis' Painting Services with the minimum of effort.

FRIDAY 20TH JANUARY

The first meeting of the Year 4 Dance Party Organising Committee was held at lunchtime today. Ms James had never met Drake and JG personally before. "And you are?" she asked, turning to the portlier of my two friends.

"JG, Ms. John Graham."

She smiled in recognition. "Ah, John Graham, the maths talent?"

If you do GSCE a year early in this place, they consider you a prodigy.

"And?" she said, turning to Drake.

"Drake, Ms. Timothy Adams."

Drake's name brought no favourable mention from Ms James, which seemed to bother him somewhat. "I'm X's business partner. We run Pete & Dennis' Painting Services together," he added.

Glancing at me with a raised eyebrow, she asked, "Do you?"

"And Rachael, how are you settling in?" Ms James asked kindly.

"Very well, thank you, Ms," Rachael replied formally.

Ms James went through her complete checklist line by line: ticket price, ticket sales, refreshments, cloakroom, staff coverage, and, most importantly, the DJ. After a lively debate, it was decided to curtail the services of Fat Terry, Marketon's sweatiest man, and instead ask a year four named Tony Dwyer, who possesses turntables, to provide the music.

"Finally," Ms James said. "Door security?"

"Sorted, Ms," I said. "A professional bouncer owes me a favour."

"How many doormen do you know?" Drake asked, sniggering gleefully.

"Now, Timothy, that's the sort of remark I'd expect a year five to make," Ms James said cuttingly. "If X says he knows someone, then that's good enough for me. However, he is now responsible for ensuring that this individual turns up. OK, X, well done on that one. Now, Team, X has come to me with this, and I've decided to back him. Still, before we go any further, can I ask, and your honesty would be very much appreciated at this juncture, is there any reason why we might think twice before going ahead with this event?"

There was a long, thoughtful silence, which was broken by JG. "Err, there's a strong history of mental illness in X's family."

As I've said, he's very matter-of-fact and a real stickler for detail.

Psycho Pete's first official job for Pete & Dennis' Painting Services was to go to the off-license and buy a bottle of wine for Rachael and me. No matter how many times I said the name, he seemed incapable of remembering it, so I wrote it down and told him to hand the note to the person behind the till when he arrived. Next up was a trip to Jenny's. The introduction was unnecessary, as she and Pete had attended Luther Parkinson together. Rather than look imitated by the brute, Jenny sat him down and made him a cup of tea, and before long, they were reminiscing about school days lost. Eventually, I interrupted them and reminded Pete that if he wanted his forms filled in, I was on a tight schedule,

"Got a hot date, X?" Jenny asked teasingly.

I was thoughtful momentarily. "Technically, *I'd say* it's not a date, but *yes*, it does involve a girl; I'm babysitting as it happens."

Jenny smiled. "Babysitting, eh? I'll remember that, X."

Pete didn't have an answer to most of the questions on the application form, so I made the responses up by working on the logic that something is usually better than nothing. Finally, as he could only think of his aunt as a reference, I put my name down, stating my title as Managing Director.

I'd never seen Rachael1989 out of school uniform until she knocked on my door this evening. She was wearing a tight black turtleneck and 501s, and I couldn't help but notice how attractive her figure was. Waving a videotape box at me, she said, "Got it!"

Mrs Rogers seemed immensely relieved that Rachael1989 was in attendance and blanked me entirely as she showed her the children's milk in the fridge, which toys were their favourites, and gave her the restaurant phone number they were going to. Meanwhile, Mr Rogers patted me on the shoulder and said, "Nice one, X. Please just make sure you're both dressed by midnight, will you?"

I nodded obediently. Frankly, the thought of either Rachael or myself undressing at any point during the evening had not even crossed my mind, but I gave a lewd smile and made a crude gesture with my fist to my neighbour, as I felt these were the required social obligations.

The children were already in bed, and, fingers crossed, Mrs R advised us that we should be in for a peaceful evening. After the Rogers headed off, we entered the lounge and played the video. Having never been in a situation like this with a girl, I was unsure of the expected etiquette, so when Rachael1989 sat on the sofa, I took the floor before her.

Angel Heart is a good movie, but a little disturbing. Usually, stories with a satanic twist would not bother a Grade 9 atheist like me. However, some of the imagery started to freak me out. The film got darker and darker, and Rachael1989 eventually sat beside me on the floor. She took my hand for the last 30 minutes, and as the film climaxed, her grip got tighter and tighter. I must confess that, at this point, I had the strangest feeling forming in the pit of my stomach, and I'm 80% certain it *wasn't* the increasingly precarious predicament of Mickey Rourke's character that was putting it there.

When the film finished, we remained stunned until Rachael1989 said, "Next time, X, *I'm* picking the movie. You pour the wine, and I'll put a record on."

Carole King's *Tapestry* was already playing when I returned from the kitchen with the drinks. We sat opposite each other, cross-legged in the middle of the lounge, and talked for what seemed like hours... well, Rachael did. "When Dad died, Mum said that it was just the two of us from now onwards, team Alison and Rachael... then she met Arthur, married him, and now we've moved here for *his* career... It's lonely being in a new town, X."

"You may be new, but at least you got invited to that party last weekend," I said consolingly.

Reddening ever so slightly, Rachael said, "Oh, you heard about that, did you?"

Raising my hands in a gesture of innocence, I said, "I didn't mean to mention... "

Smiling demurely, Rachael replied, "That's OK, X. I know what you meant, and, just for the record, I didn't kiss him; he kissed me, and *I* pushed him away... I might act differently if a boy I liked tried the same thing."

At this point, I was 60% certain that Rachael was moving her face closer to mine; however, if she had been, she soon stopped when the brat upstairs started screaming.

Rachael sighed deeply. "I'll go."

Having had no luck settling young David back down, she returned with him in her arms.

"So, what do we do now?" I asked in genuine wonder.

"Well, if you take him for a second, I'll go and warm his milk, and then we'll see if that settles him down," Rachael said calmly.

"OK," I said, holding my arms to take the toddler. Young David clung tightly to Rachael and seemed reluctant to come to me.

Approximating the type of baby voice most adults use when communicating with infant children, I said, "Come to X, David; Rachael's going to go and get your milk."

Eventually, he came into my arms of his own volition, and at first, I thought he was hugging me, but then I felt a sharp pain just below my shoulder blade.

"*Shit!* The *fucking freak* just bit me," I said and tossed the toddler back at Rachael, who, thankfully, caught him.

"*X!*" Rachael said, scolding me. "You *can't* throw children!"

"*It's* not a child; *it's* a bloody rabid dog," I protested.

Suddenly, Rachael cried in pain and dropped David to the floor. "Are you OK?" I asked, concerned.

"*No*, I'm not; the little bastard just bit me as well!" she said, sounding in genuine discomfort.

David, now sitting in a heap by Rachael1989's feet, was crying hysterically. Scooping and holding him at eye level, she said, "There, little boy, don't cry. You *mustn't* bite people; it hurts."

David listened intently to Rachael and then, without warning, threw up all over her face. I tried hard not to laugh, but couldn't keep it in.

"This isn't bloody funny, X!" Rachael said. Vomit was dripping down her face as she reprimanded me.

Biting two people and emptying his stomach on Rachael seemed to be precisely what young David needed, as, after she had taken herself off to the bathroom to get cleaned up, he was soon soundly asleep in my arms. The Rogers returned to a serene household; Rachael's still-wet hair was the only indication that the evening hadn't gone as smoothly as we were trying to make out.

When we got to Rachael's front door, I said, "Some night, eh?"

"Some night," she echoed. "Though I enjoyed every moment until Jaws woke up."

We both laughed. "Yeah, me too," I said.

"Anyway, thanks for walking me home, X. Good night," Rachael said, kissing me on the cheek. As she did, I couldn't help but notice that she still smelled vaguely of vomit.

"Goodnight!" I said and walked home.

On the way back here, I decided I'd been mistaken about the almost-kiss earlier this evening. Rachael had chosen to peck me on the cheek; that's not something you do to the guy of your dreams. Besides, it means JG's fiver is still rightfully mine.

SUNDAY 22ND JANUARY

It's been a weekend comprised mainly of painting and organising. Two bike rides and 50 pages of Wuthering Heights have been about it for leisure activity. As literary heroes go, I've decided Heathcliff is as good as they get. He's wild, women adore him, and he is truly a child of nature.

Somewhat irritatingly, there are many things to keep track of when running a business. Who did what and when, how much did a job cost, and how much profit did it make? I need a stickler for detail so you can guess where I'm headed next.

Later

It took fifteen minutes of flattery before JG agreed to join the project; I suspect he was still a little put out that I hadn't initially involved him.

"Leave it to me, X; I'll revolutionise your business model," he assured me, but I have no idea what he meant by that.

Also, I lost another 4 pounds this week.

MONDAY 23RD JANUARY

Ms James took morning assembly this morning. "Luther Parkinson, I shouldn't have to, but it would appear I do need to warn you all of the dangers of experimenting with harmful substances as a year four boy is presently very ill in hospital after drinking an entire bottle of aftershave."

Two more jobs came in today, both from unexpected sources.

Inspired by Ms James' comment in our first meeting, I have devised a new way of tormenting Mr Crackett. Occasionally, I have written the word penis in one of its various linguistic forms on his blackboard before his, usually tardy, arrival at form group. Unfortunately, I was caught red-handed this morning as Mr C's knowledge of Spanish includes the word 'pene', though the mind boggles why.

As such, I had a lunchtime appointment with Ms James. When I arrived, she was writing on her notepad. She paused to indicate the sign behind her.

"Spanish, penis, blackboard," I said as if I were playing some twisted game of Cluedo.

Choking a laugh, Ms James finally gave me her attention. "Yes, that dreadful man did mention something about it. However, the real reason I wanted to see you was *painting*."

"Painting, Ms?" I asked.

Ms James nodded. "Yes, your curious friend mentioned that the two of you were running a business of some kind…"

"That is correct, Ms James," I said, interrupting her. "I first had the idea at the end of last year. Over the Christmas holidays, I put together what I believe is commonly called a business plan. At the beginning of term, I recruited Drake, and we started a marketing campaign in the local surroundings… "

Ms James was staring at me in bemusement. "Hang on," she said sarcastically. "Would you mind starting from the beginning? I'll get Spielberg on the phone, then you tell me, and I'll tell him."

As always, her point was crystal clear. "Yes, Ms, we are doing small painting jobs in the local area," I said briefly.

She smiled. "Well, in that case, I'd like to reward your spirit of enterprise with a job."

The second came from the mother of my classmate, Jenny Wood. Jenny's dad works three weeks on/three weeks off on the rigs, and, when he's on leave, according to Mrs Wood, "He does nothing but sit on his fat arse and watch that bloody thing," she said, pointing to their television for clarity. "Anyway," she said, looking me up and down. "You ain't half turning into a right handsome lad, X; you've lost weight since the last time I saw you. Well, it's good to see a young boy trying to make something of himself; the job's yours if you want it."

TUESDAY 24TH JANUARY

There are five open jobs and four painters; I was on a recruitment drive today. However, the next two recruits to Pete & Dennis' Painting Services came remarkably quickly.

Firstly, I am still avoiding Lisa, the Repeater in form group, so I sat next to Driffid this morning. I couldn't help but notice that he was nodding his head more frantically than usual, so I enquired about the cause of his distress, "What's up, Driff?"

"Oh, hey, X… it's bad, man. The Cure are playing Wembley this year, and I have no funds."

Secondly, Matt Jacobs approached me during break time and asked, "Is there anything you need today, Captain?"

Matt can start working immediately, though Driffid has made things slightly awkward by insisting on wearing only black dungarees for work, something I have tasked JG with finding. As such, I have sent my mungo chum on a flyer distribution mission for the rest of the week at a reduced rate.

Matt and I worked at Jenny's; Psycho Pete got started at Mrs Grant's, while Drake and Cocksucker Carl finally finished our first job off at Mrs Grifton's, which meant payment.

"Here you go, young man," Mrs Grifton said, handing me an envelope. I had an instinctive urge to check the contents. However, I'm 95% certain she would have viewed such behaviour as impertinent, so I refrained.

"And here's your tip," she said, handing me a tenner.

"There's no need, Mrs G," I said.

"I insist!"

"Well, thanks," I said, smiling. "I'll split it between me and the boys."

Mrs G shook her head firmly. "No, that's for you, X; it's in appreciation for what you've done for our Peter."

WEDNESDAY 25TH JANUARY

Wendy Wood spread the word around the school about Pete and Dennis's Painting Services, which caused quite a stir. Wherever I went today, I was greeted with a "Hey, X," even by kids I don't know. Rich Wilson, all round nice guy, even asked, "The way you do your hair, X, does it have a name?"

Rather self-consciously, I ran my hand through my hair and replied, "Just go to Ray, the barber. Tell him X sent you, and ask him to Cochran you up."

"Thanks, X, I'll do that," Rich said with a grin.

I smiled. "Sensible thinking, my friend; besides, you know what they say, don't you? Life without hair wax is not *really* living."

At today's second meeting of the Year 4 Dance Party Organising Committee, tasks were dutifully allotted, and Rachael1989 and I will be selling tickets over lunchtime next week.

THURSDAY 26TH JANUARY

It is official; an attractive girl has announced that she fancies me! Her name is Claire Marshall, but she shall be known as Claire with An Eye For X. Helen Goodman, Claire's best friend, told Lisa Abbott, who told JG in Maths this morning. My friend found me during break time to relay the news.

"Oh my god," I said, a little taken aback. "She's top 10 material."

JG was thoughtful for a moment. "Number 9, to be precise," he said eventually. "Also, X, so that you know, the girl is thicker than pig shit. *Don't* let that put you off, though; strike while the iron's hot, just in case your weight loss turns out to be temporary. Now, my friend, you won't screw this one up, are you?"

As I've said, he's very to-the-point and a real stickler for detail.

My friend had further good news, as he has been telling anyone with ears at school that he is now the Financial Director of Pete & Dennis's Painting Services—Clare, Who Has Seen Drake's Phallus and has asked him to be her beau again.

Such is my enjoyment of school life now that I was still smiling when I got to English, which caused Rachael1989 to ask somewhat coldly, "Is that cat that got the cream grin because you're Luther Parkinson's most talked about student all of a sudden?"

"No," I said, turning to her. "It's better than that; Claire Marshall fancies me."

Wrinkling her nose, Rachael asked, "*She's* your type, is she?"

"Does it matter? It's nice to hear that someone finds me attractive, especially after all the effort I've been making. Can't you be happy for me?" I said, somewhat put out by her cynicism.

"If it weren't for the fact I was sitting down, I'd do a cartwheel in joy," she said dryly.

It's easy to see why she's Ms James' favourite pupil.

I snappily replied, "Listen, Rachael, you might not understand this, but I've been in this school for three and a half years, and this is the first time an attractive girl has paid me even the slightest bit of interest."

I was too snappy, as we were back to communicating through Post-it notes for the rest of the lesson.

FRIDAY 27TH JANUARY

Stuart Moor returned this morning. His eyes were full of violent intent when he glared at me in form group. However, I have learned over the years that you do not wait for him to hit you. Instead, you play with his mind. As such, I stormed over to his desk and said, as threateningly as possible, "Just because you can't handle the shave, they're cracking down on all of us now. You don't glug it, you fool; you bloody sip it! I swear, Stuart, if this happens again, we're not friends anymore!"

Behind Stuart's eyes, I could hear his brain reluctantly begin to function.

In English, I received a Post-it note from Rachael1989.

It read, "HAVE YOU ASKED CLAIRE THE TART OUT YET?"

I initially responded, "NO."

And then added, "NOT YET ANYWAY."

In classics, we departed from *The Odyssey* and ended up back at the siege of Troy.

"Now, what made this woman, Helen of Troy, so special?" Dr Harris asked.

The rest of the class remained mute, so I volunteered, "A great body, sir!"

"Like Claire Marshall?" Rachael sneered under her breath.

"Yes, X, undoubtedly, her beauty was legendary. Though I was thinking of something else," Dr Harris said.

Still, the class remained silent. "A remarkable lover?" I suggested.

"Like Claire Marshall?" Rachael sneered again.

"Undoubtedly, X, undoubtedly, my boy, but I was thinking of something else," Dr Harris said, scanning the other pupil's faces optimistically.

Rachael1989 raised her hand. "She was the ultimate status symbol, sir—the Ferrari, if you will—of ancient Greece. If you had Helen, then other men were guaranteed to envy you. That was her real power."

"Exactly, New Girl, exactly," Dr Harris said, delighted with the new resident smart-arse.

As the bell went, I expected Rachael to disappear without saying a word. However, she hung around, and when the rest of the class had left, she said, "Hey, X!"

"Hey, Rachael... Is this going to be about Claire Marshall?"

"I only asked if she was your type," she said, holding her hands up defensively.

"Do you know what, Rachael? *I don't know!* As JG constantly reminds me, I know nothing about girls. So how am I supposed to know one type from another?" I said, a little frostily.

Despite my shortness, my answer seemed to please Rachael, as she then said, "Mum and I are going to watch *Gorillas in the Mist* tomorrow night, and we wanted to know if you'd like to join us. We're having dinner out first, too."

"Yes, that would be great," I replied, a little shocked by the invite.

SATURDAY 28TH JANUARY

Ms James lives in a stylish, albeit sparse, new-build house on the edge of The Village. The place is spotlessly clean, with highly polished exposed floorboards. One look at the walls told me they had only recently been white-washed.

"It's all too clinical for my tastes," she said as she showed me into the front room. "So I'm going to be daring, four walls, all with different colours."

"Wow!" I said. "Two colours in Marketon would be considered avant-garde, Ms."

Ms James laughed at my joke. "Right, I'm off hill-walking for the day and won't return till five. I've made you a small salad and left it in the fridge; I didn't want to upset all your hard work," she said, indicating my trimmer waistline. Oh, and X, call me Catherine out of school."

By the time Catherine had returned, I'd done both coats on the walls and one coat of gloss. Frankly, I'd thought the mixed walls idea wouldn't work. However, it looked fantastic, and she has an eye for colour that I do not possess.

"Very impressive, X; I mean that sincerely," she said after a thorough inspection.

"Thanks, Catherine. I'll be back tomorrow to finish here and do the dining room, but I'm due somewhere soon, and I was wondering if I could use your shower?" I asked politely.

"Hot date?" she asked with interest.

"Sort of..."

"I'll find you a towel, X," she said, smiling.

I showered and then got changed into my new clothes. The guy in the boutique I visited after school yesterday had recommended a black shirt, and I'd also bought a new pair of 501s, which are a waist size smaller than my other pairs and fit comfortably.

As I entered Ms James' sitting room, I said, "I feel ever so slightly awkward asking a teacher this, but do I look OK, Catherine?"

"Are we off the record?" she asked.

I looked slightly confused, and Catherine explained, "Off the record, it means if you repeat what I say, then I'll deny it."

"In that case, we *are* off the record," I said.

"You look very handsome, X; who's the lucky girl?"

"Are we *still* off the record?" I asked.

"Of course."

"Rachael Williams, though it's not a date."

"Why do you say that?" Catherine asked with curiosity.

"Her mum's coming. You don't invite the man of your dreams on a night out with your mother," I said.

Ms James smiled. "Still got a lot to learn about girls?"

"Apparently, according to most people, everything," I said frankly.

"Oh well, Romeo, a male friend of mine who stays over irregularly and has left some aftershave in the bathroom, help yourself. Oh, and X, *don't*, whatever you do, drink it."

Alison took us to a stylish Italian restaurant on the road

parallel to the High Street. Rachael's mum spent most of the meal talking about the government. "I fear that your generation is going to grow up without knowing what collective action is… That bloody woman's cut the soul out of this country… If World War III were to commence tomorrow, we wouldn't stand a chance… It's that awful man, Murdoch. He's brokered a deal with half the working men in this country: 'Do what I say, vote for whom I tell you to vote for, and every morning I'll show you a pretty girl falling out of a swimming costume'."

"Sirens!" I said suddenly, in realisation.

"Yes, that's exactly what they are, X," Alison said, sounding impressed. "Sirens who are calling the British proletariat to their economic and social doom."

"Sorry, Mum's on one tonight," Rachael whispered as we left the restaurant.

"No, I like listening to her; she's very passionate," I said sincerely.

When we'd taken our seats in the cinema, Alison said, "Oh, if you two want to snog and fondle one another, or whatever it is young people call it these days, then please go ahead; I will pay you no mind whatsoever."

"*Mum!*" Rachael1989 said aghast, and even in the low lighting of the theatre, I could see that her cheeks were burning.

Halfway through the film, Rachael took my hand. Whether this act was caused by her concern for the plight of the apes or simply by force of habit, I cannot say.

MONDAY 30TH JANUARY

The Year 4 Dance Party tickets are nearly sold out. There are only about twenty left. The Asian kids never come to these events, so eight will never go, but I also noticed that no mungos bought a ticket.

Ten minutes before the bell rang, Claire Marshall came to buy her ticket. "Hey, X, I'm looking forward to the disco," she said, winking.

"Me too, Claire," I replied flirtatiously.

After she'd walked off, I turned to Rachael and sighed. "I wish people would stop calling it a disco; it's a dance party."

However, Rachael just slapped a Post-it note in front of me, grabbed her things, and left me to it. A little taken aback, I read what she had written. "GO TO HELL!!!"

Having sold a few additional tickets, I watched Dr Harris approach with a curious look. Before speaking, he looked cautiously left and right. "I've lost you to Team *James*, have I?"

Baffled, I replied, "Sir?"

Dr Harris said disapprovingly, "Might have known she'd have recruited a dirty little heretic like you first."

With mock offence, I replied in a whisper, "Excuse *me*, sir, but I thought *this*," I indicated to the poster for the dance party, which Rachael had stuck on the wall behind me earlier, "is what you wanted me to do, 'I wouldn't mind you keeping an eye on her, my boy.'", I said in my best approximation of his voice. "There's no other way to put this, sir, *I'm* undercover."

Dr Harris held his hand in apology. "Masterful, X, masterful. I should never have doubted you. You know, MI6 could do worse than recruit you when you come of age."

Really, they couldn't.

The head leaned in conspiratorially. "Anyway, are you ready to make your first report, Agent X?"

Tired of bullshitting the old boy, I replied honestly, "Sir, I couldn't think of a finer officer for the good ship Luther Parkinson than *James*. In many ways, she's a lot like you, sir, always pushing me to do more and to think bigger. Yes, admittedly, she has a style *very* much of her own, but this *is* a results-driven business, and I'll wager a fair penny she gets them for you."

Dr Harris weighed my comments momentarily. "You're sure about this, X?"

Solemnly, I replied, "I would swear to it on my tennis racket, sir."

His eyes widened. "Well, I couldn't ask you to do more, X. Really, excellent work."

Having concluded his business satisfactorily, he gave me an affectionate pat on the shoulder and took his leave.

After school, Mr Rogers called around to give me another job. "Rich bloke who owns a big house in the village and is tighter than a gnat's chuff, as they all are. Your prices will suit him down to the ground, X. Oh, and babysitting again on Friday night... bring that girl, will you? The missus approved of her."

Mr Rogers's vampiric son had not complained after Rachael1989's and mine's last feeble attempt at childcare, but then again, perhaps he enjoyed himself; maybe that's how the little bastard gets his kicks.

TUESDAY 31ST JANUARY

In form group this morning, Lisa, the Repeater, handed me a package. "For you, X." Those are the first words she has spoken to me since I declined her assistance with the babysitting assignment.

"What is it?" I asked curiously.

Lisa scowled. "I don't know, *do I*? It was with the register when I picked it up from the office earlier."

I took the package and studied it; nothing was on it besides a large 'X' written with a fat marker pen.

"Aren't you going to see what it is?" Lisa asked impatiently, having taken the seat next to me.

I opened the package and withdrew the item contained within. "It's a cassette," I said blankly.

"I *can* see that. X, what's on it?" Lisa asked snappily.

I withdrew the Walkman from my rucksack, replaced the tape inside with the new one, and pressed play. After a minute, I recognised the song. "Bruce Springsteen, 'Cover Me'," I told Lisa.

"*Who's* sending you songs all of a sudden?" Lisa asked sullenly.

"I'm guessing it was Claire Marshall," I said. "Apparently, she's got a thing for me."

"*Cover me*? Well, if you ask me, X, she's clearly into some *weird shit,* and I'd stay well clear of her if I were you," Lisa said, and, with that, she went and sat across the other side of the classroom from me.

WEDNESDAY 1ST FEBRUARY

I sat with Driffid in form group this morning and asked, "Hey, Driff, how come none of the mun… " I quickly corrected myself. "How come the goths haven't bought tickets to the Year 4 Dance Party?"

"Because, X, man, they only play pop songs at those things," he said dismissively.

I eventually managed to persuade Driffid to purchase a ticket and to encourage his fellow mungos to do likewise in return for a guaranteed play of The Sisters of Mercy's 'This Corrosion' on the big night. However, later, at the Year 4 Dance Party Committee meeting, Tony Dwyer nearly quit in protest when I broke the news to him.

Tonight, I headed over to Mr Ronson's, the rich guy whose details Mr Roberts had given me. His house is set back from the main road that runs through the village, and by the look of it from the outside, I'm guessing you could comfortably fit our house into it 14 times over. I rang the doorbell, and eventually, it was answered by a portly, well-dressed man with greying hair.

"Can I help you, son?" he said, looking at me suspiciously.

I indicated to the painting overalls that I was wearing underneath my coat. "Mr Rogers asked me to pop over, sir, regarding the painting job." Something told me that formality might work with this guy.

"A little young, aren't you?" he asked.

"Yes, sir, I am, but if you'll just hear me out..."

"You better come in, lad; it's freezing out there," he said kindly.

Once inside, I hit Mr Ronson with my full sales pitch

"So, in short, sir, we may be young, but we're motivated, keen, and committed to the highest quality of service."

After listening to me intently, Mr Ronson laughed. "They broke the mould when they made you, didn't they? Go on, why not? The job's yours."

I looked around the vast sitting room in wonder; it would take an army of us to do the work. "It's a big job, sir, but the boys and I are up to it."

Mr Ronson burst out laughing again. "I'm not letting you decorate this place, you young bugger. The job's not here; I want you to paint our Karen's place," he said, and he picked up a silver photo frame containing a picture of a student in her graduation gown. She is, without a doubt, the most attractive girl I've ever seen.

"Thing is Karen's..." he hesitated, "away now. We're hoping she'll be back next week, so if you leave your number, I'll give you a ring then, and you can make your introductions from there. The job's yours on the proviso that Karen approves. Anything our little girl wants. Deal?"

"Deal, sir," I said, and shook his hand firmly.

Afterwards, I walked over to JG's. He is once again a resident of Cloud nine now that he is safely ensconced in the arms of Clare, Who Has Seen Drake's Phallus again. Her attention certainly positively impacted his business brain, as inspiration struck him when I described the impressive effect of Ms James' four-colour living room.

When I returned, I finished *Wuthering Heights* and will share my thoughts with Mrs Simpson tomorrow.

THURSDAY 2ND FEBRUARY

On the way to school, Drake told me that he'd been given a part in a production of *Jesus Christ Superstar* at the arts centre, and, as a result, he won't be able to commit to as many hours of painting from now on. I'm pleased for him, but equally, I'm disappointed. Pete & Dennis' Painting Services was supposed to be his and my baby, but he no longer seems interested.

In English, I enquired whether Rachael was available for another shift at the Rogers' house tomorrow evening.

"Why don't you ask Claire, as she is such a big fan of yours?" She asked flippantly.

"I don't know Claire Marshall from Adam; besides, I really enjoyed myself the last time we did it together," I said sincerely.

Rachael considered me momentarily. "OK, I'll bring a video... *my* choice, remember?"

At the end of class, I hung back to chat with Mrs Simpson.

"Ah, X, I was beginning to think our extracurricular lessons had finished," she said with a smile.

"Not at all, Mrs S," I said. "The first thing I read this year was a genetics book, which I wasn't sure was your type of thing. Also, I'm running my own business now."

"A business? How very entrepreneurial of you, X," Mrs S said, genuinely impressed.

"Thanks, Mrs Simpson. However, I just finished *Wuthering Heights* and had a few questions."

My teacher smiled and said, "*Wuthering Heights*; now *that* is a classic. X, very impressive, so what did you think?"

"My favourite librarian said it was all about sex, and I agree with her."

With any other teacher, mentioning the s-word would be unthinkable, but with Mrs S, it's different.

"What makes you think so, X?" she asked with interest.

I grimaced slightly. "Well, I'm no expert."

"In literature?" Mrs Simpson asked.

"In sex, actually," I replied matter-of-factly, causing Mrs S to smirk ever so slightly. "However, I do understand that ladies are more inclined to a gentleman with a," I indicated to my crotch, "larger bat size *if* you get my meaning?"

Mrs Simpson did seem a little uncomfortable with this reference. However, she asked, "And?"

"Well, I think Heathcliff is packing a size seven down there, whereas Edgar has one of those little toy things you get in your first cricket set when you're four years old."

A smile was crossing Mrs Simpson's face. Still, I continued, "Anyway, Cathy can't get enough of Heathcliff's… you know what, and is, at best, tickled by Edgar's little alternative. However, E's *the* boy you bring home to meet your mother. He's respectable, erudite, and well-to-do—all the things a girl wants, except the size of his member. So, in life, she chooses Edgar, but in death, she comes back to Heathcliff because when you're dead, you *don't* care how nice the curtains are or how expensive the plate you're eating dinner off is; all you really want to do is scream the house down again."

Mrs Simpson laughed. "X, I'm sorry, I'm not laughing at

you."

Really, you are.

"It's just that it is by far the funniest explanation of *Wuthering Heights* I've ever heard."

I must have looked a little crushed as Mrs Simpson said, "X, that wasn't a criticism... There's something in what you said; Heathcliff is by far the more... " I saw her searching for the appropriate word, "*passionate* of the two male characters, and *yes,* that is one of the forces that attract Cathy to him, however, it might help if you thought about the novel in terms of broader themes than your err... cricket bat metaphor; untamed nature versus civilisation, for example."

I thought about what she had said before saying, "There's one other thing I don't get, Mrs Simpson."

"What's that, X?"

"Well, if we momentarily buy back into the cricket bat metaphor?" Mrs Simpson nodded. "Then we know what drives Cathy into Heathcliff's arms. However, I don't get why Heathcliff loses his mind to Cathy."

My teacher looked at me thoughtfully, saying, "Ah, well, that's something you'll learn when you... grow up a bit, shall we say?"

At lunch, I saw JG's new posters.

The Multi-Coloured Bedroom Experience

Join the revolution and get your personal space transformed today.

Brought to you by Pete & Dennis' Painting Services.

Contact JG or X for further information.

*Deposit, parental permission note and room dimensions required for booking

❖ ❖ ❖

JG has used four thick horizontal stripes, the same colours now adorning Ms James' living room, and I have to say, it's very eye-catching. Only time will tell if it is the money spinner he's predicting.

Ms James certainly noticed it, though, and summoned me to her office at lunch for a chat. "X, I *don't* recall giving you permission to commercialise the colour scheme of my sitting room."

Squirming slightly, I racked my brains for a suitable response. Eventually, inspiration hit. "Does anybody *really* own a meme, though, Ms?"

"What?" Ms James said with a frown.

"A meme," I said brightly. "A bit like a gene, but instead of genetic information, an idea transmitted via speech and the written word. Some are strong..."

Ms James held her hand to stop me. "Thank you, X, I've read *that* book. As you're so fond of ideas, I'll share another with you, shall I? If this *fad* takes off, you will agree to repaint my room *gratis,* or I will make you suffer in ways you couldn't imagine until the day you leave this school. Clear?"

I smiled grimly. "So clear, Ms, I can barely see it."

Ms James gave me two little waves of her hand to indicate my dismissal.

Tonight, I found Pete lurking outside my house; he's got the nightclub job and wanted to thank me.

FRIDAY 3RD FEBRUARY

We're a month into the new year, and yet, for reasons I'm not entirely sure of, I haven't taken a trip to Clare Anatomy's table in biology until today. This morning, though, she looked particularly alluring, and I decided to make the pilgrimage.

"Hey, X, I thought you'd forgotten about me," Clare said, smiling broadly.

"I'm sorry, Clare, I'm so busy these days that I need to pay attention in class as there's no time to catch up."

"So, I hear you're suddenly Luther Parkinson's very own man about town," she said coyly.

"Man about town"—I like that!

"And there's so much less of you as well," she said, indicating to my stomach.

"What can I say? New year, new me."

"Well, X, this new you certainly is a lot easier on the eye," she said sincerely.

At that moment, I'd have fucking hammered the Cheshire Cat in a grinning contest. However, the smile soon withered when Rachael1989 chimed in, "Hey, X, please take my seat, then *you* can drool over Clare to your heart's content, and *I* can get on with my work at your table in peace," and with that, she grabbed her books and left, returning only to deposit my things next to Clare.

"Looks like someone's cage is rattled," Clare said playfully.

"Rachael and I have a—complicated relationship," I said, sitting beside her.

Although sitting next to the second-best looking girl in year four is not without its attractions, it's almost impossible to concentrate on what Mrs Gillian is saying when your eyes are constantly drawn down the front of Clare's blouse. Besides, I'm sure Rachael1989 will soon want to swap back our places, as sitting at a table with three boys will prove to be cost-prohibitive regarding Post-it-note usage.

In English, Rachael1989 and I were back to communicating but not speaking.

"WHAT HAVE I DONE NOW?"

"YOU WERE FLIRTING!!!"

"AND?"

"WE HAD A DATE TONIGHT!"

That word again, but one of the others she'd used, gave me a more significant cause for concern.

"HAD?"

"HAD!"

Now, there is a pressing need for a clarification chat with Rachael1989; however, at that moment, I had an even bigger problem, and, at lunchtime, I grabbed my salad ration and sat opposite the solution.

"Hey, Lisa," I said brightly.

"Hey, X, have you had any more dirty songs from Claire?" she asked curiously.

"Not yet. However. I'll keep you posted, Lisa. Hey, I was

wondering. What are you doing tonight?" I asked.

"Are you asking me out?" she enquired with a smile.

"Not *exactly*," I said carefully.

Lisa rolled her eyes. "Hey, X, you know how to sweep a girl off her feet."

Delicately, I said, "If I were to say the word *babysitting*…"

Lisa arched an eyebrow. "I'd say you've got a bloody nerve; that's what I'd say." She stopped, took a deep breath, and added, "You're in luck. As it happens, I'm broke and need some new jeans. How much?"

"Lisa, I'm desperate, so just name your price."

"Tenner!" she said intently.

"OK, no problem."

"Hey, X. Do you like *Dirty Dancing*?" Lisa asked brightly.

"I can't abide it," I replied truthfully.

"Tough, it's my favourite film, and *we're* watching it," she said firmly.

Arguing, I figured, would prove futile, so I remained quiet as Lisa filled me in on the latest school gossip.

Just before the bell went for the start of afternoon lessons, JG found me in the library trying to clear some homework before the weekend.

"Guess what?" he said brightly.

"What?" I asked.

"Two bedroom painting jobs," he withdrew two fivers from his pocket. "And deposits paid."

Mrs Rogers seemed a little put out that I didn't show up with

Rachael1989. However, Lisa the Repeater soon set her at ease with her impressive baby-sitting knowledge. While chatting in the kitchen, Mr Rogers put his arm around me and said, "Two in as many weeks, X, you're getting around in all the right ways."

Halfway through *Dirty Dancing*, I started wishing that Rachael1989 hadn't cancelled. I'd really enjoyed the evening we babysat together, and this evening felt hollow in comparison. As soon as the film finished, Lisa turned to me and said, "Come on then, X," With that, she pushed me backwards on the couch, climbed aggressively on top of me, and started kissing me. Genuinely alarmed by the turn of events as I was, I saw no other course of action than to kiss her back.

We must have been lying thus for 15 minutes or so, kissing, when Lisa grabbed my hand and placed it on her left breast. This being a new sexual milestone for me, I did make the most of the opportunity and, after a while, decided to try my luck by venturing my hand further south, a journey Lisa soon aborted by seizing my hand and replacing it in its original position.

We kissed for most of the night, and as my jaw ached, I was glad when I heard the Rogers' car pull up on the driveway outside.

Lisa's house is only a few streets away, so it didn't take me long to walk her back home. Outside her house, we kissed again. "Hey, Lisa, here's your tenner. Thanks for getting me out of a spot," I said as soon as the embrace had ceased.

"No problem, X, thanks for the cash. By the way, please don't get any ideas about tonight; I'm supposed to be going out with Shaun Daniels, a year five. Please don't spread it around; I'm unsure I could live with the shame."

In truth, this was a blessed relief; the evening had been entirely unerotic, and I was starting to think that maybe

Drake's report on his first sexual adventure may not be as uncommon as I'd initially suspected.

SATURDAY 4TH FEBRUARY

JG called to inform me that I'd be painting Mary Holder's bedroom this afternoon and to give me the address. Before work, I decided to visit the library.

"Oh, my god, look at you, Mr Skinny. I bet you're beating them off like flies, aren't you?" Michelle said this when she saw me.

"Not exactly," I assured her.

"Further adventures in science, X?" Michelle asked, holding up a book on quantum mechanics.

"Something like that," I replied.

"I'm guessing you didn't understand it all?" she asked, holding a *Wuthering Heights* study guide.

"Well, I thought I did; I figured Heathcliff had a massive cock, but my English teacher reckons there might be more to it than that," I explained.

Exploding with laughter, Michelle said, "Well done, X; that's the first time I've heard that word in this place. Your English teacher's a smart lady; there's much more to love than *that*. Anyway, you'll soon find out for yourself by the look of you."

I had one more errand to run in town, and I was done.

Mary seemed thrilled with the transformation of her room, though her parents looked a little less impressed. "It's brilliant,

X, thanks!" she said with delight.

"No problems, Mary. It will look better when the second coat goes on tomorrow. Make sure you tell your friends on Monday, OK?"

"Don't worry, X, I'm going to tell everyone about this," she said enthusiastically.

I rushed home, got changed, grabbed the present I'd picked up in town earlier, and headed over to Rachael1989's. There was no guarantee that she would be home, nor, even if she was, any certainty that she would want to speak to me. However, I thought I could always leave the gift regardless.

Alison answered the door. "Oh, hello, X, how are you?"

"Very well, thank you. Is Rachael home?" I asked politely.

Alison nodded. "Yes, she's in her room. Should I call her?"

"Alison, before you do, would you know if she's still not talking to me?" I asked carefully.

Confidentially, Alison asked, "Have you done something wrong, X?"

I nodded. "Yes, I have, but I'm not exactly sure what it is."

Alison laughed. "Join the club in that case, X. Listen, Rachael's room is up the stairs, second on the right. And if she doesn't talk to you, you're welcome to chat with me, as Arthur has taken himself out for the night."

I knocked gently on Rachael's door, and she opened it briefly. She was wearing a bathrobe, and her hair was wet. Looking at me, slightly shocked, she asked in a monotone, "What do *you* want?"

"Oh, I got you this," I said, handing her the album. Rachael reached out, took the gift, and then slammed the door shut in my face. After two minutes, I realised it would not be reopened soon, so I went downstairs to join Alison in the kitchen.

"No luck, X?" she asked sympathetically.

"Not tonight, Alison."

"Never mind, would you like a coffee?"

We'd been chatting for about ten minutes when I heard Rachael's footsteps on the stairs. She froze in the doorway and studied Alison and me intently.

"Are you wearing a skirt?" her mother asked in wonder, causing Rachael to scowl furiously back at her.

Eventually, Rachael transferred her stare to me and said dispassionately, "You can come up if you want to?" and ran back up the stairs to her room.

Rachael1989's room is different. It's not very girly, and there are no pictures of pop stars, and, most interestingly, no TV. The only two posters on the wall are one of *Rainbow Warrior* and one of Mickey Rourke in *Rumble Fish*.

Taking a couple of large cushions from her bed, Rachael placed them on the floor and invited me to take a seat. "Thanks for the LP," she said as she went over to the HiFi, "I've never listened to Frank Sinatra before."

After putting a record on, Rachael sat on the cushion opposite me. "Did you sort the babysitting out?"

So, I told her, and as I tend to do with Rachael, I told her everything. After I'd recounted last night's incidents, she said, "I don't think *unerotic* is a word, X."

"Really, after last night, Rachael, it should be," I laughed.

This made her smirk. "You always tell me the truth, X; that's what I like about you best. So, why did you want to see me?"

I took a deep breath and began to recite the speech I had

mentally prepared while painting this afternoon. "I really like you, Rachael… and I think, some of the time anyway, that you really like me too. I've never had a girlfriend before, and when I say that, I mean a friend who's a girl. Though I've never had the other kind either, now I come to think of it. *Anyway*, that makes you special—different, I suppose. I like being around you; I like doing things with you. It gives me this weird feeling here," I said, pointing to my stomach. "Does that make sense?"

Rachael smiled sweetly and nodded in understanding.

I continued, "Well, I don't want that to stop, but I'm worried that I'll say something or do something, and that will be that. This is virgin territory for me here. And believe me when I say there's much-hidden truth in that last statement."

Rachael smiled. "Clare Parkin is pretty, isn't she?"

"Yes, she is," I replied.

"I think she's developing a bit of a thing for you."

Usually, this would cause an impromptu song and dance routine. However, the news bounced off me. "I didn't come here to talk about Clare Parkin; I came here to talk about you… Us."

"Clare goes with boys… she's told me… and she's done things I haven't, and it sounds like she's done quite a lot of it," Rachael said with a look of wonder.

"And?"

"You told me the truth; that's me telling you some back."

"Why?" I asked.

"I thought you might like to know because you're not the only one on virgin territory here."

I smiled at her in understanding.

"Do you think I'm pretty, X? I know I don't dress like Clare or wear much make-up..."

I held my hand to silence her. "Rachael, *you* are beautiful; that was my first thought when you first walked into English at the start of the year."

Rachael lit up like a floodlit football stadium. "Thank you, X. That was a very nice thing to say, particularly for you."

"All I wanted to say is that I like being your friend, and I think that's more important than anything else right now," I said.

Rachael nodded. "OK, I agree, but what happens? Say one night like this, when we're sitting and talking, you manage to go 30 minutes without upsetting me, and I decide it might be nice to kiss you. Is that OK?"

I nodded keenly. "I think it would be *more* than OK, but if it doesn't happen, I'm 80% certain that would be cool too... and if you decide there's someone else you want to kiss, then I'm 70% sure that wouldn't stop me from wanting to spend time with you."

Rachael frowned slightly. "What's with all the percentages, X?"

"I've *never* been 100% certain of anything in my life," I said brightly.

This made Rachael laugh, though I wasn't exactly sure why. "X, I think I understand what you're saying, friends, whatever, but maybe more?"

"Exactly!" I said. Rachael's way of saying it was so much more concise than mine, which, in its way, was ever so slightly irritating.

Rachael then insisted that we hug each other. At first, I was a little uncomfortable with the suggestion; however, as soon as I had my arms around her, the Mickey Rourke feeling returned, and I'm 92% certain it wasn't the poster of him that was putting it there.

When she finally released me, she poked me in the stomach and said, "*You* are getting skinny, Mister."

"Thanks!" I said, somewhat thrilled, having never been described by that adjective.

"Just take it easy, X; don't get hung up on how you look . *Anyway,* should we go and sit with Mum? I think she's a bit lonely tonight."

SUNDAY 5TH FEBRUARY

Tonight, I learned about a third kind of miracle courtesy of a book I borrowed from the library yesterday—the quantum variety, to be precise. In physics, there is a procedure called the double slit experiment. An elementary particle, such as a photon, is fired at a piece of card with two slits, and the results are recorded on a screen placed behind. Contrary to logic, the results show that rather than passing through one slit, the photon does indeed pass through both slits and, therefore, miraculously, can be in two places simultaneously. However, the illusion shatters if you try to observe the photon's behaviour closely, and it once again behaves like a single particle.

I'm unsure what the practical application could be for this new learning. However, you never know...

TUESDAY 7TH FEBRUARY

The Multi-Coloured Bedroom Experience has gone postal. JG reckons there are not enough of us to fill the bookings he's already taken. I've promised him I'll do more recruitment this week, and we'll send the new lads out with the more experienced ones to ensure the work is still being done to the required standard.

WEDNESDAY 8TH FEBRUARY

Other things happened today—Drake sang *Jesus Christ Superstar* songs on the walk to school. We had the last Year 4 Dance Party Organising Committee meeting, and everything was ready; seemingly, half the school wanted their bedroom walls painted in four different colours, so JG is pulling his hair out. However, only one event of real significance occurred today: I met Karen Ronson.

After rushing home from school, I showered and changed into my sharpest outfit—no white dungarees today, thank you—and then headed to the address Mr Ronson had given me. I rang the doorbell; after a moment, Karen opened it, and I realised that the graduation photo had failed to do this goddess justice.

"Can I help you?" she asked pleasantly.

"I'm X; I'm here about the painting job," I replied, unsure which part of her to check out first.

"Christ! Dad said you were young, but... How old are you exactly?" Karen asked in concern.

"Sixteen," I replied, which is the truth legally, but, as far as the wider world is concerned, a year older than I am supposed to be. I'd been thoroughly knocked off my guard by the vision in front of my eyes.

Karen looked me up and down. "Actually, you're cute. You can have the job."

I repeat, she said, "You're cute."

Now, I'm no fool; I *do* realise that I'm a sixteen-year-old virgin who has kissed a girl properly on two occasions, and she's, I'm guessing, 23 at least; however, the first time you meet somebody as beautiful as Karen Ronson, it changes you. Having long lusted after the girls at school, Karen is a potent dose of perspective. She's a petite, doe-eyed brunette, and even under the baggy jumper she was wearing tonight, it was hard not to notice the size of her breasts.

Mr Ronson bought her a three-bedroom semi about half a mile from my house. The recently deceased former occupant was a lady in her eighties who had a taste for floral wallpaper, and Karen wants the whole lot stripped and the walls painted —except the tiny box room, which, she assured me, is so full of junk that it will take her at least two months to sort it out.

After showing me around the house, Karen offered me a cup of coffee, and I sat at the table in her kitchen while she made the drinks.

"Dad is paying you for this, isn't he?" she asked in concern.

"Oh, yes, of course. He seems like a straight-up guy," I said brightly.

Karen turned to me and raised her eyebrows. "Have you been to their house?" I nodded affirmatively. "Listen, you don't get the money it takes to build a house like that by being a straight-up guy," she said intently.

I had no idea how to respond, so I quickly changed the conversation topic to, "Your dad said you'd been away—on holiday?"

Karen looked down at her feet. "It was a kind of holiday, I guess," she said quietly, and then turned back to make the coffee.

Placing the drinks on the table and taking the seat next to me, Karen studied me intently before asking, "So what kind of name is X anyway?"

"A nickname; it's a long story... Actually, that's not true, it's a short story, it's just *really* underwhelming."

Karen smiled. "Got a girlfriend, X?" I shook my head. "Playing the field, eh?"

"Underused substitute," I said flatly, and Karen laughed.

"Good-looking lad like you, the girls at your school must have something wrong with their eyes."

My cheeks burned, and I had the strangest feeling in my stomach.

"Oh God, I didn't mean to embarrass you," Karen said apologetically.

I held my hand in a gesture of understanding. "There is good and bad embarrassment, and I'm 95% certain that was the good sort."

Shaking her head and smiling, Karen said, "I reckon it'll be fun having you around here, X. So, is there going to be a whole army of schoolboys invading my house after the final bell?"

"Oh, no," I reassured her, "I'll do this job myself." This, admittedly, was an improvised policy—Karen is far too lovely to share with anyone else.

"Good!" she said, smiling.

"I'll do my best not to disturb your lifestyle," I added.

"Ha!" Karen said. "What lifestyle? I'm back in my hometown and job hunting... Don't worry, X, you'll break the monotony."

With interest, I asked, "What do you do? When you're working, I mean."

Karen sighed. "I'm a PA... I didn't want to be... I just fell into it when I moved to London. Dad made me do secretarial evening classes when I was doing A levels ... He said it would be something to fall back on. That man has a lot to answer for... Sorry, X, I'm bombarding you."

"No, that's fine," I said. Do tell me, though, what a PA is."

"Personal assistant is a secretarial job with longer hours. I usually work for overweight, pompous types who couldn't organise a piss-up in a brewery if someone wasn't there holding their hand. Also, X, without exception, all seem to suffer from wandering hand syndrome. Do you understand my meaning?"

I got the meaning and nodded in understanding.

"So, what do you want to be when you're older, X?"

"Well, not a PA if it means being regularly sexually molested by a fat man, that's for sure," I said, and we laughed.

After finishing our drinks, I told Karen I'd be back as soon as I'd gotten hold of a wallpaper stripper.

"Don't worry; Dad will have one. I'll get him to drop it around later."

"OK, then, in that case, I'll get started tomorrow," I said.

"I look forward to it, X," Karen said brightly and showed me out.

On the way home, I pinched myself three times to ensure I wasn't still in the middle of the best dream I'd ever had.

After food, I headed to JG's to solve Pete & Dennis' workload issues. We agreed to put up a poster in school tomorrow and recruit four more painters. Also, JG is concerned that the lure of the stage is proving too much for Drake, and while it's OK to pay him the going rate for the work he does, giving him a share of the profits is beyond the pale. In short, JG wants to usurp Drake as my partner. In addition, he wants *me* to break the news to him. It's an awkward situation to be put in, but JG has a point, as he's done ten times as much work as Drake has in the last few weeks. Also, as I was leaving, JG handed me an envelope.

"What's this?" I asked.

"Payday," JG said nonchalantly.

There was at least £400 inside.

Maybe breaking the news to Drake won't be so hard after all.

THURSDAY 9TH FEBRUARY

Although it was difficult to tell because, as always these days, everything Drake said was interspersed with bursts of *Jesus Christ Superstar,* he seemed to take the sacking in his stride. "I can still do the painting though, can't I, X?" he asked keenly.

"Of course," I assured him.

Drake fell silent momentarily and then asked, "You will come and see it, won't you, X?"

"What's that?"

He turned and looked at me earnestly. "The musical, you will come?"

"Of course, I'll be there," I said, silently walking on while Drake sang his songs.

In English, I was deeply lost in thoughts about Karen when Rachael1989 asked, "Are you working all weekend?"

"Most of it," I replied. "Why?"

"I wondered whether you wanted to go shopping on Saturday, not locally; maybe we could go to the city."

"That sounds great," I said honestly, "but… "

"And when we got back, I was going to cook you dinner," Rachael said coyly before I had the chance to finish.

It certainly sounded more tempting than a day of painting.

In addition, as I have a significant amount of money for the first time, the thought of some retail therapy somewhere with decent shops rather than the limited selection on Marketon High Street made it an even more appealing invitation.

"Listen, I do have this big job on at the moment, but... if I can swing it with my client tonight, I'll see what I can do. Still, if I can't make it for the shopping, the food would be great," I replied.

Rachael frowned. "No deal. Come for the whole day, or I'm asking another boy," she said frankly.

Dumbstruck, I said, "Oh!"

A smile broke across Rachael's face. "Of course, it's OK, *dimwit*."

At lunch, I sat with JG and Lisa, the Repeater. She was filling her face with as much stodge as one can fit on a plate of standard dimensions while trying to interest us in a much-recycled story about Jason White's sexual misadventure with a slinky. JG finally told her to shut up and then set out the agenda with Pete & Dennis' staffing crisis as point number 1.

"The bad news is that we have 18 outstanding jobs," JG said, holding up a sheet of paper with his left hand. The good news is that we have ten applicants," he added, holding up a second sheet with his right hand.

"19!" Lisa said that after swallowing a mouthful of food,

"Sorry?" I asked.

"*I* want my room painted four colours," Lisa said petulantly.

I sighed. "OK, no problem; we'll put your name on the list."

"Ahem!" Lisa responded. "You'll put my name at the top of that list."

"Why?" I asked, a little befuddled.

"Because, X, I helped you out of a corner last week and because I was always nice to you, even when you were a fat nobody," Lisa said, causing JG to laugh.

After school, I went to Karen's to start work. I was disappointed that she seemed so much less friendly than she had been yesterday. When I arrived, she showed me the wallpaper stripper her dad had dropped around and asked if I could start in the dining room. Beyond that, she didn't say another word until I cleared up at about 8 o'clock.

"Karen, I was wondering if it'd be OK if I didn't work Saturday..."

However, Karen didn't let me finish. "No problem. See you tomorrow," she said blankly.

And that was that. *This* Karen was so much different from the warm, friendly, and funny one I had met yesterday that, if it weren't for the testimony of my eyes, I would say that there was indeed a Karen1 and a Karen2 in existence.

FRIDAY 10TH FEBRUARY

"What do you think of whales, X?" Rachael asked in English today.

"In truth, Rach, I've never been there. I hear it's an awful place, however. Apparently, it rains constantly, and the people spit at one another when they talk," I replied truthfully.

"I'm talking about whales, the mammals, not the country, you idiot!" she laughed. It turns out she's a big fan of them. This misunderstanding aside, it was a fun lesson, and she seemed particularly pleased when I told her I was free all day on Saturday.

After school, I headed home to get changed into my painting gear. As I exited the house, I saw Pete sitting on our front garden wall. At first, I feared the worst. "Tell me you're still OK for Tuesday night." I asked nervously.

I had no reason to be alarmed; Pete had come over to announce that Jenny Fry and he were now officially *courting*.

On arriving for work, seeing Karen1 again in attendance was a relief. I had intended to work late, though she came into the dining room at seven and asked, "Do you fancy some pizza? I'm ordering a takeaway."

In truth, I was famished and could have devoured two of them; however, as I don't want to end the healthy eating regime just yet, I asked, "Could we share one?"

Karen laughed. "Don't worry, I'm paying, X."

"Oh no, it's not that; I'm still on a diet," I explained.

Karen stared at me incredulously. "You're on a diet?"

I nodded enthusiastically. "Yes, it's not a particular diet plan as such. I've been limiting myself to 1500 calories daily and swore I wouldn't stop until my body looks like Prince's on the *Lovesexy* cover."

Karen raised her eyebrows. "You like Prince?"

It turns out that Karen is as big a fan of the diminutive pop genius as I am—we were even at the same concert last summer.

She did most of the talking, following the pattern of previous evenings spent with female company. After the first glass of wine, she started to open up about her feelings towards her dad. "He's manipulative, greedy, and selfish. I wouldn't trust him as far as I could throw him."

The clock on the mantelpiece eventually chimed for 10 o'clock, and aware that I had an early start in the morning and was beginning to feel somewhat tired from the wine, I said, "I don't want to, but I've got to get going."

Karen smiled. "Don't tell your parents I've been so generous with the wine; they might get the wrong idea."

I laughed. "Don't worry; I'm not sure they care what I get up to."

"Well, those are two things we have in common then, X. We both like Prince and have unresolved issues with our parents."

She showed me to the door and said, "Thanks, X; I had a great time tonight, and she gave me a kiss on the cheek."

I floated home.

SUNDAY 12TH FEBRUARY

Yesterday's 'date' was almost a complete success. When we arrived in the city, Alison went shopping alone, and we didn't see her again until it was time to head home. Rachael picked a short black dress for the dance party, which, I must say, looked pretty incredible. Despite her suggestion of a shirt she spotted as my potential attire for the big night, I had other ideas. When I came out of the changing room to show her my choices, she asked, "And what would you call that then, X?"

"This, Rachael, *is* 'the original teenager'," I replied, indicating my leather jacket, blue jeans, and white T-shirt.

"Suits you!" she said with a smile.

The only sour point of the whole day came during a particularly competitive game of *Trivial Pursuit* we played later in her room. Having successfully filled her 'pie', she had landed in the centre, only for me to hit her with a sports question, the one category she'd struggled with all game long. She didn't know the answer, and I could see she was furious with herself. Her mood worsened when I won a few rolls of the die later.

"I'd have won if it wasn't for that *fucking* stupid sports question!" she snapped.

Genuinely taken aback, I said, "OK, we'll give that game a miss next time."

"I'm sorry, I'm sorry," she said sincerely.

"There's no need to be so competitive, Rachael; it's just a

game."

"I just want us to be equals, that's all," she said, looking at me with desperation, but the blank look I gave her must have disappointed her. "Argh! You wouldn't understand, would you?"

And on that point and that point alone, I had to agree.

After the game, I suggested we join Alison and Arthur, which Rachael reluctantly agreed to do. As we headed downstairs, I could hear her muttering under her breath, though I couldn't make out what she was saying.

As she showed me out, I thanked her for everything: "I really did have a great day, and we'll have to do it again soon."

"My turn to screw things up," she said sadly.

"Hey, nothing was screwed up," I said brightly.

However, Rachael merely said, "Just go, OK?"

So, I obeyed.

I got up early this morning and went for a bike ride. When I returned, I ate breakfast, showered, changed, and headed to Karen's.

After a couple of hours of finishing the work in the dining room, Karen came in with a coffee for me. When you've drunk that, do you fancy coming for a walk with me? It's a lovely sunny day out there."

Taking the mug from her, I said, "I'd love to, but I really should get on with some work; what would your dad say?"

Karen snorted. "Let me worry about him, X. If I say you're doing a fantastic job, then that's what he'll believe."

Reluctantly, I agreed, and we decided to head along the old railway line, which runs the length of Marketon. As we walked north, a girl with a little poodle approached us. At first, I didn't see who it was, but then she said, "Hey, X."

It was a girl from my Maths class. "Hey, Joanne," I said in response.

My schoolmate looked curiously at Karen and me and then walked on with a mischievous grin.

"She's pretty," Karen said after my schoolmate had passed us by.

"She's OK," I replied absently.

"You know, if you asked any of these girls out, they'd say yes."

As lovely as it was for Karen to say this, schoolgirls have suddenly started to lose their appeal. "What about you?" I said, changing the conversation's direction. "Do you have a boyfriend?"

Karen sighed deeply. "I did have... some time ago now... It's a long story... Do you mind if we don't talk about it?"

Fearful that I had somehow upset her, I apologised, "I'm sorry; I shouldn't have asked; it's none of my business."

Karen stopped walking and looked at me. "Don't worry, X. I'll tell you about him someday, but right now, I'm happy with you, and I don't want anything to spoil that."

I have replayed that phrase all day since. However, at the time, I just clumsily changed the subject.

On returning home, I dutifully rang JG to check that everything was running smoothly with Pete & Dennis' Painting Services. He has, as always, got everything under control, though he asked if I could do a quick audit of all the jobs in progress this week to ensure the painting is up to standard. I was slightly irked about asking what the word audit meant, and was even more irritated by his condescending explanation. I agreed to meet him in new school at 8.30 tomorrow to discuss everything. Also, I think he was trying to subtly say that he has successfully cast off his virgin robes. So, that makes it official, then; I'm the last of the three of us standing.

MONDAY 13TH FEBRUARY

JG was waiting for me in the new school hall when I arrived this morning.

"Am I right in saying congratulations are in order?" I asked brightly as I sat beside him, but my friend stared blankly at me.

"The cat is out of the bag!" I said excitedly. "That's what you said on the phone last night, wasn't it?"

JG looked baffled. "Yes, but X, sorry to be rude, but what the hell are you talking about?"

I shrugged. "I thought you'd shagged Claire."

JG frowned in consternation. "Only in your strange little mind could the phrase 'The cat is out of the bag' possibly refer to sex, X."

"Oh!" I said. "What *were* you talking about then?"

"*Your cat* is out of *your bag!*" he said, emphasising his point by poking me squarely in the chest.

Genuinely baffled, I said, "I haven't got a bag… or, for that matter, *a cat*."

JG shook his head. "*Your* girlfriend… Sorry, you and your 'stunning' older girlfriend were seen on a romantic walk yesterday, holding hands and whispering sweet nothings to one another."

"Karen?" I asked.

Starting to look somewhat exasperated, he replied, "I don't know who *she* is, X; it's not the sort of information my best friend and business partner sees fit not to share with me anymore."

Really, JG, it's not the sort of information I've ever had to share before, so go easy on the 'anymore'.

"It's all rubbish," I said curtly.

Jesus T Christ, I wish it wasn't, however.

JG ignored my denial, though continued in an accusatory manner. "Joanne Yates saw you when she took her dog for a walk yesterday; she called around Beatrice Parker's; Bea called Susan Gates; Susan called Rebecca; Rebecca came round to mine last night to copy my Maths homework and asked twenty questions about *your* love life, none of which *I* had an answer for." It's safe to say that, by this point, he'd lost his temper.

"And I guess that makes it all true," I said flippantly.

"Well, *is it?*" he asked firmly.

"*No!*" I said imploringly. "Who else knows about this anyway?"

"Everybody will soon enough," he said with a shrug.

"Listen, JG; she's the woman whose house I'm painting. She asked if I wanted to go for a walk, and I said, 'Yes'. We strolled, but the handholding and the sweet nothings were dreamt up by Joanne or by someone else further down the gossip trail."

"So, *nothing* has happened between you and this girl?" JG asked firmly.

"*Nothing!*" I said adamantly.

Adopting a humble tone, he said, "Listen, I'm sorry, I just thought there was something you weren't telling me."

"If something ever does happen, you'll be the first to know," I assured him.

"Anyway, here," he said, handing me a sheet of paper. "That's all the names & addresses of the places we're painting. Just check that nobody is doing a crappy job, OK?"

"No problem," I said obediently.

As he headed towards old school, JG turned back to me and eagerly asked, "Right, sorry. Just for clarification, you are still single, then?"

Really, I had no idea where this sudden interest in my non-existent love life had come from. "I solemnly swear, JG," I said, holding up my hand as if swearing an oath, "that unless my parents are planning on springing a surprise arranged marriage on me this evening, I will remain unattached for this day at least."

"Right," he said with a grin, "see you in chemistry, X," and, with that, he rushed off.

In form group, Lisa the Repeater couldn't wait to hear the gossip. "Tell me, I'm your oldest friend; who is she? How did you meet? *Please,* tell me first."

"Nothing to tell, Lisa, I promise you."

"Oh, come on, X, I promise I won't speak to anyone about it," she said, pulling impatiently on my arm.

I sighed. "Lisa, firstly, *you'll* tell everybody; secondly, there's not an ounce of truth in these rumours," and, with that, I took myself off and sat next to Driffid. I was comforted by the knowledge that if it were rumoured that I was enjoying an obsessive three-way love affair with twin llamas, he would still pay the matter little mind.

As I was about to take the spare seat next to the mungo, Lisa shouted after me, "You've changed, Mister. Too cool for school; that's what you are these days."

So, the truth finally dawns. That's how you become cool; you get yourself an imagined girlfriend.

In chemistry, I had just sat next to JG when House Party Helen turned around from the table and said, "Hey, X, JG, why don't you come and sit with Penny and me? There's room on the end for you both."

Frankly, it seemed like a wasted effort to me, but before I could protest, JG enthusiastically said, "Come on, X."

Mr Palmer asked us to break into twos for today's experiment—the oxidisation of hydrogen. "Excellent!" I said to JG. "That sounds like explosions to me."

JG ignored me and suggested, "Why don't you work with Helen? I'll work with Penny."

"Are we playing bloody musical chairs today or what?" I asked my friend in irritation.

However, the others paid me no attention and quickly swapped seats, leaving Helen on my right and Penny on my left.

"How are you, X?" Helen asked once we were all settled.

"Fine," I said, absently.

She smiled at me. "Looking forward to the disco?"

"Dance party," I corrected her.

Helen smiled sweetly. "Looking forward to the dance party, X?"

I shrugged. "I suppose."

She studied me momentarily. "Hey, X, that thing you do to

your hair, does it have a name?"

Self-consciously, I ran my hands through my hair. "The Cochran?"

"It suits you," she said sincerely.

I looked at my new science partner. "Well, you know what they say, Helen—life without hair wax is not *really* living."

"Hey, X, what sort of music do you like?"

Come back, JG!

The questions kept coming, and I was glad when Mr Palmer asked us to collect the required equipment from the front of the lab.

At the end of the class, JG put his arm around my shoulder and said, "That was nice of Penny and Helen to ask them to sit with us, wasn't it?"

"I guess," I said absently.

JG sighed fondly. "They're both pretty, especially Helen, right?"

"Helen? Yes, she's gorgeous, I suppose, less so when she asks so many questions, though," I said casually.

"Right," JG said. "Sorry, X. You did say 'gorgeous,' didn't you?"

"I believe I did," I said, shrugging in acknowledgement.

"OK. See you later," he said abruptly, heading down the corridor at a pace.

JG behaved weirdly, so I avoided him for the rest of the day.

During the morning, I was asked at least eight more times about Karen, so at break time, I made myself a badge with some stickers and a marker pen that read, "I DO NOT HAVE AN OLDER GIRLFRIEND!"

Bizarrely, even that didn't stop them from asking. It was Clare Anatomy's first question when I took my seat next to her in biology. "No, Clare, I do not have an older girlfriend," I said, trying to hold my temper.

"You know, X, the more you deny it, the more people will think it's true," she said teasingly.

"OK, then, fine!" I said, finally losing it. "I have an older girlfriend; happy?"

"I knew it!" she said excitedly.

Memes are fascinating, and events today are proof that an absolute lack of fact is no obstacle to one becoming successful, despite how much I may wish to the contrary.

TUESDAY 14TH FEBRUARY

Another tape arrived in form group this morning, containing Taylor Dayne's 'Tell It to My Heart'. I thought it was a lovely song for Claire to send; Lisa vehemently disagreed, though. "Nice? It's only nice, X, if you like having a psychopathic stalker on your trail!"

Each to their own.

Preparing the hall for the dance party was an uphill task. Ultimately, after following Ms James' *pro-to-col*, I requisitioned Cocksucker Carl and Driffid from their respective classes to assist. By 3.30, most of the work was done, and Rachael1989 and I stayed back to hang up the last few banners.

"Heard about your new girlfriend, X," Rachael said coyly.

I sighed. "Not you as well."

"So, you are still single then?" she asked.

"For 15 years, five months, and five days," I checked my watch. "5 hours."

Rachael smiled. "Maybe it's time for a change, X?"

After going home, showering, and changing, I looked at the clock. It was only 5.15, and as I'd agreed to meet the others back at school at 6, I had time to kill, so I decided to visit Karen.

Opening the door, she looked me up and down and said, "Hello, handsome!" After inviting me in and making me a coffee, she asked, "So what brings you around here, X?"

It was a good question, and one I didn't have an answer for. "I... just wanted to apologise... The work's not getting done very quickly, and... "

Karen smirked. "Do you want to know what I think, X?"

A little hesitantly, I replied, "Sure."

"I think you came here because you wanted me to see how good you looked in your new clothes."

I reddened and looked down at my feet to hide my embarrassment.

"Do you want to know what I also think?" she said, stepping closer. Delicately, Karen ran her finger from the base of my neck to the buckle on my belt. "I think you should go and play with the *little girls* tonight, X, then come back and see *me* tomorrow."

At first, I feared I might have become paralysed, but as Karen started pushing me towards the door, I realised my legs were still functioning as they were designed to. "*Go!* It's your night off, and you're only young once."

The walk to school was a daze, and I must have been still reeling from my encounter with Karen when I arrived. When he saw me, Drake asked, "Jesus, X, are you OK? You look like you're going to puke?"

Pete exceeded all my expectations. He was dressed in his full nightclub uniform—a black suit, bow tie, great coat, and gloves—and his head was freshly shaven. I couldn't imagine a more intimidating beast, and I thanked him heartily for his efforts.

However, Ms James did seem a little suspicious of him and eventually pulled me to one side for a little chat. "Tell me, X, who's the doorman? He looks the part, but for all I know, you led him here straight from the fruit farm with the promise of a milkshake."

"Let me assure you, he's well-qualified," I said sincerely.

"How so?" she asked with interest.

"Are we off the record?" I asked, and Ms James nodded. "He's only recently been released from Backton jail for GBH, aggravated assault, and disturbance of the peace. He's a member of the security team at The Place nightclub, holds the required license, is well on the road to rehabilitation, and is a former, if not somewhat ill-remembered, pupil of this fine establishment," I said proudly.

Ms James looked impressed. "Wow! The real deal, eh? Well done, X. For a moment, I thought you were trying to squeeze one on me while the lights were out."

"I wouldn't dream of it, Ms," I replied, and, for once, I was being entirely sincere with the woman.

The dance party was due to start at 7.30 pm, and, at ten past, Ms James called together the organising committee and the two members of teaching staff who had offered their services for the evening, Mrs Simpson and, rather unfortunately, Mr Crackett. "Right everyone, thank you for volunteering to help this evening. I'm here purely in an oversight capacity tonight, so I'm handing you over to X, who is running the show."

This elicited a groan from Mr Crackett; however, Ms James soon silenced him with a piercing glare.

"Thanks, Ms James," I said. "The plan is simple. Rachel, Pete, and I will work the door. Rachael, you collect tickets. I'll check everyone to ensure they're sober enough to come in, invite them to deposit contraband in the large black dustbin, and Pete will look at them scarily to ensure they do as I've requested. Once inside, pupils are invited to leave their coats and other belongings in the cloakroom, which is being run by Drake, whom Jimmy will ably assist." I smiled smugly as I said my form tutor's Christian name.

Mr Cracket pointed at me. "If you bloody address me like that again, I'll … "

"Now, now, *Jimmy*, we're all one team tonight," Ms James said, suppressing a smile.

I continued, "As I said, coats and bags can be deposited for 10p; pin or tape a raffle ticket to the item and hand the matching ticket to the student."

"No problem, X," Drake said, nodding.

Mr Cracket was staring at me blankly.

"Would you like me to go through that again, Jimmy?" I asked patronisingly.

Again, he raised his finger at me and was about to threaten me in some way or another when Ms James interjected, "Don't push your luck, X!" she said firmly.

"Yes, Ms," I said obediently. "Right, the refreshments stall is being run by JG and Susan."

Mrs Simpson beamed at me.

"Finally, Tony, here is our man on the decks and lights. Please play an hour and forty minutes of pop, fifteen minutes of acid house, and five minutes of The Sisters of Mercy."

"No problem, X," Tony said.

"When The Sisters of Mercy track is played, it may be wise for us to all help on the refreshments stall, as it's almost guaranteed to clear the dance floor of everyone except the mungos."

Even Mr Cracket laughed at that comment.

I looked from face to face and asked, "OK, is everyone happy with what they're doing?" They all nodded in acknowledgement.

Drake looked at the head of year. "What are you doing, Ms?"

She seemed a little put out by his impertinence but furnished him with a response regardless. "If you *must* know, Timothy, I will be in my office, reading. I have precious little interest in watching tipsy teenagers sexually molesting one another, and if I wanted to study the mating rituals of apes, I'd watch an Attenborough documentary. In short, I do not want to be disturbed unless the matter is so grave that word of it may reach Dr Harris' ears tomorrow. Is that understood?"

We all nodded obediently.

"Oh," she continued. "And Peter, I'm aware that some of the students smoke, but could you dissuade them from doing so directly in front of the school? If the headmaster were to drive past and see them, he'd likely have a coronary."

Enthusiastically, Pete replied, "Don't worry, Catherine, I'll tell them to *fuck off* and do it in the bus shelter across the road."

With a face that was half smile and half grimace, Ms James said, "Thank you, Peter," and she headed off towards her office.

With five minutes to go, a significant and increasingly rowdy gathering of pupils stood outside the main new school entrance. Everything appeared ready, and I was mindful that we didn't want any misbehaviour before the event commenced, so I unlocked the door. As I did, I was greeted with both cheers and invective.

"Hurry up, X; it's bloody freezing out here."

However, as soon as Pete came and stood beside me, a fearful silence descended upon the rabble, and I said, "OK, tickets to Rachael, please. If *you are* carrying any booze, please deposit it in the bin by the table."

Like a platoon of well-drilled army cadets, my fellow students obeyed my every word. Watching the contraband bin filling up rapidly was an eye-opening experience. Pete's presence had the desired effect. I'm guessing that 90% of the students decided instantaneously, after seeing the hulking brute, not to risk incurring his wrath by being later caught in possession.

It was amazing to learn how cunning the average 15-year-old, particularly the girls, could be when carrying a concealed bottle or can. Most people, it was plain to see, had partaken of some libation or other. However, everyone seemed in control and, more importantly, in the best spirits.

Nearly everyone was inside within ten minutes, and I was about to suggest that we close the door and leave Pete on sentry duty when Clare Anatomy and Amanda James came stumbling along the path towards us.

"She looks a little unsteady," I said discreetly to Pete and Rachael.

"She looks drunk, X!" Rachael said it indiscreetly.

"She looks fit; that's how she looks," Pete said indelicately, causing Rachael to issue a disapproving sigh. However, Pete's assessment was spot-on; Clare was looking fine even by her high standards.

While Pete questioned the newcomers about their intoxication levels, Rachael pulled me aside. "You can't let her in!" she said imploringly.

"Clare's harmless enough; she'll be OK," I said calmly.

"You're only saying that because she's dressed the way she is!" Rachael said it accusingly.

"That's got nothing to do with it!" I said defensively, "I don't want to turn anyone away if I don't have to. It doesn't seem right."

Rachael's features softened. "You're a big softy; that's what you are, X. I'll turn a blind eye to Clare if you do one thing for me."

"What's that?" I asked.

"Dance with me later," she said intently.

Dance?

"I can't dance!" I said it honestly.

Rachael put her arm around me and pulled me closer to her. "Don't worry, I'll show you how."

Dancing *is* the human mating ritual. How did I miss it when I was putting together my grand plan for 1989? I started to feel a little unwell at the mere thought of it.

With the evening safely underway and everyone seemingly having fun, I chatted to Pete, who remained stoically by the main door. After five minutes, we were joined by JG. "Bloody hell, X, that English teacher of yours is a sex maniac."

"Mrs Simpson?" I asked in confusion.

"Yes!" JG said. "She keeps saying how inspiring it is to watch all these slender young men gyrating in time to music and wishing she could jump on the floor and join them. Frankly, I'm a little scared of her."

I laughed. "Stay here with us for a little while then; Pete will keep you safe."

"Hey, X!" A familiar voice spoke, and I turned to see House Party Helen.

"Hey, Pete, come and join me on the stall for a second," JG said, promptly led Psycho away, leaving me alone with the newcomer.

Helen, like all the girls I find attractive, is a brunette. She has shoulder-length hair, which has plenty of what I'm sure the ads on TV would describe as 'bounce'. Her figure is athletic, and her backside is regarded as the very finest in the school.

"Well done tonight, X," she said.

"Thanks; as long as everyone has a good time, that's all that matters," I replied.

"I was wondering whether you would like to dance with me later?" Helen asked coyly.

I sighed. "Thanks, Helen, but I've already promised Rachael. I can't dance, so being humiliated once will be sufficient."

"Rachael and you, are you?" Helen asked.

I smiled. "Oh no, we're just friends. Best friends."

Raising her eyebrows, Helen asked, "So, you are *still* single then?"

"For 15 years, five months, five days," I checked my watch. "And 8 hours," I lied.

"Maybe it's time for a change, X," Helen suggested.

The dance party had been underway for an hour when Rachael found me lurking by the cloakroom talking to Drake. She grabbed my hand and dragged me towards the hall floor. "Come on, we're dancing, Mister."

Leading me to the centre of the crowd, she turned me to face her. "Listen, I *really can't* dance," I said, raising my voice so she could hear me over the music.

"And I said, 'I'll show you how'. Now, put your hands on my hips," she said obediently; I did as I was told. The record ended, and Tony put on Neneh Cherry's 'Buffalo Stance'. Rachael put her hands on my shoulders and slowly started to move. Reluctantly, I tried to do the same.

"That's it, X; you're getting the hang of it," Rachael said enthusiastically. As the song continued, her hips moved closer to mine, and eventually, with every gyration, her groyne was brushing mine. This was not an unpleasant sensation, but as the song continued, she exaggerated her movements so that we were no longer just touching one another; we were, there's no other word for it, *grinding*.

This was now undoubtedly the most delightful experience of my life thus far. Unfortunately, there was an inevitable reaction in my loins. "Err, Rachael, this is nice, but if you keep doing that, I'm going … " I started.

Rachael touched my lips. "Just go with it, X."

I then had what I believe is commonly called a moment of clarity. *Of course*, if you are *ever* going to have an intimate encounter with a girl, then there is one thing you just must be prepared for: you need to be able to get an erection in front of her without feeling embarrassed. I looked into Rachael's beautiful eyes and had my second moment of clarity; it was about to happen with *her*. Of course it was—it was *always* Rachael. Why hadn't I seen this earlier?

This time, I was 98% certain that our mouths were moving closer together, and I closed my eyes in anticipation.

Then I heard a voice—JG's. "X, sorry to interrupt, but we've got a problem,"

"Five minutes, then I'll be all over it," I said, hoping he'd disappear quickly.

JG coughed loudly. "X, it's a *major* problem." My lips must have been an inch from Rachael's.

"Right," I said irritably, pulling back from her mouth. "I'm coming, and if this isn't important, *I am* going to hurt you!"

I allowed JG to lead me off the dance floor; as he did, he turned back to me and said, "Judging by the scene I've just witnessed, I'd say you owe me some money."

"Don't worry; you'll get your fiver," I assured him.

JG groaned. "X, *this* is why you weren't asked to sit your maths GCSE a year early; you owe me a tenner!"

Really, everyone hates a smart arse.

His interruption had not been without good cause. He led me into the girls' toilets, where a very drunk Clare Anatomy was sitting on the floor being looked after by House Party Helen. Looking at Clare's scant dress and the empty bottle of vodka beside her, my mind did boggle as to how she'd smuggled the contraband past us early.

"Shit!" I yelled as I saw her.

House Party Helen looked at me in dismay. "X, are you going just to swear, or are you going to *do* something?"

I racked my somewhat Rachael-addled brain. "Look after her; I'll be back in five minutes," I said decisively.

I gave three knocks, allowed a polite pause, and entered.

"Ah, X, you know, you were right; this was a good idea. The booze in that contraband bin will take care of the next two staff parties nicely," Ms James said brightly.

I asked, "Are we off the record, Ms?"

"Yes," she replied.

"I have a dilemma. I don't know what to do, and I need your advice."

Ms James rolled her eyes. "Oh yes, I bet the earth *shook* the day your balls dropped, Hercules," she said sarcastically.

Ignoring her wit, I said, "We have a drunken girl on the premises."

Looking concerned, she asked, "How drunk exactly?"

After careful consideration, I gave her my best estimate. "Between very and smashed."

Ms James scowled and advised sternly, "Well, *you* need to get her out of here and get her home safely without my on-the-record self finding out anything about it."

I nodded in understanding. "I thought you might say that

—it's just that the other thing I mentioned about tonight. The thing that hasn't really happened to me before—I think it's just about to."

Ms James smiled. "Then you have a choice: take one for yourself or the team, because if I'm forced to pick up the phone and call that girl's parents, then you and your friends can say *goodbye* to dance parties."

"Right," I said with resignation.

I was about to leave her office when Ms James advised, "Oh, and X, if you are planning to escort her home, take a girl with you."

Clare doesn't live too far from the school, but she was so incapacitated that it took House Party Helen and me twenty minutes to get her home. Our drunken schoolmate's mother then insisted we come in for a cup of tea, her way of saying thank you for our kindness to her daughter.

As we returned to school, Helen asked, "Do you fancy coming over to mine on Friday, X?"

Finally, I got invited to a party!

"Yes, that would be great, Helen," I replied.

By the time we got back to school, Rachael had already left.

WEDNESDAY 15TH FEBRUARY

At lunch, I tried to speak to Rachael1989, but she gave me the brush off.

After school, I decided to resolve my dancing dilemma. My sister used to go to lessons in the community centre in The Village, and I thought I'd try there first. "I remember you; you're poor little Lizzy's brother. What can I do to help?" Miss Richards, the dance teacher, asked.

"I need to learn to move my arms and legs in time to music," I said plainly.

With a look of bemusement on her face, she asked, "X, I teach ballet, tap, modern, and jazz to mainly under 12-year-olds. Exactly which discipline do you think will suit you best?"

I withdrew fifty pounds from my back pocket. "Actually, Miss Richards, I was hoping to arrange one-to-one lessons."

The dance teacher's face lit up when she saw the cash. "Well, X, I'm sure something can be arranged."

When I got to Karen's, I found Karen2 in attendance again, and I busied myself with the painting and kept out of her way.

If it weren't for the fact that I'm a Grade 9 atheist, I might start suspecting there is a curse on me regarding the fairer sex. Then again, maybe it's the girls that are the problem. Perhaps I'll go to school tomorrow and ask Claire With An Eye For X out.

THURSDAY 16TH FEBRUARY

As it happened, I didn't ask Claire out; instead, I spent a tense hour in English exchanging words via Post-it notes with Rachael.

"SORRY, I'M STILL ANGRY ABOUT TUESDAY."

"WHAT CAN I DO?" I replied.

"GET LOBOTOMISED?"

"REALLY, WHAT WAS I SUPPOSED TO DO?"

"LET SOMEONE ELSE SORT THE DRUNKEN TART OUT."

"MS JAMES SAID IT WAS YOU OR THE SCHOOL."

"OH, AND YOU PICKED THE SCHOOL. THANKS!"

"YOU KNOW, SOMETIMES YOU DRIVE ME INSANE."

"YEAH? WELL, YOU'RE A FUCKING TWAT SOMETIMES."

And I guess that's that for the time being. Karen was moderately more friendly than the previous evening. However, there was no return to the intense flirting of Tuesday.

Just an ordinary girl, that's all I ask for: someone attractive, funny and, smart. Honest, I'll be the best boyfriend I can be.

My apologies; that *might* have sounded like a prayer.

FRIDAY 17TH FEBRUARY

Today, when I was least expecting it, my 'like a prayer' was answered, and I was, there's no other word for it, seduced.

Rachael and I are not even exchanging Post-it notes in English anymore. Really, it's *that* bad, and I guess we won't see one another over half-term.

At Karen's, I tried to ask what I'd done wrong in the past few days, but when I broached the subject, she said, "X, spare me; I don't have the patience to deal with schoolboy angst right now."

Fucking twat?

Schoolboy angst?

At about eight, I was lying on my bed, idly toying with the Rubik's cube, when I suddenly remembered House Party Helen's invite. So, having quickly showered, I threw on some new clothes and headed to The Village.

Helen looked ever so slightly irritated when she opened the door to me. "I thought *you* weren't coming."

Keen not to alienate yet another female who, occasionally, seems to quite like me, I politely responded, "I'm so sorry, I was waylaid."

Folding her arms with suspicion, Helen asked, "How exactly?"

"I was working and then brooding," I replied honestly.

Helen's face finally broke out in a smile. "And are you brooded out now?" she asked, and, after I'd nodded in the affirmative, she invited me in with a wave of her hand.

Much to my surprise, it turned out that Helen was throwing a party for just the two of us. Also, the shocks didn't stop there.

"I've got a thing for you, X," she said sweetly as we sat in front of the fire in her sitting room.

The light bulb finally illuminated. "Right, I get you now; you weren't just being weird in chemistry when you kept asking all those questions, were you?" I asked.

Helen looked at me, dismayed. "Strangely enough, X, *no*. That's called flirting! JG did warn me you'd be slow to catch on, but *Jesus*, this is off the scale."

Flippantly, I replied, "Oh great, JG is involved in this too, is he? This is like some nightmare date in a Franz Kafka novel."

Then, suddenly, I stopped myself.

X, this girl is beyond lovely; what's more, she likes you. Get over yourself right now and make this right.

I held my hand up in apology. "I'm sorry, Helen, please ignore what I just said. In here," I tapped the side of my head. "I'm still the chubby kid that no one pays a great deal of attention to, and it will take a little while for the rest of me to catch up. I'm utterly flattered that someone as gorgeous as you would want to spend the evening with me."

Judging by how Helen beamed at me, I knew my mini-speech had worked. "Well, X, it seems we have similar opinions of one another."

After a couple of beer cans had been drunk, Helen held out her hand and asked, "Would you like to come upstairs with me, X?"

Fortunately, I behaved appropriately and didn't burn the carpet in my sprint to her bedroom. What followed ... well, it was delightful. Don't get me wrong, we didn't do *it*, though I don't think 'courting' covers it.

"Sorry I was a bit slow to catch on," I said later, as we were laid together, half-naked, upon her bed.

"That's all right; you got warmer as the evening progressed," Helen said, kissing my ear.

I heard a thud downstairs but paid no mind to it.

"Just one thing, X," Helen said with concern.

"What's that?" I asked.

Reaching down, she scooped my jeans from the floor and deposited them on my bare chest, "Would you mind throwing your clothes on quickly, climbing out of my window and shimmying down my drainpipe? I think that's my parents!"

As I climbed out the window, Helen smiled and said, "Another time?"

"I'd like that; maybe on the next occasion, I'll just come in through your bedroom window," I said eagerly.

"I look forward to it!" she said, giving me one final kiss.

So, at last, I have crossed the Rubicon. I know I haven't done *it*, but I have shared intimacy with a remarkable young woman whom I think I will ask to be my girlfriend. With life like this, who knows the heights I could reach in 1989? I knew it was my year; I could feel it. Maybe it's time to stop writing about it and get out there and really live it.

PART 2

Welcome to the Pleasuredome

FRIDAY 2ND JUNE

After climbing up the drainpipe, I rapped lightly on the pane. I couldn't see in as the curtains were closed; however, the light was on. When Helen opened the window, she stared at me, dismayed. "You took your bloody time, didn't you?"

"I was waylaid," I replied humbly.

Teasingly, Helen said, "You know, if my dad were to catch *you* in my bedroom, he'd probably drop down dead in shock."

"Really?" I asked.

She sighed. "Oh, come off it, X; even you must know that you're the teenage cautionary tale to end all teenage cautionary tales?"

There is a phrase, 'famous last words,' and after reading that last page I wrote in February, I am now more in tune with its meaning than I was previously.

"What the hell happened, X?" Helen said, looking at me in bewilderment once I'd climbed into her room and sat on her bed.

I sighed deeply. "Helen, you must believe me when I say this, but it was the first Monday evening of the half-term holidays, and I was about to come over here and ask you to be my girlfriend."

"And?" Helen asked in wonder.

"And instead, I answered the siren's call," I replied.

Really, it's all chaos.

If I'd left for Helen's just one minute earlier, I'd never have taken Karen's call. "Please, X, I need you; come over; I wouldn't ask if it wasn't an emergency," she pleaded down the phone line.

The woman had hardly said a pleasant word to me in a week, and yet I, *sucker*, dutifully went over to hers as requested. When I arrived, there was a guy, unknown to me then and still unknown to me now, trying to push his way into the house while Karen vainly attempted to block his path. As for what happened next, something snapped. Before I knew what I was doing, I'd grabbed the back of his jacket and dragged him away from the door.

When the unknown aggressor finally caught sight of his opponent, he laughed sadistically, and said, "Fuck off, kid, before you get yourself hurt."

I'd never been brave before, but suddenly it was easy. "Make me!" I said intently.

I saw his swing coming out of the corner of my eye, but it was too late to duck out of its way. His fist connected with my face, but fortunately, his punch lacked, *well*, punch. In response, though, my body flooded with adrenaline, and before I knew what I was doing, I'd landed a blow and heard cartilage snapping as my knuckles crashed into his nose. It wasn't exactly a technical knock-out; however, as he tried to stem the blood flow with his hand, I could see him weighing up the pros and cons of further pugilism. Eventually, he decided and, pointing at Karen, said, "You're fucking bad news; do you know that?"

I watched him return to his car, get in, and drive off. After that, I pushed past Karen and stormed into her house.

"Oh god, X, are you OK?" she said, following me.

I angrily threw my coat to the floor and saw that my T-shirt was splattered with blood. At the time, I didn't know whether it was mine or his. I removed it and threw it to the floor in a rage.

"X, let me look at your face. Are you hurt?" Karen said, looking at me intently.

"Who *the fuck* was that?" I demanded to know.

"Nobody," Karen said submissively, and then, somewhat unexpectedly, she started kissing me. Pushing her back against the wall aggressively, I kissed her right back. Next, we were ripping each other's clothes off. We didn't even get upstairs; we just made love on her kitchen floor. I swear, it was the most exciting two minutes of my life. *Still*, I did beat Drake by thirty seconds.

Later, lying in her bed, I asked, "So who was he?"

"*He* was a mistake, but it doesn't matter now; I've got you!" Karen said this and immediately started kissing me again.

I left at about eleven, and when I returned the following day, I wasn't sure which Karen would open the door to me, but we were doing *it* again within five minutes of my walking into her house.

Later that evening, I told Mum, "Hey, I need to finish my job this week. The lady I'm working for says I can work late and sleep in her spare room."

"If you need to work, love, you need to work," she replied absently.

Sex is like cycling; the more you do it, the better you get. When I returned to school the following week, Karen and I were on fire. She was all I could think about.

In English, Rachael asked, "What happened to you over half term? You seem different."

"I grew up!" I replied, and to celebrate this fact, I started smoking.

Helen was as friendly as ever, but although I was not rude to her, I made it clear that I was no longer on the market.

As Karen was due at a party at her parent's house on a Saturday evening, I agreed to go and watch *Rain Man* with Rachael. I had intended to inform her about my change of status. Unfortunately, I didn't get the chance before she kissed me halfway through the film.

I gently pushed her away and said, "I'm sorry, but there's someone else."

Rachael stormed out of the theatre, and I reluctantly followed her. I never did find out whether Dustin Hoffman's and Tom Cruise's characters found a way to get along, which is a shame as, just before our departure, I was starting to feel that they really needed one another in each other's lives.

When I got outside the cinema, I was somewhat alarmed to find Rachael being pinned against the wall by the throat by an irate-looking Karen, who looked at me and screamed, "What *the fuck* is going on, X?"

Holding my hands in appeasement, I said sincerely, "She's just a friend, Karen. *No one* could compare to you." Eventually, after considerable persuasion, I got Karen to see reason, and she released her grip on Rachael.

Calmly, I told Karen, "Let's go home together."

We quickly got into her car and drove off.

I feel dreadful writing this now, but I have no idea how

Rachael got home that evening. All I could think was that Karen must *really* love me.

In English on Monday, I was anticipating total silence from Rachael; however, 20 minutes into the lesson, I received a Post-it note. "YOUR GIRLFRIEND IS A PSYCHO!"

"YOU WOULDN'T UNDERSTAND."

"I'M NOT ANGRY. JUST KNOW I'M HERE FOR YOU."

The next afternoon, as I stood outside the school gates talking to JG and Drake, Karen pulled up in her car and yelled, "Get in, stud!"

That was it; the next day, the news was everywhere. Other boys looked at me with awe reserved for someone who had just won the jackpot on the pools. I hadn't just gotten myself a girlfriend—I'd pulled Helen of Troy.

Not everyone seemed happy for me. Geoff Travis, school heartthrob and football hero, and I had a little set-to in the canteen. "Check out, X. You think you're a big man suddenly. So that you know, I remember when you were a fat loser."

"Geoff," I said diplomatically. "I have no problem with you whatsoever, and I'm not sure what I've done to upset you," Thankfully, as Geoff didn't seem to be able to verbalise his issues with me, the tension rapidly dissolved.

Really, who *does* have time for schoolboy angst?

"I thought you handled that situation very well with Geoff earlier," Rachael1989 said approvingly in classics.

Thoughtfully, I responded, "I'm a lover, not a fighter, Rach."

Life with Karen was exciting. She bought me an expensive suit with her dad's credit card to ensure I would get into her preferred pubs and clubs. We even went to an illegal rave one night, and as soon as we arrived, Karen put a pill in my mouth and told me to swallow. Stuart Moor was there, and we exchanged pleasantries while simultaneously punching our fists into the air in time to the relentless beat and chewing gum ferociously. Following that evening, the school thug sat next to me in form group, telling me his tales of mischief as if we were the oldest of friends.

You don't realise you are changing at the time; however, with hindsight, it's easy to see the signposts, and the day I fought with Mr Shaver was one of them.

It must have been a couple of weeks after I'd started seeing Karen; I was walking to class when a year-one boy barged into me, "Watch where you're going!" was all I'd said to him.

"Go screw yourself, X!" he replied, running down the corridor.

I'd entirely forgotten about the incident when, as I was getting changed for gym class, Mr Shaver marched in, grabbed me by the shirt front, threw me against the wall, and held me tightly around the throat. "You hit one of my lads this morning, didn't you?"

Perplexed and terrified in equal measure, I squeaked, "What?"

"You heard me. Just before the second period, you hit Alex White!" he snarled.

Alex being the cocky little brat who had bumped into me earlier, Mr Shaver's interrogation started, at last, to make some vague sense.

"I didn't touch the kid," I said defiantly. "He was rude to me."

Mr Shaver's grip on my throat tightened. "Don't tell lies to me, *boy*."

By now, the fear had begun to dissipate and was being replaced by adrenaline and, I'll admit, a fair amount of self-righteous indignation. "I'm not lying, and get your *fucking* hands off me," I said. The rest of the gym class had stopped changing and were now watching the scene unfold with intense interest.

Mr Shaver laughed sadistically. "That's right, you think you're a big man all of a sudden, don't you? Now you're screwing that *slut* who lives over the road from me?"

And with that, I saw lots of red.

Usually, as at all schools, I imagine, when a fight starts at Luther Parkinson, a howling, blood-thirsty crowd soon forms to watch the combatants slug it out. However, as Mr Shaver and I rolled around on the floor, hell-bent on inflicting as much damage on each other as possible, my classmates watched on in horrified silence. Fortunately, before either of us had the chance to cause any lasting harm to one another, Big Wilson, the burly gym teacher, pulled us apart and marched us both to Ms James' office.

"What were you thinking, X? He's saying you threw the first punch," Ms James asked in wonder.

"He insulted my girlfriend," I replied, opening another can of worms.

Ms James' face registered disapproval. "Yes, well, X, I've heard everything about this new *lady friend*, and she's *too* old for you!"

"I'm not sure what you're talking about, Ms; my girlfriend is seventeen," I lied.

There was a flash of anger on the head of year's face. "X, that's the first and last time you ever try to take me for a fool in this office, do you hear me?" She said it threateningly. "Now," she said, quickly regaining her composure. "I appreciate that you probably have powerful feelings for this individual; however, and you'll just have to trust me on this one, some things are doomed from the start."

Snappily, I asked, "Oh yeah, and how many girls in year four dating older guys have you pulled in for the same chat, Ms James?"

"It's different for girls, X," she said soothingly. "Trust me, this one's going to end in tears—*your* tears, to be precise."

After uber-brat Alex White hastily withdrew his accusation during Ms James' inquisition, it was looking like I was in the clear, while the woodwork teacher seemed to have booked himself an appointment with the dole office; however, that night, as I sat upon Karen's doorstep smoking, I saw Shaver's car pull up across the street. As he got out, he briefly looked in my direction before quickly averting his gaze, but when his wife got out the passenger door and I saw that she was at least eight months pregnant, I nearly threw up.

Later, Karen unsympathetically advised, "I wouldn't change your story one little bit, X. Remember what he said about me?"

"He's just about to become a father, Karen; it's no surprise he's wound up so tightly," I replied reasonably.

The following day, I went straight to Ms James's office. "I want to change the statement I made yesterday. Mr Shaver said nothing to incite me; I just hit him."

"What on earth for?" she asked, looking appalled.

Unfortunately, I hadn't done much planning for this faux confession, so after a moment's thought, I said, "Actually, Ms, this may sound a little strange, but it's just always been an ambition of mine to punch a teacher in the face."

The head of year fixed me with a piercing glare. "You could get expelled for this! I hope you know what you're doing, X, and, *off the record*, I don't believe a bloody word you're saying."

For a little while, I thought I would be expelled, but in the end, I was handed a five-day suspension. When explaining my actions to Dad, I opted for the truth, except for the little fact that the 'nice' lady whose house I was painting was now, in fact, my lover. "You did a good thing, son, a good thing," he said, and the home discipline committee rested.

At first, I thought getting suspended would make other pupils wary of me. However, it seemed to have the opposite effect. Interest in me soared, and my sex appeal doubled with everyone except Rachael.

"I thought you were a lover, not a fighter," she asked dispassionately in the first English class after my enforced absence.

Thoughtfully, I replied, "Actually, Rachael, I think I might be a bit of both."

A few days later, Mr Shaver stopped me in the corridor and said quietly, "I owe you, X."

My suspension soon looked like a blip compared to my subsequent controversy—I was arrested, and this one was all thanks to Karen.

When you're adrift in an insane, unstable relationship, you

need to develop a system to see you through—it's called lying to yourself. However, it's a less-than-perfect mechanism, and just like the maddest of inmates in the darkest of asylums, you still have moments of clarity. I had such an epiphany that Saturday evening.

It'll be all right, X; she's just gone for a drink with a friend; that's what people do.

Listen, X, I'm your authentic inner voice, the one you stopped listening to after your first shag. How can she go out for a drink with a friend when she has none? The only person who gets in touch with her is that psycho-ex of hers who calls in the early hours when he's shit-faced, and, as it's you that usually takes the calls from him these days, he's more likely to ask you out for a beer as the two of you have now built up something of a rapport.

I spent the early evening fretting like a soon-to-be-jilted groom. Eventually, in search of sympathy, I called Rachael.

After explaining the cause of my turmoil to her, Rachael, in a voice dripping with sarcasm, said, "Oh, the nice lady who assaulted me for the heinous crime of going to the cinema with you? The woman who's turned you into a tragic, self-obsessed love-junkie? She's gone off somewhere, has she? Well, maybe she's been involved in a high-speed motorway collision, X. Don't worry though, I'll send flowers to the funeral… *or perhaps not!*"

I sighed. "You know, you'll never get a job with the Samaritans if this is your idea of making someone feel better about life."

"I'm not trying to make you feel better—I'm trying to make you see sense. That's what real friends do, X."

"Can I ask you something without you freaking out?"

"OK."

"Are you jealous?"

There was a long pause before she replied, "A little... at first, but my feelings for you, X... they fluctuate...like you wouldn't believe. Don't get me wrong, you're one of my favourite people... ever, but you can be an utter arsehole when you put your mind to it."

It was my turn to pause before speaking, the Mickey Rourke feeling having crept into the pit of my stomach again. "Hey, Rach, what are your feelings for me right now?"

Her answer wasn't exactly what I'd hoped for. "Honestly? Concern! I want you to wake up to yourself, that's all."

"Listen, I appreciate what you've said; I do... and I need to do some thinking. Thank you, Rachael. See you Monday?"

"See you, X."

As I hung up the phone, it rang immediately. I desperately wanted it to be Rachael, but instead, it was a paralytic Karen, and I duly fell straight back to sleep.

Despite her almost incoherent speech, I figured out that Karen was pissed in a village pub about five miles out of Marketon, and I, *sucker,* answered the siren's call *again.*

At best, the lights on my bike are ineffective, and it was a miracle that I wasn't killed on the journey to Long Sawton. As I arrived, the landlord politely suggested that Karen call it a night. As I approached the table where she was slumped, he beamed at me in relief. "Oh, here you go, love; your little brother's here to take you home."

Drunken people weigh more; it's a fact, possibly twice as much as when they are sober. After I'd practically carried her from inside the pub to the car, she had the second worst idea in history. "Don't worry, X, I'll drive us home," she slurred.

Rest assured, though, I had that one beat. "No, don't be ridiculous; you're smashed; I'll drive. How hard can it be?"

It is *really* hard as it happens.

After stalling five times, I'd finally got us on the road back to Marketon when, forty yards ahead, I saw a large saloon reversing out of a driveway. Having forgotten which pedal was which, I thought I'd play it safe and press all three simultaneously. It was a shit idea; I missed all of them, and the full Isaac Newton followed.

To say the guy whose car I'd *remodelled* was pissed off would be the understatement of the century. I'd never heard someone shout quite so loudly before. The crash had one positive effect, though, as Karen seemed much soberer as she repeatedly countered his every outburst by retorting flippantly, "Oh, fuck off, mate, it's only a scratch."

She was correct; it was just a scratch *and* an enormous dent. Karen's car, meanwhile, had come off even worse.

With other villagers now appearing to watch the scene unfold, the shouting man gave up on Karen and began venting his spleen at me. "Why didn't you stop? How old are you anyway? I've bet you have no idea how much a car like this is worth, do you?"

I understand he was angry and needed to get it off his chest, but he kept repeating the same three questions. Whether he was in shock or I'd just triggered a speech impediment, I cannot say. I asked him—scratch that—*begged* him to stop, but he kept going. In the end, just to shut him up, I hit him. And that's when things went even further south… a siren, flashing blue lights, and eight words you really don't ever want to hear.

Mercifully, Karen drew the short straw and was questioned by the young, rat-faced bad cop, while the older, overweight good cop took me to one side. "What's your name, son?"

"X," I answered uncertainly. My breathing had become irregular, and my heartbeat was so loud that I could have danced to it.

The police officer smiled warmly. "Cool name, but I need

your real one, X."

As I answered, I turned and saw Karen, who was shouting obscenities, being led to the police car by Bad Cop.

Good Cop sighed. "OK, what happened, X?"

Good question, X; what happened?

I looked down at my feet. "Really, I don't know. I was just *so* tired of being an utter nobody that girls looked through like glass, so I devised this big action plan: lose weight, get rich, raise my profile, and be cool. Honestly, I never meant to do any harm; it's just that, someway along the line, I lost the plot, and everything's gone horrifically fucking pear-shaped suddenly."

The policeman looked at me in bemusement. "No, I meant what happened here *tonight*, X?"

"Oh, sorry," I said with embarrassment and pointed at the wrecked vehicles. "Err, I drove that car into that one really fast."

He nodded. "And do you have a driving license, X?"

I shook my head.

"I'm going to have to arrest you now."

Top job, X. Tomorrow, you can get your 'Fucked for Life' tattoo, an addiction, and a dead-end job because that's about all existence has to offer you now.

Difficult as it was, I fought back the tears, nodded in acceptance, and then the strangest thing happened. Bad Cop got out of the car, walked up to Good Cop, whispered something in his ear, and Good Cop said to me politely, "Just wait there for a minute, X."

The police officers then turned their attention exclusively to Shouting Man and, after much resistance, made him do a breathalyser test, which he failed. Eventually, after a lengthy three-way discussion, Good Cop returned to me and said,

"Come with me, X."

A little confused, I asked, "Am I under arrest?"

He laughed. "Probably not."

As we drove back to Marketon, leaving Bad Cop behind, I remained ignorant of my situation. Good Cop refused to answer my questions, and Karen passed out in the back seat beside me.

Rather than being taken to the station, our destination was the Ronson House. Good Cop spoke briefly with Karen's father, John, on the doorstep. After which, her mother came out of the house and, with considerable effort, managed to escort her semi-comatose daughter inside. The policeman soon followed her into the house. This left John Ronson eyeing me curiously from the threshold of his home.

After casually walking to the police car, hands in pockets, he opened the rear passenger door and said, "Evening, X."

"Good evening, sir," I replied. Now more than ever, I thought formality might be an excellent idea with this guy.

Sighing deeply, he said, "Let me guess, Karen got plastered and tried to drive home, but you stepped in and did the honourable thing?"

I smiled meekly. "That's about the long, the tall, and the short of it, sir."

John nodded approvingly. "Good for you, lad. Need a ride home?"

I shook my head. "No, it's fine… " In sudden realisation, I quickly added, "*Oh shit*, my bike is back in Long Sawton."

"Valuable, is it?" John asked with interest.

I shook my head. "I bought it second-hand for £20, but the

emotional attachment to it is beyond measure."

John smiled. "Well, far be it from me to keep you from a treasured possession; I'll drive you down there and take you home."

I smiled warmly, but then my expression turned severe. "Sorry, sir. Just one question before we proceed. Will I get arrested?"

Mr Ronson laughed. "Not unless you're planning any other mischief tonight, X."

After we returned to my house and retrieved the bike from the boot, I said, "Hey, Mr Ronson, I'm not sure quite what you did tonight, but I'm pretty sure you did *something*, and that *something* is the reason why I'm not in a police station facing a tough conversation with my parents."

Mr Ronson ruffled my hair affectionately. "Don't worry, you young bugger. If there is nothing else in this life, you can always rely on a copper to take a payoff."

Not exactly sure how to respond, I said, "Oh, I'll be sure to remember that, sir."

Karen's dad hadn't quite finished with me. "Listen, X, what you did tonight, well, you probably saved my daughter's life… though *whether* she deserved it or not is an altogether different matter," he added. "Anyway, there's nothing I appreciate more than loyalty. Here you go, son, treat yourself to something nice," and with that, he handed me a roll of notes.

It wasn't until I was back in my room that I could count the money he'd given me: two hundred quid! *My* pay-off, I suppose. It was a mightily generous gesture, but it would have been much cheaper if Karen had just gotten a bloody cab from the pub.

The following day, rather than going for the usual bike ride, I lay in bed and wondered about my great escape from the previous evening. Really, I should have been screwed, but instead, I'd been let off scot-free. I hadn't even had to suffer an 'X, treat this as a sign, and get your life back on track' lecture. A less rational mind might have divined the hand of fate or a fairy godmother at work, but I knew why I was in the clear; I was banging the daughter of the town bigshot, simple as that. Life isn't fair, but occasionally, it can offer you a soft landing.

Lesson learned, though—I was resolved to send Karen's and my relationship the way of the dinosaurs.

The following day at school, though, the airbag that had cushioned my fall burst. Good Cop was the father of Carol Shipley, a girl in my maths class; the news was everywhere.

Most pupils looked at me as if I were a celebrity, except my friends and Ms James.

After 15 minutes of Mr Crackett referring to me as Jailbird, I was summoned to the head of year's office.

"Wanting to raise your profile in the school is one thing, but mindless self-destruction, which is what this behaviour is starting to resemble, is another matter altogether."

I responded solemnly, "I've had a warning shot across my boughs, and from this day forth, I'm going to be a changed man."

I later repeated the same speech, almost verbatim, to Rachael1989 in English.

After school, I dutifully called Karen and walked over to her house. When she answered the door, she wore an incredibly short silk robe, and I immediately felt the strain of turning my new leaf.

"My dad says I'm a very naughty girl who owes you a big apology. So, to say sorry, I'm going to be naughtier than I've ever been with anyone before," and with that, she took the robe off. Underneath, she wore the sort of black lace underwear rarely seen in this part of the world.

What followed, well, I'm not telling, but it was like Prince said: *I can't tell you what she did to me, but my body will never be the same.*

The next evening, I went over to Rachael1989's to confess. "I'm sorry, Rach. I know you're not going to approve, but Karen and I are still together. Please don't get mad; it's out of my hands. Genetics has got me by the balls on this one. Anyway, I've been thinking this doesn't stop me from being the best friend you could ever have, and that's what I solemnly swear to be from this day forth."

To my amazement, Rachael replied, "That would be good, X."

As I was packing away my things after classics that Friday, Dr Harris wandered over to my desk and leaned in confidentially. "Icarus," he said quietly.

I nodded. "Flew too close to the sun, didn't he, sir?"

The head looked me up and down. "Those wings of yours are melting, my boy; take heed."

My next step towards notoriety followed shortly afterwards. Doubtless, with a mind to levering me back onto the straight and narrow, Ms James offered Pete and Dennis' Painting Services the opportunity to decorate the school library one weekend. Before we even got the chance to get started, though, someone broke into the school store and stole the cans of paint intended for the job.

With my previous brush with the law still fresh in the hive mind, it didn't take the school meme machine long to do its thing and declare me a prime suspect in the break-in. When the police came to the school, they questioned me for nearly an hour. They even asked if I had an alibi. As it happened, I did; however, as it involved a presumed 15-year-old sleeping with a 23-year-old, I decided this wasn't necessary information to share with law enforcement officers, so I lied and said I'd been with Rachael1989.

"You *bastard*, you *utter shit*, X! Is this your idea of being the best friend I could ever have?" Rachael screamed at me after I'd caught up with her on the way home from school.

"What did you say?" I asked nervously.

"Oh, don't worry; I got you off the hook. When they asked what we'd been doing, I said, 'What do teenage boys and girls normally do when they get together, PC Hanson?' Though the thought of it, frankly, turns my stomach." Rachael said before exploding into tears. I can't believe you stole that paint and got me to cover for you."

"Listen, Rachael, I can explain… " I didn't get the chance as she ran off towards the village. We've hardly spoken since.

Suspicion seemed to grow at school that I had been involved in the burglary; even JG confronted me. "X, just tell me straight. Was it you?"

"I promise you it wasn't me," I said solemnly.

Two days later, in form group, Stuart Moor asked if I would be interested in buying some paint at a knocked-down price.

"Jesus, Stuart, do you know how much trouble that paint has

caused me?" I asked in an angry whisper.

"Sorry, X, mate, we were bored; you know how it is?" Stuart said it flatly.

Really, I don't.

As the week progressed, Stuart became increasingly worried, as the police still visited the school daily.

"What am I supposed to do, X?" he asked desperately.

Leaning close to him, I said, "I have an idea, Stuart, but you're not going to get anything out of this other than a clear conscience. Is that understood?"

"What's the plan, X?" he asked in wonder.

Really, I *was* trying to do the right thing.

My scheme wasn't exactly *The Italian Job*, merely breaking into the school and putting the paint back.

Sitting in Pete's car, waiting to go—Stuart was in the back—the ex-offender eyed me suspiciously from the driver's seat. "If I end up going back to nick for this, X… " he began.

"Pete, I'm not even sure what we're doing is illegal," I said firmly.

Pete shook his head. "*This* is breaking and entering, X; trust me, *it's* illegal."

Reasonably, I replied, "Listen, if we play this right, people will stop thinking I'm a thief, Stuart won't be sent to a young offenders institute, and the school won't be out of pocket."

Pete sighed. "X, does the phrase 'two wrongs don't make a right' mean anything to you?"

"This isn't two wrongs, Pete," I said imploringly. "This is a wrong and a right. Frankly, I'm unsure what that makes, but that's our situation here."

"A wring?" Stuart suggested from the back seat, but as I've already said, undoubtedly, pound for pound, the stupidest boy in the school.

However, to his credit, the school thug turned out to be a masterful burglar, and Pete, judging from the handiwork he displayed that evening, was no stranger to illegal break-ins. We soon had the paint back in place, and, as we'd smashed a window to gain entry, I even left a £20 note taped to the wall of the store cupboard to cover the cost of the damage.

Mistakenly, I thought replacing the paint would restore my reputation with my fellow pupils. However, it had the opposite effect and only confirmed my guilt in their eyes. This wasn't helped by Stuart proudly telling everyone who would listen to him, "X and me put the paint back."

The school meme machine did the rest. So began the process of my isolation from the student body.

At the time, I thought, *Screw them; I've got a business making me more money than I know what to do with, a girlfriend other boys can only dream of, and enough real friends left.*

Not for long, though. Pete and Dennis' Painting Services was the first to go.

Tensions regarding enterprise management had been slowly growing between JG and me, and things finally reached boiling point one Sunday evening when I went over to pick up my share of the profits.

"Do you even know what's going on anymore, X?" he asked accusingly as he handed me an envelope full of cash.

Testily, I replied, "Of course I do, JG; it's *my* business."

JG scowled. "It's *our* business, X, remember? *I* do all the work; I check everything's going OK and ensure we get paid, and the boys get their wages. *You* spend your entire life around that woman's house, shagging. The only thing you turn up on time for is payday."

In response, I flipped. "I knew it; you're jealous. Well, my apologies that I'm not the school nobody anymore, and I least have sex with my bloody girlfriend, unlike you!"

JG reddened with anger and embarrassment; however, his response was conciliatory. "X, you're my friend; I know you didn't mean what you just said. Just sort it out, or I quit, OK?"

Ignoring the door marked 'You Can Still Save This Friendship, X!' I yelled, "Quit now! I started this thing and can run it perfectly without you!"

"Fine!" JG said it flatly, and we haven't spoken since.

Two weeks—that's all it took for Luther Parkinson's number one student business to end up as dust. I swear, I'll never paint again as long as I live.

Drake was next. His performances of *Jesus Christ Superstar* were spread across a weekend, and although I'd agreed to go away with Karen, I was sure I would make it back for the final performance on Sunday. However, Karen and I got so smashed on Saturday night that she could not drive until late in the evening, and we arrived too late to make the show.

When I called for him the following day, he said, "Don't come around for me anymore, X; you only care about yourself."

That one really stung.

Karen was the last thing to go. After an intense six weeks together, cracks began to show. I've been around antidepressants for as long as I can remember, and I immediately recognised them in her bathroom cabinet the first night I slept with her. However, over the following weeks, I noticed that the amounts in the bottles didn't decrease, and I convinced myself that whatever problems Karen may have suffered from, they were now safely in the past.

With a week or so to go before the Easter holidays, Karen2 started making appearances again. At first, I dismissed it as a phase and got out of the way when the clouds gathered.

"I think I need to work, X," she declared one night and promptly took a temp job in a neighbouring town. I thought this would improve her mood, but she grew more distant. Also, she began working every hour that she could. As I had keys to her place, I could let myself in whenever I wanted; however, when she arrived home from work one night and found me there, she just said, "*Jesus*, X, give me some space, will you?"

That was fine for her to say, but she was all I had left. After leaving things to cool down for a few days, I resolved to confront her. When I entered her house, an older guy wearing a suit stood in her hallway.

Turning to me with a look of bemusement, he said, "If you're delivering a paper, lad, it's polite to put it through the letterbox, not walk into the house." Next, Karen appeared at the top of the stairs, held her hand to her mouth in horror, and said, "Oh shit!"

I'm reliably informed, even by teachers who hate my guts, that I'm a bright kid, and, as such, it didn't take long to figure out the plotline of the scene I'd just walked into. In short, I lost it and started throwing punches wildly at the interloper. Unfortunately, I was hopelessly outgunned on this occasion, and he began striking me. Karen was screaming wildly, and he, I never did find out his name, grabbed hold of me, dragged me outside onto her front lawn, and began issuing what I hope will remain for some time, the beating of my life. I was lying on the ground, trying desperately to protect my head from his kicks, when, rather curiously, my assailant tumbled motionless to the floor beside me. At first, I thought Karen had intervened, but when I finally looked up, I saw Mr Shaver rubbing his fist above me.

He smiled at me and winked. "The real trick, X, is to knock them out with the first punch."

Breathlessly, I replied, "Sir, as long as I live, *I swear*, I'll never forget that piece of advice."

Mr Shaver's wife, Sarah, tended to my numerous injuries while the woodwork teacher watched on curiously. Eventually, he said, "If you want my advice, X, start screwing girls your age, mate."

"Leave him alone, Trevor. Look at the poor lad; I reckon he's learned his lesson well enough," Sarah said compassionately.

I looked at Mr Shaver. "I reckon this makes us even."

"Not yet," he replied with a firm shake.

Unfortunately, Sarah wasn't entirely correct, and I was still convinced I could salvage my relationship with Karen. After school the next day, I went to her house, which was deserted.

The following day, as I came out of my house, I saw Mr Ronson's Jaguar parked 20 yards along the street. "Get in, X," he said as I approached the car.

I was ever so slightly terrified. If Karen is to be trusted—and let's face it, the jury's still so far out on that particular issue that you'd struggle to see them through a mighty telescope—the word gangster would not be entirely ill-placed if it featured in the same sentence as Mr Ronson's name. However, I was desperate to know where she was, so I obediently hopped into the passenger seat beside the older man.

Despite my trepidation, Karen's father immediately struck a conciliatory note by saying sincerely, "I'm sorry, X."

As I had expected his opening statement to be more like, "I was paying you to paint the house, X, not to ravish my daughter 42 times without paying the slightest heed to the notion of safe sex," I relaxed somewhat.

Mr Ronson continued with resignation, "That daughter of mine has been driving men insane since she was old enough to wear a bra. However, what she did this time with you was wrong, and you have my sincere apologies."

Eagerly, I asked, "Where is she?"

He shook his head. "She's gone away again, X," he said flatly.

"Where?" I asked desperately.

He turned to me. "You're a bright lad, X; figure it out for yourself."

I nodded in realisation. "Is she OK?"

Mr Ronson sighed. "We'll get her back. God knows this isn't the first time. Just one thing: X, you can't see her again. Please don't make me have to stop you, understand?"

I nodded again.

"Here!" he said, throwing an envelope into my lap. Buy yourself something to cheer yourself up."

When he drove off up the street, I investigated the cash-stuffed envelope with wonder. It must have been three times more than the last wad. Buy something to cheer me up. No problem, I swear; I spent every single penny of it on drugs.

You see, some brave people can pick themselves up and march boldly on when they have just had their guts ripped out, as I had. What I learned that day was that I was not one of them. I would need help to get through this, and figured a call to the Samaritans wouldn't do the job.

Up to that point in my life, I had tried soft drugs courtesy of Karen, although I wouldn't have known how to secure them myself if it hadn't been a chance detour Pete had made a month or so earlier, after he had driven me over to a DIY store so I could procure supplies. Pulling into one of the estates on the other side of town, he'd parked the car, got out, and made a quick house call.

"What was that all about?" I asked when he got back in the metro.

Pete sighed. "That was me politely requesting that Doffo, the drug dealer who lives there, no longer shows his face at The Place because if he does, I'm under strict instructions to pull his head from his torso."

When Doffo answered the door to me, he sneered and said, "I don't deal to kids."

I took the envelope with cash from my back pocket and waved it in his face, saying, "You'll deal with me."

Doffo's eyes lit up at the sight of the money, and politely gestured for me to enter. "In that case, *welcome!*"

I'd already passed my entry exam in weed, speed, and ecstasy, and now it was time to upgrade. Coke was a riot, and if I'd continued to ingest it, I would have undoubtedly started one. However, it was a little noisy, and I didn't want to take anything that would give me away. So, eventually, after trying an array of narcotic options, I settled on something Doffo referred to as 'oblivion'.

When he sold me my first batch, he looked at me with slight concern and said, "Just go easy with those, X; they're the pills they give to the most hopeless cases in the loony bin."

Smirking, I replied, "Ideal!"

"I'm serious, X, one a day, no more," he added.

"Drug dealing and health advice—it really is an all-round service you are offering, isn't it, Doffo?" I asked sarcastically.

"One does what one can, X," he replied with a smile.

The pills hit the spot, and sweet oblivion was duly forthcoming. That's when I started to drift and, although I didn't realise it then, also to disappear.

Over the next month or so, several people tried to make me see sense. House Party Helen was first. "X, I think you should talk to someone; you don't look well. It doesn't have to be me, but my mum's a nurse; she would know how to get help," she said after chemistry one day.

"Helen, I'm fine; please just leave me alone," I replied sullenly.

I was in the habit of occasionally babysitting for Pete and Jenny until the big man said one night, "We can't leave you with the kids again, X, not until you've sorted yourself out. And I'd do it quickly, mate. Don't make me do something about it!"

Although we rarely spoke, Rachael1989 still sat next to me in English. One morning, I found a Post-it note waiting for me. "WHATEVER IT IS THAT YOU ARE DOING, PLEASE, JUST STOP!"

Ms James tried a more subtle approach. "We've all been there before, X, and taken the ride; the trick is in knowing when to get off."

Though everybody knew what I was doing, proving it was the tricky part. Drugs make you ingeniously sneaky, and you will take every precaution to ensure nothing stops the good times from rolling. Besides, for the first time in years, I wasn't causing any trouble when it came to school. I sat through lessons quietly, made a token effort with the homework I was assigned, and then, when I was done, I washed yet another pill with a large vodka, lay down on my bed, and drifted off to a better place.

No one spoke to me at school anymore except for Cocksucker Carl, Matt and Driffid, whose mungo chums now looked at me with something approaching awe.

Whenever I passed Dr Harris in the corridor, he would pause as if he were about to speak to me, but then give a sad shake of his head and walk onward. In classics, he ignored me and adopted Rachael1989 as his new favourite student. Sure enough, my name was missing when the team sheet for the first tennis match of the season was pinned up on the sports board.

By now, I was looking for a way back, but I didn't know what to do as I'd cut off all my channels. Finally, I resolved to talk to Rachael; however, the next time I walked into English, she'd taken the seat next to Jack.

At about this time, I received another tape in form group, the Sid Vicious version of 'My Way'. Very funny, Claire!

Dad was, as always, oblivious to it all. "Some woman from the school called me today. She said she thought you might be taking drugs," he said one night as we watched TV together.

"Only idiots take drugs," I scoffed.

Dad slapped his thigh in approval. "That's *exactly* what I

said, son. Anyway, rest assured, I told her to mind her own business."

The ball was back in the school's court, and Ms James duly took her best shot. I prepared myself for the inevitable interrogation when I was summoned to her office the next day.

I'd barely sat down when she asked me formally, "X, could you roll up the sleeves of your shirt and show me your forearms, please?"

Whatever I had been expecting wasn't this. "I'm sorry, Ms James. I don't understand," I said in confusion.

Ms James straightened the papers in front of her as newsreaders do at the end of a broadcast. "OK, X, let me explain what happens if you do not comply with my request. My next call will be to social services; they will visit you at your home and make an assessment. If they are unhappy with your health and judge you as at risk, you will be placed in a care home or a foster environment. There is no guarantee that this will be arranged locally, so you may have to leave the school," she had her poker face on that day.

I was baffled momentarily, but eventually, the penny dropped. "You think I'm on smack, don't you?" I asked incredulously.

"*Everybody* thinks you're on smack," she said defensively. "Why do you think you are so popular with the mungos these days?"

"Smack?" I asked. "Are you serious?"

Ms James studied me momentarily. "Do you know what they've taken to calling you these days?"

I shook my head.

"The school spirit," she said.

"Why?" I asked in wonder.

Ms James leant forward purposefully. "Because the ghost of a former pupil stalks our corridors because a boy whom many people care about has volunteered to join the ranks of the living dead, because X... " Ms James was yelling now, "You're starting to disappear! Now show me your bloody arms!"

Angrily, I undid the cuffs on my shirt, rolled up my sleeves, and thrust my forearms forward for her to see.

"There you go. Satisfied?" I asked defiantly.

Ms James studied my arms momentarily and sighed with relief. "Oh, thank God for that. X, I'm sorry, it's just that you've lost so much weight, your eyes are permanently bloodshot, and we've had endless reports that you spend long periods locked in a cubicle in the new school toilets, only to emerge looking wasted. What exactly is it that you're doing in there?"

"You really want to know?" I asked, barely restraining the tears.

Ms James banged her fist on the desk. "I *have* to know, X."

My emotional dam was giving way. "I cry, Ms James; I cry, and I cry, and I cry. Are you satisfied? This is the moment you get to say, 'I told you so!'"

"Oh, X," her face softened; she got up from behind her desk and, to my utter disbelief, offered me a hug. Shorn of close human contact for weeks, I threw my arms around her and burst into tears.

Sometime later, having regained my composure, I finally broke the silence. "May I please smoke, Ms James?"

Ms James sighed. "X, you know the school policy on smoking... Oh, do you know what? *Fuck it;* I'll have one too."

She opened her top drawer, withdrew an ashtray, and placed it on her desk between us.

After taking a deep inhalation of smoke and exhaling, Ms James said, "I think we might be able to keep this… " She waved her cigarette in a circular motion, "Within the bounds of the school… I fear you are far too fragile a leaf to entrust to those *disgusting* commie zealots in the local authority right now."

Relieved beyond words, I replied, "That is appreciated, Ms James."

"There are a few conditions, though, and both are non-negotiable," she said firmly.

"Anything; I'll do anything," I pleaded.

Ms James leant forward in a business-like manner. "X, there is an institution in this school *so* secretive that no one except those in the very highest authority, the smallest dinner lady, and Stan, the caretaker know of its existence," she said confidentially.

"What is it?" I asked in wonder.

"X, I'm sending you to the Eating Disorder Club," she said plainly.

This was new to me. "Eating Disorder Club?"

Ms James nodded. "Yes, Thursday lunchtimes in the computer suite."

I was somewhat baffled and said, "I didn't realise we had one."

Smiling wryly, she said a touch superciliously, "Why would you? As I said, *it's* top secret."

I shook my head. "Actually, I was referring to the computer suite, Ms."

"*Oh*, neither did I; now you come to mention it, but I'm reliably informed it's in here somewhere. You're a bright boy; I'm sure you'll find it," she said brightly.

I was confused. "Is lunch the best time to hold it, Ms James?"

"Well, X, it's not as if these people eat, am I right?" Ms James asked plainly.

She had made a sensible point, so I let the matter lie. Finally, I asked, "What's the other condition, Ms James?"

"You'll need to see the school's psychiatrist, X."

After my heart-to-heart with Ms James, I resolved to sort myself out. As the final bell rang that day, I felt optimistic for the first time in weeks. On returning home, I had every intention of disposing of my stash of pills, tipping the large bottle of vodka, which had become a permanent resident in my sock drawer, down the sink, and eating a proper meal.

As I headed home, Geoff Travis, heartthrob, school football hero, and, as I've now discovered, all round fucker, caught up with me. Foolishly, at first, I thought he was being genuinely friendly until he said, "Hey, Super Freak, why don't you do the school a favour? Fuck off and kill yourself."

With that, he slapped me around the back of the head, and ran off laughing towards his football cronies, cheering him on from thirty yards away.

"Super Freak?" So that's what they thought of me now? Well, if I were going to be a freak, I'd be damned if I wasn't going to be the biggest and best this school had ever seen.

The transformation was straightforward enough. Having been nowhere near Ray's barber's shop in months, The Cochran had long since grown out, and my hair only required the addition of a cheap black dye to create the desired effect. My mum's abandoned make-up store provided face-whitening materials, mascara, and blood-red lipstick. And when it came to looking skinny, well, I already had the entire school beaten hands-down in that department.

The effect I hoped for was 'shock'; however, upon entering my form group the following day, I was greeted only with suppressed smirks. However, it wasn't until Mr Crackett walked in that I realised the true extent of my miscalculation. As soon as he caught sight of me, he burst into hysterics and, when he could finally breathe, said, "Sorry, 4F, I'll be back in a minute. I'm going to find a camera; I've just got to get a photo of him looking like that."

Only Driffid seemed impressed. "Hey man, X, you've joined us... You could lead us!"

"Driffid," I replied confidentially, "call them *all* together at lunchtime. I will address the brothers and sisters then."

As I was about to go into maths, Ms James tapped me on the shoulder and said sternly, "Follow me!" When she finally caught a proper sight of me, she suppressed the urge to laugh. "This one's not getting solved over my biscuit barrel, X. It's straight to Olympus for judgement this time. Would you *please* walk at least four paces behind me? I don't want people to realise I'm *quite* fond of you."

I was oblivious to the alleged misdeed, which was the cause of an urgent summons to the head's office. However, the charge soon became apparent once I was sitting facing a red-faced Dr Harris. "Now I'm a tolerant man, X... and I've cut you a lot of slack this year—the painting and decorating scam, the obsessive love affair, the drinking, the drugs, the arrest, even the eating disorder."

I was quivering beneath him in the chair opposite his desk. For the first time, the man was genuinely intimidating me. Sheepishly, I asked, "You knew about all that stuff then, headmaster?"

"Yes, of course, I did," he roared. "You even assaulted a member of my teaching staff, and I cushioned your fall. However, and here you would be wise to mark my words well, my boy—you would have to crucify me upside down before I allow the captain of *my* school tennis team to walk around dressed up like a *fucking mungo*!" As he finished shouting at me, he slammed his fist down on the desk.

I know! I was shocked, too; you don't expect language like that from a justice of the peace, do you?

Meekly, I replied, "I didn't know I was still captain, sir."

Dr Harris waved his hand irritably. "Of course, you're still captain, X. It's a school appointment written in stone; only God Almighty himself could strip you of the title. To the best of my knowledge, he hasn't started intervening in everyday school affairs yet, although if things get much worse around here, I wouldn't entirely rule it out."

"Problems, sir?" I inquired, keen to divert his anger in any direction other than mine.

Dr Harris was thoughtful for a moment. "Where do I start? The year fives are drooling hopelessly into their exam papers; year four aren't responding as we'd hoped. Most pupils view the uniform as optional these days, and we've never performed so badly on the sporting field."

"What is to be done, sir?" I asked timidly.

"Well," he said, raising his voice, "it doesn't help when so-called example pupils take a one-way trip on the Narco Express!"

"I'm sorry, sir; I've let you down," I said, shamefully lowering my head. I could feel tears beginning to well.

The headmaster's features softened upon spying my distress. "Now, X, keep your chin up, my boy. I know you've had your heart broken; rest assured, though, that it happens to the best of us. Life goes on; always trust in those words. And if you need to cheer yourself up, look around you; this place is full of the bloody creatures, and at least you have girls at your disposal. *I* had to make do with boys when I was your age, and understand me when I say this: That's a *whole different* system of pain—I could tell you stories that would make the mascara run from those eyes, my boy."

Dr Harris was lost in the contemplation of an, no doubt, uncomfortable memory momentarily before eventually adding, "If you get knocked down, X, there's no point just sitting there crying into your life-givers; you've just *got* to get back up and give it another go!"

I sighed, "Yes, sir."

Pointing at me, he continued, "It won't be long till you're saying goodbye to this place, you know? Ask yourself, 'How do I want to be remembered?' As an upstanding, hard-working, and team-playing citizen of this school or as Alice Cooper's pansy-bastard love child?"

I nodded. "You're right, sir."

The head looked at me curiously. "What's that, 'right', you say? Of course, I'm bloody right, X. I can see it a mile off; you're suffering from a monumental dose of self-absorption. A good bit of service is what you need. I'd pack you off to the army for a week, but going on how you look, they'd no doubt shoot you at first sight."

Whatever he was saying, and I wasn't exactly sure what he *was* saying, it worked. "Service, sir?" I asked.

Dr Harris' eyes widened. "Yes, *service*; God damn you. You've done a mighty fine job serving yourself these past few months, so if you need something to get you out of bed every morning, give this a try—serve the school!"

"Serve the school," I repeated, as much to myself as in

response to the head.

Dr Harris banged the desk with his fist. "That's right, X, serve the school! And you can start by removing that degrading Halloween costume, getting yourself fit again, and getting back on that tennis court; do you hear me, my boy?"

"I hear you, sir," I said, jumping to my feet. "Serve the school!"

"That's the ticket, X," Dr Harris said encouragingly.

Politely, I asked, "Permission to de-mungo immediately, sir."

The head finally took a seat. "What's that, 'de-mungo', you say? Well, yes, the sooner, the better, my boy."

I breathed deeply. "Thank you, sir," I said sincerely.

"Not a problem, X; just get me that win, my boy!" The head replied, making a fist.

And that was all it took—a pep talk from an older, albeit potentially senile, father figure—and I saw the light.

I was so inspired that I immediately pulled Rachael from class. "I need your help, Rach."

She stared at me in wonder. "You look ridiculous, X."

"And what exactly are we doing here?" Rachael asked after I'd led her into the boy's toilets in old school.

"Rachael, I've been an idiot; I know that now and want to change. There's something I desperately need your help with," I said sincerely.

She folded her arms and eyed me suspiciously. "What's that, X?"

I pointed to my head. "Can you help me get this black shit

out of my hair, please?"

There is a phrase, 'letting off steam', which I was more in tune with the meaning of when Rachael had finished yelling at me. "It's not your bloody hair that's the problem, X, *awful* as it looks. You need to stop pouring whatever *crap* you have into your bloodstream. *You* need to start eating and sleeping again like a normal person."

I held up my hands defensively. "Rachael... " I began.

"Shut it, X; I'm not bloody finished yet. Do you have any idea what it's like to watch someone you... care about go on a self-destruction mission?" she yelled.

"Err... " The sound had barely escaped my lips when Rachael interjected.

"Don't answer that one, X, because you don't. This has all been easy for you, wrapped up nice and warm inside your little drug bubble, *hasn't it?* Have you ever asked yourself how *I* might feel about the suicide mission you've been on these past few weeks?"

"Err... "

"Don't answer that, X," Rachael shouted threateningly.

Stop asking questions, then.

When she had finally finished yelling, I pointed to my hair and meekly asked, "Sorry, was that a yes or a no to helping me wash this stuff off?"

Irritably, she said, "Oh, bend over the bloody sink, you imbecile."

After we'd finished, as I attempted to dry my hair with a paper towel, I asked, "Hey, Rach, does this mean we're friends again?"

Rachael's eyes narrowed. "Not even close. Sort yourself out. I mean it; get the old X back."

"OK, and then?" I asked.

"Then we'll see, won't we?" she said sullenly and walked out.

Rachael1989 was right about many things but wrong about one. When you've hit rock bottom and want to turn it around, there's something you need to do first; really, you've just *got* to get the hair right again.

"What happened to you?" Ray asked later as he surveyed my matted locks with horror, still dotted with cheap black dye despite Rachael's best efforts.

I looked at the barber in the mirror and smiled. "Ray, it's fair to say I've been lost, my friend. I took too many wrong turns, and for a while there, I thought I would never find my way back. However, I was fortunate enough to see the light this morning, and I intend to follow that bad boy all the way back home. In short, today's the day I start turning it all around. So, if you'd be so kind, squire, Cochran me up," I replied intently.

Ray continued investigating my formerly sculpted hair. "X, it would be my distinct pleasure. As I may have cautioned you, life without hair wax is not *really* living."

When I got home from town, I stripped off and took a good, long, hard look at myself in the full-length mirror in my room. It wasn't pretty; I was emaciated. Really, I reckon I might have looked better fat.

Next, I gathered every harmful substance in my room—pills, spirits, fags—even the glue I'd sniffed one Sunday evening when I was feeling particularly nihilistic. After stashing them all in a carrier bag, I dumped them in the bin outside the local shops.

Aside from the severe disappointment of 24 mungos at

lunchtime, it had been my best day in weeks.

The following days were not easy, but I got through them. Cold turkey at school wasn't on the menu, so I convinced my dad that I had contracted a particularly virulent spring flu and got down to sweating it all out of my system.

Empty hours, previously spent getting higher than a hair-sprayed quiff, drag like you wouldn't believe. I needed a distraction, something to focus on, so I got domestic.

In truth, Dad and I had been living like animals for weeks. While I'd barely eaten, he'd existed entirely on takeaways. Cooking and cleaning—how hard could it be?

Before long, I'd learned a great deal, including how to put an ironing board up and turn on a vacuum cleaner. Best of all, though, I finally realised the purpose of the little tray on the top left-hand corner of a washing machine—genuinely fascinating. Soon, I had the old place looking as good as new.

Within days, we were once again settled into a routine. Dad would dutifully ring to advise of his ETA from work, and I'd set about preparing dinner. Meat and two vegetables—three if I felt ambitious—were back on the menu. Admittedly, it wasn't exactly fine dining at the start. However, cooking is like sex; the more you do it, the better you get.

Next, I had to start restoring my fitness. After jumping on my bike for the first time in weeks, I managed to cycle only five miles before my body revolted and refused to go further. Undeterred, the following lunchtime at school, I took myself off to the gym changing rooms, where Big Wilson discovered me and, with suspicion chiselled into his granite features, asked, "What are *you* doing here?"

Innocently, I replied, "Listen, sir, I'm not here to cause any trouble. It's just that I'm a physical wreck, and I was going to run around the track this lunchtime to rebuild my fitness."

The gym teacher was thoughtful momentarily, then said, "Wait there!" and headed towards his office. I was 90% certain that he would ring Ms James and report me; however, when he returned, he had changed into his shorts.

"Come on then!" he said enthusiastically, and I followed him to the track, around which I managed to complete four slow and intensely painful laps before collapsing to the ground. While I lay on the grass, overwhelmed by dizziness and nausea, Big Wilson loomed over me and asked, "Are you serious about this, X?"

Between gasps of air, I managed to reply, "Yes!"

Big Wilson nodded. "OK then, same again tomorrow."

And so, it came to pass that those lonely lunch hours ended, and instead, I spent the time circumnavigating the athletic track in the company of the muscular gym teacher.

The following Thursday, I duly attended my first session of Eating Disorder Club and almost got kicked out before it even started. Really, it wasn't my fault, but rather a simple misunderstanding. Upon entering the computer suite, I spied Fatty Jacobs sitting in the circle of pupils in the centre of the room and said politely, "Sorry, this must be *overeaters*; I was looking for *undereaters*."

The next thing I knew, the school nurse dragged me back out of the room by the collar. "I'm warning you, X, one more remark like that, and I'll kick you straight back to Ms James. There are children in there with real issues, and I'm not going to allow you to undo all the hard work I've done."

The school nurse had her game face on, so I apologised to her and the rest of the group.

The format of EDC is simple: we sit around and talk about our problems and how we feel about them. I'm not 100% sure I have an eating disorder, so I just sat there in silence, listening intently to the others. Halfway through the session, the school nurse asked me, "Is there anything you would like to share, X? It doesn't necessarily have to involve eating. You may wish to talk about some of the challenges you have faced with drugs recently, for example."

After a moment's contemplation, I said, "There are many challenges with drugs, though a lot of those, I believe, can be overcome simply by establishing the right rapport with your dealer. If you take the time to explain… " I stopped as the school nurse stared at me, stunned.

"X," she said eventually, "I was thinking more about the problems *caused* by drugs."

Finally catching her drift, I dutifully shared tales of panic attacks, paranoia, and insomnia, which were well received. I rather enjoyed myself, and by the time it ended, I was already looking forward to the following week's session. Really, the school should run more clubs like this.

The next day, I asked Big Wilson for a favour. "While we work out today, could you possibly summon Rachael Williams, sir?"

The gym teacher looked at me in wonder. "Why?"

"I'm trying to impress her, sir."

After completing ten laps of the track, Big Wilson held my legs in position while I did some sit-ups. As it was gloriously sunny, we had both removed our tops.

"You wanted to see me, sir?" I looked up, saw Rachael, and smiled at her. However, she just dissolved into a fit of giggles. "Sorry!" she said apologetically, "This is just *way* too homoerotic," and walked off laughing.

Big Wilson looked at me curiously. "Was that the impact you were hoping for, X?"

I shook my head and said, "Not really, Big Wilson, I'll be honest."

The next time I walked into English, there was still no Rachael in the seat beside me. However, a Post-it note on my desk read, "KEEP GOING!" After looking at it, I felt like I'd just had a shot of pure adrenaline to the heart.

Today, after my appointment with the school psychiatrist, I went to Ms James' office to hand in the slip signed by the Dr Peters.

"Three down, three to go," I said brightly.

Ms James eyed me curiously. "And how was it?"

I nodded. "You know, it's not as painful as I thought it would be, and although she is fond of asking some astoundingly awkward questions, Dr Peters is one good-looking woman."

Ms James' face was a picture—*The Scream*. After a moment, she shook her head. "Actually, no, you're right. It makes perfect sense. How else does one get over an obsession with a wholly unsuitable older woman? That's right; you develop another obsession with an even older, equally unsuitable woman: *genius!*"

Shifting uncomfortably, I replied, "I was only making an observation."

Arching an eye, Ms James remarked, "Yes, well, please keep your appreciation of the good doctor on an observation-only basis. Besides, I think you could benefit from these sessions if you can keep your brains and balls apart for a reasonable time.

Anyway, will you be making an appearance tonight?"

I grimaced. "I'm not sure, Ms, I am still the school outcast."

Ms James smiled warmly. "Well, you'll just have to be brave then, *won't you?* Besides, we wouldn't even be having a dance party if it wasn't for you. I'll give you sanctuary here if it all gets too much for you."

Next, I headed to my lunchtime appointment with Matt Jacobs on the old school tennis courts. I've only played a few games this year; however, as I'm keen to avoid ending up as the only tennis team captain never to play a match for the school, I thought I'd test my mettle against the young pretender.

With a coin poised, ready to be tossed, I asked, "Heads or tails?"

"Heads, please, Captain," Matt answered politely.

"Tails," I said after studying the coin on the ground. "I'll serve."

"In that case, I'll take the swimming pool end," Matthew said. "Oh, and Captain, I just wanted to say how good it is to finally see you on the court. You probably don't know this, but I got involved in drugs at my last school."

I nodded in understanding. "Got a bit messed up, did you?"

"A little, I suppose," he said and smiled. "I fucking loved it, however. I'd still be doing it now if I thought I could get away with it."

I searched for some words of consolation. "There's always university, Matthew. You'll be able to do what you want there."

"I suppose," he said mournfully, "seems a long way away. Listen, Captain; you don't know where I could score some… "

I held up my hand firmly to silence him. "That's all in the

past for me, Matthew."

The one-set game only lasted twenty-five minutes. I took all my service games and two of his. After shaking hands over the net, I said, "Thanks for the game, Matt. Sorry to rush off, but I've got to go and see Dr Harris urgently."

"Dr Harris can't possibly see you right now; he's working on the school budget," the headmaster's secretary informed me sternly.

"Rosie," I said gravely, holding up my racket. "This is important; it concerns *tennis*."

Her face turned serious. "In that case, you better go right in, X."

Dr Harris was busily engaged in practising putting a golf ball into an upturned coffee mug. As he saw me enter, he ceased playing, leant on his club, and appraised me. "So you've finally crawled out of Creep Street and picked up a racket again, eh?" he asked.

"Yes, Headmaster, I'm ready," I said firmly.

"What's that, 'ready', you say?" he barked, and I nodded in the affirmative. The headmaster pointed at me with his putter. "You weren't ready at the start of the bloody season, were you? While you were off playing dominoes with the dream fairy, we played seven and lost seven," he scoffed.

I held my hand up in a gesture of remorse. "I'm sorry, sir. I really am, but now I'm ready. I've been training hard every day and I just took James apart 6-2."

This news immediately impacted the head's mood. "Well, I never doubted you, X. Not like some of the malcontents in the staff room. There was a sweepstake on how long you'd last—I bet you didn't know that, did you?"

Somewhat bemused, I replied, "No, sir, actually, I didn't."

Ignoring me, the head continued, "The next match is on Thursday, Marston Private, so we don't stand a chance. Still, we'll know we did our best with you out there."

"I look forward to it, sir," I said sincerely.

Dr Harris nodded and quickly waved his hand. "Right you are, X, now on your way, my boy."

Despite the dismissal, I remained where I was. "Sir, I just wanted to thank you for the pep talk you gave me last month; it really did do the trick."

"What's that, 'pep talk', you say? Well, X, it's all part of the service. Anything for our miracle man," Dr Harris said fondly. "Oh, I'm not here next week—at a conference as it happens, so Little Wilson is in charge of the team; make sure he knows you're available."

"Yes, and sir, *serve the school!*" I said proudly.

Dr Harris smiled. "That's right, X. Serve the school!"

After leaving the headmaster's office, I searched for the diminutive gym teacher.

When I got home from school this afternoon, I pondered long and hard whether I should show my face at the Year Four Dance Party. Eventually, after much consideration, I decided Ms James was right. Sometimes, you've just got to be brave. As such, after a bit of searching, I showered, set the Cochran just right, and rediscovered 'the original teenager'.

The weather is permanently glorious, and I can't recall a time it's ever been so good. "This could be the best since '76," my dad reckons. As such, I took a slow walk to school with the leather jacket hung casually over my shoulder. As I got to the gates, though, I had a sudden attack of nerves. I may have given up pills, spirits, and nicotine, but wine and beer are still fair game to my mind, and, at that point, even two cans of weak lager would have been most welcome.

No one paid me any real attention at first, except for Geoff Travis, all round-fucker, who, clearly drunk, spat his predictable concoction of yourself, off, fuck and kill in my direction. With no other distractions and using my recently acquired skills in coordinated movement to music, I took myself to the middle of the hall and danced. After ten minutes or so, I was joined by Clare Anatomy, who was even drunker than Geoff. While we danced, her hands were *everywhere,* and I soon learned that there's something remarkably unpleasant about being molested in public when you're stone-cold sober. As such, I excused myself and walked straight into Claire with An Eye For X.

"Here we are again, X, she said brightly.

I thought long and hard, but I couldn't divine *any* sense in what she'd said.

"Hey, is it safe to be this close to the school, bad boy?" she asked mischievously.

I sighed and, over the De La Soul track that Tony was playing, said, "Claire, I'm seemingly the only person in this hall who hasn't drunk anything tonight. Moreover, before coming here, I cooked a beef stew, vacuumed, and put a white load in the washing machine. When I get home, I'll hang it out to dry."

I thought for a second that she'd been struck dumb, but then her eyes widened. "That's *so* cool!"

You could have said anything; she'd have responded with the same three-word inanity.

To be polite and to conclude this awkward conversation, I said, "By the way, thanks for the songs, Claire."

Shuddering as if given some form of electric shock, she

smiled unconvincingly and said, "No problem, X."

As I left the hall, I saw Rachael conversing with my two ex-best friends; only JG looked in my direction and casually fired the international symbol of the too-frequent self-abuser at me. I felt my middle digit adopting the position, but my inner voice advised sternly against retaliation.

You earned it, X; now, be a grown-up and take it.

Dutifully, I looked away and caught House Party Helen's eye, who smiled warmly and gave me a little wave, which I reciprocated.

Ms James seemed pleased to see me when I called into her office, and we had a pleasant half-hour conversation. "You're not the first to go off the rails, X, and you won't be the last. Let me tell you, I did it myself more than a few times. My advice is, when you lose your way, return to where you were before everything went wrong."

These words of wisdom inspired me to knock on House Party Helen's window after the dance party.

When I finished my long story, Helen looked at me, wondering. "X, when Miss James said, 'the place you were', *really*, do you think she meant geographically?"

"How do you mean, Helen?" I asked, somewhat perplexed.

"Well, perhaps she meant that you should go back to what you were doing," Helen explained. "Still, you weren't nearly as bad as some of the stories suggested," she added thoughtfully.

The school meme machine really had gone into overdrive about me this time. Amongst other malicious rumours, I had been dealing drugs within the school, robbed Katy James' older brother at knifepoint, stolen cars, made three unsuccessful attempts on my own life—and one successful one (?)—and impregnated Lisa Bond.

"The problem is, X, you stopped talking to everyone, so as

people didn't know what you were getting up to, they just made stuff instead," Helen said sagely. "Still, it just goes to show, all that trouble over one girl?"

"Oh, I'm not sure anymore, Helen; I think it's all just chaos, though my psychiatrist…" I began.

"*Wait!* You're seeing a psychiatrist?" Helen asked in wonder, and I nodded in acknowledgement. "How *thoroughly* modern of you, X… sorry, you were saying?"

"Well," I continued, "she says it's all about my mother."

On Saturday, 18th February, I returned home to find my mother out cold on her bed, with half a bottle of gin and an empty box of tablets beside her. She wouldn't have made it if another 20 minutes had passed before being discovered. And what thanks did I get for staging this intervention? Let me tell you, her very first words to me in the hospital afterwards were, "Oh, X, I wish you'd just left me to die."

Really, the ingratitude of some people knows no bounds. As she didn't show remorse for her actions, they've kept hold of her ever since.

"Oh, you poor thing, X, of course, it's all been about your mother, if only I'd known," Helen said as she hugged me.

After returning here, I sat in front of the computer for an hour while toying wildly with the Rubik's cube. Finally, I started writing, and it felt better than good.

"Go back to where you were before things went wrong." Catherine James is one intelligent lady. I'd never say that to her face, but she really is damn clever.

It's 5 a.m. now, and you've kept me up talking. You know, I am still in recovery.

SATURDAY 3RD JUNE

After a long, hot bike ride on Thursday evening, I stopped on the way home at the local shops to buy a drink, and when I got outside, my pride and joy had been stolen. In the past few weeks, cycling has greedily gobbled up empty hours previously invested in less beneficial pursuits, and, as such, a replacement was urgently required.

When Ron spotted me entering Ripton Cycles this morning, he looked at me sourly and said, "I thought you'd given up like the rest of them."

I laughed. "I think I'm about to make your day, Ron."

The income from Pete & Dennis' Painting Services had accrued far faster than I could spend it, and, as such, I'm flush. Cycling has become a true passion, and I wanted the right bike.

As Ron carefully counted the money I'd handed him, I asked, "Hey, could you use an extra pair of hands around here?"

Ron shook his head. "If it's a Saturday job you're after, then I can't afford you, I'm afraid."

"I was offering to volunteer," I said brightly.

Ron looked at me suspiciously. "Work for free, why?"

"*Well*, I want to learn more about bikes; truth be told, I need as many distractions as possible," I said sincerely.

Ron laughed. "Been getting up to no good hanging around on street corners, have you?"

Really, I have no idea what that phrase means.

I looked at Ron intently. "If you *must* know, I had an obsessive love affair with a much older woman, and when it all fell apart, I fell into a whirl of drink, drugs, and anorexia."

The bike shop proprietor looked surprisingly impressed. "Well, at least that's original, I suppose." After further thought, he added, "Listen, X, I certainly wouldn't mind you being here once a week. If you want, you can start next Saturday."

SUNDAY 4TH JUNE

This morning, I found Pete lurking outside the house. It was a good news/bad news call. Jenny has finally sold the house, but this means they are moving away. Once I'd demonstrated that I was over my recent issues, I'd been welcomed at their place again, and it has proved to be a sanctuary over the past month or so. With the four of them leaving, my circle of close friends now nears the square root of fuck-all. As such, after Pete had said goodbye, I resolved to act.

When I reached Rachael's, Alison answered the door. "Oh, hello, X; it's been a while. Madame's out at present; would you care to wait inside?"

When we entered the kitchen, Rachael's mum asked, "Tell me, X, have you ever had an espresso?"

I smiled. "Never, but you know me, Alison; I'll try anything once."

Rachael's mother fiddled nervously with the back of her hair. "Err, yes, so I've heard, X."

Mine isn't the only household missing someone; Arthur's gone. It turns out that his frequent absences were eventually explained by a letter from one of his undergraduates that Alison found in the pocket of a pair of trousers.

"Really, an affair? He doesn't look the type." I asked in wonder.

"Oh, X, *he's* a man, isn't he?" Alison replied. "Sorry, I shouldn't say that in front of you," she added quickly.

It was at this point that she burst into a flood of tears. I've had my heart broken in similar circumstances, and now I know what the word means: *empathy* comes naturally. Besides, I've spent enough time in the company of my inconsolable mother to be prepared for such circumstances. It's fair to say that I've learned to hate the sound of a woman crying.

Eventually, as the tears were still flowing, I hugged her. At this point, Rachael walked in dressed smartly. "What's going on, and what is *he* doing here?" She asked accusingly.

Alison angrily slammed her hand down on the table, stood up, and shouted, "*He* is a guest in my house, young lady; don't be so *bloody* rude!" I thought Rachael was about to respond, but she stormed off towards her room instead.

Wiping her eyes with a tissue, Alison said, "You'll have to forgive my daughter; there's something of the conformist about her." She smiled at me and added, "You, X, are more like her father. He wasn't one for doing what he was told, either."

Eventually, Rachael returned, having changed into shorts and a vest top, and I couldn't help but notice how nice her legs were. She looked at me and said, "You can come up if you want."

After I'd sat on her bed, Rachael looked at me suspiciously and asked, "My mother and you, should I be worried?"

"What?" I replied dumbly.

"*Well*, now you've got the taste for older women; maybe there's no stopping you," she said sarcastically.

"Oh, please, as if I'd ever… " Keen to change the subject, I asked, "Where have you been all dressed up anyway?"

Rachael, hanging up the clothes she had just changed out of, said, "If you must know, X, I've been to church."

"Why?" I wasn't being flippant for once; I was genuinely curious.

Rachael peered at me over her shoulder. "I'm hedging my bets. I'd rather see my father again, and I wouldn't want to be turned away from the pearly gates on a technicality," she explained.

"You should try Grade 9 atheism," I replied sincerely.

Rachael laughed. "Oh yes, and maybe I could be the next school nihilist; I have to say, you *really* sold that one to us all so well, X."

"All in the past," I said reassuringly.

"What do *you* want anyway, X?" Rachael asked sharply.

On the way there, I'd rehearsed my lines. "I miss you, Rach. You *were* my best friend. I'm incredibly sorry for the *many* wrongs I have done to you. I'm here to ask—no, make that *beg*, for your forgiveness."

Rachael studied me briefly and asked, "Are you prepared to earn it, X?"

MONDAY 5TH JUNE

"Save the whale?"

Rachael couldn't have picked a worse person to help her collect money for her favourite cause. I may look dramatically better than I did a month ago. However, it's no longer like anyone gives me the time of day.

When I saw Ms James approaching, I figured I could at least count on her to donate. "Save the whale, Ms?"

The head of year looked at me in utter disgust. *"Certainly not!"*

Undeterred by her rejection, I rattled the collection box in front of her face.

"X, it's nothing personal; it's just that natural selection has served the planet perfectly well these past four billion years, and I feel it would be arrogant in the extreme to start meddling with its inner workings now," Ms James said politely.

I smiled. "But, Ms, they are beautiful creatures, aren't they?"

Ms James frowned. "Spend a lot of time underwater with your big dumb friends, Captain Nemo?"

Vainly, I rattled the box one last time at the head of year.

"X, I swear, if you shake that thing at me one more time, I will weaponize it." With that, Ms James walked on.

Weaponise? I like that word.

When I took my usual seat in the back corner of the chemistry lab this morning, House Party Helen came and sat next to me. I have a friend again and couldn't ask for a better one.

As I handed the collection tin to Rachael at the end of the day, I thought I'd check if I'd doubled my number,."Friends again?"

"I'm still considering the matter," she replied flatly.

TUESDAY 6TH JUNE

A strange thing happened at school this morning—fellow pupils again acknowledged my existence. Six or seven kids must have said, "Hey, X", as they passed me to classes.

At lunchtime, I went to the sports board, where the team sheet for Thursday's tennis match had been posted. My name was missing from it, and, in my place, Geoff Travis'. As such, I headed to the gym in search of Little Wilson. As often, he sat with his feet on his desk, smoking. Meanwhile, Big Wilson was tapping slowly on the computer's keyboard at the adjacent desk.

"How come my name's not on the team sheet, Little Wilson?" I asked politely.

The gym teacher looked at me absently, took a drag on his cigarette, and exhaled slowly. "I didn't know you were available, X," he said.

Brightly, I replied, "You did; remember, I came and told you last week?"

Slowly, with a vague sense of recollection, his head began to nod. "Yes, now that you mention it, you're right; you did tell me that, X. Sorry!"

"No problem, Little Wilson. Can we get it corrected, please?" I asked expectantly.

Shaking his head, the diminutive teacher said, "Sorry, X. The team's been named; I can't change it now."

I was overwhelmed by a feeling of righteous indignation. "Little Wilson, I'm a better player than Geoff is; besides, he's an all-round f… " I stopped as I saw the frown forming on his face. After all, I was about to insult his beloved football team captain. "Geoff is an all-round sportsman; *yes*, I grant you that," I said, backtracking, "but me, *I'm* a specialist; we stand a better chance of winning if I play."

"We don't stand a chance, with or without you, X," he said blankly.

Resolutely, I said, "Little Wilson, *I'm ready* for this. Just ask Big Wilson."

We both looked at his colleague, who said, "He's ready," and returned to typing slowly.

Little Wilson nodded in understanding and then looked back at me. "Still can't change the team, X."

I thought I'd try a different tactic. "Listen, sir; I'm the captain of the tennis team. *That's* a school appointment, written in stone; only God Almighty could strip me of the title, and as far as I'm aware, he hasn't started intervening in everyday school matters yet."

The gym teacher seemed utterly unmoved by my speech. "I can't change it, X," he said plainly.

I tried one final angle. "OK then, I'll play him for the right!"

Finally, Little Wilson smiled. "You're on, X. Tomorrow lunchtime, old school courts."

WEDNESDAY 7TH JUNE

I may have been surprised by how friendly my fellow pupils were yesterday, but today was overwhelming. It wasn't just, "Hey, X," either; I was getting compliments from every direction. At morning break, Penny Chemistry threw her arms around me and said, "Oh, X, you're an inspiration to every single one of us." For a moment, I thought she wasn't going to let go of me. At the time, I didn't know what I'd done to deserve all this attention; however, after the isolation of the past few months, I wasn't about to start complaining.

Geoff Travis, all-round fucker, turned out to be a far feebler tennis opponent than I had imagined. I beat him 6-1. Every time we changed ends, he did his level best to elicit a reaction from me. "Hey, X, I'm guessing you're such a good player because of all those drugs you took. Isn't that right, smackhead?"

Whatever anger he managed to generate, I invested in my shots and thoroughly enjoyed every moment of the game. I finished him off with an ace, and as we shook hands at the net, he said, "Yeah, well played, X; let's just hope you don't go home tonight and find that your nutter mum has killed herself."

I squeezed his hand, pulled him closer, and punched him so hard on the jaw that he hit the ground—Mr Shaver would have been most impressed.

Little Wilson, who had been umpiring, jumped out of his chair and went to Geoff's aid. Looking up at me, the gym teacher asked, "*Jesus*, X, what did you do that for?"

Calmly, I relayed the insult Geoff had thrown at me to the man, word for word. After nodding his head in understanding, Little Wilson grabbed my opponent by the scruff of the neck and pulled him up from the ground. Looking at me sympathetically, he said, "Sorry about that, X." Turning to Geoff, he angrily barked, "It's a trip to Ms James's office for you, Travis. There are some things you don't say—*not even in a school!*"

On returning home, I headed out for a bike ride and afterwards collapsed on my bed in exhaustion. I was fast asleep in no time. When I awoke, Rachael sat in front of my computer screen.

"Hey!" I said drowsily.

"Hey, X," she said while continuing to read. "I didn't know that you wrote a diary."

"It's not a diary; it's a document," I replied irritably. Suddenly, realising what she was looking at, I leapt out of bed and stood behind her. "Hey, Rach, exactly how much of that have you read?"

"Oh, just a little," Rachael said absently, sniffing the air. "Do me a favour, would you? Take a shower; you smell odd. Meanwhile, I'll make us a coffee, should I?"

After showering, I found Rachael sitting at the patio table with two steaming mugs.

"Thanks!" Taking one of the drinks, I said, "I just want you to know I *didn't* steal that paint."

"You *did* break into the school, X, though, and two wrongs

don't make a right," Rachael replied disapprovingly.

I sighed. "I appreciate that *now;* however, at the time, I thought we were dealing with a wrong and a right... and, as everyone knows, *that* makes a wring."

Rachael shook her head in dismay and asked, "Why didn't you tell me about your Mum?"

"We weren't talking that weekend," I said awkwardly.

Rachael scowled. "Oh, for god's sake, X, that's a perfectly ridiculous thing to say. It's dangerous to bottle things up. I'm your best friend, and *you* should have come to me," she said testily.

I sighed. "You sound like my psychiatrist."

"You're seeing a psychiatrist?" she asked, sounding impressed. "How *thoroughly* modern of you, X. Hang on, *that's* why you're not in English on a Friday morning, isn't it? I did ask Mrs Simpson, but she just said that no one ever tells her anything and, for all the attention she gets paid in life, she might as well be dead—by the way, I think she's having a breakdown. *Anyway*, I know you've got your new *girlfriend* running all over school, telling everybody that you're just a poor victim who went off the rails because an unfortunate incident occurred at home, but *I'm not* buying it," Rachael said.

I held up my hand defensively. "If you're referring to Helen, she's *not* my girlfriend, *and*, as it happens, *I* agree with you," I said, but Rachael ignored me.

"You see, sorry as I am for what happened with your Mum; I think you would have done all those things regardless. You may not have gotten away with as much, but *you* would have tried your best regardless," Rachael continued.

"I agree," I said intently, but Rachael ignored me again.

"The thing is, I think you subscribe to a life philosophy called 'just say yes'. I've devised a new scientific rule called

X's law: The more foolish an endeavour is, the more you'll be tempted to try it."

The longer she talked, the angrier she got. "You see, X, I don't think you loved that woman; *you* were just obsessed with the idea of her. You only fell to pieces when she dumped you because it was the first time this year that something hadn't gone your way. Suddenly, you didn't have the girlfriend everybody envied, so you went and threw a gigantic, narcotic tantrum. It was just Helen of bloody Troy all over again!" Rachael took a sip of coffee and burned her mouth.

"I agree," I said again.

Rachael screamed, "And stop saying 'I agree'; it's *pissing* me off." With that, she jumped to her feet, picked up her mug, and angrily threw its scalding contents over my chest.

"Oh shit, that's hot!" I yelled, jumping to my feet. Quickly, I removed my T-shirt and threw it on the grass.

Realising what she'd done, Rachael covered her mouth with her hand in horror. "Sorry," she said meekly.

"It's all right!" I said it testily. "I'm sure the burning sensation will stop eventually. *For the record*, I agree with everything you've said, but if Helen wants to run around the school restoring my reputation, then good luck to her because, believe me, Rachael, being Luther Parkinson's outcast really isn't much fun. It so happens that the one thing I've wanted more than anything else this past month is to be close to you again, dangerous as that might be to my health. I missed you; you're my dearest friend. Are we done here, or were you planning on throwing some hot fat over me to complete the job?"

Rachael still had her hand over her mouth. "There was something else, but now may not be the most opportune moment to ask," she said meekly.

"Oh, ask away!" I shouted with a wave.

Through her fingers, she enquired, "Can I go out for a bike ride with you, please?"

I was somewhat surprised by the request but replied, "OK, yes."

"Your girlfriend won't mind?" Rachael asked.

Snappily, I replied, "She's *not* my girlfriend."

Rachael let her hand drop, said brightly, "Date!" and gave a little clap.

Just as she was leaving, she turned to me and said, "Oh, and no one's ever said that I have nice legs before, X."

At first, I didn't know what she was talking about, but then I remembered that she'd been reading *this*.

Really, only a few pages?

THURSDAY 8TH JUNE

There is a phrase, 'You can't please all the people all the time.' After attending form group this morning, I am more in tune with its meaning than before.

Lisa the Repeater sat next to me for the first time in weeks. "Listen, X, I just wanted to say I'm *so* sorry for being such a bitch to you over these past few months."

Confused, I replied, "I didn't realise we'd even spoken."

"Oh god, X, *please* don't make me feel any worse than I already do," Lisa said emotionally.

Keen not to cause any further distress, I moved and sat next to Driffid, who, sounding deflated, said, "You broke my heart, man. I put you on a pedestal, thinking you were trying to destroy yourself for the hell of it, and now it turns out that you were just this big, emotional mess."

"Right, everyone except X, off to classes," Mr Crackett said as the bell rang.

After the rest of the class had shuffled off, I approached my form tutor's desk. Mr Crackett looked ever so slightly uncomfortable as he began. "Listen, I know you and I haven't always seen eye to eye, X, but what you've been through these past few months, well, that must have been tough, and I just wanted to say that I'm here if you need me, son," he said compassionately.

Son?

"You'll be the first person I come to, *Dad*," I laughed.

Reddening, the form tutor, yelled, "Get out of my sight! Oh, and Ms James wants to see you; I *hope she bloody expels you this time*!"

Once inside the head of year's office, I asked meekly, "Geoff Travis?"

Ms James looked at me and smiled. "Oh, good god, no, don't worry about that." Her face turned serious. After all, there are some things you *don't* say… *not even in a school*. No, X, I brought you here to congratulate you. I think it's courageous that you've decided to share what happened to your mother with your fellow pupils. It's good to have you back on the team."

The most welcome sight of the day came when I walked into English and saw that Rachael had taken the seat next to me. A Post-it note was waiting for me on my desk, which read, "IT'S GOOD TO BE BACK, SHITHEAD!"

I replied, "IT'S GOOD TO HAVE YOU BACK!"

After English, as our post-class chat ended, Mrs S looked me up and down and said, "You know, X, you are developing into quite a remarkable-looking young man."

Unsure how to respond, I walked back towards the door, giving her my politest smile, and then quickly headed off to Eating Disorder Club.

The tennis match was a disaster; Marston Private destroyed us. Afterwards, the evening ride with Rachael wasn't exactly a success either. She owns a Dutch town bike, which appears to have the same mass as a small car.

"Weight is the key, Rachael; your bike's heavier, so you're

going slower. Also, look how thin my tyres are and how fat yours are," I said after we'd stopped five miles out of town.

"Well, as you're the better cyclist, why don't you ride my bike, and I'll ride yours?" Rachael suggested. Frankly, it sounded like an awful idea; however, as I was determined to ensure our first 'date' in months went as well as possible, I reluctantly withdrew the set of Allen keys from my jersey pocket and adjusted the seats accordingly.

"Oh, yes, I see what you mean. X, I don't know why you didn't suggest this earlier," Rachael said as she sped off on my bike, leaving me struggling behind on hers.

FRIDAY 9TH JUNE

After I'd told Dr Peters, the school psychiatrist, about the incident with Geoff Travis, all-round fucker; she was thoughtful for a moment. "Well, there are some things you just don't say—not even in a school! However, having said that, X, this is yet another act of violence to add to the growing list you have committed this year; what are your thoughts?"

I considered the question, then replied, "To be honest, Dr Peters, I think I've been rutting."

The school psychiatrist smiled ruefully and then said, "X, and please don't take this the wrong way, but *you* are not, in fact, *a deer*."

And so followed one of our frequent disagreements, which Dr Peters tried to end by uttering, "All I'm saying, X, is we all have to exert a measure of self-control in life if we are going to get on successfully in society."

"Self-control?" I said, somewhat outraged. "I cook, I clean; how many kids my age do you know who do all those things?"

Dr Peters looked at me curiously. "Well, that just sums you up. X, *you* go to extremes."

Tonight, I decided to visit House Party Helen, and, as I passed the row of shops in the village on the way to her house, I heard a familiar voice.

"Hey, X," Rachael said from behind me.

I turned and smiled. "Hey, Rach, how are you?"

"I'm fine. I just rented a video. Do you fancy watching it with me?" she asked keenly.

"I'd love to, but I'm heading to Helen's. I thought I'd better say thank you for everything she's done for me this week," I said truthfully.

"Ok," Rachael said, disappointed. "See you in English on Monday?"

"I look forward to it!" I said it with a smile.

After entering through her window, I dutifully thanked Helen for single-handedly restoring my reputation at school.

"It's my pleasure, X; just go easy in the future, yes?" Helen advised.

I smiled. "Absolutely, you're looking at a genuine Paul the Apostle here. Screw Damascus: nothing but bad shit is going down there. I've seen the light, heard the word, and bought the T-shirt. From this day forth, I'm serving the school."

Helen shook her head and giggled. "How exactly?"

I was thoughtful momentarily. "I'll be honest; at this precise point in time, I have absolutely no idea, but I'm sure I'll figure it out."

Helen laughed again. I'm so glad you're back, X."

Instinctively, I leaned in for a kiss, but Helen froze.

"Listen, X; it's very tempting as it happens. But I've been doing some thinking, and there's something you should know about me: I'm *nowhere* near as together as the other kids at school think I am. And getting it on with the school's 1000-piece jigsaw might be a recipe for disaster."

1000-piece jigsaw? It's not a compliment, is it?

I withdrew my face from hers. "I understand you don't want to kiss me; it's cool."

She flushed slightly. "Well, I do, X, but how about we become best friends instead?"

This offer was as good as any snog after weeks of loneliness. "OK, you've got a deal. You'll need a nickname; let's see, I've got it! From this day forth, you will be known as *Flan*."

"Flan?" she asked a little sourly.

I held my hand up. "I can see you're not loving it yet; that's not a problem, though. Nicknames are like new shoes; wearing them can take a couple of weeks before they feel comfortable."

"X, are you sure that's the best you can come up with?" Flan asked, clearly still far from convinced.

I didn't have time to answer as there was a knock at the door. Catching Helen's eye, I pointed at the window to suggest my departure, but then her mother said, "Would either of you like a drink?" Flan and I looked at each other in confusion. "Oh, and X, you're welcome here anytime, but in the future, love, could you just use the front door like a normal person, please? We're terrified you'll fall off that drainpipe and break your neck," Mrs Flannigan said kindly.

Flan and I exchanged a look of wonder and then burst out laughing.

SATURDAY 10TH JUNE

When I heard Rachael's voice, I was busy de-greasing and re-greasing an old racing bike at the back of Ripton Cycles. "What's this, X, and the art of bicycle maintenance?"

I looked at the door. "Hey, Rachael, what brings you here?"

"I want a proper bike; mine's rubbish," she said absently.

Laughing, I replied, "Really? I hadn't noticed."

Alison joined her daughter in the doorway. "Oh, hello, X, I didn't realise you worked here."

"Hello, Alison," I said politely, "I'm volunteering."

"Oh, yes, Alison," Rachael said conspiratorially. "X is something of a dark horse; he doesn't tell people where he's working, and he doesn't tell people when he's got a new *girlfriend*."

Irritably, I replied, "I have *not* got a girlfriend."

Rachael ignored me, though. "Actually, Alison, we shouldn't even be talking to him; his *new girlfriend* might get upset; besides, now that X has a *new girlfriend*, I imagine he wants some time alone to think about his *new girlfriend*."

"*Stop*, will you?" In frustration, I threw the tube of grease I'd been using on the floor. "Stop doing that weird repetitive *Rain Man* thing; it's driving me nuts."

"*See?*" Turning to her daughter, Alison said, "It's not *just* me who thinks you're strange."

I sighed. "If it *is* Helen whom you are referring to, then, for clarity, let me just explain that Flan, as I now call her, is part of my tiny, rather select, group of friends," I said.

Rachael smiled sweetly, turned on her heels, and disappeared into the shop.

After wiping my hands on a cloth, I stood up and joined her mother in the doorway. "Why is she calling you Alison?" I whispered.

We both watched Rachael casually peruse Ron's selection of bikes as Alison explained, "She's been doing it all week. That's why we're here. I am at a complete loss, so I've decided to try and buy my way back into her affections."

"Good luck with that!" I said discreetly.

At that point, my boss returned from his lunch break. "Potential customers for you, Ron; I'll leave you to it," I said, returning to work and listening in to the conversation next door.

"If it's a road bike you're interested in, you'll need one specifically designed for a female. I don't have any in stock, but ordering one won't take long," Ron advised pleasantly.

"I want the same bike X has," Rachael said firmly.

"The difference with a lady's bike is this top bar; it's angled differently to allow for… " Ron continued.

"I want the same bike X has!" Rachael repeated.

"If I just show you a picture, then you'll see the difference," Ron said to explain.

Angrily, through gritted teeth, Rachael said, "I want the same *bloody* bike that X has!"

After making the purchase, Rachael popped her head around the door and asked sweetly, "Would you like to go out for a ride tomorrow? It's going to be another lovely, sunny day."

"That would be great," I replied, smiling.

Ron opened the till and looked mindfully at the cash inside. "I think she's got a thing for, you know?" he said, giving me a friendly nudge.

"Who, Rachael? Maybe once, I think we might have had something for each other, but I can't risk losing her again, so *that* is strictly off the menu," I replied.

"Pretty girl, a bit weird, but *very* pretty," he said thoughtfully, and after thrusting the two notes he had taken from the register into my hand, he added, "Here you go, X; profit share."

SUNDAY 11TH JUNE

Looking somewhat flustered, Alison opened the door to me this morning. "All I'm saying is, after two hours of shopping last night and another hour spent preparing it this morning, you'd better bloody appreciate this picnic, X."

In the kitchen, I found Rachael wearing the same outfit as last Sunday. Walking behind her, I whistled and said, "Those legs again."

"It's hot, that's all," she said defensively.

"Hey, speaking of the sun, I brought you one of these to keep it off your eyes." I reached into my rucksack, pulled out a baseball cap, and placed it gently on her head.

"*No*, X, it'll make me look ridiculous," she said objectionably.

I looked at her. "No, leave it on; it makes you look cute."

Rachael glowered. "Cute?"

And that's the last time I will try to compliment you today.

With Rachael's mood erring towards the tetchy, I meekly acquiesced when she suggested we cycle to Griarsly Water, a reservoir 15 miles from town. Eventually, we set off. I seemed to be carrying the world's weight, while Rachael had a light rucksack on her back.

The new bike certainly had the desired effect on Rachael's speed, and, as such, it took no more than an hour and a quarter to reach our destination. On arrival, we laid the bikes on the grass, walked up the steps to the water, and laid out the picnic blanket. We sat quietly in the sunshine until Rachael suggested, "A swim might sharpen our appetites."

A swim?

"Unfortunately, I haven't got any trunks with me," I said, hoping this news would curtail her plan before it developed further.

Rachael eyed my shorts curiously. "What have you got on under there?"

"Boxers," I replied ruefully.

She looked at me and smiled. "*Well*, you can swim in them; they'll dry in the sun."

"And what are you going to wear?" I asked in wonder.

"Oh, I've got a bikini on underneath," she replied casually.

I looked at the water—even in the streaming sunlight, it had a murky quality, making it entirely unappealing. "Listen, Rach, farm fields surround this reservoir. With concern, I said, "For all we know, it's full of chemicals."

Rachael, already up and unbuttoning her shorts, looked down at me. "The water's used for irrigation; why would the farmer put chemicals in it?"

With her shorts removed, she took the vest top off and threw it carelessly to the floor. Rachael's body is beautiful, but as difficult as it was, I endeavoured to maintain eye contact with my friend.

"I'm just saying, don't blame me if you dip your toe in there and the bloody thing falls off," I said dramatically.

Impatiently, Rachael said, "Oh, *come on*, X."

Reluctantly, I got to my feet and, feeling intensely self-conscious, removed my T-shirt. As I did, Rachael wolf-whistled. When I started to pull down my cycling shorts, she said, "Hey, X, if you're wearing embarrassing boxers, then I promise I won't laugh."

I was wearing white ones with red hearts, and she promptly exploded with laughter. After Rachael had finished giggling, she asked, "Tell me, you didn't buy those thinking girls would be impressed?"

Thoughtfully, I replied, "I don't think *I did* buy them. It was Mum, if memory serves me correctly."

"Then your mum must be insane!" Rachael giggled, and then, realising what she *had* said, her face dropped in horror.

"I'm sorry, I'm sorry, I'm sorry, I'm sorry," she said with her face buried in her hands.

"Rachael, it's OK," I said reassuringly and hugged her. "I know you wouldn't say something like that intentionally," as I placed my hands on her bare back, I felt suddenly, and rather dramatically, aroused.

Control yourself, X; we discussed this. Rachael is far too important to risk a hormonal urge for. This is the new you standing here, with added self-control. Yes, her backside is perfectly formed, and her breasts are more substantial than you'd imagined. However, this girl is your best friend, a status only recently regained after a tumultuous three months. Keep it together, sunshine, and we'll take care of the monster in your, frankly, ludicrous, underwear when we are safely ensconced in your bedroom later.

You can tell the size of the dilemma I was having. Eventually, to avoid the black hole of temptation, I suggested we do the last thing I wanted to. "Come on, let's go in the water."

Rachael is an elegant swimmer whose strokes look effortless. As she glided to the centre of the reservoir, all I could do was splash hopelessly behind her. Once she had reached the centre, she gracefully trod water, and patiently waited for me to join her.

"I'd imagined you'd be a better swimmer than you are," Rachael said playfully.

Desperately trying to keep my head above water, I replied, "Sorry to disappoint in that case."

Rachael giggled. "That's all right, X; I like it when I'm better than you at things."

"Hey, I'm going back to the bank; I'm starting to fear drowning is a real possibility," I said after spitting out a mouthful of water.

"OK, I'm going to stay in for a bit longer," she replied and swam off.

When I returned to the picnic rug, I found what I wanted in Rachael's bag: a towel. After drying myself off, I lay on the blanket and placed the towel strategically to protect my modesty. The boxer shorts also had the disadvantage of becoming see-through when wet.

I watched Rachael glide up and down for 10 minutes before she swam back to the bank and joined me. "Throw me the towel, please," she said, shielding the sun from her eyes.

"No can do," I said plainly.

Sounding needy, she said, "Please, X, I'm freezing."

"Penises shrivel in the cold; it's a well-established scientific fact. That towel is staying right where it is," I said firmly.

"Well then, I promise *I* won't look, X," Rachael said sincerely.

Reluctantly, I threw the towel at her, and true to her word, Rachael averted her gaze. Whether that is a sign of her utter disinterest or a difference between the male and female of the species, I do not, in truth, know. Suffice to say, if the situation had been reversed, then I'd have made a liar of myself instantly.

As we lay next to one another, warming in the sun, she asked, "So, do you think you'll be able to get to the end of the term without... well, you know, going off the rails again?"

"I'm a changed man, Rachael; no more madness. And I really need to find a way to repay the school for standing by me," I said thoughtfully.

"It is *only* a school, X. Besides, it's part of their job to look after your well-being," Rachael said dismissively.

I propped myself up on my elbow and looked at her. "It's more than a school to me; it's different for you, I suppose, because you haven't been there for long, but Luther Parkinson and me, well, we're tight. Anyway, I'm not sure what *I can* do now, except for winning a tennis match, obviously, but I'm sure it will come to me—I think I'm just waiting for a sign."

"*A sign?*" Rachael asked incredulously. "X, for a self-professed Grade 9 atheist, you do sound like a religious lunatic sometimes—do you know that?"

After we had dried under the sun, Rachael took the picnic contents from the rucksack. The first offering was a small, malformed, black, greasy ball. "Olive?" she asked.

Dutifully, I placed one in my mouth, bit into it, instantly gagged, and spat it towards the water. "No!" I said objectionably. "Say, Rachael, have you got any scotch eggs in there?"

"*No*, I haven't. Here, try this," Rachael said, offering a small Tupperware dish containing a substance with the colour and consistency of dog vomit: "it's hummus; dip the pitta bread into it and give it a try; it's delicious."

Hummus is much tastier than olives, and the picnic contained many other delights. After gorging, we lay on the blanket together, and Rachael asked, "Can I rest my head on your shoulder?"

"Yes, of course," I replied politely.

After positioning her head appropriately, she gently touched my stomach.

Fortunately, I drifted off to sleep before my teenage mind could lead me astray. Rachael was still fast asleep when I awoke, and as I gently placed my hand upon her arm, the strangest feeling overcame me. I cannot recall an occasion on which I have ever felt such a sense of utter contentment. Eventually, the sun disappeared behind a thick white cloud, so, trying not to disturb my friend, I carefully reached for the towel and placed it over her. After lying there for another half an hour or so, Rachael finally stirred. "Thanks for putting the towel over me, X," she said, stifling a yawn.

"No problem. Hey, you were really out of it. I managed to take off your bikini top and put it back on without waking you up," I said cheekily.

Rachael slapped my stomach. "Shut up, X. You're not funny." However, as I looked down, I could see that she was smiling.

Later, after packing up, we cycled back to Rachael's house. As I stood on her doorstep, hoping for an invitation inside, I exclaimed, "I had a great time."

Rachael beamed, kissed me on the cheek, said, "That was my favourite day!" and promptly slammed the door shut.

MONDAY 12TH JUNE

I reconnected with another friend today. When JG took the seat opposite me at lunch, I was discussing England's chances in the Ashes series with Cocksucker Carl.
"Hey, X," he said a little uncertainly
"Hey, JG," I replied brightly.
I could tell something was eating JG, as he didn't touch his food. Instead, he impatiently tapped his fingers on the table, glaring intently at Carl. Finally, he said, "Hey, Carl, could you go and sit somewhere else, please? I want to speak to X without you hearing it."
As always, very matter-of-fact.
"Don't be rude, JG. Stay where you are, Carl," I said testily.
"Don't worry, X, I'd finished anyway," Carl said sullenly, and, taking his plate, he left us.
"Sorry, what I have to say is not for Cocksucker's ears, OK?" JG said it defensively.
"Well, say it then," I replied.
"Firstly, I didn't know about your Mum... and, if I had, *well*, it does put a different perspective on things, I suppose," JG said. I held my hand up in acknowledgement, "Listen, it's me who should be apologising. I'm sorry for letting you down over the business, and I'm *particularly* sorry for what I said about Clare. I heard you two broke up, by the way."
JG was thoughtful momentarily and then said, "We did, but now I think it was fate... Anyway, friends again?"
"Absolutely," I said, then added, "How's Drake?"

Sheepishly, he said, "Oh, we've fallen out."

"Why?" I asked curiously.

"Oh, it was about Rachael," he replied. "Yes, we both fell for the same girl when we were working with her on the committee for the last dance party, but, X, what's a beautiful creature like her going to see in a boy like Drake? He is, and I don't mean any disrespect when I say this, so *utterly* beneath her, both intellectually and physically."

I laughed. "And I just know you said that directly to his face, *didn't you?*"

"*Obviously!*" JG said it rather superciliously. "I'm trying to save the lad from a fall. I don't want him humiliating himself in front of a girl so far out of his class that it would be like Eddie Large asking Michelle Pfeiffer if she fancied sucking him off in the back of his Ford Granada."

I burst out laughing, and when I'd finally stopped, I noticed that those around us had started paying attention to our conversation.

"Anyway," JG continued, "there I am trying to save him from himself, and how do you think he repays me for this kindness?"

I shrugged my shoulders in ignorance.

"How? By telling me to shove my head up a dog's arsehole, that's how. Can *you* believe it, X?" JG asked in astonishment.

Ironically, I replied, "Unbelievable!"

He looked at me expectantly and asked, "Well, can you help me, X?"

Shaking my head, I responded, "To make up with Drake? I'm not sure I'm the best person for the job. We're not speaking, remember?"

"Oh, I couldn't give *a fuck* about Drake, X; all I care about is

Rachael... I think I'm in love with her. Now, there's a girl who would prize the meeting of minds over the meeting of, well, you know what I mean." JG was speaking so loudly that half the people in the canteen had already turned to listen to our conversation.

I said calmly, "Keep your voice down, JG. Listen, what do you want me to do?"

"You are friends with Rachael again, aren't you?" he asked expectantly, and I nodded. "Well, you could talk to her; tell her all the good things you know about me."

Mumbling under my breath, I said, "I'll start with your delicacy and tact."

"What did you say?" JG asked.

"I said, 'I'll see what I can do,'" I replied clearly.

TUESDAY 13TH JUNE

I got the other friend back today...
There was a knock at the door at 8.25; it was Drake. "Hey, X, want to walk to school with me?" he asked brightly.

Halfway to school, with the conversation yet to move on from his burgeoning obsession with Rachael and keen to change the subject, I said, "Listen, Drake, I just want to say that I'm sorry I missed your musical."

Dismissively, Drake said, "That's OK, X; sorry for being a bit of a crybaby about it."

"No, you were right to be angry; I let you down. I say—have you got anything else coming up soon?" I asked with interest.

He replied casually, "We're doing a Pinter play on Saturday night, but, you know, it's fairly low-key."

"I'd love to come. Can you get me a ticket?" I asked.

Drake smiled warmly. "Of course; that would be great, X."

I added, "Actually, Drake, get me two tickets, will you?"

"Anything you want, X; you will talk to Rachael for me, though, won't you?" he asked expectantly.

Uncertainly, I replied, "Err, I'll see what I can do."

THURSDAY 15TH JUNE

This situation with JG and Drake is complicated. Firstly, I must admit that my feelings for Rachael have grown more intense, particularly since Sunday, in a way I find hard to define. However, they are my friends, and I've missed them over the past few months. So, in English today, I decided to do the right thing for a change. "Listen, Rachael, I need to be careful how I put this because, let's face it, this concerns two of my friends, and just before I go any further, I just want to say that you should consider me neutral in all of this."

Rachael looked at me in dismay. "X, what *on earth* are you talking about?"

I proceeded with what I mistakenly thought was delicacy. "Right, it turns out that both JG and Drake have a major crush on you, and they've asked me, individually, to speak to you on their behalf. Needless to say, that's put me in an *incredibly* awkward position. Still, before you take things any further with either of them, I just wanted to say I believe the choice should be *entirely* yours."

There was a look of horror on Rachael's face though.

"You've got two guys ripping chunks out of one another over you; isn't that every girl's dream?"

Angrily, Rachael scribbled on a Post-it note, ripped it off the pad, and slammed it down on the desk before me. It read, "PLEASE, DIE!"

Next, after trying to do the right thing *again*, I was

kicked out of Eating Disorder Club. Halfway through English, I could feel my stomach rumbling, so I asked, "Excuse me, Mrs Simpson, I have… an appointment over lunch, which will prevent me from visiting the canteen, and I was wondering whether I could leave class 10 minutes early to go to the shops across the road."

"As you asked so nicely, X, then, of course, you can," my English teacher replied with a smile.

While stuck in the bakery line, I decided to buy a sausage roll. However, it might have appeared a little selfish if I had turned up with just something for myself, so I duly bought a selection.

After sprinting back to school, I arrived at the computer suite and offered the food to the other pupils. Fatty Jacob's hand shot so fast into the bag that I thought he would punch a hole in the bottom. However, the other kids shrunk back from my offering, like I were waving a snake at them. The school nurse came in and started yelling at me, "Ms James' office, X, *now!*"

The head of year considered her response momentarily. "No, you weren't wrong in your actions, X; you were just *wildly* insensitive."

I thought for a moment. "Actually, Ms, now you say that I think I may have been *not* wrong, just *wildly* insensitive with Rachael earlier," I said through a mouthful of food.

"Well, X," Ms James said with a polite smile, "why don't you run along and find her instead of bothering me unnecessarily?"

"OK," I said brightly. "So you're not mad at me, Ms?" I added it cautiously.

"No," she said casually. "Though don't go back, *ever!* Besides," she frowned slightly, "your appetite seems to have returned now."

Having already polished off a pork pie and a sausage roll while we'd been chatting, I was working through a steak slice.

"I suspect there was an appetite suppressant in whatever rubbish it was that you were taking," Ms James said thoughtfully. "Oh, and X," she peered curiously at the bakery bag in my hand, "what have you got left in there?"

I looked inside. "Cheese and onion pasty."

Ms James smiled meekly. "Would you mind? I'm starving."

FRIDAY 16TH JUNE

Dr Peters, the school psychiatrist, waved the floppy disc casually. "Thank you for letting me read some of your diary, X."

With a groan, I replied, "It's not a diary; it's a document."

"Well," she said with a smirk, "thank you for letting me read your *document* then. Tell me, X, would you call yourself a grown-up?"

This was a good question, so I dutifully considered my response. "What is a grown-up? The government draws the line at sixteen and says, 'Off you go, kids, go screw each other senseless and smoke fags together when you're done,' Peter Pan certainly had his theory, and that's why he fucked off to Neverland when he did." Much to my chagrin, Dr Peters flatly refuses to react when I swear, "There were times this year when I felt like a man… "

Dr Peters leant forward intently. "And which times were those, X?"

Stroking my chin, I said, "When I was making good money, and when I was… " I looked at the psychiatrist and quickly raised my eyebrows a few times in a suggestive manner.

She nodded immediately in understanding. "Right, yes, I get you. That would make sense."

I was thoughtful for a moment before continuing, "You know, I'm like that song that's playing on the radio all the time, 'Manchild'. *Do* you know the one I'm talking about?" The good doctor nodded in affirmation. "I mean, we guys don't get much support through *our* change, do we? The girls are taken off for their period chat, aren't they? What do we get? *Nothing!* That's what. Instead, we wake up one strange, sticky night and discover that we now have two unpinned grenades with *the most remarkable* recharging capabilities swinging between our legs. Just a brief chat, a little heads up on how much trouble these things... " I indicated to my crotch, "can land you in. Is that too much to ask, *really*?"

"Didn't your father talk with you?" she asked, and I rolled my eyes incredulously. "*That's* a no, then," Dr Peters added quickly. After a pause, she asked, "Do you think about sex a lot, X?"

Flippantly, I replied, "Just take the hours and minutes I'm awake in the day and subtract a big fat zero."

"Really?"

I stared at her intently. "I'm thinking about it right now, with you as it happens, Dr Peters."

The psychiatrist blushed slightly and shifted uncomfortably in her chair. "Well, I hardly think that is appropriate, X!"

Aggrieved, I replied, "*You asked!* Besides, you told me last week that I was a master at... " The word had gone.

"Evasion?" she suggested.

"That's it! Anyway, I finally opened up and told you something truthful, and the first thing you did was freak out."

Dr Peters raised her hand in a gesture of apology. "I'm sorry, X. You caught me a little off-guard. *Anyway,* as you're in the mood to answer my questions truthfully *for once*, would you mind me asking a few about your mother?"

Oh, bravo! You turned that back on me spectacularly well, Dr P.

I issued a deep, irritable sigh. "Here we go!"

"You know, you stopped writing this the day it happened," she said, tapping the floppy disk.

It was my turn to shift uncomfortably in my seat. "That's a coincidence, Dr Peters; as I've told you many times before, don't look for answers because all you'll find is chaos."

She leaned forward purposefully. "I think that's an excuse; saying everything is chaotic is just a way of abdicating responsibility for everything that happens in your life, isn't it, X? All I want to understand is how you felt when your mother tried to commit suicide."

For four weeks, I'd employed every form of, in the good doctor's favourite word, *evasion* possible in avoiding answering that question, but today, I just snapped. "If you *must* know, I felt embarrassed, *OK*? I'd just turned my life around—I was finally becoming the person I wanted to be, and she went and pulled that trick. Suicide is ugly, Dr Peters. I*t's a stain,* and I didn't think it suited my image, so I buried it. That's why I didn't mention it in that." I pointed at the floppy disc, "There you go—what does that make me?"

Dr Peters smiled sympathetically. "Human, X, just human."

After classics, I caught up with Rachael in the corridor. "Listen, about yesterday, I just wanted to say I'm sorry for being *wildly* insensitive to you."

Rachael looked at me curiously. "Who told you to say that to me, X?"

Rumbled, I replied, "Actually, if you must know, I stole it from Ms James, but I am *truly* sorry; it's none of my business whom you go out with."

Smiling warmly, Rachael replied, "Apology accepted, X.

Please pass on to your friends that, although their offers are flattering, I must decline because I have my eye on somebody else."

"Oh," I said with a shrug. "Anyone I know?"

She raised her eyebrows. "Everybody knows him, X."

"Well, if you can still fit me in, would you like to come and watch a play with me tomorrow night that Drake's acting in?" I asked.

Rachael's eyes narrowed with suspicion. "X, if you're trying to set me up..."

"Scouts, honor," I replied, giving the three-fingered salute as I did. "I would feel honoured if you spent the evening in my company."

"Ok then," she said sweetly. "Burger first?"

"Cool, but you'll have to meet me at work," I replied.

"Oh, will you have the overalls on?" she asked with interest.

Shrugging, I replied, "Maybe; why?"

Absently, she said, "No reason," and smiled curiously.

SATURDAY 17TH JUNE

Rachael quickly devoured her food. "Yum! Burgers are dirty food. Most of the time, I like to eat healthily, but occasionally, I get the urge for something filthy. I imagine it will be much the same with sex," she said casually.

I was so shocked that I spat a mouthful of lemonade across the table.

"Not that *I'd* know, of course," she continued. Noticing the mess on the table, she said kindly, "Don't worry, X, I'll get some napkins to clear it up."

As she approached the counter, I noticed Geoff Travis receiving service at one of the tills. Rachael and the football captain exchanged a few words first before he looked over his shoulder in my direction. Eventually, he headed towards the exit, food in hand, and as he did, he nodded in my direction. I'm unsure if he was trying to be friendly; regardless, I gave him the finger in response.

"That wasn't very adult, X," Rachael said disapprovingly as she wiped the table.

"I don't care. I hate him; besides, he's an all-round fucker," I said sullenly.

With the mess now taken care of, Rachael took the seat opposite me. "I suppose it's natural that you are rivals. You are the two best-looking boys in the school, after all."

I looked at my companion in horror. "*Please* don't tell me you find that creep attractive." I said it with a mouthful of burger.

"*You* find Clare Parkin attractive!" Rachael countered.

I really dislike it when she says something clever that I can't quickly formulate a response to.

Drake's play was excellent; it was called *The Caretaker*. Afterwards, in the bar, he joined us for a drink, and when Rachael went to get another round in, he said, "Thanks for coming, man, and I can't believe you brought Rachael. You're the best friend a guy could have, do you know?"

Really, I'm not.

He seemed so happy that I didn't have the heart to break the bad news to him just yet. I resolved to give the matter due consideration and devise a way of delivering the body blow as gently as possible by tomorrow.

Leaving the arts centre, we entered streets teeming with drunken violence, and, as such, I suggested to Rachael that we avoid the danger inherent in waiting for a bus and jump in a cab instead. When we arrived at her house, Alison sat in the kitchen. "Oh, hello, you two. Good play?"

"Very," I replied.

Bossily, Rachael said, "Bit late for you, isn't it, Mum? Why don't you take your cocoa with you to bed? There's a good girl."

Alison sighed. "I know when I'm not wanted. Nice to see you, X," and retreated upstairs.

"That *wasn't* very nice, Rachael," I said reprovingly once Alison was out of earshot.

"She doesn't mind. Besides... " Rachael took both of my hands in hers. "There's something I wanted to say to you."

"Oh yeah, what's that exactly?" I asked absently.

Rachael leaned in close to me. "That was a lovely evening, and I want it to end especially too." With that, she kissed me. I mean, she *really* kissed me, and I kissed her back.

I've only kissed four girls properly, five counting Rachael, but nothing in the past could compare to this. My whole body was alive with the Mickey Rourke feeling, and it pleased the rational side of my brain to see that there wasn't a picture of the bastard anywhere in sight. I feel embarrassed writing this, but it was like our mouths were made for one another—*scratch that*—I'm not ashamed! That's *exactly* how it felt. I must have been kissing her for five minutes when the X alarm in my brain sounded, and I pulled my mouth away from hers.

X, we discussed this!

"Wait, stop. Is this a good idea?" I asked.

"The best idea I've ever had," Rachael said breathlessly, kissing me again.

Another minute passed before I pulled away again. "Listen, Rachael, this is important; I don't want to lose you."

"Keep kissing me like that, and I promise you that you won't," and we embraced again.

Resolutely, I stopped again and stepped back. "Listen, *please*, can we just talk about this for a minute?"

Rachael frowned. "You don't find me attractive, do you?"

"There is nothing unattractive about you, Rachael," I said sincerely. "You look great, you feel great, and you even taste great."

Somewhat testily, Rachael asked, "So, what is it then?"

I placed my hands on her shoulders. "I want to; believe me, I don't want to stop, but I just got you back, and I'm genuinely terrified of losing you again."

Looking concerned, Rachael asked, "What can I do, X?"

"Can you give me some time with this?" I asked.

"Yes, if you need it," Rachael said, adding quickly, "How long exactly?"

I shrugged as I edged backwards towards the door. "I don't know; a couple of weeks?"

"OK, that's fine. Listen, X, are you OK?" Rachael asked with concern.

"OK? Of course, *I'm not* OK; I'm seeing a psychiatrist, *remember?*" I was starting to sound ever so slightly hysterical. Eventually, with my hand on the door, I said, "Listen, Rachael, I think I should go. I'll see you on Monday."

SUNDAY 18TH JUNE

Today, I went out for a sun-drenched, exhausting three-hour bike ride. It was a blessed relief, as it was the only part of the day I didn't agonise over Rachael.

MONDAY 19TH JUNE

Despite my best intentions, I failed to tell Drake the news this morning on my way to school. Similarly, when JG asked for an update during the morning break, I also evaded the issue with him.

"*Well*, what did Clare send you this time?" Lisa the Repeater asked impatiently in form group after I had listened to the latest tape to arrive with the register.

"'The Lovecats' by The Cure," I replied.

"The Cure? Well, there you go. The poor girl got so depressed over you that she's turned into a mungo. I imagine she'll hang herself next. Still, at least the school will get on the local news, I suppose," Lisa said casually.

"What's good about that?" I asked in wonder.

Lisa scowled. "Oh, don't be ridiculous, X; *everybody* wants their school to be on the local news!"

THURSDAY 22ND JUNE

It was another tennis defeat today. Dr Harris managed to remain upbeat, though. "I still believe, X. As mad as that might make me, I still believe," he said, giving me an affectionate pat on the shoulder.

FRIDAY 23RD JUNE

After last week's drama, my appointment with Dr. Peters passed without incident. We talked about Rachael.

"Trust me, X, she won't mind that you want to wait to make sure you are doing the right thing; on the contrary, I'm sure she finds it quite endearing," Dr Peters said reassuringly. I would only advise this: Remember, she's just a girl."

As opposed to what exactly, just a post-box?

"And what I mean by that is that sometimes when you talk about Rachael, it sounds like you worship her. That might be why you're struggling to be intimate with her; you may feel like you are committing blasphemy. Try not to make her into something she can never be. By your admission, you have distant relationships with your family, you frequently fall out with friends, and it seems you are channelling everything in your heart into one person. If you want my advice, share the love, X."

"Share the love?" I asked.

"Yes, share the love, oh, and X, take it easy for a little while, yes?" Dr Peters added.

"Ok. So, that's it; we're done, and I'm now free?" I asked, rising from my chair.

"You are, X." the psychiatrist said with a smile. "Remember, the next time you feel the train is going too fast, simply apply the brakes."

THURSDAY 6TH JULY

So, I had been following the good doctor's orders. Frankly, the last two weeks have been relatively uneventful and dull. Rachael and I are still on the best of terms. Every time I mention our Saturday night kissing, she says, "Tell me at the year four camp, OK, X?"

I'm getting along exceptionally well with JG and Drake, though strictly on a one-to-one basis, as they still can't stand the sight of one another. Admittedly, I have yet to break the news of Rachael's disinterest in them. However, the ideal opportunity will present itself before the term ends.

The doctor at the loony hospital tells us that there's every chance Mum will be home before the end of summer. If that's the case, Dad has promised a family holiday to remember. In the next breath, he did say "Wales," Tragically, when he did, there wasn't the slightest hint of irony in his voice.

The endlessly sunny weather has done wonders for business at Ripton Cycles, so I am now a paid employee. Ron has set one condition: I must always wear the overalls, even when not in the workshop. This is because he believes the attire positively impacts our female customers. This is known as exploitation, which, as I had been led to believe, is a largely negative phenomenon. However, I'm pleased to say that such reports are groundless, and it really is quite fun.

Yes, it has been a quiet time until today.

In English, Rachael was flirting via Post-it-note.

"YOU LOOK HANDSOME TODAY!"

I replied, "THANK YOU."

"IT'S LESS THAN 2 WEEKS TO YEAR 4 CAMP!"

I am now 93% certain that Rachael and I should be together, and even though I still have a few doubts, I think I'm ready to commit. My main worry has been that, from what I've seen, when two people break up, it's rarely civilised. My other worry is my libido. It's been over three months since I last had sex, and after being neutralised by my narcotic binge, the beast is awake again. I am a raging hormonal time bomb, and just as English finished today, I exploded.

The rest of the class had already departed for lunch, and Mrs Simpson and I were alone. "I think you'll enjoy *Tess of the D'Urbervilles*, X. As an atheist, you'll find it right up your street," she said enthusiastically.

In truth, I wasn't paying Tess too much attention at that precise point. On the contrary, I was somewhat entranced by my English teacher. She'd been making the most of the fine weather, as she was nicely bronzed, and her hair had been freshly highlighted.

"X, are you OK… X?" She asked with concern, as I had ignored her question.

"Your hair looks great today, Mrs Simpson," I said dreamily.

My English teacher's face lit up. "Why, thank you, X; that's the nicest compliment I've received in a long time."

I wasn't finished yet, though. "Well, in that case, Mr Simpson should book himself an appointment at the opticians because *you* are a beautiful woman!" I said passionately.

Mrs Simpson launched herself at my face and started kissing me without warning. After a few moments, though, she aggressively pushed me backwards, and I naturally assumed that she had realised the madness of the situation.

"Sorry, Mrs Simpson," I said in fear. "I'm not sure what I was thinking," I said, unsure why *I* was apologising.

My English teacher had a twisted smile on her face that made her look ever so slightly demented. "I've just got two words for you, young man: *store cupboard!*"

Even though it sounded more like an order than an invitation, I willingly followed her.

The English cupboard isn't an ideal place to do *it*. Firstly, it is so packed with fading texts that there is little room for manoeuvring. Secondly, and more significantly, there is no lock. So, as a security measure, we did *it* up against the door—another 1989 first for me right there. Mrs Simpson is a vocal lover, and, terrified we'd be overheard, I pressed my hand into her mouth to silence her and, during our lovemaking, she bit down on it so hard that she drew blood. Next, in a passion, she lashed out with her left arm so wildly that she brought a shelf and its contents down on top of us.

"Ouch!" I shouted in agony.

Mrs Simpson was entirely unsympathetic, though. *"Don't stop!"* she said in a voice that reminded me of the demonic teen in The *Exorcist*, a movie I'd watched a ropey pirate copy of a few weeks ago. As I was ever so slightly afraid, I did exactly as I was told.

Afterwards, I noticed she'd been crying, and I was about to ask why when a familiar voice asked, "Is everything OK in there?"

After quickly restoring our dress, I opened the door and saw Mr Jacobs' kind face.

"Oh, John, I was just reaching for a book, and the shelf collapsed. X rescued me," Mrs Simpson said in a faltering voice behind me.

"Oh, well done, X!" Mr Jacobs said, beaming at me, and,

turning to Mrs Simpson, he added, "Oh, look at you, poor dear, you're crying; that must have been quite a bang you took in there." He offered a hand to Mrs Simpson, who promptly burst into a fit of giggles, which she disguised, quite brilliantly, as further upset.

Leading Mrs S from the cupboard in a gentlemanly manner, Mr Jacobs said, "You're a hero, X; I shall inform Ms James of your bravery. There's a shame there isn't more like you in this place."

Mrs Simpson cast me a dirty look. *"I'll say!"*

"Now, come on, my dear, we need to get something hot and sweet into you," Mr Jacobs said with concern to the English teacher as he led her down the corridor, which only caused her to burst into another fit of giggles.

"You poor thing, you're hysterical," I heard him say as they strolled away.

I, however, went off to search for a plaster for my bleeding hand.

This injury led to a relatively poor showing on the tennis court after school this afternoon.

"Sorry, sir," I said. "It's the hand, see?" I said this while holding up the bandage so the headmaster could see it.

"Ah, dog, was it?" Dr Harris enquired with interest.

"Something wild, sir, that's for sure."

"Well, you'd better get it looked at, X. After all, you don't know where it's been," the headmaster advised sagely, and with that, I resolved to buy some condoms.

"Still, sir, one more game to go, eh?" I said brightly as we wandered towards the changing rooms.

"I… still… believe, X," Dr Harris said, but it was clear to me from the look on his face that he didn't.

Tonight, I have reflected on the 'incident' with Mrs Simpson, and my thoughts are as follows:

> 1. Rachael and I are not an item, so I am under no restrictive monogamous clause.
> 2. Dr Peters advised me to 'share the love', and only the fool ignores solid, well-intentioned psychiatric advice when it's offered.
> 3. I obeyed a teacher's direct instruction, as the Luther Parkinson code of conduct instructs all pupils to do without question.
> 4. Mrs S and I have a special relationship. I think sex is *far* too simple a word to use to describe what passed between us this afternoon. To me, it was more of a rite of passage. What could have been a more appropriate way to celebrate our bond than with centuries of literature raining down upon us?
> 5. I was horny.

I'm glad I went through this process; I'm sure I'll sleep better tonight.

FRIDAY 7TH JULY

Clare Anatomy has developed a new game in biology. Subtlety, under the table, she has taken to running her fingers along my inner thigh, almost to the point where she touches... *Well,* you know what I mean. Admittedly, it's a bit of a risk with Rachael in the room. However, I'm sure it's all in the spirit of harmless fun and makes the lesson more interesting.

MONDAY 10TH JULY

Lisa the Repeater was mid-way through telling me about Kerry Watson's shoplifting arrest in form group this morning when a spotty, year three kid came in and said, "X, to Ms James' office."

"You wanted to see me, Ms," I said as I entered.

"Ah, the hero of the book cupboard, do take a seat. Now, X," she said, studying the timetable in front of her. "As the school is broke and supply teachers are not an option until next term, Mr Shaver will be covering your English class on Thursdays and Fridays. I trust you two can be in the same room without trying to beat the living what-have-you out of one another?"

Reassuringly, I said, "You'll be pleased to know that Mr Shaver and I are on the very best of terms these days."

Ms James raised her eyebrows. "*Good lord*—that's the only response I can think of."

"Err, what's happened to Mrs Simpson?" I asked with concern.

"Well, X, I was rather hoping you would tell me," Ms James said, folding her arms and staring at me intently.

I gave her my best *blank* face.

"Let's see, what *has* happened to Susan Simpson? Forgive me for referring to my notes, X, *it's* quite a list," Ms James placed her notepad in front of her. "She has called in sick for the rest of the term, submitted her notice, is leaving her husband, *and* has decided to travel the world. *Strange*, no?"

"Unbelievable," I replied in wonder.

Ms James smiled sweetly. "I was rather fond of Susan,— well, as fond as one *can be* of a hippy. The husband is a brute, however. I'm happy for her. Too many good women squander their precious lives on an oaf. Although, I think it's rather bizarre that all it took was four copies of *The Old Curiosity Shop* to fall on her head to see the light," she said incredulously.

I smiled ruefully. "If you ask me, Ms James, women *are* the greatest mystery."

"*And one...* " Ms James slapped her hand on the desk angrily. "I would appreciate you trying to solve outside of school hours in the future! If there's one thing I can't stand, *Romeo*, it's unnecessary timetable disruption. *Is that clear?*"

I gazed innocently back at my interrogator.

Ms James sighed deeply. "Oh, don't worry, X, I'm hardly likely to bring a teacher/pupil sex scandal down upon the place, am I? We all want Luther Parkinson to be on the local news, but not *for that*! I can't imagine being the only one bright enough to put two and two together, so don't come crying to me if you find yourself on the receiving end of some alarmingly smutty innuendo."

My face remained impassive. "Was there anything else, Ms?"

"Yes, of course, *there is*. I'm not in the habit of inviting students to my office for idle chat," Ms James said crossly.

"Now, why haven't you won this tennis match yet?"

Relieved to be off the subject of Mrs Simpson, I could speak freely. "It's a complicated issue, Ms. There are many factors at work. The doubles partnerships haven't quite clicked as I would have hoped. Also, first-serve percentages... "

Ms James frowned. "If I wanted waffle, X, I'd go to Belgium.

Now, the absence of a victory is upsetting Dr Harris, who in turn is upsetting me, and *I* do not like being upset. So, it would be very much appreciated if you would invest your not inconsiderable energies into a pursuit suitable for your tender age for once and win that bloody match this week."

"No problem, Ms, I am always happy to serve the school!" I said it proudly.

With an irritable wave of her hand, Ms James said in disdain, "Oh, get out, X. *Really*, I am in no mood for oversexed teenagers today."

The incident with Mrs Simpson, as incorrectly relayed by Mr Jacobs, has given my popularity another significant boost. I'm sad that Mrs Simpson is leaving; she was my favourite teacher. However, if our brief encounter has given her the confidence to take her life in a new and exciting direction, then, like Ms James, I'm happy for her. Maybe Dr Peters is correct—sharing the love might be the way forward.

TUESDAY 11TH JULY

"Letter for you, X", Lisa the Repeater said in form group this morning as she handed me an envelope. "Who's it from?" I asked.

"How should I know?" Lisa replied petulantly. "And the secretary requested that you get your fan mail sent to your home address in the future, as the school is chronically under-resourced."

Ignoring Lisa, I took the envelope, opened it, and read.

> Dearest X,
>
> By now, I'm sure you've heard about my decision not to return to Luther Parkinson. You have set me free, X, and I just wanted to say that those five minutes in the store cupboard with you were among my happiest. Take care, my love, and keep reading!
>
> Yours,
>
> Mrs Simpson (Susan)

"So, who's it from, and what does it say?" Lisa asked with interest.

Hiding the note behind me, I said confidentially, "It's from Claire Marshall, but I can't show it to you. The contents are, I'm afraid to report, *utterly* obscene."

"That girl has *real* issues; stay clear of her, X," Lisa said, flashing me a cautionary glance.

"If anyone cares," Mr Crackett said flatly, "due to year four camp taking place on Tuesday, Wednesday, and Thursday of next week, the end-of-year awards ceremony will take place on Monday afternoon at 2.30; however, you lot," he scanned the faces of his charges dispassionately, "don't get too excited, though, as I can't imagine any of you winning a bloody thing."

Clare Anatomy was at it again in biology.

"*Seriously*, why do you do that, Clare?" I asked in wonder.

The older girl leant in confidentially, and what she whispered in my ear *really* was obscene.

WEDNESDAY 12TH JULY

Last night, I dreamt about Rachael. It was one of those dreams, if you know what I mean. I woke up so happy that I could have flown to school. At lunchtime, I sat with her and said, "Rach, I just want to let you know that I'm finally..."

Putting her finger to her smiling lips, she said, "If this is about us, tell me at year four camp, OK, X?"

I sighed. "What is it with this trip, Rachael?"

She fluttered her eyelashes. "I think it's going to be *very* special!"

There is significant interest in a school tennis match, for the first and most likely *only* time in the history of Luther Parkinson. The school meme machine randomly connected my recovery from recent troubles and my 'heroism' in the cupboard with Mrs Simpson to the upcoming game. As a result, people now believe that *I am* a miracle man. This extra attention adds to the pressure; I feel as sick as a dog. House Party Helen grabbed me after the final bell and announced, "Hey, X, I'll be net-side tomorrow—your very own cheerleader."

I'm just like a prayer-ing that there is something to cheer about.

THURSDAY 13TH JULY

During form group, I was summoned to Dr Harris' office. On arrival, the head gleefully asked, "Ah, X, my boy, how are you feeling?"

"Hunky-dory, sir," I lied.

"That's the spirit, my boy. You've got the hopes and dreams of the entire school on your shoulders; what a privilege that must be, eh?" the head said with sickening enthusiasm.

Really, it isn't.

"And far be it for me to increase your burden; however, if you could just bear in mind that if we do lose, I will owe the bishop a hundred pounds of my own money," Dr Harris said awkwardly.

"*A hundred quid?*" I asked in astonishment.

Dr Harris put his face in his hands. "Oh, I know, X, I know, I'm a fool; what was I thinking?"

Curiously, I asked, "What is with you and the bishop, sir?"

"Teddy? Old school chum—buggered me then, still trying to bugger me now... professionally speaking, obviously, X," he said, holding up his hand defensively.

"Obviously, sir," I said in reassurance.

Dr Harris sighed. "He got my goat; that's how he did it. He said Luther Parkinson was a school full of losers and there was more chance of the Revelation of John coming true this term than of us winning a tennis match. Something inside me just snapped, X."

Something inside me snapped, too. "*Screw him*, sir!" I said adamantly.

Dr Harris looked taken aback. "Now, steady on, X, that's a man of the cloth you're insulting."

There was no stopping me, though. "I meant what I said, sir; *screw him*. No one insults *our school* and gets away with it. We'll take his money by winning that match this afternoon... *and cheat if we must.*"

Dr Harris leapt to his feet, slammed his fist down on his desk, and pointed at me. "That's the spirit, X. Now, just keep that fire in your chest alive until this afternoon, and you'll soon have put them to the sword."

At lunchtime, Rachael walked up to me, quickly kissed me, and said, "Good luck; I know you'll do it." As I headed off to class, she pinched my bottom. I've never seen her so much as even dent a school regulation before, but that was two rules broken in under a minute.

It was blisteringly hot on the courts; by a quarter to four, an ominously large crowd of students and teachers had gathered to watch. Our opponents, who travelled 40 miles to play us, were late. Finally, by a quarter past, they'd arrived, changed, and the match was ready to start.

School tennis games consist of six one-set matches, two rounds of doubles, and four games of singles. If the teams are tied on sets won at the end of the match, the victory goes to the side that has won the most games.

It was honours even in the doubles. John and Charles, our numbers 3 and 4, respectively, lost narrowly 7-5, but Matt and I won ours 6-4. Their number two was a weak player, so we consistently returned the ball to him, avoiding their six-foot Herculean number one. I can serve fast, but this guy had thunder in his arms. I was starting to 'like a prayer' that we'd win the other three games of singles, as attempting to beat this guy would be a labour.

The single matches got underway, and my opponent won his first service game to love. Instantly, I felt the buzz of the crowd begin to fade. House Party Helen was umpiring our game, and as we changed ends, I hung back to talk to her.

Helen said thoughtfully, "Stand further back for his services, X."

"Any other top tips, Flan?" I asked.

Irritably, she said, "Yes, X, *try* hitting the ball back at him occasionally."

My service game was also won to love, slightly aided by Helen calling a service, which was three inches long, good.

"Hey, umpire, are you blind?" my opponent said, looking shocked with his hands on his hips.

Helen jumped to her feet and pointed at him accusingly. "Any more of that, and *you're off!*" she yelled back at him.

At the change of ends, I said to her confidentially, "I don't think you can send people off in tennis, Flan."

"I can do whatever I want—I must say, I'm rather enjoying this," she said with a little giggle.

The match continued with serve until, with the score at 4-5, I had a bit of a wobble and was 15-40 down. However, I recovered and served the rest of the game out.

With my opponent 5-6 up, we changed ends and paused for refreshments. The other games had now finished, and Matt came over to update me, "We're 3-2 up, but Charles lost 6-0, and we're tied on games. You've *got* to win, Captain," he said intently.

I looked behind the court and saw Dr Harris nervously chewing on his fingers. Rachael stood a few places along from him, and she gave me a little clap, a big smile, and a two-thumbed-up salute.

As we retook the court, the crowd gave a loud round of applause, and despite the increased nerves, I won the game easily.

At 6-6, the supervising teacher from the visiting school shouted, "Tie-break."

"Regulations say it's the umpire's call," Dr Harris yelled from behind me, and everyone turned to Helen, who looked at me questioningly. In response, I gave her a slight shake of my head.

Jumping to her feet, she yelled, "*No tie-break. Play on!*"

My opponent groaned loudly.

The game continued stubbornly with serve. Helen did her best to assist my efforts by making dodgy calls and issuing my opponent two racket violations. In fairness, the first time, he did throw it in anger. However, on the second occasion, even I thought the guy was trying to get something out of his tennis shoes.

At 10-11, I thought I'd blown it. My first serve began to falter, and I was forced to rally it out for points. The game dragged on for 10 minutes, and on my opponent's fifth break point, I thought he had me. Before I served, I stared over at a nervous-looking Rachael, who mouthed, "I love you," and the effect was more potent than any form of performance-enhancing drug ever could be. On the next point, I served my fastest ace of the match, then another, and finally won the game with a serve volley. At this point, I got somewhat carried away with myself. I pumped my fist at the crowd like I'd won the match. Next, I ran to the back of the court and started hitting my racket against the fence to incite them further.

"Oh, *come on*, umpire, what's that if not racket abuse?" my opponent asked reasonably.

However, Helen looked at him dispassionately and said, "Oh, *do* shut up!"

In my exhilaration, I hadn't even noticed the visiting school's teacher walk onto the court. When I finally did, I, like everyone else, looked at him in wonder.

He shouted, "Match to Luther Parkinson!"

There was a stunned silence.

"*What?*" my opponent screamed at his teacher. "*You can't!*" He promptly fell to his knees in anguish.

Looking down at his charge with a bemused expression, his teacher replied, "I can do what I want, lad; besides, if we don't leave now, I'll miss *Brookside*. Luther Parkinson wins."

"*We win!*" yelled Dr Harris. "*We win!*"

My opponent was in tears, imploring his teacher to change his mind.

"Listen, you daft bugger, that minibus is leaving in 10 minutes, with or without you," was the curt response he received.

The next thing I knew, Helen had sprinted over and jumped on top of me. My teammates did likewise, and it soon felt like I was underneath the entire school.

"You did it, X, you *bloody* did it," Helen yelled in my ear.

Eventually, I shouted, "Can you all get off me, please? I'm struggling to breathe under here."

The rest of the day was a dream.

FRIDAY 14TH JULY

When I entered form group this morning, I received a round of applause and dutifully gave a slight bow. There was no sign of Mr Crackett, though. Ten minutes in, a year one boy with ginger hair came in and said, "X to Dr Harris' office."

As I arrived at the headmaster's study, Rosie smiled and said, "Well, look who it is, Luther Parkinson's miracle man! You can go in, X, just keep your head down; it sounds like they're ready to kill each other."

As I got to the door, I could hear raised voices, so I knocked loudly.

"*Come in!*" Dr Harris barked.

Upon entering, I saw the headmaster sitting behind his desk with a resolute look, and a red-faced Mr Crackett stood before him.

"X plays, Crackett, and that's the end of the matter," Dr Harris said firmly.

"Plays what?" I asked innocently.

Dr Harris rolled his eyes. "Good god, my boy, the cricket match—Luther Parkinson versus Marketon High—is being played this afternoon."

"X left the team!" Mr Crackett said plainly. "I have no dealings with quitters."

Dr Harris reddened. "*I don't care!* He's the miracle man, our very own lucky charm. The boy's going out there today."

I turned to Mr Crackett and said, "Listen, sir. I quit because you gave me out when I was clearly in."

"What's that, 'not out', you say?" Dr Harris asked with interest.

"Not out, sir," I clarified.

"Well, I only gave you out because you'd left that drawing pin on my chair in form group that morning, and when I sat on it, it bloody hurt," Mr Crackett said sulkily.

"*Good god*, it's sedition!" Dr Harris said, sounding alarmed. He stood up, opened the door, and yelled at Rosie, "Call the palace guards, woman. We've caught ourselves a traitor." Closing the door and calmly retaking his seat, he looked at us both expectantly and asked, "Well?"

Mr Crackett sighed, "X, I'm sorry I gave you as out when you were clearly in."

I savoured the moment before replying, "In that case, sir, I'm sorry for the drawing pin incident and any discomfort it may have caused you."

Dr Harris fixed me with his gaze. "And?"

"And it would be my honour to play, sir," I answered sincerely.

"That's *my* boy! Good to see there's still *some* bloody heroes left in the world," he said, giving Mr Crackett a look of utter disdain.

"Who do I drop, Headmaster?" Mr Crackett asked with a sigh.

Dr Harris looked at him in horror. "Good lord, man; you're the manager; decide! I'm not picking your bloody team for you," he replied, and immediately started chuckling.

"Yes, Headmaster," Mr Crackett said in resignation.

School cricket is 20 overs per team. We lost the toss, and Marketon High elected to field first. Mr Crackett put me fourth in the order with Rich Wilson, all-round nice guy, and Geoff Travis, all-round fucker, opening.

Rich was out, caught, and bowled in the first over, but Geoff and Jack Parker, the next batsman, put on 20 runs before Jack was eventually run out. I must admit that I was nervous as hell as I walked to the crease. Mr Crackett and Dr Harris were umpiring, and as I readied myself to receive the first ball, the headmaster gave me the thumbs up and a broad smile. The lad bowling was a medium pacer; I played a defensive stroke and watched the ball dribble along the grass away from me when Geoff yelled, "Single!"

As my teammate was already yards down the wicket, I sprinted in the opposite direction. Bat outstretched, inches from the crease, my heart sank as I saw the bails explode off the stumps.

Oh well, X. Your time as Luther Parkinson's sporting hero was enjoyable, if not somewhat brief.

The shout went up. "*Howzat!*"

"Not out!" I looked up in amazement at the somewhat guilty-looking face of Mr Crackett, who added unconvincingly, "He made it… *just*."

There was debate from the opposing team, but Dr Harris barked, "Umpire's decision is final."

So much for school spirit; Geoff was planning to run me out!

When the next ball bounced forward off Geoff's pad, I tried his same trick by yelling, "Single," and sprinting for the opposite crease. My plan failed, though, and we scored a clean run. On the next ball, the bowler pitched short, and I really should have been thinking about hitting a boundary, but instead, I aimed my shot straight at Geoff, who, with something less than grace, managed to duck out of the ball's way. Smiling, I watched the ball bounce away for four.

"*Watch it, X!*" Geoff snarled.

"My sincere apologies; it must be the sun," I said, pointing to the sky with my bat.

After scoring two runs off the next ball, I played a clumsy defensive stroke, which, if the bowler had been atletic, would have been caught. Dr Harris called, "Over," and summoned Geoff and me to the middle of the wicket.

"What, in the name of Judas Iscariot's carwash, do the two of you think you're doing exactly?" he barked, glaring at us alternatively.

"*He* started it!" I said it accusingly.

Dr Harris looked at me incredulously. "I don't care who started it, X. Just bury whatever bloody hatchet there is between the two of you now. You're both capable sportsmen, so play like it and, for god's sake, hit out, will you? The run rate's too ruddy slow!"

So, for the next three overs, that's exactly what we did; we hit out and added another 40 runs to our total between the two of us. However, after hitting two consecutive fours, Geoff was clean-bowled. The next batsman, Paul Bishop, hit a single off his first ball, and, on the next delivery, I tried to hit a six, and was caught out 10 yards from the boundary.

Still, I enjoyed the applause as I returned to the pavilion. Eventually, we were all out for 97.

Marketon High are Boycott disciples, as they chased our total with a measured five runs per over. I bowled twice, even though I was out of practice. My first delivery was an embarrassing three yards wide, so when the facing batsman said sarcastically, "*Look!* I'm over here," I did lose my temper somewhat and gave him the finger in response.

"*X!*" Dr Harris bellowed, "Remember, it's a gentleman's game, my boy."

"You tell him, Granddad," the facing batsman responded cockily, and this time, it was my headmaster who, with a somewhat twisted smile on his face, gave the Marketon High boy the insulting gesture with his middle digit.

As I walked past Dr Harris to take my run-up, he whispered, "Never mind this one's stumps; just bowl it straight into his face, will you, my boy?"

"It would be my honour, sir," I replied with a smile.

Trying to obey the head's wishes, I overpitched my delivery and took the batsman's left-hand stump with a full toss.

By the beginning of the 20th over, Marketon High were 90 for seven, and our defeat looked all but assured. Geoff bowled the last over, taking a pair of further wickets off his first two balls. Our opponents scraped a single off the next, before hitting a boundary off the following delivery. There was a loud shout for LBW on Geoff's fifth ball, but Dr Harris sadly shook his head as the batsman was at least a yard out of his crease.

One more ball was to be bowled, one more wicket remained, and only two runs were required. The facing Marketon High batsman looked more than a little ill at ease at the crease, and Geoff dutifully added 10 yards to his run-up to intimidate him further. My least favourite pupil bowled a high-speed ball, and the batsman— no doubt with a mind to avoiding bodily harm—placed the bat defensively between himself and the oncoming projectile without even attempting to play a stroke. The lucky swine caught a thick edge, which raced past me in slip just out of my reach. I chased the 10 yards required to catch the ball, cleanly scooped it from the turf, and turned to see Rich Wilson, the wicketkeeper, ready to receive my throw behind the stumps.

As it turned out, I threw the ball hard and true—too hard and too true. It went straight through Rich's gloves and smashed into his face. Fortunately, Rich's skull absorbed the energy from the throw, and the ball fell directly onto the stumps.

"Out!" yelled Dr Harris, and I duly jumped heavily on top of the scrum of bodies piling on top of Geoff, as the all-round fucker was at the bottom of it.

Thankfully, when the mass of bodies finally untangled, I saw Rich being helped up to his feet and led away for the required medical attention.

I was about to write that life can't get any better than this, but up next is the end of term, the year four camp and Rachael.

Well, let's not jinx it, eh?

MONDAY 17TH JULY

The end-of-year awards ceremony was held this afternoon. Dr Harris conducted the event as always. "Before we finish for the day, Luther Parkinson, there is just one more prize to give out. It's a new award, and I would like to invite Ms James to the stage to make the presentation." The headmaster still pronounced 'Ms' slightly resentfully.

After collecting the final award from the trophy table, Ms James walked to the centre of the stage and smiled in recognition of the polite round of applause she was receiving. "Thank you, Headmaster. Thank you, pupils. As Dr Harris mentioned, this is the first time the following prize, the School Spirit Award, has been presented. It's a subjective accolade, so how best to define its essence? Simply put, we are giving the trophy to the pupil, without whom the first half of 1989 would not have been the same. Today's winner has had his fair share of highs and lows this year, and, even though he wasn't old enough for most of the former and almost all the latter self-inflicted, he has shown a remarkable, some might even say *unnerving*, ability to bounce back with style. Headmaster, colleagues, and pupils, it gives me great pleasure to name X School Spirit: 1989."

There was a roar from the crowd, who turned to see me stepping forward to collect my award.

"Err," Ms James said in confusion. "X?"

Still, I didn't come forward to collect my trophy.

"Oh, good lord, what's that dreadful boy up to now?" Ms

James finally asked with concern.

"Excuse me, Ms James," Penny Chemistry said, raising her hand. "Clare Parkin fainted in biology this morning, and X kindly saw her home."

My fellow pupils sighed in appreciation, and then JG added, "That must have been over three hours ago now, Ms James."

As I've said, he's a real stickler for detail.

"Well, how like our school spirit," Ms James said through gritted teeth, "to excuse himself from school to *sort out* a fellow pupil." Apparently, the emphasis was all hers.

"Ms James!" a year three boy suddenly shouted, pointing out the window at the old school gates. "Here's school spirit now."

I admit it; I'd been waylaid.

It all started in biology this morning. We watched a dull video on plant reproduction, and Clare and I sat behind everyone else. I must be honest; last week's double-sporting triumph has caused a slight case of inflamed ego syndrome, so when Clare started her under-the-table tease and whispered in my ear, "Success is a big turn-on, X."

I responded, "So, why are you only playing tease down there? Haven't I earned something more thorough?"

That was all the encouragement Clare needed, and she took a tight hold of, well, you know what. In return, I pulled her skirt up and gently slid my hand between her legs. As I did, she let out a squeal of delight.

"Quiet, at the back!" Mrs Gillian shouted grumpily from her desk.

After a couple of minutes of entertaining one another under the desk, Clare whispered in my ear, "I'm about to faint, and I think you should take me home." She then performed a remarkably convincing swoon, falling sideways into my arms.

"What's going on back there?" Mrs Gillian barked.

"It's Clare, Miss; I think she's fainted," I replied falsely.

Somewhat impatiently, Mrs Gillian said, "Well, who better than Luther Parkinson's resident knight in shining armour to take care of her? Off you go, X,"

"Yes, Mrs Gillian," I said eagerly.

Supporting Clare as I led her from the lab, I was relieved the lights had been dimmed for the video, as I still had the best part of an erection. As we got to the old school entrance, I saw the headmaster's secretary receiving a delivery. "Hey, Rosie, Clare fainted in class, so I'm going to walk her home," I said innocently.

"Oh, X, that's *so* sweet of you," she said with a smile.

Really, it isn't.

A blast of sunlight shining on my face woke me up. Clare was already awake, absently studying her ceiling.

"Hey, what time is it?" I asked.

Clare looked at the radio alarm on her bedside table. "2.30," she said casually.

"Shit!" I yelled. "I'm missing the end-of-year awards."

I had intended to sneak into the back of the hall unnoticed, but as I walked in, everybody was looking in my direction, clapping and saying two words repeatedly: "School spirit."

"And *finally,* he arrives. School Spirit: 1989, X." Ms James announced from the stage.

Utterly bemused about what was happening, I stood looking dumbfounded until several fellow pupils pushed me towards the front of the hall. I had won something, but I needed clarification as to what exactly.

I walked up the steps and stood alongside Ms James, who handed me an eight-inch-high cup, the inscription on which read, 'School Spirit: 1989 X.'

"Thanks!" I said it sincerely to the head of year four.

However, I could tell Ms James' smile was forced. Leaning in closely, she whispered menacingly, "I want a word with you when we're finished here."

I nodded in understanding and turned to face the audience, who had risen and given me a standing ovation—another 1989 first. I held the award aloft in acknowledgement. A shout of "Speech!" came from one of the year fours at the back, and soon the request was repeated across the hall.

"Oh, I'm sure X is *far* too modest to make a speech," Ms James said, flashing me a warning glance.

Really, I'm not.

I politely said, "Actually, Ms James, if it's not too much trouble, *I would* like to say just a few words."

"Well, OK, X will make a *brief* speech," Ms James said uncertainly, and, with that, she took a few paces backwards and invited me to take centre stage.

After waiting for the noise to subside, I cleared my throat and began, "Wow! I'm truly speechless."

Really, I'm not!

"This is the first trophy I've ever won. Actually, that's not true. I did win a table tennis tournament when I was 11 years old, though not entirely by fair means; I now feel able to confess. Even though it has spent the last four years in pride of place on my bedroom shelf, I have always felt that it has exuded an ominous aura. This, however," I looked at the new trophy fondly, "will soon be replacing it. I really should say thank you to certain people while I'm here. Firstly, Dr Harris." I looked over to my right, where he was standing. "A headmaster in a million, I'm sure you'll agree, Luther Parkinson." There was a tiny ripple of applause. "And thanks to Ms James," rather embarrassingly, the applause was noticeably louder than it had been for the head. "I, like many of you, I imagine, did wonder exactly what it is that a head of year does. However, it's all credit to Ms James that she's made the role her own. Really, these last two terms would not have been the same without her."

I took a deep breath and racked my brain for other names to mention. "Thanks to my form group." Twenty or so pupils cheered, and, raising the trophy again, I yelled, "Crackett said we'd never win, but he was wrong. The revolution starts today, brothers and sisters!" And with my free hand, I beat my chest three times.

"Thanks to Helen Flannigan for... well, Helen, you know why. Big Wilson, you're my running soul mate. To Cocksu... correction... Carl Rogers, Drake, JG, Driffid, and all the boys who helped make Pete & Dennis' Painting Services an almighty, if not somewhat brief, success. Thanks to Matt Jacobs and the rest of the tennis team, lads, I'll see you all in eternity. A big thank you also to all the members of the school cricket squad, except for Geoff Travis, all-round fu..."

Ms James stepped forward. "Thank you, X; I'll stop you there as nightfall will soon be upon us."

I tried to make a sly escape to the side of the stage, but Ms James grabbed the back of my shirt and kept a tight hold of me.

Ms James continued, "Well, Luther Parkinson, I can *finally* bring the 1989 awards ceremony to a close. This is a reminder to year four that the bus leaves for the Moors at 10 am sharp tomorrow. The dress code is casual. You can use the communal areas as it's only five past three. However, no one is to leave the grounds until they hear the final bell; thank you."

Ms James kept holding me until all the pupils and staff had filed out. Finally, I turned to her and politely asked, "You wanted to see me, Ms?"

Ms James scowled. "Don't play the innocent with me, X; I know what you've been up to, you *grotty* little boy!"

"I was just helping a fellow…"

She cut me dead. "Don't *bloody* lie to me, X. Good god, when you said you wanted to serve the school, I didn't realise you had *that* in mind." This, I'd safely say, was the angriest I'd ever seen her, so I tried a different approach.

"I'm truly sorry, Ms, she got me at a weak point," I said humbly.

Ms James made an irritable sound. "Yes, well, your… *weak point* had better remain in your trousers during this bloody camp or else! I mean it, X, you're out of control again, and you'd be wise to keep your head down for once in your life. Now, we may have a personal relationship, but do not make the mistake of thinking that it will stop me from expelling you if you push me too far. Do I make myself clear? *Now*, get out of my sight before I decide to take that bloody trophy back," she said threateningly.

I needed no further encouragement and quickly headed outside to the sports fields, where most of the school had congregated. As I walked through the various groups sitting and lounging in the sun, I received plenty of congratulations. Every time someone shouted, "School spirit," I responded by repeatedly blowing and fluttering my fingers to appear spirit-like. Finally, after soaking up the attention, I found who I was looking for. Rachael had taken a spot at the far side of the football field, facing the small, wooded area that marked the school's boundary, and sat with her back to me as I approached.

"Hey, gorgeous!" I said it brightly.

"*Go fuck yourself, X!*" she screamed.

OK, I'm guessing I've done something wrong; what, however? Oh my god, I didn't mention her in the speech.

"Rachael, I'm so sorry I didn't thank you when I got the award. That was thoughtless of me," I said sincerely.

As she stood up and turned to face me, I saw Rachael had been crying, and as I was trying to figure out what I was missing, I felt her fist connect with my jaw. The blow was so unexpected that it almost knocked me off my feet. Rubbing my chin, I stood looking at her in utter bemusement. "What... in fuck's name... was that for?"

Tears were now streaming down Rachael's cheeks. "*Howzat, X? You ruin everything! I never want to speak to you again.*"

And with that, she ran off into the trees.

OK, you don't punch someone for forgetting to thank them in a speech. There's something I'm missing here...

Then, something else hit me, which hurt far more than the punch. I swear at that precise moment, if it weren't for the fact that I'm really attached to it, I'd have run to the school kitchens and cut my penis off with the sharpest knife I could find.

Oh my god! Clare... Biology... Rachael was in the classroom! X, what have you done?

Despite the temptation to run after her, I reasoned that doing so would only lead to another punch and further upset Rachael. So, after finding out what I'd missed in the assembly from Drake, I retreated home to do some thinking.

'*Share the love?*" *Well, that was a shit idea.*

My chances of saving things with Rachael would be

non-existent under normal circumstances. However, sweet chaos has delivered the year-four camp tomorrow, changing everything. Now, I'm 93% sure Rachael will endeavour to avoid me with every ounce of energy she possesses. However, I'll pursue her across the moors until she swoons helplessly into my arms. After all, I'm 'the original teenager'; I'm nature's child. I'll tell you *exactly* who I am: Heathcliff with a smaller penis, *that's who!*

TUESDAY 18TH JULY

I dreamt about Rachel again last night; the plot line wasn't the same as the last one. This time, I was in a cricket net, batting, while Rachael, dressed in an appropriate pullover and an alarmingly short white skirt, maliciously fired balls at me from a machine, performing a not-bad at-all cover version of Sherbet's 'Howzat'. I'm sure this is my subconscious trying to tell me something, but right now, I can't get over how bloody sexy it was. Christ, I hope I can fix things up with her today.

Later

As I arrived in the schoolyard this morning, I saw a large crowd of students standing in a circle, yelling, *"Fight, fight, fight..."* Curious, I wandered over to find out who was battling it out when I heard someone shout, "That's it, Drake, kill him."

"Get him, JG," I heard someone else yell.

Concerned, I shouted, "Right, get out of my way!" The crowd eventually parted, allowing me to get to the front, where I found my two friends rolling around on the tarmac, doing their level best to beat each other half to death. Noticing Rich Wilson, all-round nice guy, standing next to me, I said, "Here, Rich, hold this, would you?" and I handed him my School Spirit trophy—yes, I admit, I am rather fond of it, so I took it with me today—and proceeded to drag my friends to their feet. "What the hell are you two doing?" I shouted at them.

"It's that moron's fault; he just can't accept that Rachael

Williams would never look twice at an oaf like him," JG spat furiously.

"Keep dreaming, fat boy," Drake responded angrily.

"Listen to me, the pair of you." It was taking all my strength to keep them apart. "There's something I've been meaning to tell you both for some time now. I knew an ideal opportunity would present itself before term's end, and all the signs tell me that now is that time. I have it from the girl's lips that she has no interest in you. So, bearing that in mind, you two can shake hands, we can go off to this camp together, and you can both find someone else to obsess over whilst we're there."

They both seemed a little shell-shocked at first hearing the news, and I was starting to think the matter was finished when I saw Drake's eyes narrow and his fist coming towards my face. I moved to duck out of the way, but he caught the top of my head. Next, I felt an impact of what felt like a foot from behind. Furious, I punched Drake on the nose, spun around, and took JG in a headlock. Soon, the three of us were rolling around on the floor, fighting one another. With the combat resuming, the crowd re-ignited and started chanting again. A few moments later, I was dragged to my feet by Little Wilson and marched in the direction of new school.

"Don't forget your trophy, X," Rich said, handing me the cup, and I nodded in thanks.

"I never thought I'd say this, but with the poor example set by you three, I'm beginning to miss the year fives!" Ms James was furious.

"I agree with you, Ms," I said, and both JG and Drake looked sideways in disbelief.

"Did you just speak, X?" Ms James asked incredulously.

I nodded. "I just wanted to say that I agree with everything you said. These *boys* started a brawl in front of the lower years; worse, they both assaulted me when I tried to break it up."

Ms James looked me up and down. "If you are the innocent party in all this, X, then why are your hands covered in blood?"

"Ah, that was self-defence," I assured her.

Ms James looked at Drake and JG and said, "Well, is this true? Did X try to stop the fight?"

"This fight would never have happened if it hadn't been for X," Drake sneered.

"That's a lie…" I started.

Ms James scowled. "Right, you've pushed me into this. I'll call your parents this morning, and none of you will join us at the year four camp."

"That's not fair!" I said it firmly.

"What did you say?" Ms James snapped furiously.

"I'm sorry," I said humbly. "Listen, Ms, following *pro-to-col*, may I please request a word with you in private?"

Ms James sighed. "You two," she said, looking at Drake and JG. "Please take a seat outside; I'll be with you in a moment."

After they'd left, I said, "You can't do this. I *must* go on this trip."

Ms James glared at me intently. "No, X, you *must* learn to follow the rules. You *need* to stop hurdling over every boundary that you see."

I put my hands together like a prayer. "*Please*, Ms James, I did nothing wrong."

"Sorry, X. You're out of chances," she said flatly. As I turned to leave the office, Ms James added, "Leave the trophy here, X; you can have it back when you've earned it."

As we were not trusted to return home and change into our school uniforms, we spent the whole day standing out like sore thumbs in our casual clothes. Ms James instructed us to report to year three's head, Mr Clarke. I felt sick when I heard the year fours heading out to the buses.

In the morning, we were sent to a vacant classroom with an assignment to write entitled *What I have learned today*.

I wrote the following:

Today, I learned that intervening when two fellow students are brawling is utterly foolish. Instead, in the future, I will join in chanting with the other mindless idiots, cheering them on, and allowing the combatants to continue beating each other to death uninterrupted. Also, I have learned there is a greater chance of finding a Martian polishing the school motto in Luther Parkinson than there is of getting a fair hearing. Finally, I have learned that I need some new friends.

The End!

When I handed my response to him just before lunch, Mr Clarke looked at me in horror and said, "You're going to hand that in, X?"

"You asked the question, sir; that's my honest answer," I said flatly.

In dismay, Mr Clarke shook his head. "I'll be showing these to Ms James; you are aware, X?"

"Well, *in that case*, sir, let me just make sure my name's nice and clear for her." I took the sheet of A4 back from him and drew a large X underneath my writing.

This *may* have contributed to our spending lunchtime

scraping other pupils' dinner crockery. One cocky little year one even said, "Hey, School Spirit, clean my plate, *you loser!*" Only the certainty of expulsion stopped me from smashing it over the little fucker's head.

For the afternoon, we were told to go and make ourselves useful around the school, as Mr Clarke was clearly out of ideas. As such, I took myself to the gym and helped Big Wilson take athletics for year two.

I called via the supermarket on the way home to get a couple of steaks, as I thought a good meal might soften Dad up after receiving a call from Ms James at work.

However, once I'd told him my version of the story, he took my side. "They shouldn't be banning you from a trip for breaking up a fight," he said through a mouthful of beef.

I nodded enthusiastically. "That's *exactly* what I said!"

"I reckon I should have a word with this James woman," he said firmly.

Bad idea, X; she has a charge sheet against you longer than your arm.

"Thanks, Dad, but I can handle myself. However, I'm not sure I can stand another two days of being the school's dogsbody. Any chance you could sign me off sick till Friday?"

Dad eyed me suspiciously. "You're not just going to sit around moping, are you?"

"Certainly not," I said firmly. "I'll go cycling."

FRIDAY 21ST JULY

I was hoping the last day of the term would pass without incident…

The campers had returned a little gloomy. While Marketon had bathed in sunshine and I had cycled over a hundred miles in two days, the moors had seen raging thunderstorms.

Really? What a shame.

We were 10 minutes into German when Flan came in and said, "X to Ms James' office."

Outside the class, I looked at Helen and asked, "*Christ*, what does that bloody woman want with me now?"

"Calm down, X; she doesn't want you; I do. Have you heard?" She said it with a look of concern.

"Heard what?" I asked irritably.

My friend took a deep breath. "It's about Rachael, X; she got a little drunk on Wednesday night, very drunk as it happens, and… well, she changes; actually, it's quite scary. *Anyway*, she went off with Geoff Travis and… "

I was beginning to feel sick.

"Well, he's saying they did *it,* and she's saying they didn't. Now, *that wanker* is spreading his version of events around the school."

I was a riot of emotion, anger, jealousy, and self-hate, but anger mainly.

I took a deep breath, ran my hands through the Cochran, and asked, "Where is she?"

Flan said, "In the girl's toilets, she won't stop crying; I don't know what to do. Rachael and I have become good friends over the past few weeks, but this is beyond me."

"I'll come and see her," I said firmly.

"No!" Helen said sharply. "You're the last person she'll want to see, X."

"Why?" I asked desperately, but Helen just raised her eyebrows.

Sheepishly, I asked, "Oh, you know about that then, do you?"

Helen rolled her eyes. "Everybody knows, X. Did you two really do it on her staircase?"

"Yes, but it *is* carpeted, so the bruising isn't as bad as you are probably imagining." I said, but then, regaining my focus, I added, "That's not really important right now. What *is* important is how I can help Rachael."

"Well, X, I thought *that* would be perfectly obvious; you've *got* to stop Geoff," Helen said impatiently.

I sighed. "I'd like nothing better, Flan, but do you know how close I am to being expelled?"

She looked at me expectantly. "Come on, X; you're the miracle man; think of something."

That's it!

"Bloody hell, you're right, Helen; that's *exactly* what we need —a miracle!" I said it excitedly.

Helen sighed. "I'll just go and get Jesus, should I?" She asked flatly.

I ignored her sarcasm as I was on a roll. "A quantum miracle, to be precise. Listen, there's something I need you to do. Also, we need someone that I can trust… Helen, go pull Matt Jacobs out of class and tell him to meet me right here at break time. Also, you don't happen to know where Ms James is for period 3, do you?"

There was no sign of Rachael when I got to English. I approached Mr Shaver's desk and leaned in close. "In 10 minutes, I'm going to jump out of the window. I'll be back in 20 minutes, and I would *really* appreciate it if you didn't notice," I whispered.

Mr Shaver looked at me, concerned. "X, you're a marked man; if you want my advice… "

"*I need this*!" I said intently.

"OK," he said with a nod. "In that case, I won't see anything."

We'd been told to read *To Kill a Mockingbird* quietly. At precisely 11.45, I jumped out of the ground-floor window and landed on the grass below.

"Get on with your reading!" I heard Mr Shaver shout at the rest of the class.

According to the book I'd read, if I were observed at any point, the miracle would shatter, and my scheme would end, no doubt, in expulsion. So, bearing this in mind, I sprinted towards the fence and ran to the head of year's office along the school's boundaries.

When I got to Ms James' window, it was wide open, and I jumped through the gap head-first. Landing hard on the floor, I was pleased to see that the head of year had been duped by Helen's fake call requesting her to visit the old school office. I allowed myself a few moments to catch my breath and then grabbed the spare key hung on the wall that I had noticed on my numerous previous visits.

Taking the key, I waited patiently by the entrance. Two minutes later, there was a knock, and I opened the door. Geoff stepped in, and I slammed it shut and locked it quickly.

Geoff looked confused when he saw me. "What have we done, X?"

Rather than answer, I grabbed him by the throat and pinned him to the wall.

"What are you doing, X?" He asked with horror.

"I'm getting even for Rachael, *you fucking bastard.*" I practically spat the words at him.

Recovering his poise somewhat, Geoff sneered, "Good for you, X, but just one thing: when you're done here, I'm going straight to Ms James. They'll kick you out for this."

"Good!" I said. "I don't give a shit about the school; I only care about her."

Mistakenly, Geoff cringed in fear.

"Listen, Geoff, there's something you should know. All those rumours about me, they're all true," I lied, "There's a madness inside me, and my psychiatrist reliably informs me that I don't know when to pull the brakes. I operate to a life philosophy that reads, 'Just say yes.' There's even a new scientific rule called X's law, which states that the more foolish an endeavour, the more I'll be tempted to give it a whirl. And let me tell you, Travis, the idea of smashing your skull repeatedly against this brick wall is just starting to turn me on a bit. Do you know that?"

Geoff, I'm pleased to report, looked suitably terrified.

"Ok, ok, ok. What do you want me to do, you bloody nutter?" he asked desperately.

"I want you to spend the rest of the day retracting that foul story you've been telling everyone. I want you to tell every year four, is that clear?" I said it through gritted teeth.

Helplessly, he said, "There's not enough time!"

I tightened my grip on his throat. "Do I look like I'm giving a shit today? Make time! Now go, get to work, Geoff."

I released him from my grip, unlocked the door, and pushed him into the corridor.

So far, so good, but I was far from home and dry. Firstly, Geoff Travis is a rat, and I knew, without a doubt, that he'd report me immediately. Secondly, I still had to get back to English *and* take the long route by which I'd come.

I was utterly out of breath when I climbed back through the window into the English class. I stumbled back to my desk, slumped in my chair, and breathed in large gulps of air. The rest of my class stared at me in amazement until Mr Shaver barked, "What's wrong with you lot today? Get on with your reading!" They all returned to their books obediently.

With five minutes of the lesson remaining, Ms James knocked on the door. "Excuse me, Mr Shaver. There's been a report that X has... been out of class. Is that the case?" She asked politely.

Mr Shaver gazed at her blankly, then looked over at me and then returned his gaze to Ms James. "X hasn't left his seat."

Ms James frowned slightly. "Trevor, this is important; a serious accusation has been made."

Mr Shaver shook his head in disbelief. "Catherine, I think *I'd* know if a student had left this classroom or not. Pupils, as Ms James thinks I'm losing my marbles, maybe she'll believe you instead. Did anyone see X leave the room?" As he asked the question, he gave my fellow pupils *the stare*.

Terrified, no doubt, the class dutifully shook their heads.

"I'm sorry, Trevor, I am. I wasn't trying to be rude. Obviously, X is in the clear." And, with that, the head of year shot me a glare, and I fired one right back at her.

I bought a sandwich at lunch and took it outside onto the field to eat. I was nervous; the plan had gone off like a dream, but there were still a few hours before I reached the safety of the summer holidays.

After I had finished my food, I lay down to soak up the sun when I felt a shadow cross me.

"Now, that's what *I* call a miracle," my co-conspirator said.

I stared up at my friend, shielding my eyes from the sun. "He went straight to Ms James, Flan."

"Maybe so, but whatever you said to him has worked. He's told everyone he can that he made the whole story up. It looks like Rachael can regain her virginity if she wants it."

"If I make it to the end of school without getting expelled, I'll join the celebrations," I said flatly.

Gleefully, Helen said, "Don't worry, Ms James is off your case, X. I was just with her, and I dropped Geoff in it like you wouldn't believe. She even said she'd like to neuter him with hot tongs."

"As I said, Flan, at the final bell, I'll party like it's 1999; until then, please forgive my caution, OK?" I replied.

"OK, X, do you fancy getting together over the summer?" she asked.

"That would be good, Flan."

Period four passed without incident, and when I got into classics, I was amazed to see my School Spirit trophy waiting for me on one of the empty desks. A thoughtful gesture from Ms James—yes, she approved of my actions this morning; no, the quantum miracle hadn't fooled her, and yes, I will be remaining a Luther Parkinson student next year *purely* by her good grace. I was hoping Rachael would show up, but she didn't, nor did Dr Harris, so I had Mr Shaver for the second time that day. At the end of class, I shook his hand and said, "Now we're even."

He nodded in acknowledgement.

And that's it- school's, as the song says, out!

PART 3

Power, Corruption and Lies

MONDAY 28TH AUGUST

Over the first week of the summer holidays, I had time for reflection and reading, and, consequently, I kissed goodbye to chaos and welcomed cause and effect into my life. Resultantly, I had some people I needed to apologise to. Firstly, JG and Drake, who both forgave me without reservation. That still left Rachael1989, which I knew would be significantly trickier.

The following two weeks were spent covering Ron's holiday at Ripton Cycles. My boss was so pleased that he and his family could, for once, get away during the summer that he allowed me to recruit an assistant for the fortnight—I picked Flan. The state of Rachael's and my relationship became evident when she came calling into the shop in the first week. Helen and I were leaning over the counter together, looking at her photos of the year four camp, and even though the bell on the door had rung, we'd paid no attention to it. Eventually, there was an unsubtle cough, and we looked up to see Rachael holding her bike and staring at us intently.

"This looks cosy," she said, stony-faced.

"Oh, hey Rachael, I'm just helping out X while his boss is away for a few weeks," Helen said guiltily.

"So, I see," Rachael said, her face impassive.

Brightly, I said, "Hey, Rachael."

She did not look my way and said, "Helen, please ask *the*

mechanic not to address me directly."

Helen turned to me and dutifully said, "X, please don't… "

"I heard," I said, interrupting, and knowing I was not wanted, I went into the workshop.

Curious, though, I listened in to the rest of the conversation.

"Helen, if you could tell *the mechanic* that my bike is not presently changing gears efficiently, I would greatly appreciate it," Rachael said.

"No problem, Rachael, it'll be ready for you tomorrow," Helen said politely.

"Thank you. Also, Helen, I must warn you that *the mechanic* is a sex maniac incapable of controlling himself around attractive girls. Therefore, I advise you to always carry a sharp dagger with you," and with that, Rachael departed.

No other course of action was available; as I was head over heels in love with the girl, I needed to make a bold gesture, so I declared myself celibate.

A week in Wales followed, during which my parents paid me little attention, allowing me to explore the endless, incredible scenery on my bike. True to my new vow, when the possibility of a holiday romance arose, I was ready. "Sorry, Abbey, I'm flattered, but I'm 92% certain that I'm gay. Please don't tell anyone." I lied.

Rather than put the girl off, this revelation appeared to make her feelings for me even more robust. "Oh, X, it's so cool having a gay pal. It's just like being with one of the girls… I suppose I don't even have to ask you to leave my room when I get changed," she said brightly one evening.

"Of course you don't!" I assured her.

Oh, X, you are *awful!*

Next up was a short trip to London with my auntie L. Traditionally, these breaks have been a highlight in the calendar; however, this year, she seemed constantly tired, and it was as if she didn't want to be there.

My final getaway was a few days camping in the Peak District with Dennis Loveday. As he was known at school, Prince Dennis is three years older than me, but we became friends as, desperate for players, I was signed up in year one for the tennis team he was then captain of.

The trip was Dennis' treat for securing the tennis win we had never managed under his leadership. He's been awarded a place at Oxford, which, he assured me, is entirely his stepfather's dream and not his. He intends to follow all the greats and get kicked out of there as soon as possible.

Those sunny days in glorious scenery, spent either hiking or getting drunk in the local pub, were, by some distance, the happiest time I've spent in 1989.

When we returned, I found an invitation waiting for me.

Dear X,

I have done a lot of thinking this summer, and no matter how strong my feelings *were* for you, I have concluded that you would make for a *terrible* boyfriend. However, I have missed you and would be more than happy if we resumed our friendship *strictly* on a platonic basis. As such, you are kindly invited to my house for a barbecue on Sunday at 3 pm. I hope to see you there.

Love Rachael1989

Forgiveness is in vogue in the Jackson/Williams household,

as Arthur opened the door to me on barbecue day. His return was not the only surprise awaiting me, though, as, when I walked into the garden, I was greeted by the sight of Rachael and Rich Wilson, ex-all-round nice guy, with their faces glued to one another's.

Really, I never liked the kid.

Watching Rachael kiss another boy was as painful a sight as I'd ever witnessed; however, following the logic of my new guiding principle of cause and effect, it was an *entirely* self-inflicted phenomenon. As such, I behaved with the utmost propriety and did my best to ignore them, even going so far as to only sit or stand in positions where my back was always to them. I passed the time speaking to JG and Penny Chemistry. However, after I'd wandered into the house to use the bathroom, Rachael1989 grabbed me by the collar and dragged me into the sitting room.

It must be said, I'd never seen her look so alluring. Bronzed from a sun far more robust than the one that they have in Wales, wearing more make-up than usual, and with fresh curls in her hair, she will, no doubt, be challenging Helen Heaven for the title of Luther Parkinson's most desired female student on our return to school.

Her arms folded tightly across her chest, she asked, "Are you ignoring me?"

"No, you seem to have sufficient male company," I replied.

"What can I say? *Young love*," Rachael said dreamily.

"I'm happy for you," I lied. "Anyway, I just wanted to say what happened with Clare. That was despicable, and I'm fortunate that I can still call you a friend." My head was hanging in genuine shame.

"Yes, well, how can you break down when I try to kiss you and yet jump into bed with that... *girl* just because she whispers something filthy in your ear in class? I'll never know," Rachael said in bewilderment.

I looked directly at Rachael. "It's like this. Doing *it* with Clare meant nothing, but making love to you would be... I mean, it *would have been...* everything. Trust me, the more you think about it, the more it makes sense."

"Thank you for saying that." Rachael seemed genuinely impressed by what I'd said. "How about you? Is there anybody?" she asked with interest.

"I'm now celibate, if you must know," I said sincerely, prompting Rachael to giggle.

When she'd finally stopped laughing, she said, "Anyway, Helen told me earlier what you did for me on the last day of term. *That* was very sweet of you. Though I think you're mad; you could have been kicked out of school for it."

"You're worth getting expelled for, Rachael," I said intently. My friend seemed a little lost for words, so I added, "Hey, I know we're on a *strictly* platonic basis these days; however, I just wanted to say, in an 'I'm not about to grab your arse' way, your hair looks great."

Rachael1989 smiled sweetly. "Are you going to compare me to a rose, X?"

"No, actually, if you must know, you look like a goddess," I replied, then excused myself quickly and headed back out to the garden as I suddenly felt an overwhelming urge to cry.

"Are you OK, X?" Flan asked, sitting beside me.

"Fine," I replied.

Helen sighed. "You're not OK, are you X?"

I shook my head. "No, I was giving serious thought to grabbing some cans of beer from the stash in my bedroom, taking them over to the wasteland near the old railway line, and getting trashed in what remains of this glorious day. Care to join me?"

After walking Flan home, I stumbled back here. As I entered my room and saw my recently polished trophy sitting proudly on my shelf, I had what a less rational mind perceives as *a vision*.

I'll show Rachael, Ms James, and all of them. Friends, the age of the individual is over; *this* is the dawn of school spirit.

MONDAY 4TH SEPTEMBER

I knew I would need to hard-talk my way onto the start of the term assembly's agenda, so I knocked on Ms James' door at 8 o'clock this morning. For some reason, I'd convinced myself on my solo walk to school that she'd be almost glad to see me. However, I was soon set straight when, upon spying me entering her office, she turned strangely pale and asked somewhat desperately, "Oh, good lord, the school doesn't open for another hour; what could you have possibly done to get sent to me already?"

Politely, I replied, "Actually, I'm not in trouble; I was wondering whether there was a slot for me in the assembly to make my first speech as school spirit."

Ms James looked at me in genuine horror. "*What?*"

"Speech," I said, taking my notes from my rucksack. "If you ask me, it's just the right mix of Abraham Lincoln, Martin Luther King, and John F. Kennedy, but not *too* over the top, you understand?"

"X, we gave you a bloody trophy; we didn't appoint you to a position of authority," she said incredulously.

I held up my hand in acknowledgement. "I appreciate that, Ms James, but, rather fortunately, on Sunday evening, I had what I believe could be interpreted by a less rational mind as a vision, and I'm determined to live it out," I said sincerely.

"X, there are *far* too many announcements to make at the start of the year's assembly already. There isn't the time to allow a pupil to say a single word, never mind make a speech," Ms James said frankly.

I put my hands together as if in prayer. "Please, Ms, this is important."

Ms James sighed deeply. "Listen, X, the hours I spend in this school before nine o'clock are my favourites. Do you know why?" she asked patiently, and I shrugged my shoulders in ignorance. "It is because they are devoid of pupils, and right now, for a fair reason or foul, *you* are soiling my solitude. As it happens, I have nothing to do with the start of term assembly; Dr Harris will be addressing the school; why don't you go and upset him instead?"

Dr Harris was equally curt. "Absolutely out of the question, X, there are far too many announcements to make at the start of the year's assembly already. There isn't time for a pupil to say a word, so never mind making a speech. Didn't that *bloody* woman tell you all this?"

"Sir," I said passionately. "I hope you know by now that I'm not the kind of man to force a favour from another just because he owes me one; however, having said that I did perform the miracle and won you a hundred quid into the bargain."

Dr Harris looked at me intently, tapping his desk. "Will you play next season, even with the exams?"

"It would be my honour, sir," I replied solemnly.

"Deal!" Dr Harris boomed, hitting his fist on the desk for emphasis.

I beamed delightfully. "Right, sir, I've already prepared my speech. If you ask me, it's just the right mix of Abraham Lincoln, Martin Luther King, and John F. Kennedy, but it isn't *too* over the top, you understand?"

Dr Harris made a dismissive gesture with his hands. "Oh, say what you want, X. Lessons can wait. After all, as I've always maintained, a school is built upon announcements."

Dr Harris gave the worst speech I've seen him give in the four years I've been at the school. He mumbled most of it, and I was relieved when he said, "Now, Luther Parkinson, I would like to hand over to X, School Spirit: 1989, who wishes to address you."

As I walked onto the stage, I received a far more significant round of applause than expected. After all, six weeks is a long time. However, the embers of school spirit still burned brightly.

As I stepped up to the lectern, my mouth felt suddenly dry, so I took a sip of water from Dr Harris's glass. After clearing my throat, I commenced. "For those of us in year five, our journey through Luther Parkinson is almost at an end, and I would ask you to spend just a few moments contemplating the state in which we will leave our beloved school in nine months. Before I joined this fine educational institution, I was somewhat intimidated. After all, the pupils of this establishment were the smartest dressed in Marketon, the sports teams dominated the leagues, and our founder's name was a byword for academic excellence. Only four years later, we've corrupted the uniform; we're the opposition the other schools look forward to playing, and the former year fives have just smashed the existing town record for exam failure."

I allowed a moment for the murmuring to subside.

"Who is responsible for this, friends? Well, people are always looking for someone to blame. The Jacksons blamed it on the boogie. The Bee Gees blamed it on those nights on Broadway, but let's take accountability for *ourselves*. Now, I know we won't change all these things in a solitary academic year;

however, what we *can do*, brothers and sisters, is set the good ship Luther Parkinson right again."

The assembly broke out into applause, and I took the opportunity to take another sip of water.

"So, as *your* school spirit, I would ask that *you*, when you wake up tomorrow morning, ask not how to corrupt the uniform but how best to honour it. Also, whilst we cannot turn our teams into winners overnight, consider the boost we could give them if 100, scratch that, 200 pupils came out to cheer them on, and think of the fear that would strike into our opponent's hearts. And, more importantly, when it comes to studying, fellow pupils, we all *must try harder*."

There was further applause.

"I *also* have a dream, Luther Parkinson. I believe school spirit is so much more than a mere trophy. Do you want to know what I think it is?"

There was a murmur of approval from the hall and a few shouts of "Yes!"

"I think it's a movement *of* the school, *by* the school, and *for* the school. We, dear pupils, must unite as one... *even the mungos*."

There were a few snorts of disapproval.

"No exceptions, brothers and sisters, no exceptions!" I said it sharply, prompting further applause.

"From this day forth, let it be known, there is *no* old school, there is *no* new school, there is only *one* school, *our* school! *Luther Parkinson rules!*" I yelled out the last line and proceeded to lower my head and raise my fist in a salute—I'd seen a picture of some black American athletes making such a gesture at an Olympic medal ceremony, and I'd decided to adopt it as my own.

The hall burst into applause and rose to their feet.

"Thank you!" I said, and I left the stage.

In maths, I asked Rich Wilson, ex-all-round nice guy, "Hey, how are things going with Rachael?"

He turned to me with a sour look. "They're not. She dumped me."

"Wow, I'm sorry to hear that; what happened?" I said it as sincerely as I could.

"Get this, X. We were supposed to go to the cinema together, so I called around for her, and she said, "Sorry, Rich. I think I've made a little mistake; I thought I liked you, but it turns out that I don't." Women, eh?"

"Women!" I echoed and gave Rich Wilson, all-round nice guy, a consoling pat on the shoulder.

This is partly welcome news; we have three hours of maths a week, which is a long time to sit next to someone you despise. However, on the negative side, it illustrates Rachael's oscillating temperament. Imagine that I go to great lengths to win her heart, only for her to decide that she doesn't like me two days later. After all, it was only a week ago that she couldn't keep her mouth from his. Why did she change her mind just like that?

Throughout the morning and lunch, I got the strangest looks from my fellow students. They appeared—there's no other way to say this—ever so slightly in awe of me. I'll admit the speech went far better than I could have imagined. However, this reaction did seem ever so slightly over the top. Just before the bell was due for afternoon classes, Rachael sat beside me on the old school sports field, and I soon understood the cause of this newfound sense of wonder.

"You've got to do something, X. This is already getting out of hand," she said curtly.

Confused, I asked, "What's getting out of hand?"

"School spirit, *that's what.*"

"Oh, come off it, Rachael; even you have to admit it was a good speech," I replied.

Rachael shook her head. "It's not that; it's Katie Pritchard and Martha Johnson. They've been telling everyone that on the last day of term, when you got *Geoff*," she struggled to pronounce the word, "you didn't leave your seat in English, and as *he* has told everyone that you were waiting for him in Ms James' office at the same time, well, there's now a belief stirring amongst the dimmer members of the school that you can be in two places at one time."

"Really?" I asked, intrigued.

Rachael looked suddenly stern and pointed a finger at me. "Oh, no, *you* don't, X, you can tell everybody exactly what happened and end this; that's what you can do."

"Is it right to mess with other people's beliefs, Rachael?" I asked innocently.

"Said the Grade 9 atheist," Rachael said under her breath.

I ignored her sarcasm. "Besides, no one with half a brain will believe that rubbish. And those that do, well, are the ones I really need onside. Don't you see, this could be quite useful?"

Rachael didn't have a chance to respond, as a year four mungo named Roger Hunt interrupted us by saying, "Dr Harris would like to see you, X. Sorry, I meant, School Spirit."

I looked at him blankly. "I haven't done anything wrong."

"Dr Harris said you'd say that X—sorry, I meant, School Spirit—and asked me to relay to you that he wishes to see you only to commend you," Roger said. Before returning to old school, he raised his fist in salute and yelled, "Luther Parkinson rules!"

"Oh, good lord," Rachael said with something approaching horror.

"Oh, yes, that was something, School Spirit; that was *really* something. Just the right mix of Abraham Lincoln, JFK, and Martin Luther King, but not *too* over the top, you understand?" Dr Harris said it earnestly.

"Thank you, sir. I'm glad you approved," I said, smiling with pride.

The headmaster played with a Newton's cradle in front of him on his desk. "What's that, 'approved', you say? Of course, I approved. Although, I must say, X, it made me just a little sad watching you up there this morning. If only I had half your zest, my boy. No, the bells are tolling for Dr Wilberforce H. Harris, JP. Retirement calls to me like the enchanting song of an alluringly sordid mermaid. It offers nothing more than the company of my beloved rose bushes, an easily irritated wife, and an incontinent dachshund."

In four years, I'd never seen him look so low. School spirit would die in its infancy without the backing of a motivated, committed, *and* alarmingly eccentric headmaster; however, the right course of action was obvious: I must now do for him what he had once done for me.

"Excuse me, sir. May I speak plainly?" I asked.

"What's that, 'plainly' you say? Of course, *you* can, my boy, be my guest," he said politely.

"Sir, school spirit didn't come about because I was handed a trophy at the end of last term; he was born right here in this office," I said firmly.

Dr Harris looked baffled. "I'm not sure I understand you, X."

"That day, sir, in the spring, I was lost in a whirl of drink, drugs, and an eating disorder. Worse still, I was dressed up as a mungo. Remember?"

"Well, yes, of course, I remember it, X; it's an image that's difficult to forget. What's your point exactly?" Dr Harris asked.

I leaned up his desk. "Well, sir, it was on that very day that school spirit began. I walked in here a broken man, but, thanks to you, I burst forth reborn. Remember what you said, sir, 'Serve the school!'"

Dr Harris sat up straight. "My god, man, you're right… but that makes school spirit, well, there's no other way to say this, X, *our baby*. Does that sound wrong?"

Resolutely, I replied, "No, sir, *I don't*. I'm not sure *anything* has sounded quite so right in the entire history of language."

The headmaster pointed at me and smiled. "We're going to take this all the way, you and I, *all* the bloody way. I'll see about finding you some office space so you've got somewhere to work during your lunch hour."

"That would be handy, sir," I nodded.

"There's one in new school which Stan, the caretaker, stores mops in at present," Dr Harris said, thinking aloud.

I waved my hand dismissively. "Whatever you can spare, sir."

"*Good god, man*, not for you; we'll move Redwood in there; you can have his. Anyway, we'll get to that; you go home tonight, X, get all your ideas together, and we'll meet for lunch tomorrow. Oh, and I know you two get along, but not a word to *James*. Remember, X; he is *our baby*."

"Absolutely, sir. Oh, and I'll be needing a two."

"I gave you a two, X, Jacobs, remember?" Dr Harris replied.

"Of course, sir."

In French, Diane Best asked, "Hey, X, I'm not sure I can be in full uniform by tomorrow, but from Monday, it'll be tip to toe. OK?"

"That's fine, Diane," I said reassuringly.

"Oh, and X, is there any particular kind of underwear you'd like to see me in?" she asked with a smile.

Waving my hand in dismissal, I replied, "Out of my jurisdiction, Diane; however, for what it's worth, I've always been a comfort-first man regarding undergarments."

After recalling the incident, it's only now that I've realised that my answer probably wasn't what she'd been hoping for.

TUESDAY 5TH SEPTEMBER

Ten minutes before the lunchtime bell, I was summoned to Dr Harris' office.

"Ah, X, my boy, let's grab something to eat before the hordes arrive and the food begins to fester," Dr Harris said keenly.

The lunch hatch had yet to open when we arrived at the canteen, and the headmaster hovered impatiently, coughing loudly to catch the catering staff's attention.

"We're working as fast as we can, Dr Harris," a harassed voice shouted from within the kitchen.

When the shutter was finally raised, the head eagerly studied today's offerings while I looked in horror at the food selection. "This is wrong, sir," I said with concern.

"Oh, I know, X, I really should queue like everyone else, but it's one of the few benefits of the job. The extra salary hardly compensates for all the additional hours I put in," he said distractedly.

"No, sir, the food is wrong," I said. The cooks, who had been waiting to serve us, were now glaring at me suspiciously.

Dr Harris flashed me a look of concern. "What is it, my boy?"

"Sir, this *is not* the lunch of champions—fat, stodge, salt, and sugar," I said with disgust, pointing to the various food items as I went. "Cause and effect, sir."

"Say again, my boy?"

"Cause!" I said, pointing to the food. "The effect? Obesity, heart disease, lethargy, the inability to concentrate for long periods, and, quite possibly, though I'm entirely sure on this one, *paranoia*. In short, ineffective performances on the sports field and poor grades."

Dr Harris' eyes widened. "Right, that does it then… "

The headmaster was interrupted by a ladle clattering on the floor. We both looked at the head cook, who had dropped the utensil and whose cheeks had turned a distinct shade of scarlet. "Headmaster, I have been cooking this same food here for 22 years now," she said. Her lips trembled slightly as she spoke.

Dr Harris looked at me, raised his eyebrows in a gesture of disbelief, and then looked back at her. "You should be ashamed of yourself then," he said accusingly.

I found myself smiling ruefully and nodding in agreement.

Head cook took a deep breath. "It was never a problem until *he* opened his mouth," she said, then shot me a look of pure hatred.

"You're trying to kill him and his fellow pupils off; what did you expect him to do? Leap over the counter and try and kiss you, woman?" The headmaster smirked at his comment; however, the cooks remained ashen-faced.

"Listen, X," Dr Harris said, leaning in close and whispering. "I reckon if we stand here too long, the cholesterol queens might just turn us to stone, my boy."

"What should we do, sir?" I asked discreetly.

"Well, X, I've just two words for you, my boy: *salad bar!*"

We collected our food and returned to the headmaster's office for a working lunch.

"It's not exactly filling this stuff, is it?" Dr Harris said, curiously eyeing a piece of lettuce on the end of his fork.

"There are other ways to eat healthily, sir, besides salad," I said brightly.

"Such as?" Dr Harris asked eagerly.

"Truth be told, sir, it's not my field of expertise. I can diet with the best of them, but that's not what we want here. We want to energise and invigorate," I said.

Dr Harris banged his fist on the desk so hard that his salad plate bounced up. "I like it, my boy. What do we do?"

"I could speak to Mrs Ransom in home economics." I suggested.

Dr Harris looked alarmed, "Good god, man, have you seen the size of the woman? I tell you, X; if a pupil ever went missing on the school grounds, she'd be the first one I'd haul in for questioning."

I racked my brains, and inspiration hit. "I have it, sir, *Williams*. Rachael Williams. She's a healthy eater."

"New Girl?" Dr Harris asked with interest.

"Yes, sir," I replied.

The head nodded. "In that case, I'll have her sent for, my boy."

My first two suggestions were approved without question: a Shakespeare production at the end of term, a former cornerstone of the academic year at Luther Parkinson, and a lunchtime fitness club to be run by Big Wilson.

"Excellent, X, excellent, just the ticket; what else have you got there?" Dr Harris asked eagerly.

As I was on a roll, I thought I'd try and slip the next one past the old boy. "We'll need a cheerleading squad," I muttered quietly.

"What's that, 'cheerleaders', you say?" Dr Harris barked.

"Obviously, sir," I replied, attempting to sound earnest.

"Well, I'm not sure about that, my boy; the last time I looked, it still said 'Church of England' on the sign above the door. Could we pass it off as Christian?" the head asked uncertainly.

"*Sir*," I leant forward and placed my hands upon his desk. "The point of a cheerleading squad is not so *our* boys can ogle *our* girl's legs. We can do it at our leisure every week in swimming lessons. The real purpose is that *their* boys can look at *our* girl's legs. If they're so distracted… "

"Then their eyes won't be on the ball," Dr Harris said, finishing my sentence.

"*Exactly*, sir. I might be going out on a limb here, but I'm 82% certain that if Jesus Christ sat opposite me right now, he'd sign this off in a heartbeat," I said passionately.

"Well, now that you put it like that, I suppose it would be ungodly not to have one," Dr Harris replied.

"Bravo, sir, it's good to see we're… " I pointed at my head and then at his.

"Oh, absolutely, X, our minds are as one. I suppose we better give that task to the female gym staff," Dr Harris suggested.

With an approximation of innocence, I said, "Actually, sir, I'll take that one; I don't want to put too much on other people, after all."

"Well, if you're sure, X. I don't want you to overdo it. Right, what's next?"

I smiled brightly. "A talent contest. We'll do it on the final afternoon before Christmas. I thought it also might help reduce the incidences of vandalism on the last day of school."

"Motion passed!" Dr Harris bellowed, "What else?"

Delicately, I said, "Well, it's the Asian pupils, sir."

"What about them?" Dr Harris asked with interest.

"It's just too 'us and them' at the moment, sir."

"Well, different religions and cultures. That's just the way it is; I'm afraid, my boy," Dr Harris said sympathetically.

Firmly, I said, "Sir, they're all good Luther Parkinson students; we'll be stronger if we stand united."

"Well, I agree in principle, but what can be done, my boy?" Dr Harris enquired.

Passionately, I said, "Integration, sir; that's the key."

"What's that, 'integration', you say? Well, tell me more, my boy, tell me more," Dr Harris asked with genuine interest.

The head approved the rest of my ideas without dispute, and then, with just 10 minutes left until the end of lunch, there was a knock on the door.

"Strange, I'm not expecting anyone," Dr Harris said, looking slightly bewildered.

Politely, I said, "Williams, sir, New Girl, you sent for her, remember?"

"Good god, my boy, you're right. You know, X, I could do with you around here full time; you don't miss a trick," Dr Harris said gratefully.

I asked, "Should I call her in, sir?"

"What's that, 'call her in', you say? Yes, X, however, before you do, pull your chair round to this side, my boy," Dr Harris said with a wink.

Once seated alongside the headmaster, I shouted, "Enter!"

Rachael1989 came into the room timidly, but as soon as she spied me behind the desk, she rolled her eyes and said quietly, "Here we go."

"What's that you say, New Girl?" Dr Harris bellowed.

"Nothing, sir," Rachael said innocently. "You wish to see me?"

"That's right, I did," Dr Harris said, but he appeared confused. He turned to me and gestured uncertainly to himself, and I nodded in assent. "New Girl, I called you here today so X could ask you a question," he said eventually.

Rachael turned her gaze towards me. "Yes, X."

With a serious look, I asked, "Rachael, do *you* think they feed a Grand National winner French fries?"

Rachel folded her arms and said flatly, "Almost certainly not, X, because, to the best of my knowledge, horses *do not* eat chips."

I sighed. "I think you're missing my point."

Rachael smiled wryly. "Then I would politely invite you to sharpen it."

"OK, then I'll be direct," I said.

Rachael sighed deeply. "The day had to come sooner or later."

I had the distinct impression that this conversation may have been operating on more than one level; however, like a true professional, I stuck to the task at hand: "In short, Rachael, the lunchtime food selection is atrocious, and *we'd* like *you* to work with head cook and design a healthier menu."

She frowned. "Is it right to be telling people what to eat?"

"We're not telling them what to eat; we're just limiting their choices, which are two entirely different things," I said righteously.

"Here, here!" Dr Harris barked.

"Why can't *you* do it?" Rachael asked.

"Out of the question!" Dr Harris exclaimed. "School spirit has a multitude of responsibilities."

"Sir," Rachael said, addressing the head directly. "I want to gain straight A's for my GCSEs, which means…"

Dr Harris held his hand to silence her. "So does X, New Girl, but you don't hear him making churlish, namby-pamby excuses, do you? It's a question of service, of duty."

The headmaster was making a valiant effort, but I knew how to get Rachael onside: "New Girl, sorry, Rachael. Do you know that the Northeast has the second highest rate of heart disease in the United Kingdom?"

"Heart disease!" Dr Harris echoed.

"Thank you, sir. We're beaten only by Scotland," I said solemnly.

"Scotland!" The head repeated. "It's barely civilised."

"Thank you, sir. In short, I, for one, am not prepared to stand back and allow the pupils of this school to be senselessly murdered."

"Senselessly!" Dr Harris added support.

Rolling her eyes, Rachael said, "*OK*, I'll do it."

The head banged his fist on the table approvingly. "That's the spirit, New Girl; good to finally have you on the team. Run along now and provide an update to School Spirit by the end of the week, please."

After Rachael had departed, he said, "You're learning fast, my boy. Delegation is the key to success. I even delegate my delegation these days. I swear, I get home some days and can't think of one thing I've achieved at work. That's organisation for you!"

"Yes, sir," I said as the bell rang. "I'd better be going."

Dr Harris waved his hand dismissively. "No rush, X; after all, there are more important things in a school than education. Speaking of which, if this all gets too much for you, we could always provide a little assistance with your exams if you catch my meaning?" The head said it conspiratorially.

I was 86% certain I did and replied, "Thanks, sir, but I would prefer to get my qualifications under my own steam."

"Noble sentiments, my boy, but just so you know, the examiners play their games, and we play ours," the head said and tapped the side of his nose. "One final thing, X, some of this is going to cost a bob or two, and the school's mired in debt."

"Don't worry, sir, we'll have a sale," I said reassuringly.

Dr Harris scoffed. "But the sales start in January, my boy."

I smiled. "Then, sir, the advantage is ours for the taking."

As the nights were cutting in, I needed an alternative sport to focus on this winter, and so, after school, I went to the football team trials. It was a significant error of judgement. Geoff Travis, all-round fucker, is the best player in this school by a considerable margin. However, he's also one of the pupils who believes I can be in two places simultaneously. Over the summer, according to Rich Wilson, he's had something of a personal crisis, lost his faith, and, with it, his much-needed midfield dynamism. At one point during the game, I got the ball, ran around seven players, and scored. This wasn't due to any skill on my part. Instead, it was because no one attempted to tackle me. It was simple: if their captain was terrified of me, then his team felt likewise.

After the trials, I visited the shorter gym teacher in his office. "Something must be done, Little Wilson," I said firmly.

"I can't help it if my best player has lost his poke, X," the gym teacher said defensively.

"Leave Geoff to me, Little Wilson; I know how to handle him. You focus on the rest of the team. For starters, your defence needs *stiffening*," I advised.

"Right you are, X," the gym teacher said, lighting a cigarette.

I looked at the man in horror. "Excuse me, Little Wilson, but what *exactly* do you think you're doing?"

"I'm smoking, X," he replied calmly.

Taking the cigarette from his hand, I stubbed it out in the ashtray. "Not here anymore; this, I have just decided, is now a non-smoking establishment. We must set the right example, Little Wilson. Now, *you* stay off the gaspers during school hours, and *I* will restore Geoff to his previous powers. After all, you don't see the winning horse in the Grand National with a Benson & Hedges in its mouth at the end of the race, do you?"

"Not in personal experience, no," Little Wilson said irritably.

After going home and changing, I headed over to Rachael's. When I arrived, she was in her room doing homework.

"Hey, Rachael," I said upon entering.

"Hey, Big Brother," she replied brightly.

So, she now views me as a sibling now; this will never do.

Sitting on her bed, I said, "Thanks for helping with the menu."

Rachael sighed. "*Must* you get me involved in all your little schemes, X?"

"Did it ever occur to you that I like involving you in my schemes because it means I get to spend more time with you?" I replied honestly.

This pleased Rachael, who smiled sweetly. "OK, you've won me over. What else do you want?"

"Fancy a bike ride tomorrow? We could both cycle in, get changed, and head off after school," I asked.

"I'd like that very much," Rachael said, then added, "Oh, but I've got detention in the library first. Will you wait for me?"

With a laugh, I asked, "How did *you* get a detention?"

"If you *must* know, I asked Mr Smith not to put his arm around me when explaining things. My request may have been a little abrupt, as it turns out," Rachael said coyly.

With a dismissive wave, I said, "Oh, Mr Smith's just friendly, that's all."

"Really, X, *he isn't!*" Rachael said it sharply.

"What did you say, anyway?" I asked.

Rachael sighed. "I believe I said, 'Will you please take your hands off me, you dirty old bastard!'"

I looked at her in disbelief before saying, "If you're not careful, you'll get a reputation. Anyway, we almost share a birthday, don't we?"

"It's on Friday," Rachael replied.

"Mine's Saturday; we could…"

"Go to dinner?"

"Ok," I replied.

"Date!" She said it excitedly and gave a little clap.

"Right, well, good chatting to you; got to get to Helen's," I said, and Rachael raised her eyebrows. I sighed. "It's not like that. Besides, as I told you, I'm celibate. My only love affair is with the school," I said sincerely.

"Lucky school!" Rachael said, but I wasn't in the mood for

her sarcasm, so I just bade her farewell.

The moment I'd closed her door, I realised something, reopened it, and poked my head back around. "By the way, I just got the Big Brother reference, but, as I've got to get going, can we save that argument for another day?"

"*Clever boy*, I look forward to it, X," Rachael said without turning around.

Helen, too, was busy with homework when I got to hers. "You look great, Flan," I said brightly as I walked into her room.

Helen continued to write. "You want something, don't you, X?" she asked absently.

"Helen, I ask nothing of you. It's your school that requests this service from you." I said intently.

"Oh, yeah, what's that then?"

I'd thought that convincing her to take on the role of cheerleading team captain might prove to be a hard sell, but Flan seemed delighted.

Brightly, she said, "OK, yes, I accept; it sounds like good fun."

Now, that is school spirit!

"Who else should I put on the team?" Flan asked keenly.

"Well, as captain, it's your choice as to who gets selected. However, I feel a squad of six will suffice, and, as a precaution, I've prepared a list of five names for you," I said, handing her a slip of paper.

"Right, X, I get you," Helen said, frowning as she took the note from me.

WEDNESDAY 6TH SEPTEMBER

After sharing my 'smoking ban' idea with Dr Harris first thing, I made my way to form group. As I wouldn't say I liked the idea of Rachael serving her first detention alone, I decided to act.

"Mr Crackett, I was watching a film last night, and do you know, sir, you are the spitting image of the starring actor?" I said sincerely.

"Who's that, then?" Mr Crackett asked with genuine interest.

Scratching my head and looking puzzled, I replied, "Oh, what *is* his name? It's on the tip of my tongue; it is."

"Come on, X, think!" my form tutor urged me.

I looked directly at him. "Oh, I remember, Richard Gere," I said flatly.

When I walked into Ms James' office, I clicked my fingers and pointed to the sign behind her desk.

"I just told Mr Crackett that he looks like Richard Gere. Could I have a detention, please?"

Ms James laughed, composed herself, and then looked up at me. "I thought *you* were setting an example this year."

"Quite right, Ms; normally I would consider this behaviour beneath me. However, Rachael has her first detention tonight, and I don't like the idea of her doing it alone."

Ms James smiled. "Gosh, X, that's quite romantic." I patiently waited for the sarcastic follow-up, but it never came. Perhaps it was too early *even* for her. "Actually, X, I'm glad you're here. I want your help organising the first year five dance party," she continued.

Firmly but politely, I replied, "Out of the question, Ms, I've got too much on."

"And whose fault is that, X?" Ms James said wryly.

"Really, I would love to help, but..." I started.

"Well, let's make a trade then. You help *me* out, and I'll give *you* the detention," Ms James proposed.

I smiled. "You've got a deal on one condition: may I use your office at lunchtime, Ms?"

Mrs Simpson has been replaced by Mr Bentley, who looks fresh out of teacher training college. He is handsome and intelligent, and I have instantly taken a dislike to him. This is with foundation, though, as Rachael and seemingly every other girl in the school has something of a soft spot for him, and, as such, she pays me much less attention in class than she did previously.

"What sounds better, The Lutherettes or The Parkinson Babes?" I asked Rachael after we had taken our seats in his class.

"Go with the Lutherettes; the Parkinson Babes sound like ill children. What are we talking about here, X?" she asked absently.

"The school cheerleading team, obviously," I replied enthusiastically.

"Good lord!" Rachael said this with alarm.

"You know, you'd make a great addition. You're gorgeous;

you can dance…" I began.

"Over my dead body, X," Rachael said sharply, and that put an end to that fantasy.

Geoff Travis, all-round fucker, dutifully knocked on Ms James' office door at a quarter to one as requested. However, as soon as he saw that it was me and not the head of year sitting waiting for him, his face dropped in horror. "Oh god, not you again."

Holding my hands up in a gesture of non-aggression, I said, "Geoff, I mean you no harm; please take a seat."

Reluctantly, the football captain took the chair opposite me. "Listen, X, I am sorry for spreading that story about Rachael, but I did pass the word that it never happened, just like you asked," Geoff said sincerely.

With great solemnity, I shook my head. "Geoff, you are a bad boy; there is no denying it. However, *I* believe in second chances, and I invited you here today to offer you a chance at redemption."

"Really?" he asked in wonder.

"Absolutely; I only ask that you immediately commence playing football again to your usual standard. Your playmaking skills are essential to the team, and the team is of great importance to the school," I said matter-of-factly.

"And that's it?" Geoff asked expectantly.

I shook my head again. "Not quite. Before your self-inflicted downfall, you were a popular boy, and under the right guidance—*my* guidance—I'm sure you will be again. The school spirit project is far bigger than I could have imagined, and I could use the support of someone like you."

"So, I'd be what, your number two?" Geoff asked with

interest.

"No," I said bluntly. "Jacobs is two; you'll be three."

Geoff was thoughtful momentarily, then said, "OK, you're on... Oh, and X, could I wear a badge saying, 'School Spirit 3'?"

"That, Geoff, is an excellent idea," I said, smiling.

Just as he left, Geoff asked me, "Say, X, that last day of term, when we had our... *meeting* here. You weren't really in two places at once, were you?"

I smiled. "It would be imprudent of me to comment upon the matter, so I will simply say this instead: School spirit moves in mysterious ways."

Geoff nodded and said, "Right, thanks, X," but his face was consternated.

Only Rachael was in detention when I got to the library, and no teacher showed up to supervise. "Are you sure it was in here?" I asked.

"I thought so; who gave you yours? Didn't they tell you where to go?" Rachael asked.

"Oh, I asked Ms James for mine. I thought you might appreciate some company."

Rachael looked at me and smiled. "You know, X, sometimes, *just* sometimes, mind, you can be lovely."

"Thanks, Rachael."

"Oh, I spoke to the head cook at lunch and gave her my suggestions for the new menu," she said. "It's difficult to know how much of it she took on board, though, as I couldn't stop her from crying."

The bike ride lasted 20 minutes before the sky darkened and Mother Nature unleashed a thunderstorm upon us. Futilely, we tried sheltering under a tree; however, after five minutes, we were soaked and decided to head back.

As we cycled home, Rachael said, "Come over to mine, X; we'll get you sorted out there."

When we got to Rachael's, the place was empty, as Arthur and Alison had yet to return from work. Upon inspection, I found that my rucksack, schoolbooks, uniform, and all had been soaked.

"X, I'll sort this out. You must be getting cold. Go shower, and I'll change into my robe, put the heating on, and start drying these books. Just leave your clothes in the bathroom, ok?" Rachael said it kindly.

Obediently, I headed off to the bathroom. After showering, I grabbed a towel from the rail, wrapped it around my waist, and left my clothes where they were as per Rachael's instructions. Walking back into her room, she gave a little wolf whistle and giggled.

I reddened slightly, and she said, "Don't be embarrassed. Put a record on and relax," and headed to the bathroom herself.

Songs for Swinging Lovers, the Frank Sinatra album I'd bought her, was already on the turntable. I switched on the Hi-Fi system and put the needle on the record. As Rachael's bed was unmade, it didn't feel right to sit on it, so I had a nose around her room with nothing else to occupy myself. On her desk were a half-finished history essay and her diary; the entries for today read 'Detention' and 'Bike ride with *HIM!*' After that, I must have got a little carried away with the music as I started dancing, sort of. Somewhat away with the moment, I failed to hear the door open, and when Rachael exclaimed excitedly, "Are you dancing, X?" I nearly died of shock.

The sight of her wrapped only in a small towel swiftly extinguished any rising embarrassment. Feeling my eyebrows rise, I tried desperately to suppress the grin spreading rapidly across my face. She looked gorgeous.

"Oh, I thought we could be embarrassed together," she said, pointing to the towel. And I thought *you* didn't dance?"

"Actually, I took a few lessons. Remember the first dance party?" I asked.

Rachael rolled her eyes. "How could I forget?"

"Well, after the sheer terror of that experience, I resolved to learn a little," I said, trying not to stare too intently at her legs.

"Show me," she said it firmly.

The combination of Rachael, looking as hot as she did, and Frank Sinatra was too good to miss, so I put self-consciousness to one side and took her in hold.

I still need to learn a great deal, but I know enough to manage a slow ballroom dance. Rachael giggled a lot as we moved around her room. It wasn't a silly giggle, though; it was, in fact, sexy as hell, just as every moment had been since she'd walked back into the room.

As the song ended, Rachael gently rested her head against my shoulder. My attention was grabbed suddenly by Alison, who was standing by the door, arms folded and wearing a face like the thunderstorm we had cycled home through earlier. "X, get out of this house *now* and never, ever return!" she screamed. And then there was shouting—lots and lots of shouting.

Twenty minutes later, wearing Arthur's somewhat musty-smelling dressing gown and sitting opposite Alison at the kitchen table, I took a sip of coffee and listened to Rachael's rather red-faced mother's explanation for her earlier outburst. "*You* see how I jumped to the wrong conclusion, don't you,

X? I mean, a steamy shower, clothes strewn hither-thither, a ruffled bed, Frank Sinatra, and two moist teenagers, wearing nothing but towels, in each other's arms. Well, I saw only one thing, X, I tell you, *a romp!*" Alison said defensively.

"A romp?" I asked, arching an eyebrow.

"Yes, X, *a romp!*" she replied.

"Just a wet bike ride and a dance, not even a kiss," I said calmly.

Alison buried her head in her hands. "Oh Christ, it will take her forever to forgive me for this one."

"Quite possibly," I said flatly, having failed to think of any appropriate words of comfort.

At that point, Alison's husband walked in and stared at me in horror. "Really, Arthur, this isn't what it looks like," I said innocently.

After my school clothes had dried, I changed and knocked on Rachael's door.

"If that's you, Alison, you can f… " she started.

"It's me," I said, popping around the door. "Listen, she's very sorry. *So* sorry that she's sending us somewhere *very* special on Friday evening."

"Paris!" Rachael said intently. "I'll forgive her for Paris. How special anyway?"

"Apparently, I have to wear a suit," I replied.

After returning home, my parents announced, "We're off for some late summer sun!"

To clarify, *they* are off for some late summer sun. The

October half-term was too expensive, so they are going the following week. I will be staying here.

I really couldn't care. My thoughts are on more critical things, Rachael, to be precise. I may not be the best in the world at reading women's minds, but even *I* know enough to realise that, after tonight's interrupted *moment*, my residence in the doghouse is officially at an end. So, Friday, it is then—an expensive restaurant, formal attire, and the exchange of gifts. Really, what can go wrong this time?

THURSDAY 7TH SEPTEMBER

Drake and JG became the newest members of School Spirit's flock today. As they couldn't agree upon who should be four and who should be five, we now have two fours, and the next joiner will be six. Also, the three of us are going out with Flan on Saturday to celebrate my sixteenth birthday. There is a pub in the nearby town of Arn where casual underage drinkers are always reliably welcome.

At the break, Matt Jacobs grabbed me. "Excuse me, Captain, I couldn't help noticing Geoff Travis is wearing a School Spirit 3 badge; can I wear one too?" he asked politely.

"Of course," I replied.

"Also, can mine be bigger than his?"

I touched his shoulder and said, "Absolutely, Matt."

After school, I took the double-bus journey to Garnborough to search for a present for Rachael.

FRIDAY 8TH SEPTEMBER

Lisa, the Repeater, sat next to me in form group and requested to join team school spirit. I consented and told her, our new number 6, to round up numbers 2, 3, 4a, and 4b for a lunchtime meeting.

After grabbing a sandwich from the canteen, I met the others in the old school hall, in which now, as year fives, we are entitled to be in pre-school, at breaks, and during lunch. The plan, as I explained, is simple. The team will arrange to sell items donated by pupils and their families. However, rather than the usual bric-a-brac and rubbish usually handed over for such events, we are interested in things of actual value. Team school spirit grasped the idea immediately, and I told them I was already looking forward to seeing the results of their labours.

Located a 25-minute taxi ride south of Marketon, just off the dual carriageway, the Lone Oak restaurant was like visiting another world for me—besuited waiters, cloth napkins, not paper, and a cutlery puzzle teasingly laid out in front of me, awaiting resolution.

"Start from the outside and work in," Rachael said when she noticed my look of dismay.

"Hey, Rach. Do you think having a beer would be okay in this place?" I asked.

She smiled. "It's your birthday. Have what you want, X."

Having ordered a pint of bitter and a bottle of white wine, it was time to exchange gifts. I had, admittedly, splashed out a little. The necklace had cost much more than I was planning to spend, but it wasn't a case of showing off; I had just seen it in the jeweller's window and bought it impulsively.

"Oh, my god, X, how much did you spend? It's beautiful; thank you. You'll think I'm such a cheapskate when you see what I've got for you."

"Here, I'll put it on for you," I said, standing up and positioning myself behind her. Normally, I'd never have dared to volunteer for a task requiring high dexterity. However, yesterday evening, I had practised putting the necklace around a Rachael stand-in in my bedroom, cunningly constructed by sticking an inflated balloon into an upturned toilet roll tube.

After delicately securing the chain around her neck, I retook my seat, and Rachael pressed her hand to the necklace and smiled. "Oh, here you go; I got you a book."

She withdrew the present from her bag.

"Cheapskate!" I said, laughing.

"Don't! I need a Saturday job. It is my *favourite* book," she said.

"A crafty cheapskate, then," I added.

The book was *Great Expectations*, and I thanked Rachael sincerely for the gift.

Every course was delicious, and the evening seemed to go beautifully. However, when I headed to the gents after we'd finished dessert, I was washing my hands, and the middle-aged man at the sink next to me started chatting. By how he talked to me, I guessed he'd assumed I was somewhat older than my seventeen years.

"You've got to bring them somewhere like this occasionally, haven't you? It makes them feel special," he said, and I could tell he'd had *a few*. I shrugged in acknowledgement. Unfortunately, my new friend had not finished; he was *nowhere* near finished, and this one-sided conversation dragged on for some time. Exiting the situation was not straightforward as he leaned against the toilet door, physically blocking my escape.

Finally, when I could take no more of his moaning about his wife or his reminisces of skirt-chasing as a youth, I said, "It's been a pleasure talking to you, sir, but I might be missed if I don't return to my table."

"Well, don't let me stand in your way, young man," he said, finally standing away from the door.

When I returned to the table, I apologised for taking so long. Rachael, though, waved the apology away and gave a little snort.

"Two pints is enough for me; I'll try the wine." However, when I took the bottle from the holder, it was empty. "Oh, look at that," I said politely. "You've finished it."

Rachael giggled hysterically and said, "Listen, X, I talked to Mum last night." My companion was slurring her words as she spoke. "I said, 'Alison, I'm 16 years old now, and I should be able to do it in my room with whom I like when I like'." Her voice was raised to a level more suited to the football terraces.

"Right, err… " I said it uncertainly, desperately looking around for our waiter.

Rachael leaned closer to me. "So, what do you say, X? Do you fancy doing *it* with me tonight, yer *sexy* bastard?" She burst out laughing hysterically.

"Sshh!" I said with my finger placed on my lips. Rachael mirrored my gesture but then let out another loud cackle.

The waiter suddenly appeared on my shoulder. "Can I help you, sir?"

I asked, "Could we get the bill, please?"

With refined politeness, the waiter advised, "There is no bill, sir. Mrs Jackson took care of everything when she made your reservation."

"Oh, OK, in that case, could we have a taxi… quickly." I asked.

"I'll do what I can, sir." The waiter was distracted by Rachael, who was yanking on his sleeve.

Addressing the man bluntly, she said, "Hey, *you*, listen to me."

"Yes, Miss?" he enquired patiently.

Rachael looked at the waiter but pointed at me. "I'm allowed to do it in my room now, and tonight, I'm going to do it with him," and she immediately started cackling to herself again.

"We'll get that taxi here as soon as possible, sir," the waiter said, freeing himself from Rachael's grip and heading towards the reception.

"Hey, Rach, do you fancy waiting outside?" I asked.

Rachael giggled. "I know what you're up to, Exy, you *dirty* boy."

Once outside, Rachael took a pack of cigarettes and a lighter from her bag and lit up.

"What are you doing?" I asked in shock.

"Smoking! I'm sixteen now, and I'm allowed to smoke, and I'm allowed to screw!" Rachael looked a little unsteady on her feet now.

"It's really unhealthy. Just throw it away, Rachael," I pleaded.

Rachael frowned at me. "*You smoked,* you hypocrite. You drank, and you took drugs. *School smackhead*, that's who you were, Exy." Once again, she laughed.

Mercifully, the cab arrived within 10 minutes; however,

once in the backseat, Rachael seemed drunker than ever and slurred, "Come on then, Exy, give us a snog!" and grabbed me by my tie.

To appease her, I said, "Hey, why don't we wait till we get back to yours?"

"No, I wanna snog now!" she said firmly.

Madonna's 'Like a Prayer' was playing on the driver's radio. "Hey, Exy, you know what this song's all about, don't you? *Blow jobs!*" She practically screamed the words at me. "Play your cards right tonight, and you just might get one, sunshine." Rachael laughed so hard that she fell sideways into my lap. I swear, those three words will never mean the same thing to me again.

After recovering her position, she once again moved to kiss me. "What about the driver?" I said, indicating the front of the car with my eyes.

Shouting forward, she said, "He doesn't mind, *do you*? Come on, Exy, what are you waiting for? Go on, my son, stick your hand up my top; that'll get you in the mood," Rachael said, and then started laughing hysterically again.

"Listen, Rach, let's just cool it till we get back, hey?" I asked as politely as I could.

Rachael looked at me in disgust. "Oh, god, you're going to do it again, aren't you?" She leaned forward to speak to the driver. "*Hey, you, listen!* He thinks he's too good for me. It's been the same all year. He's happy to shag anyone else at the drop of a hat, but craps himself every time I lay a finger on him. He calls himself *School Spirit,* but I think he should be called *School Shit!*"

Geoff and Rachael's *incident* at the year four camp was suddenly making a lot more sense. The abuse continued until we were back outside Rachael's. I tried to help her out of the cab. However, she shouted, "Get off me, you big freak."

Alison answered after I'd pushed the doorbell, looking a little perplexed. "I didn't expect you back so early. Is everything OK?"

"No, it's not; *School Shit* doesn't fancy me! Out of my way, Alison," and, with that, Rachael barged past her mother into the house.

"Bit too much to drink, I'm afraid," I grimaced.

Alison looked at me expectantly. "Oh, you don't fancy helping me out with her, do you, X?"

"Not tonight, Alison; I think I've had quite enough, thanks," I said honestly.

When I got back here, I was still annoyed, so in pure spite, I burst the balloon that composed half of the stand-in Rachael, which was perched next to the computer.

Oh well, at least there's still tomorrow night. After all, it would take a miracle to turn out as badly as tonight did. Still, I've learned an important lesson today: I now understand why Rachael gets so angry when I screw things up for us.

SATURDAY 9TH SEPTEMBER

"I thought you'd forgotten about me!" Helen said it accusingly as she stepped out of her front door.

"A cake-cutting ceremony at home waylaid me," I replied.

"Here, happy birthday, X," she replied, and then handed me a card.

The four of us were having a great time, and, for once, I'd succeeded in putting thoughts of Rachael to the back of my mind. At about 9.30 pm, I was going to the gents when a familiar scent filled my nose, and someone stepped before me.

"Hello, X," she said.

"Karen?"

"You're not going to see her again, are you? You *can't* see her again!" Helen spoke imploringly as the cab drove us back to Marketon.

I replied defensively, "It's not like I'd want to be with her again. I want to understand a few things; that's all. She seemed really together tonight."

Helen sighed deeply. "X. I'm not going to lecture you, but just remember where that relationship got you last time."

"I will keep it in mind," I said thoughtfully.

SUNDAY 10TH SEPTEMBER

This morning, I rang the number I still know by heart and said, "The railway line in ten minutes."

"I'm sorry for what happened with James, X. It started one night at work, and I didn't know how to stop it. I never meant to hurt you," Karen said as we strolled north along the old track.

I laughed. "I think your boss did, though."

"You, if memory serves, threw the first punch, X," Karen said disapprovingly.

Dr Peters had talked about confronting demons, which I was there to do. Really, I had no idea how it would play out. After all, demons are ugly, reptilian creatures from the underworld, whereas mine's got the face of an angel and tits to die for. However, now that I was standing before her, I realised that my gene-carrying machine had served me well. Having already suffered one near-fatal dose of Karen Ronson, it had built up its immunity in the months since our last encounter. I was now safe from harm and in control, which, given the history of this relationship, was a first.

"Do you ever think about us, X?" Karen asked.

"What do you want?" I asked bluntly.

"I miss you, X; I miss my little friend. I'm lonely!" she said earnestly. "I just pulled myself out of a depression, and I'd like to avoid slipping straight back into another one. Can I see you again? I want the opportunity to make things up to you."

The last thing I expected to feel was pity for the girl. Mindful that I didn't want to be anywhere with her, should I momentarily drop my guard, there was a chance of us ending up in bed together again. I racked my brains for an appropriate solution. "Squash," I said eventually.

"Squash?" she said in bemusement. While we'd been together, Karen had bragged of being a county-standard player in her school days.

"Yes, *I* need an alternative to cycling, and *you* need to get out of the house more; teach me." I said enthusiastically.

"Not exactly what I was expecting, but OK, X, you're on," Karen said, smiling.

"Oh, and one more thing, Karen, your dad indicated that if I came near you again, something awful might happen to me. Could you please ensure *this* is OK with him?"

Karen looked at me in disbelief. "You're joking, aren't you? I think he missed you almost as much as I did."

MONDAY 11TH SEPTEMBER

"**M**um would like me to pass on her sincere apologies for giving birth to me," Rachael said humbly in English.

"Her apology is accepted," I replied.

"And mine? Or am I getting the silent treatment?" she asked delicately.

I smiled. "Yours is accepted, too."

At lunch, I was summoned to Dr Harris's office. "Ah, X, my boy, are you certain about this no-smoking policy?" he asked with concern.

"Absolutely, sir," I said assuredly.

"I just can't stand the sight of them all standing around chuffing outside the school gates," Dr Harris said in disgust.

Resolutely, I replied, "I'll talk to the pupils in question."

The head looked bemused, though. "What's that, 'pupils', you say? It's the teachers who are upsetting me, my boy. I counted twenty of them out there at break time today."

"Right, sir, it's probably best you address that with them then."

"Well, I suppose that would be appropriate, but it's not popular, you know, X?" Dr Harris said it with concern.

Firmly, I replied, "Sir, Luther Parkinson isn't going to get back on top without a fight. Stand in the way of progress, and it'll mow you down like a partially sighted pensioner driving a Volvo; that's *my* motto!"

Dr Harris made a fist. "You're right, my boy; you're right. Good god, I'm glad I've got you by my side. Where are we at with the Shakespeare play, by the way?"

"Mrs Gates has proposed *Romeo and Juliet*," I replied.

"Good lord, suicides at Christmas? We'll do *La Traviata* as well, shall we? Make it a double bill." The headmaster started smirking and remarked, "No, it will never do. Tell her to come up with something jollier, X."

Mrs Gates was in the drama studio, eating a sandwich. "Sorry, Miss. Orders from the top, no tragedies."

"*Much ado about Nothing*, X?" she asked.

"Off the record, Miss, I agree, but I think we'd be wise to keep the old boy happy," I replied sincerely.

Mrs Gates smiled pleasantly. "No, X, *that's* the name of a play —it's a comedy."

"Right, in that case, it sounds perfect," I said, trying to hide my embarrassment.

TUESDAY 12TH SEPTEMBER

Collections started at lunchtime today for Luther Parkinson Sells Out. Lisa the Repeater is putting School Spirits 2, 3, 4a, and 4b to shame with her passion for the project. She's appropriately firm with the pupils when they are donating their items and will only accept items of genuine value. "If your parents want to get rid of rubbish, tell them to hire a skip or visit the incinerator. Now take it back!" she said to one particularly frightened-looking year three kid.

When a year 1 had a change of heart about a toy Transformer he had just handed over, she dealt with the situation brilliantly. "Sorry, I'm having second thoughts; could I have that one back, please?" the boy asked politely.

"This one?" Lisa asked, holding up the truck in question for clarity. The boy nodded eagerly. "You *can* take it back. However, as it is now the school's property, I may *have* to report you to the police." Lisa said firmly. The boy took one last look at his toy and then slowly walked away.

I beamed with delight. "That's the spirit, Lisa. After all, you don't see a Grand National winner sulking when it's forced to donate its possessions to a good cause, do you?"

Flan grabbed me at the final bell. "'The Lutherettes' will be ready for your inspection tomorrow, X."

"Great!" I replied. "So, who's in the team?" I asked, perhaps a little *too* eagerly.

Tapping the side of her nose, she said, "I won't ruin *the* surprise for you."

WEDNESDAY 13TH SEPTEMBER

As the poster for the *Much Ado About Nothing* auditions went up yesterday, Drake was naturally excited on the way to school this morning. "Hey, X, any chance of you helping me out, you know, making sure I get a big part?"

"Yeah, sure; which one do you want?" I asked casually.

"Benedick."

Finally, I have defined a purpose for Stuart Moor, school thug. He and his band of equally thick mates are regulars at the local football team's home games. I imagine they are not far from becoming fully realised hooligans; however, with this afternoon's big opener to the football season, Luther Parkinson versus Marketon High, their often misguided energies can finally be put to good use.

"Really, X, I'm in charge?" Stuart asked eagerly.

"Stuart, you only report to me on this one. I want you to take the large crowd of students and weaponize it!"

"So, can I be a school spirit too?" he asked.

"Yes, Stuart, you can. You will be school spirit 13," I replied.

"Oh, and X, would you please show me how you do that thing when you're in two places at the same time?" Stuart asked eagerly.

Naming Stuart School Spirit 13 wasn't a slight; far from

it, I'd already allocated positions 7—12 for six extraordinary ladies.

Inspecting the Lutherettes was a dream job; whether or not they had intended to go for the 'St Trinian's with pom-poms' look, I have no idea, but they pulled it off with style. Helen had recruited Helen Heaven, Clare Anatomy, Claire With An Eye For X, Penny Chemistry, and a rather shy-looking girl, shifting her feet nervously on the far left of the group. Dutifully, I gave every team member the once-over. I thought Helen Heaven winked at me momentarily when I stopped before her, but my eyes must have been playing tricks on me. I congratulated every one of them on their quite magnificent efforts. When I came to the last recruit, I leaned in close and whispered, "Over your dead body?"

"This is my way of saying sorry; what do you think?" Rachael, or school spirit 12, as she is now known, whispered back.

"I like it. I like it a lot. Say, what would you do if you'd been naughty?" I asked cheekily.

"Maybe you'll find out one day," Rachael said with a cute little giggle.

As difficult as it was to drag myself away, I was due in the drama studio to help Mrs Gates run the auditions for the play. When I arrived, Mark Hardy was up on the stage reading from the text. "Ah, just in time, X, I'm thinking of Mark for Benedick," Mrs Gates whispered.

Decisively, I said, "Don't you worry, Miss; I have found you a Benedick!"

"Oh, really, who?" she asked with interest.

I replied, "Drake, I mean Timothy."

Mrs Gates looked concerned. "Oh, a talented young actor, for sure, but I'm not certain he's my, or, in fact, *anyone's*, idea of a Benedick, X."

"Those were my exact thoughts too, Miss, *until* he came around to mine last night, and he blew my mind frankly. I thought *he was* Benedick," I lied.

"Really?" Mrs Gates asked with interest.

I nodded. "Absolutely; besides, the Shakespeare play is one of school spirit's flagship projects; it's not like I'd do anything to jeopardise it, is it?" I said it sincerely.

The drama teacher smiled warmly. "*Right*, we'll go along with your choice, X."

Drake had only begun reading his chosen extract when Mrs Gates exclaimed, "First class, you'll be our Benedick."

The other pupils, both those still waiting to audition and those who already had, seemed a little disgruntled; however, Drake had used his initiative this morning, and a poor school will remain if we knock back students who choose to think their way around obstacles.

The last pupil to audition was a somewhat out-of-breath and dishevelled-looking Rachael. "I would like to read for the part of Beatrice," she said clearly before commencing. She was fantastic—an incredible performance—or maybe I was still picturing her in the cheerleader's outfit. Really, who can tell? Regardless, I leant in closely to Mrs Gates and whispered, "Far be it from me to interfere with key casting decisions, but I'd say we've found our Beatrice, wouldn't you?"

"I couldn't agree more, X," she replied. "Will you be looking for a part yourself?"

"No way! I was once on stage, Mrs Gates, in the Christmas school play when I was seven. I only had one line, "Merry

Christmas, everyone," and I said it incorrectly. It is, I believe, what my former psychiatrist would refer to as a mental scar."

This afternoon, I saw the first fruits of the school spirit project. Over 250 pupils must have turned out to watch the football match against our biggest rivals, Marketon High. School Spirit 13 and his hooligan posse worked their magic, and within five minutes, the crowd roared every time we were in possession and jeered loudly when Marketon High got the ball. As for the Lutherettes, some refinement is required, but the raw talent is there for all to see. Helen Heaven and Clare Anatomy are very good at doing cartwheels; everyone could see their pants each time they did one. This distracted the opposition and the referee, Little Wilson, allowing Geoff to elbow the boy, marking him in the face without caution.

Although it was 0-0 at the break, we took the game to them in the second half, and Geoff rediscovered his scintillating form. It ended 4-0, with the captain helping himself to a hat-trick.

Really, I could have wept with pride.

THURSDAY 14TH SEPTEMBER

"So, how was your first cheerleading experience?" I asked Rachael in English.

"I enjoyed it, and *I* got a date out of it," she said, giving a little clap.

Sorry, it sounded like she just said, 'date'.

"*A date?*" I asked sharply,."With whom, exactly?"

"With Rob, the captain of Marketon High, *all* the other girls were saying how handsome he was, and, after the game, he walked straight up to *me* and asked if I wanted to go to the cinema with him on Saturday," Rachael said with an almost sickening level of glee.

A date?

I must admit to not seeing *this one* coming, and I immediately went on the attack. "You know, Rachael, I always knew there would be traitors to the cause in this school, but I never figured you'd be one of them."

Rachael stared at me in disgust. "A traitor? Do you have *any* idea how pathetic you sound, X?"

I shook my head and sighed. "Listen, if you want to start sleeping with the enemy, then go right ahead, but be it on your head; that's all I'm saying."

Looking at me with something approaching horror, Rachael said furiously, "Who said *anything* about *anyone* sleeping with *anybody*, you prat?"

Despite her anger, I remained defiant. "Listen, *I am* school spirit, and I can already feel the place turning against you. I'll do all I can to protect you, but I can't make any promises."

Looking close to tears, she said with disgust, "Do you remember all those months ago in my bedroom? 'Hey, Rach, I'm pretty sure that if you wanted to kiss another boy, then I'm 70% sure that would be OK too'. I should have known you were talking crap. I thought you were different, X. How wrong was I?"

At that moment, I realised that Mr Bentley and the rest of the class had been listening intently to our conversation. "Can this lover's tiff possibly wait until the end of the lesson?" the new teacher asked with an arched eyebrow.

"Yes, sir," Rachael and I replied in unison.

Mr Bentley shook his head with mild disbelief. "Right, now *Love Story* has been paused; I can tell you about today's lesson, class. We're going to do something a little different—we're having a debate, and the topic is school spirit—good or bad?'"

Rachael's hand shot up. "Oh, Mr Bentley, can I be on the bad team, please?"

The English teacher shook his head. "No, Rachael, you'll be on the good team, and X, you'll be arguing against it," he replied.

"He made you do what?" Dr Harris roared. After English, I headed to his office to report Mr. Bentley's heresy.

"It was, sir, just as I said," I replied honestly. "I had to stand up in front of my flock, and denounce myself... and what's *really* irritating is that I did a pretty decent job of it, too."

Dr Harris nodded. "Well, good for you, X! I admire your spirit—more than a touch of *Bridge over the River Kwai* in that behaviour. But don't worry about *Bentley*—I'll soon have him dancing to the school spirit beat."

During lunch, at a hastily convened meeting with five out of the six Lutherettes, I opened the proceedings by explaining Rachael's treasonous behaviour, proposed that her immediate expulsion be decided by ballot, and closed my introduction by saying, "Girls, you are at the vanguard of the Luther Parkinson revolution, and far be it from me to try and influence your decision. So, I will leave it entirely in your own hands, but ask yourself, Do you want to carry on with a sly, backstabbing, good-for-nothing rodent in the troupe, or do you think it's better to kick her in to touch?"

Flan shook her head vigorously. "For the record, though he is an excellent friend, I entirely disagree with X, and I think that Rachael should be allowed to go out with whomever she wants to."

Penny Chemistry sighed. "Yes, that's all well and good, but what's the point in doing what we're doing if, at the end of every game, we shack up with the opposition?"

"Who said anything about shacking up, Penny?" Flan asked reasonably.

Catching my eye, Clare Anatomy winked at me and said, "I'm with Penny; Luther Parkinson rules!"

As I shifted my gaze to Helen Heaven, she looked conflicted and asked, "I'm seeing a guy who works on the rigs. Is that a problem?"

Smiling warmly at the school beauty, I said, "As he's not at Marketon High, no."

Looking expectantly at the fifth member, Claire With An Eye For X, I motioned for her to register her opinion. "Err… I agree with the others," she said finally, after a significant gesture on my part.

How can you agree with the others when they're in disagreement?

Ignoring my inner voice, I clapped my hands together, looked at Flan, and said decisively, "*Right,* I make that 4-1 in favour."

Sighing deeply, Flan said, "OK, I think we're doing the wrong thing here, but I'll respect the majority's decision. We kick her out. Just one thing, X, who do we replace her with?"

I smiled brightly at my friend, anticipating her question. "It's entirely up to you, but I'd say School Spirit 6 would make an ideal replacement."

You see, I'm not being harsh; it's just that this situation with Rachael 1989 *can't* be taken lightly. And yes, I know this is entirely my fault under the rules of cause and effect. God, I miss chaos sometimes. Anyway, regardless, we're talking about the girl I love here. There's no point in playing passive here; really, there isn't. Ladies and gentlemen, we are at DEFCON 1, and it's time to launch my weapon of mass destruction.

Karen looked slightly confused when she opened the door to me. "I thought this was a Wednesday night-only thing."

Pushing past her, I said, "I did for you; now you do for me!"

"What's this all about, X?" she asked behind me.

I turned decisively to my former lover. "Karen, let me ask you a question: have you ever fancied a career in sabotage?"

FRIDAY 15TH SEPTEMBER

In English, Rachael was defiant regarding her dismissal from the Lutherettes. "You know, I don't care if I'm on that cheerleading squad. I only joined to say sorry to you."

I shook my head. "*I* don't care either. All *I* care about is the school and that *we* have a suitable replacement. She's an old friend; if you broke her in half, you'd find Luther Parkinson written inside her like a stick of rock. That is what I'd call a result, Rachael."

Teasingly, she asked, "So, you're not bothered about me and Rob then?"

I was in the mood to fight fire with fire. "*Nope*, not in the slightest. Sorry, schoolgirl crushes are so far under my radar that you wouldn't believe it. I am in love, and always have been, with the same girl."

"And who's that?" Rachael asked with interest, though I didn't get the chance to answer as Mr Bentley told us both to shut up.

"Right, now *Kramer vs. Kramer* is on pause; I have something to say," our teacher began. "Yesterday, I started an inappropriate debate topic. The fact that a student, who happens to be in this class as I speak, wants to do his utmost to improve his school, is a commendable effort, and encouraging people to find fault in his actions was a misjudgment on my part. My apologies if I offended any of you."

There was a banging sound from the desk beside me. "I

can't believe this!" Rachel said it with disgust. She quickly packed her things into her school bag and stormed out of the classroom.

Well, someone else seems to be struggling to dance in time with the school spirit beat!

However, by the end of the lesson, my anger at Rachael had subsided. My normal protective urges towards her had finally kicked in, so I hung back to speak to the new English teacher. "Listen, Mr Bentley, I just wanted to say… " I began.

He raised his hand to silence me. "X, if you're about to say thanks for what I said earlier, please realise I only did that to save my bloody career, which is still in its infancy. Sorry, to check, I can talk to you, man to man, can't I, or will you run to Dr Harris again?"

I'm feeling genuine shame.

Taking a deep gulp and with my head pointed shamefacedly to the floor, I said quietly, "Actually, sir, it's about Rachael; please don't come down on her too hard for storming out."

Mr Bentley seemed pleasantly surprised. "I'm glad you said that, X, because, after yesterday, I wasn't sure what to make of you. For your information, I picked the topic of school spirit because everyone's guaranteed to have an opinion about it, and I picked you for the 'No' team to test your skills as a debater, not because I disagree with what you're doing," he said intently.

"Sir, permission to swear?" I asked humbly.

"Permission granted, X," he said kindly.

"I'm a complete wanker, and you're a good guy," I said remorsefully.

"*I am* a good guy, X. And, as such, I can say this… fresh start?" Mr Bentley offered his hand out to me.

I let out a big sigh, and we shook. "Thank you, sir," I said with a smile.

"And don't worry; I won't come down on your… *friend* too hard," he assured me.

I smiled. "Thanks, sir. Listen, your predecessor and I had what can only be described as a close relationship."

He smirked. "So, I've heard, X."

"Her absence has left a gaping hole in my school life. I love books and would discuss whatever I read with her after class. It would be my honour, sir, if you would oblige me similarly," I said genuinely.

"X, you know what, I think I'd enjoy that," he said with a smile. "Just one thing though, *I'm not* going to the store cupboard with you."

SUNDAY 17TH SEPTEMBER

"OK, let's rule *The Fly 2* out of the equation immediately," I said, studying the posters outside the cinema last night.

Karen sighed. "They'll go and see *Lethal Weapon 2*, I promise you, X."

Resolutely, I said, "There is no way Rachael would go and watch it."

"Listen, X, it's what *he'll* want to see, and, right now, *he's* Mr Right, so *she'll* want to see it too," Karen replied patiently.

I said commandingly, "Karen, trust me. *I* know this girl; she'll want to watch *Talk Radio*."

Five minutes after the film had started, I scanned the empty theatre and said humbly, "OK, I'm now willing to admit that you may have had a point."

Karen flatly replied, "X, I don't think a career in sabotage is for you." Then she playfully threw a piece of popcorn at my head.

Still, the advantage was ours. The film we saw was the shorter of the two. Therefore, we could hang around discreetly and discover if they were going on elsewhere. After 20 minutes of waiting, Rachael, Rob, and the rest of the crowd of fellow patrons emerged from the cinema, and the new couple headed towards the arts centre next door.

They were already seated in the far corner of the bar when

Karen and I entered. "What are you drinking, X?" my partner for the night enquired.

"Pint of bitter," I said, looking intently towards the lovers.

"X, be cool," Karen said patiently. "And no fighting; trust me, it won't work. Just look in any direction except theirs."

Given that she had been right about the film, I was willing to go along with her, though I did struggle to keep my envious eyes from seeking out Rachael and her new beau as Karen and I made idle conversation.

A few minutes later, I heard Rachael's voice. "Well, *this* is a surprise, *isn't it*?" Thankfully, her face was full of genuine concern.

Casually, I replied, "Hey, Rachael, what are you doing here?"

Karen gave her a bitchy sideways glance.

"I was going to the cinema with Rob, remember?" she asked expectantly.

"Nope," I said flatly, and Karen toyed affectionately with a button on my shirt.

Politely, she enquired, "Err, would you two care to join us?"

"Ok," I said.

Petulantly, Karen asked, "X, do we have to?"

"Please, for me?" I asked her intently.

Rather smuttily, she replied, "I'd do anything you asked me to."

"Right, we're over here," Rachael said brightly, and we both followed her to the corner of the bar.

When we reached the table, Rachael commenced the introductions. "Rob, this is X, my *best* friend, X, and this is Karen, his…"

"Girlfriend," Karen said, holding out her hand to Rob, whose mouth had fallen open at the sight of my companion.

"So," Rachael said, "what have you two been up to?"

Nonchalantly, I replied, "Cinema."

"So have we. What did you see?" Rachael asked with interest.

"*Talk Radio*," Karen said, giving Rachael a bitchy stare. She then put her hand on my thigh, *really* high up.

Flatly, Rachael said, "Oh, that's what *I* wanted to see."

Joining this somewhat awkward conversation, Rob said, "*Lethal Weapon 2* was good, wasn't it?"

"Yes, I enjoyed it," Rachael said unconvincingly. She then placed her hand on Rob's thigh, though it was far closer to his knee than Karen's hand was to mine. After sipping her glass of wine, she asked, "So when *exactly* did you two get back together?"

"*Love never dies!*" Karen replied, sounding ever so slightly deranged.

Rachael rolled her eyes in dismay, then glared at my partner for the evening. "Karen, I haven't seen you since... oh, I remember, since you had your hand around my throat just for going to watch a film with X," she said cattily.

Karen sighed deeply. "Rachael, I was a bit out of it back then; I was off my medication; I didn't know what I was doing, and if I frightened you, I offer you my heartfelt apologies. Deep down, I always knew X wouldn't cheat on me with someone like *you*."

"You scared the hell out of me!" Rachael said it accusingly across the table.

"Take it easy, Rach; Karen's apologised," I said firmly.

"Don't worry, X," Karen said, putting her arm around me

and leaning her head against my shoulder. "Some people will always *hate* the mentally ill. I've grown used to it over the years," she said sadly.

Rachael looked aghast. "That's *not* what I meant," she said defensively.

Abruptly changing the direction of the conversation, Rob enquired, "So, how does the age gap affect you two?"

Karen took her hand from my thigh and placed it on Rob's knee under the table. "Fortunately, Rob, X makes love with the ferocity of a man ten years his senior."

Seriously, I thought the boy was going to faint. Karen acted her role exceptionally well, and as much as I wanted to play along, I was somewhat distracted by Rachael, who looked more alluring than ever.

Just as I was drifting into a daydream starring the girl sitting opposite me, Karen said brightly, "Actually, speaking of sex, I want to do it right now, X." Taking her hand from Rob's knee and placing it delicately on my face, she asked demurely, "Back to mine, stud?"

After fluffing my crucial line, "No, I can't wait that long, let's just go and do it in the toilets." I made amends by purposely leading Karen out of the bar, down the stairs, and into the first available taxi.

When we returned to Karen's, we shared a bottle of wine. After listening to her tales of her recent experiences in a private mental health hospital, I eventually drifted off to sleep on the sofa. There was no sign of her this morning. I read a note advising me to help myself to breakfast and to let myself out when I was ready.

As I walked back along my street this morning, I saw Rachael perched on the front garden wall. "I'm not here to argue; I just want to talk. OK?" she said, holding her hands up in a gesture of non-aggression.

"Ok," I replied, "let's talk."

"You know, your parents do the perfect impression of not caring about you," Rachael said as we reached the end of the street.

I smiled ruefully. "I used to think, you know, that it was an impression, but it's not."

We'd reached the wasteland that runs in a long, rectangular strip from the old railway line, passing the end of my street to Swan Lane, where Luther Parkinson proudly stands. After we climbed the fence, Rachael asked, "Which way, left or right?"

Pointing to our left, I said, "Let's head to the railway line; there's less broken glass that way."

After walking silently for a few minutes, Rachael said irritably, "By the way, for two minutes last night, you had me fooled, but *I* know you, X. The first time you were with Karen, you used to look right through me; however, in the bar last night, you couldn't take your eyes off me."

"Oh," I said with a shrug, "that bad, were we?"

Rachael snorted. "Actually, Karen was convincing, but you were pretty terrible, and, for the record, that was an *incredibly* cruel trick to pull on me."

"Sorry!" I said sincerely. "I was jealous."

Pleasingly, Rachael was still looking for further clarification on my, at present, non-existent sex life. "What *is* going on between the two of you anyway?"

"Oh, we had a chance encounter a few weeks ago. She's lonely, so I said I'd hang out with her. *Strictly* on a platonic basis," I replied.

Rachael sighed. "That's the thing with you, X—your

intentions, *only* your intentions, though—are nearly always good."

For the first time, I'm 50:50, whether that's an insult or a compliment.

"You know what I wish, though, X?" Rachael said wistfully as we strolled onward.

"No," I said blankly.

Looking at me intently, she said, "I wish *just once* that instead of putting all your efforts into your hare-brained schemes, you could have used *some* of that energy and told me how you feel about me."

Resolutely, I said, "Well, let me give it a go. Right here, right now."

"It's too late, X," she said sadly.

I grabbed her arm and turned her to face me. "Don't give up on me, Rachael."

I saw a tear in her eye. "X, I'm not giving up on you; I'm leaving Marketon next weekend. Mum broke the news to me first thing."

Alison's mother is ill and can barely look after herself at home. The decision has been made that Rachael and her mum will move back to Reading as soon as possible. Even though Alison still has a few weeks' notice to serve at the poly, she wants her daughter to move in with her gran as soon as possible, act as a carer in the interim, and limit the disruption caused by the change in schooling.

It wasn't much of a walk. As soon as she broke the news, Rachael couldn't stop crying. Eventually, she said, "Sorry, I can't handle this," and ran off. The moment she was out of sight, I started crying too.

MONDAY 18TH SEPTEMBER

I tried to talk to Rachael in English, but she started crying again. "I can't talk to you right now, X; I'm sorry."

After class, I hung back and talked to Mr Bentley. "Problems, X?" he asked kindly.

"I've hit an iceberg this time, sir," I said solemnly.

The English teacher gave me a firm slap on the shoulder. "Time to start swimming, my friend." I've decided he is my favourite teacher, along with Dr Harris.

WEDNESDAY 20TH SEPTEMBER

I got a letter from Rachael today.

    X,

    Sorry, I can't talk to you right now; I'm too emotional. I would love it if you would come and say goodbye to me at five on Saturday.

    Love Rachael1989

At lunch, Dr Harris summoned me to his office. "The word on the corridor is that school spirit has lost his mojo; what can be done, my boy?" he asked brightly.

"I'm sorry, sir; I just had some bad news, but I'm intent on soldiering on," I said solemnly.

The headmaster was thoughtful momentarily. "I know just the thing to cheer you up! Leave it to me."

THURSDAY 21ST SEPTEMBER

In form group, Mr Cracket read an announcement from Dr Harris. "It is kindly requested that teachers and students alike now refer to the pupil formerly known as X as School Spirit at all times."

It cheered me up… a little.

Rachael was silent again in English. We didn't say a single word to one another. I don't understand; I want to say so much, but she won't let me talk.

"Got a book you want to discuss, X?" Mr Bentley asked after the rest of the class had left.

"Actually, no, sir, I tried reading last night, but after three lines, I felt like vomiting," I replied honestly.

Mr Bentley smiled kindly. "If you ask me, X, one of the greatest rewards of literature is the consolation it can offer us when life is cruel."

"Really, sir, would you know of a book entitled *I Want to Beat Myself Over the Head with a Cricket Bat for Being Such a Massive Twat*? Because if you do, that's the book for me right now," I said flippantly.

Mr Bentley smiled. "At least you've still got your sense of humour, and, if I may say so, you sound a little wiser, too."

FRIDAY 22ND SEPTEMBER

I wouldn't blame Mr Bentley if he were sick of the sight of my face, but the man seems limitless in his kindness to me.

"My advice, X, when you say goodbye tomorrow, don't hold back. That way, you won't chalk up any more regrets," he said gently.

"Should I prepare a speech, sir?" I asked eagerly.

He shook his head. "No, X, just tell the girl how you feel."

Geoff sat with me at lunch. "Hey, X, if the fashion is to go out with Luther Parkinson girls, then we're going to need some year four girls invited to the Year 5 Dance Party as the girls in our year are getting fussy these days."

"No problem, Geoff, just get me a list," I replied absently.

SATURDAY 23RD SEPTEMBER

Today, I offered Flan the chance to work at Ripton Cycles, as I had a busy schedule.

Luther Parkinson Sells Out was an outstanding success. It looks like we've managed to make over £1,000. That will pay for the costumes for *Much Ado About Nothing* and uniforms for the Lutherettes, and plenty will still be left afterwards for other worthy causes. I wish I could enjoy it more.

At 4.30, I took a slow, reluctant stroll to Rachael's. It felt like I was walking to my execution.

At first, she was all bright-eyed and smiling as she put the last things in Alison's car. Finally, when she'd finished, she came over and hugged me. Holding back the tears took a monumental effort, but I was determined to be brave.

"Rob must be upset." Obviously, I was being insincere.

Rachael laughed. "I don't care about Rob, *silly*. I care about you!"

"Back to your old school, eh? It's not all bad news," I said, sounding upbeat.

"I liked Luther Parkinson better. I think it's probably the best school in the world," she laughed.

I smiled. "Here, here,"

Her face turned suddenly serious. "Hey, X, don't use *this* as an excuse to go off the rails again. *Promise me!*"

"I promise you!" I said with it sincerity. "Listen, Rachael, there are so many things I want to say."

Rachael placed her finger delicately on my lips. "There isn't time, X, so you'll just have to tell me everything with just one kiss."

As we embraced, I could feel the hot tears streaming down her cheeks. I'm not sure how long we kissed, but eventually, I heard Alison coughing impatiently, and our lips parted. "Thank you, X," Rachael managed to say before dissolving into floods again. I couldn't respond; it was like I'd gone into shock. I didn't even say goodbye.

When the car drove away, I fell to my knees, and I wasn't sure I was going to be able to get up again. The last time I felt like this, I went into a spiral of drugs and anorexia. However, it's true what they say: you live and learn, so I went over to JG's and, this time, I just got blind drunk.

SUNDAY 24TH SEPTEMBER

There's no point in writing when there's nothing to write about.

WEDNESDAY 27TH SEPTEMBER

I saw Ms James at lunch, hoping she would cheer me up.

"Ah, X, good to see you. How are you?" she asked with concern.

"Actually, Ms James, the general practice these days is to refer to me as school spirit," I said with a smile.

Her expression darkened. "Right, let me throw that one back at you, and we'll find out together whether you catch like a sissy, shall we? *If* you want me to refer to you by that *preposterous* name, all you need to do is shoot me down in the town square, *Cowboy*, and then form the words 'School Spirit' yourself with my cold, dead lips. Does that make my position clear enough for you on this matter?" she asked.

"Crystal, Ms James," I replied with a grimace.

"Good! Now, what can I do for you?"

I adopted a business-like tone. "Actually, Ms James, I've been thinking that there should be more interaction between years five and four, and I thought…"

Ms James scowled. "Oh, *do* shut up, X. The year five boys want the pretty year four girls to come to the dance party because the females in their year have too high standards to consider kissing them. I am head of year, you know, even *I* hear some of the gossip," she said irritably.

"Right, well, yes, 19 girls and Matt Jacobs, he's on the list because he's my two," I said honestly.

Casually, she said, "If you want to, I have no problem with it."

"Really? I thought you... " I began.

Ms James eyed me sharply. "What? You thought I would take that list from your grubby little hands, roll it into a ball, and throw it back into your unbearably smug face?"

"That's *exactly* what I thought you would do," I replied with a nod of confirmation.

She smiled demurely. "Normally, *I would*, but the clouds have gathered over you, X. There's that doomed romantic look to you again, and I'm worried. After all, look where we ended up last time," she said with concern. "As such, I'm cutting you *a little* slack."

Resolutely, I replied, "*This* is different; I promised her I wouldn't go mad again, so no matter how crap this feels, and trust me, it does feel incredibly crappy right now. I'm going to keep it together—for her."

"Good for you, X. And let this be a lesson. Never let a good thing slip through your fingers again!" Ms James advised.

"Never! Ms, now that Rachael has left, does this mean I'm now your favourite pupil?" I asked with interest.

Ms James looked at me in bemusement. "Don't be ridiculous, X; you're *a boy*. Helen Flannigan is my favourite student now; rest assured, you will always be my second."

Delicately, I asked, "Sorry, Ms, I may be wrong, but isn't that, in fact, prejudicial?"

Sneering, she replied, "Prejudicial? Try a day in the life of a black person in Soweto, you big crybaby."

The head of year had made a valid point, and I dutifully laid my argument to rest.

THURSDAY 28TH SEPTEMBER

Jack came and sat next to me in English today again. "Sorry, I know you'll retake your place someday soon, but just while I'm grieving, could you please leave the space empty? I feel closer to her that way." I said it miserably. Jack just nodded and took his usual seat behind me by himself.

Halfway through class, I wrote on a Post-it note and slapped it on the empty desk beside me. It read, "I MISS YOU!"

Tonight brought another football victory, and we were away from home this time. Our support outnumbered theirs by 100-1; for clarity, there were 100 of us and only one lonely boy cheering on the opposing team.

FRIDAY 29TH SEPTEMBER

On the way to school, Drake asked if I would mind spending the evening helping him learn the lines for *Much Ado About Nothing*. I agreed to assist as if Drake isn't anyone's idea of a Benedick; as Mrs Gates pointed out, there is plenty of time to take the appropriate corrective action.

Of all people, Helen Heaven took the seat opposite me at lunch. There are pretty girls in this school, but Helen is pin-up-gorgeous. It is not uncommon for younger boys to walk into walls after passing her in the corridor. Her raven hair always looks effortlessly fabulous and beautifully frames her adorably sweet, pixie-like face. In short, she's hotter than heavy lifting.

"Hey, School Spirit; you look nice today," she said brightly.

I swear, just eight months ago, *those* words from *that* mouth would have knocked me off my chair. Today, however, they just bounced harmlessly off me.

"Thanks, Helen; how are you?" I asked.

Coyly, Helen said, "I have a dilemma, actually, and I thought you might be able to help."

After swallowing a mouthful of lunch, I replied, "I'll endeavour to."

"It's my 16th birthday next Saturday, and a few of us are going out for a meal. My boyfriend, Dean… "

"The guy who works on the rigs?" I asked.

"Yes, he can't make it due to work, and it would be strange if I were by myself, while my girlfriends are all with their other halves," she explained.

I held my hand up. "No problem, I understand the situation; you want me to set you up, don't you?" I quickly scanned around the tables and saw Geoff sitting nearby, "Hey, Geoff!" I shouted over at him.

Turning his head to me, he replied, "Yes, School Spirit?"

I pointed at the school beauty. "Helen here needs a date next Saturday. Can you oblige, my friend?"

I thought his eyes would pop out of his head. "In a heartbeat, X."

"Good man!" I replied and looked back across at Helen, "OK?" I asked.

Helen smiled politely but shifted uncomfortably in her chair. "Thanks, X. That was, err… very efficient. Though Geoff is nice, I wondered if you would be kind enough to escort me."

"Err, yeah, sure, why not?" I said it uncertainly. Looking back in Geoff's direction, I shouted, "Hey, Geoff, change of plan; you're the first reserve, OK?"

Keenly, Geoff replied, "No problem, X, that's good enough for me. I'm just happy to be on the team sheet."

I looked at Helen and smiled. "It's settled now; you may consider yourself escorted."

"Date!" she said with a smile.

Really, there's only one pair of lips I wanted to hear those words from, and it wasn't hers.

SUNDAY 8TH OCTOBER

As the week progressed, I felt my mood slowly brightening. When kids shout, 'School Spirit!' at me in the corridor, I start blowing/finger-rippling back at them.

Helen's birthday party was dull, as I knew no other guys there. After the meal, we got a cab back from the restaurant, and outside her house, she gently took hold of one of the lapels of my jacket. "You look very handsome dressed up, X," she said sweetly.

"Thanks, you look beautiful; you always do, Helen," I replied.

Smiling sweetly, she asked, "Would you like to come in for a bit? I'm pretty sure my parents will be in bed."

The offer was not without its temptations, as I figured I'd get at least a snog out of it if I accepted her invitation. However, would kissing another girl make me feel any better, no matter how beautiful she may be? After a moment's consideration, I decided it would be an unwise move. "Thanks, but I'm going out for a bike ride tomorrow morning first thing. I'd better be getting back."

Rather than offend her, my restraint seemed to have the opposite effect on Helen. "You're a gentleman, X. Do you know that?" With that, she kissed me on the lips and went inside.

MONDAY 9TH OCTOBER

The first poster went up today, advertising the end-of-term talent show. Applicants are invited to add their names, acts, and onstage experience to the A4 sheets Lisa the Repeater has kindly prepared.

TUESDAY 10TH OCTOBER

It was the Year 5 Dance Party tonight, and although it was supposed to be a school spirit team effort, as soon as the evening was underway, Geoff, Drake, and Matt quickly made their excuses and disappeared onto the dance floor in search of one of the 19 year four girls.

There was a perfect atmosphere to the whole event, and although that made me happy, I wasn't really in the mood for dancing, so I spent most of the evening sitting by the new school entrance chatting to Ms James. "I have to say, X, I'm proud of you. I know the last few weeks can't have been easy for you, but your conduct has been admirable," she said sincerely.

"Thank you, Ms James; that means a lot," I replied.

"Just one thing, though, X. You're only 16 once. You've organised this evening, and there is only half an hour remaining. Please stop talking to me at once and go and join your friends. That is an instruction, not a request," she said intently.

I saluted her and headed towards the hall to join the others. As I got to the dance floor, I felt slightly uncomfortable as fellow pupils started staring at me expectantly. Desperately, I looked around for Flan, but she was busily engaged snogging Rich Wilson, all round nice guy. As the record ended, Tony Dwyer, from behind the decks, said, "Luther Parkinson, please give it up for your school spirit."

Now, *everyone* was staring at me in anticipation—for what?

I had no idea. Tony put on 'Miss You Much' by Janet Jackson, and, as the situation became slightly uncomfortable, I started dancing. Well, sort of. Unfortunately, although the other pupils had started dancing again, they did it in a wide circle around me.

I froze because I had no idea what they were waiting for me to do. Thirty uncomfortable seconds passed before inspiration finally hit me. I started by pointing at my fellow pupils in time to the beat, and thankfully, they mimicked my actions. Next, I started waving my arms, and my fellow students did likewise. I then began working my way through various dance moves, duly mirrored. After pulling off a passable *robot*, I overstepped the mark by suggestively rubbing my hand over my groin. This move, I must report, was repeated by just a minority of the crowd and only members of the male contingent at that. At a loss as to what to do next, I looked at everyone helplessly and asked, "Will somebody dance with me?"

Hands were raised; however, Helen Heaven stepped forward from the crowd and joined me in the middle.

"Thank you," I whispered in her ear as we started dancing.

"My pleasure," she said, putting her hands on my waist and pulling me in closer as she did. Helen then proceeded to brush herself against my groyne as Rachael had done all those months ago.

A little concerned, I asked, "Err, what about your boyfriend?"

"He's not here!" she said, smiling brightly.

That was a perfect answer, X; on you go. Remember, 'Never let a good thing slip through your fingers again!'

Resolved, I joined in the dance, and, as the song finished, I was about to acknowledge our audience when Helen started kissing me. As no other action seemed appropriate, I kissed her right back. The rest of year five clapped and cheered in approval.

Rachael's gone, and she isn't coming back. My period of celibacy is at an end!

WEDNESDAY 11TH OCTOBER

School spirit has never felt better. I bolted out of bed this morning, eager to get to school.

"So, are the two of you an item then?" Lisa asked in form group.

I shrugged. "I'm not sure; I think she has a boyfriend, but he works away, and she gets lonely. I'm so busy with school spirit work that I probably wouldn't have time for a girlfriend. If you think about it, this could really work out well for the three of us. You never know; maybe all relationships will be like this in the future."

The kissing had gone on after the dance party last night. We snogged outside the school, on her front doorstep, and finally in her kitchen. Still, I wasn't sure if that meant there would be a repeat performance soon. However, my fears were quickly allayed as, at lunchtime, Helen walked straight up to me and planted her lips on mine, even though I was in mid-conversation with JG.

"Walk me home tonight?" she asked after our lips had parted.

After more post-school snogging, Helen suggested we skip school tomorrow, and I spent the day around hers. There was more than a hint of sexual promise in the invite; however, duty called. "I'd love to, Helen, but tomorrow's the big one. Hug an

Asian Day".

"Obviously," she replied a little sourly.

THURSDAY 12TH OCTOBER

"Call it off, X!" The head of year five was angrier than I'd ever seen her.

"Ms James, *please* remember, this is an attempt to integrate the school; I don't think we should give up on it just yet," I pleaded.

She took a deep breath to regain her composure. "Integration is a process that takes time; it *can't* be achieved on a whim. Now, I have 37 terrified children who have barricaded themselves in the computer suite because the rest of the school won't desist from molesting them. *Please* see reason and cancel it."

"Dr Harris *has* approved this project," I said defensively.

"Oh, he's madder than you are!" she said snappily. What followed can be best described as an awkward silence. "*Obviously*, I didn't mean for that to come out *quite* the way it did, X," Ms James said coolly.

"*Obviously*, Ms., and even if you had, he wouldn't have heard about it from these lips," I said sincerely.

"Well, that is appreciated, X. And listen, I know your intentions were not impure today. Your idea is not wrong; as such, it is *simply stupid*. *Please*, just come with me to the secretary's office and make the announcement over the school's Tannoy system."

"Good afternoon, Luther Parkinson; this is your school spirit speaking. Thank you for your enthusiastic support of our inaugural Hug an Asian Day. Unfortunately, due to health and safety concerns, I must close the event prematurely and insist that all interracial embracing cease *immediately*. However, I hope to announce an alternative date sometime soon... *Ouch!* Oh Christ, that *really* hurt, Ms... or perhaps not. Thank you!"

"Ms James, I can't believe you stamped on my toe!" I said this as soon as I had turned the microphone off. The pain was so great that I was hopping up and down in agony.

"It serves you bloody right, X. I mean it—if I ever hear the words 'Hug an Asian Day' from your lips again, then that heel will end up contacting an altogether more sensitive part of your anatomy," she said firmly.

Really, she wasn't joking—there was actual intent in her face.

"Will there be anything else today, Ms, before I limp back to classes?" I asked sarcastically.

Ms James sighed. "Yes, there is, X. Could you and Miss Wells *please* tone down your public displays of affection for one another? They seem to be having a strange effect on certain members of the male teaching staff."

SATURDAY 14TH OCTOBER

A fter we'd sunk our third can of nuclear-strength lager tonight, JG hit me with a bombshell. "X, I'm gay."
"How do you know?" I asked in bemusement.

Friends, here's a little advice: If someone close to you chooses to share the same information that JG did with me tonight, I am now reliably informed that you *should not* ask that question. Also, you may be wise to avoid my follow-up enquiry. "So, how gay are you?"

Finally, after my somewhat inebriated brain had absorbed the enormity of the information, I could be a more effective confidant. "Who else knows? I asked.

"Just you at the moment," he replied.

"OK, I understand you want to keep this on a need-to-know basis, but I'm 99% sure we can trust Flan. Also, when I was on holiday this summer, I acted gay in front of this girl who fancied me, as I was celibate then. She was *so* convinced by my performance that she undressed in front of me twice, so I think I might really be *one* with the homosexual consciousness, you know?" I thought JG might be impressed by this, but he just shook his head in dismay.

Just before leaving, I asked, "Listen, just one more thing, JG, I'm curious. Do you fancy me at all?"

JG sighed. "You are tragic sometimes, X. Do you know that?"

"Humour me, please?" I asked.

After giving me a quick look up and down, he answered, "A little bit, I suppose."

'A little bit'? He's not 100% gay. Clearly!

SUNDAY 15TH OCTOBER

I woke to find a note from my parents saying they had gone out to the Lake District for the day. After a quick bike ride, I rang Helen Heaven and invited her over for lunch, and when I said lunch, I meant sex.

Fifteen minutes before she arrived, the heavens opened, and I feared my sleazy little scheme was about to fall at the first hurdle; however, 10 minutes later, the doorbell rang.

"Let me in; I'm soaked!" Helen said it in a cute little voice.

I stood aside, allowing her to enter. "Purely in the interest of your well-being, I think we should get you out of those clothes immediately," I said with mock concern.

She giggled, "OK then."

Helen and I's relationship is not exactly what I'd call profound. I'd go as far as to say that it is entirely superficial. Our conversations run no deeper than, "Did you see that thing on TV last night?"

"No."

"It was ok!"

"Oh."

Still, it's a more than effective distraction to see me through this challenging time, and it was on this very matter that I was contemplating, lying in bed, quite contentedly, with the school beauty, when the doorbell inconveniently rang.

"Are you going to answer that, X?" Helen asked.

"If it was important, I'm sure they'd kick it down," I replied.

Helen hit me with a pillow. "Go and see who it is, you lazy sod."

Reluctantly, I dragged myself up. My T-shirt had been thrown lord knows where in the passionate frenzy that had followed Helen's arrival, so I just slipped my jeans on and headed downstairs. Whoever this ill-timed caller was, they would have to suffer my half-nakedness. When I opened the door, though, my mouth hit the floor.

"Rachael?" I said it in utter disbelief. The rain was still hammering down, and she was soaked.

"I've run away. I'm sick of her dragging me up and down the country on her whims. I need a place to stay," she said desperately.

X, I am your inner voice, and I must regrettably inform you that there is no way out of this one, Sunshine.

"Right, OK, well..." sentences were refusing to form.

"Can I come in, please?" she asked expectantly.

"Err... of course," I replied hesitantly.

Rachael stepped into the hallway. "Why are you undressed, X?"

She didn't have to wait long for the answer. Helen *clearly* remembered where she had thrown my T-shirt as she proceeded to walk into the hallway wearing nothing aside from it. "Is everything OK?" she asked innocently.

"Oh, I might have *bloody* guessed!" Rachael yelled. Storming out of the door she had just walked through, she took off at a pace.

I looked at Helen in disbelief, but she frowned and said, "Don't just stand there like an idiot; X, go after her!"

So, shirtless and shoeless, I sprinted after her through the lashing rain.

"Rachael, wait up, Rachael." I yelled.

As she had a large rucksack on her back, slowing her down, I caught up with her quickly enough. Taking her by the shoulder, I turned her to face me.

"Just *once; I* needed you to be there for me," she barked at me.

Frustrated, I asked, "Rachael, how was I supposed to know you were coming? Don't you call ahead in the south?"

"Three *bloody* weeks; that's all it took for you to find someone else. Did I mean so little to you?" Rachael spoke, crying.

Trying to remain calm, I said, "Listen, this isn't what it looks like. Just come back to the house and let me help you out."

Miserably, through floods of tears, she said, "I came back *for you*, but you don't even care about me."

I was also angry. "If you think she means a fraction of what you do to me, please run right back home. I mean it, Rachael. It broke my heart when you left, and I thought I would never see you again."

Rachael looked me up and down and then said intently, "X, you *really* need to put on a shirt."

She was correct; I was bloody freezing. "Please, just come back to mine, will you? Let's get you dry, and we'll sort things out, I promise."

Rachael shrugged, and I put my arm around her and led her home. When we got back inside, Helen had dressed in some of my clothes and was standing ready with a large bath towel.

"Thanks," I said, making as if to take it.

"This is for Rachael; you can get your own," Helen said sharply.

By the time I'd dried myself, dressed, and got back downstairs, the sisterhood was in full effect. "X, don't just stand there; make the poor girl a cup of tea," Helen said with an irritable sigh.

After Rachael had changed into fresh clothes and the storm had finished, Helen took charge of the situation, "She doesn't want to go to her stepdad's place, so I'm going to take her to Ms James'," she said.

"We need to let her Mum know she's OK," I suggested.

Helen rolled her eyes. "Oh, really, I'd never have thought of that, X."

I'm unsure how I became the bad guy in this scene, though I'm 85% certain I was the victim of sexism this afternoon. After they'd left, I went upstairs, laid on my bed, and tried to make sense of everything that had just happened. Clearly, it had all been too much for me, as I was fast asleep within three minutes.

Later, I retrieved Rachael's clothes from the tumble dryer, ironed them, and headed to Ms James's house.

When Catherine opened the door, she looked at me and sneered. "And here he is, the *Marx Brother* of love himself. Nice work this afternoon, *Romeo*."

"Oh, come off it; how was I supposed to know she was coming back? Besides, *you* planted that meme in my head about not letting a good thing slip through my fingers again," I said irritably.

Catherine rolled her eyes. "It was a guide to life, not an

instruction to jump into bed with the first willing volunteer."

I took a deep breath to control my temper. "Is she here?"

"She is, but she doesn't want to see you," Catherine said flatly.

"I just *knew* you were going to say that," I said defiantly.

"You're getting good at this now, aren't you?" she smirked.

I handed her the bag. "Her clothes; I pressed them."

Catherine took the rucksack from me. "X, don't get yourself all worked up. This one's going to take time, OK?"

MONDAY 16TH OCTOBER

Ms James didn't come to school today, so I am none the wiser about Rachael's situation.

Someone, and when I say *someone*, I mean Helen Heaven, has spread the news of yesterday's events throughout the school, and, as such, the male contingent has been rapturously applauding me for performing the miracle of bedding her, while the female half has taken to looking upon me as vermin, the very same ones, I may add, who were applauding Helen and me when we kissed at the dance party last week. On more than one occasion today, I heard the word 'Snake' being hissed at me as I walked along the corridor.

At lunch, Flan came and sat next to me. "Want to talk about it?" she asked delicately.

I reluctantly shrugged in ascent.

"X, there is, I'll admit, an *enormous* amount of bad timing in this unfortunate incident, but I must say, as your friend, this does make you just ever so slightly cheap," Flan advised.

"I was just trying to take my mind off Rachael, that's all." I pleaded.

Flan sighed deeply. "Next time, maybe try fishing, X?"

I tried saying thanks to Helen Heaven for helping with Rachael yesterday, but when I approached her, she said, "Don't stand anywhere near me, you *awful* boy!"

TUESDAY 17TH OCTOBER

"Don't sit next to me; you are a filthy animal," Lisa spat as I was about to take the place beside her in form group this morning.

"Right, *fine*," I said sulkily, and I decided to go and sit next to Driffid instead.

As I approached, he smiled at me. "You're one *bad* motherfucker, do you know that X?" he said, genuinely impressed.

"Thanks, Driff," I said sincerely, patting my mungo friend on the shoulder.

"Mail for X," Mr Crackett said, holding an envelope. I went to the front and took it from him. "I imagine it'll be Rachael William's suicide note," he said, and he promptly burst into hysteria.

Thankfully, form group was quick as Dr Harris took the year five assembly this morning. I would have declined the invitation to speak out of my genuine fear of being stoned by the female contingent of the audience. However, the letter I had just received contained exciting news that might reverse my recent opinion poll dive. I managed to grab Dr H just before he got underway and update him on the latest developments in the school spirit revolution.

After the head had delivered a general, keep up the excellent work message, he said, "Just one further announcement: year five, Rachael Williams, will be re-joining the school from Thursday." He paused for thought. "Williams? That's New Girl isn't it, X, my boy?" he asked, catching my eye.

"That is correct, sir," I replied.

"Well," Dr Harris said. "I'll be damned—I suppose she'll just have to be New New Girl now then," and he started chuckling. "*Right*, I would like to hand you over to School Spirit."

As I stood up, all the boys cheered wildly while the female contingent of the hall booed and hissed as loudly as they could.

When I reached the lectern, I held up my hand to silence them. "Thank you for the mixed reception," I said holding up the letter. "I have received some good news. Though, after my treatment at the hands of certain individuals yesterday and this morning, I was tempted, after reading the contents of this envelope, to set it on fire and throw it out of the nearest window." I paused to let the murmuring subside, "I only have one question for you today, Luther Parkinson. Would you lot like to be on TV?" I asked grumpily. There was an instant buzz of excitement. "I didn't hear you, Luther Parkinson; what did you say?"

"Yes!" they shouted back.

"Yes, *who*?" I asked teasingly.

"Yes, School Spirit," they roared back.

"A few weeks ago, I wrote to the local news station and mentioned how the large turnouts at our school sports matches were positively impacting our performances on the field, and they would like to come along on Thursday and film us." There was a swell of excitement around the hall. "My next question, Luther Parkinson, is simple. Will there be *any* further mention of that unfortunate incident I was *innocently* caught up in on Sunday?"

The hall mumbled, "No, School Spirit."

"I didn't hear you, Luther Parkinson," I said coyly.

"No, School Spirit!" they roared so loudly that I couldn't prevent a big grin from breaking across my face, "I just have one last question for you, Luther Parkinson—who loves you?"

"School Spirit!" they yelled back.

"I didn't hear you, Luther Parkinson," I said with my hand cupped to my ear.

Honestly, I could have gone on like this for hours. Still, morality be damned, I say; all people really want is to be on the telly.

After I'd finished, Dr Harris retook the stage. "Thanks to School Spirit for, as I'm sure you'll all agree, Luther Parkinson was, an almost *remorselessly* smooth announcement. We will now bring the assembly to a close by singing hymn 7, 'Back to Life' by Soul II Soul.

It took more than a bit of time to persuade Dr Harris to switch from Christian hymns to pop songs, and, admittedly, we are on a strictly trial basis only at present. However, I think we've struck gold, as everybody loves it!

At lunch, I was in the old school hall playing a game of table tennis with Drake when Helen Heaven came over and started kissing me—as I said, *entirely* superficial. I was also pleased to note that there wasn't so much a murmur of disapproval from the other year fives during our somewhat elongated reunion.

Only now that I'm back at home, has the news sunk in. Rachael's back!

WEDNESDAY 18TH OCTOBER

I took a trip to the drama studio at morning break to see Mrs Gates and get back into Rachael's good books. "As she won the part fair and square, now that Rachael's returned, it's hers by rights. It would be wrong not to give it back, possibly even illegal," I said intently.

Mrs Gates looked at me in bemusement. "Hardly illegal, School Spirit, but it's up to you. If you insist on re-casting Miss Williams, you can also tell Wendy Moore, who will be heartbroken."

Heartbroken was an understatement; I couldn't stop the girl from crying. Perhaps a busy corridor wasn't the best place to break the news to her after all. "It's nothing personal, Wendy; it's just that the play will be much better with Rachael in it than you," I said, as gently as I could.

My efforts were fruitless, though I couldn't get the girl to see sense.

"Oh, Christ, what have *you* done now?" a passing Flan said upon spying on Wendy's somewhat hysterical distress.

"Nothing, just a casting change for the school play, that's all," I said innocently.

"Go away, X!" Helen said it threateningly as she put her arm around Wendy.

Quickly, I added, "You don't see a Grand National runner crying just because he didn't win the race, do you?"

"*Now, X!*" Flan said it rather scarily.

Flan wasn't the only one to lose her temper with me today; when JG caught up with me at lunch, he looked furious. "Stop being bloody chivalrous to me, X!" he whispered angrily.

"Sorry?" I asked in wonder.

"*Stop* holding doors open for me; *don't* pull chairs out when I'm about to sit down, and I *do not* need your help putting my coat on. Ok?"

"Right, not the way forward, then?" I asked meekly.

"No!" JG looked down at my hand, which I gently placed on his upper arm as we spoke. "Stop doing *that!*"

<u>3 am</u>

I was woken from my sleep by a most alarming thought. If placed in the wrong hands, the power of school spirit could be put to significant misuse. I will visit Dr Harris first thing tomorrow morning. Together, I'm sure we'll come up with the right solution.

THURSDAY 19TH OCTOBER

I can name my successor. It's a school ruling, written in stone; only God Almighty himself could strip me of the right to it, and to the best of my knowledge, he's not interfering with everyday school matters just yet.

"Well, at least you kept my seat free for me, if not your bed," Rachael said, taking her place next to me in English this morning.

"Listen, Rach, before you start... " I began.

"I'm pulling your leg; I was very emotional on Sunday. After all, you weren't to know," she said pleasantly. "You were getting on with your life, that's all."

Suspiciously quick forgiveness; something's going on here.

"Besides, I'm back with Rob and 100% *in love*," she said smugly.

Oh yes, the old 'I'm going to date someone I don't like just to piss you off' manoeuvre. Well, Miss Williams, two can play that game.

"Oh," I said disinterestedly. "So, where are you living?"

"Ms James' for now; Mum will be back next week. We'll be finding a place for Gran somewhere locally," she said.

"Wow! You must have put your foot down," I said, sounding impressed.

Rachael turned to me. "I told you, X, *I'm* a Luther Parkinson girl!"

Practically, the whole school turned out for the football match, and Geoff and the boys dutifully delivered a 5-0 thrashing for the TV cameras. As the Lutherettes' uniforms arrived, they were more modestly dressed than usual. In addition, their practice is paying off, and now, on occasion, they look coordinated.

When the local news reporter was interviewing Dr Harris, he called me over to him. "Here he is, our school spirit, X," the head said proudly. We owe him a debt of thanks for all his hard work."

The TV reporter shoved a microphone under my nose,."How did you get the name X?"

"It's a long story. Actually, that's not true; it's a short story, but it's really underwhelming," I said flatly.

"What exactly is school spirit?" he asked.

"It's a movement of the school, by the school, and for the school," I replied.

"The school's motto, *Semper ruminat inmunda cibum tuum ante deglutire*, could you tell our viewers what it means?" He asked finally.

"Always chew your food before you swallow."

FRIDAY 20TH OCTOBER

"Are you seeing Helen this weekend?" Rachael asked in English.

"No, her boyfriend's home from the rigs at the moment, so I can't," I replied absently.

"Well, I really would like my boyfriend and best friend to get to know one another, so will you come out with us tonight?"

"Fine, but I'm bringing Flan as backup," I replied.

"Whatever," Rachael replied abruptly.

Somewhat predictably, the destination for drinks tonight was that favourite haunt of the eager underage drinker, the arts centre bar. It started as an OK evening. Rachael and Flan gossiped, while Rob and I managed to converse well. He wasn't drinking, as Marketon High is playing Luther Parkinson tomorrow morning at rugby. It was only when the girls disappeared off to the toilets for what seemed like an excessive amount of time that things suddenly turned sour.

"Listen, X, I appreciate you and Rachael were close, but she's *my* girlfriend now, and I don't want you seeing her anymore," Rob said, trying his best to sound threatening.

I glared at him. "Not a chance," I said clearly.

"Listen, X; it's obvious you still have a thing for her. Unfortunately, you didn't have the stones to do anything about it. Stay away from her, or I will make you sorry. Is that clear?"

he said, staring back at me fiercely.

"Listen, Rob, please just understand one thing: if you ever suggest that I keep away from *that* girl again, I will put you down so hard, you'll feel like a fat man has just fallen from the sky and landed right on top of you. Am I making myself clear?"

"You're all talk, X," he sneered.

Really, on that front, I'm not.

At that point, the girls returned, and we feigned civility for the rest of the evening.

SATURDAY 21ST OCTOBER

No doubt, since it was the start of the half-term holidays, rather disappointingly, only Geoff, Matt, Rachael, three of The Lutherettes, and I turned out to watch the game this morning. Still, not one single soul turned up to support Marketon High, which was pleasing to note.

As Rachael's rather possessive boyfriend was playing, I spent the entire game talking to her. Occasionally, I put my arm around her and asked if she was warm enough.

"What's got into you? You're being quite the gentleman today," she asked with a smile.

Really, I'm not!

Marketon High edged the game with a disputed late try. Big Wilson and the opposition's teacher were still shouting at each other about it on the pitch when Matt, Geoff, and I followed our lads into the dressing room to offer our words of consolation.

Luther Parkinson 0: Marketon High 1

"Well played, Luther Parkinson. You did the school proud. Sorry, you didn't have the support you deserved," I said, patting Stuart Moor on the back. Suddenly, I was grabbed by the throat and thrust against the wall.

"You've got this coming, X," Rob said, glaring at me intently. Out of the corner of my eye, I saw Matt and Geoff move towards him.

"Wait! Leave him alone; I'll handle this," and with that, I

dislodged his hand from my throat and punched him in the jaw. He went down so quickly that I thought it would be the end of the matter. However, at that point, one of their forwards hit me so hard that I thought I would pass out. Then, the whole place just *erupted*. As soon as I was back on my feet, I leapt onto the back of a guy who had Matt in a headlock. I repeatedly hit him on the head until he let Matt go, at which point School Spirit 2 punched him so hard that his assailant and I crashed to the floor.

Stuart Moor was magnificent; one moment, he was trapped in a corner by three of theirs. Then, seemingly seconds later, he stood triumphantly over some rather sorry-looking individuals.

It took the combined efforts of Matt, Geoff, and I to wrestle the big guy who had hit me to the floor. While engaged in the task, we heard Big Wilson roar, "What the hell is going on here?"

The scuffling ceased immediately, and everyone looked fearfully towards the muscular gym teacher. At that moment, he was joined by his opposite number, who sneered, "Oh, this is bloody typical. Luther Parkinson, bad losers on the pitch and bad losers off the pitch."

The Marketon High teacher enjoyed the moment for precisely three seconds before Big Wilson's fist connected with his jaw, and the changing room duly exploded again.

It took another five minutes, but with seven of us still standing and all our opponents felled, I put my fist in the air, lowered my head, and shouted, *"Luther Parkinson rules!"*

A wheezing voice piped up from the floor: "Actually, there were more of you than there were of us," but Geoff dutifully kicked the big mouth in the stomach before he could say anything else.

Luther Parkinson 1: Marketon High 1

After the enemy had traipsed miserably back to their minibus, Big Wilson sat us all down in the changing rooms for some good, old-fashioned man-chat.

"Lads, what happened today happened," he opined.

And there you have it, right there—surely the single finest nugget of gym teacher philosophy in the history of education.

"They started it; you all stood up for one another and your school. I'm proud of every one of you. However, for several reasons, my career in particular, I would appreciate it if we kept this battle within these four walls," Big Wilson said, and there was a murmur of ascent from us, the victorious.

In the yard, safely out of earshot of the others, Matt, Geoff, and I joined Rachael, Helen, Lisa, and Penny.

"Go on then; what happened?" Flan asked with a mixture of concern and interest.

"Massive fight, we won!" Geoff said it proudly with his hands in the air.

Flan then caught sight of me, and her face dropped in horror. "Oh my god, what happened to your face, X? Right, you three, back to mine, *now*!"

"Stop doing that—it really bloody hurts," I said as Flan placed an icepack against my face.

Looking at me with concern, Rachael asked, "Did *he* do this to you?"

"No," I replied, "his big, bloody mate did."

Flan's kitchen was a hive of activity. Her Mum was helping by treating the wounded, while her dad was more interested in learning about the details of the fight.

"I think you're all overgrown children," Rachael said dismissively.

Irritably, Geoff said, "Rachael, your bloody boyfriend started this. X acted in self-defence."

"Is this true?" Rachael asked Matt, hopeful she was more likely to scare the truth from a year-four boy.

"Rob attacked X," Matt said sincerely.

Rachael turned to me again. "And you did *nothing* to provoke him?"

"I *only* went there to commiserate with *our* boys," I replied intently.

"Hold on a second, Rachael," Flan said irritably. "You know me, I'm no fan of violence, but I'm with the boys on this one. Your nutter boyfriend just turned a harmless game of rugby into a bloodbath this morning. It's *bang* out of order."

"Well, *obviously*, he's not going to be my boyfriend anymore after this," Rachael said defensively.

Luther Parkinson 2: Marketon High 1

"Good!" Geoff said. "Because I tell you what, Luther Parkinson has declared war on Marketon High!"

Pete, Helen's dad, who was studying the damage to my face from behind his daughter, looked at me and said, "That one's going to need a trip to the hospital, young man."

Flan kindly stayed with me for the four hours I was in A&E. After being given an X-ray, I was reassured that there appeared to be no lasting damage.

I've got to stop writing, as my face *really* hurts.

SUNDAY 22ND OCTOBER

I could hardly sit up this morning. "Stay in bed; you've got a concussion, that's all. That will teach you to stay out of fights!" Mum said it disapprovingly.

MONDAY 23RD OCTOBER

This isn't a concussion. I can barely stand. Mum sent for the doctor.

TUESDAY 24TH OCTOBER

A concussion doesn't usually come with a fever. A blood test was administered.

WEDNESDAY 25TH OCTOBER

"You will try and get better, won't you, love? Your dad and I are off on holiday next week."

Don't worry, you bastards, leave me here to die.

THURSDAY 26TH OCTOBER

Even worse, I can hardly move. My immune system has disappeared. I've seen the ads, and I know what this is. My friends, this is where carefree lovemaking will lead you. Live life fully, but please take the precautions I never did!

FRIDAY 27TH OCTOBER

It's not AIDS, as it happens, but glandular fever, the mother of all doses. Whatever I wrote yesterday, forget it, OK?

FRIDAY 3RD NOVEMBER

I really thought I'd died on Monday morning. I woke up in an unfamiliar box room, which, I calculated from the standard dimensions, was undoubtedly situated within a post-war, three-bedroomed, semi-detached house.

Oh, fucking great, I've got the whole atheism thing wrong, and I'm in heaven, where you get issued with the exact accommodation you had on earth.

What am I thinking? I'd never be allowed in there. This is the other place where everyone lives in a three-bedroomed, post-war semi in Marketon.

Pinching myself a few times, I eventually convinced myself I was still on *this side* rather than the *other.* The fever had abated somewhat, but I wasn't sure I had the energy to sit up.

I tried calling out, but my mouth was too dry, and I made a soft droning sound. Eventually, I stretched out and knocked a bottle of water from the chest of drawers beside the bed onto the floor.

The trick worked. I heard the pad of feet on the stairs, and the door opened, "You scared the living hell out of me, X!" It was Karen.

OK, back to the heaven and hell hypothesis.

"You didn't call about squash last week, and I got worried, so I came over. Your mum said you were too ill to see people, but I just barged in. Anyway, she said they had a holiday booked and seemed keen not to miss it, so I offered to look after you.

Indeed, a new zenith for parental indifference right there?

"Dad helped me get you over here. That was Saturday afternoon. You were out of it, and you just kept getting hotter and hotter. I had you in an ice bath at one point. Then you just collapsed asleep. You've been out for nearly thirty-six hours, X."

I still couldn't talk, but I pointed to my lips.

"Drink?" Karen asked, and I nodded feebly.

Three glasses of water later, I could finally talk. "Karen, thank you. I see you finally got the box room cleared out, then." I said that and promptly fell asleep again.

The doctor said on Wednesday, "You've got it as bad as you can get it. It will take a long time to bounce back from this; there's nothing to do but rest, I'm afraid."

It's a blessed relief that Karen and I have been intimate in the past, as my trips to the toilet require assistance.

As I started feeling slightly claustrophobic this morning in the small room, Karen helped me down the stairs and put me on the sofa. "X, I've got your house keys. Is there anything you'd like me to fetch?" she asked.

"Books, computer, and Frank Sinatra, please," I replied.

When she returned, she complained, "That *bloody* computer weighs a tonne, X!"

I replied, "Sorry."

"Don't worry, it's fine. Oh, and X, sorry to inform you about this, but you're dead," she laughed.

According to my guardian, at least eight bouquets on my front lawn express sympathy for my passing. "Did you ring the school?" I asked curiously.

"No, I thought your parents would have done it," she said distractedly.

"In that case, can I use your phone, please?" I asked politely.

"This is Catherine James speaking; how can I help?"

In the spookiest voice I could muster, I said, "Ms James, this is X; I'm calling you from the *other side*. You must continue the work of school spirit, or I will haunt you in this life and the next."

"Oh, good god, you're a ridiculous boy. Where are you? I've been worried sick," she asked.

SATURDAY 4TH NOVEMBER

"Your parents will be back tonight," Karen said brightly, opening the curtains in my room this morning.

As I enjoyed my stay, I casually asked, "Is there any chance I could remain here for a bit longer?"

Karen seemed delighted rather than looking put out. "For as long as you want."

Admittedly, it would have been nice if my parents had put up a bit more of a fight to get me back home; however, as they both have work commitments, they jumped at the chance for Karen to keep a hold of me.

WEDNESDAY 8TH NOVEMBER

'Long, slow recovery', they got that right. I'm still exhausted and can hardly stand by myself.

THURSDAY 9TH NOVEMBER

Rachael showed up today. When she walked into Karen's lounge, she looked angry and concerned.

"I'll leave you guys to it. I'm just going to pop to the shops," Karen said delicately from the doorway, "Do you two want anything?"

"Twix, please," I said politely.

"Lion Bar." Rachael said testily before adding, "Please."

"Do you have any idea how worried I've been? I barely slept for four nights straight," Rachael said irately after the front door had closed. "You could have rung. And what the hell are you doing here of all places?" She said, looking around in bemusement.

"Karen's been an angel. She makes me soup," I replied.

"*I can make soup!*" Rachael said it furiously.

Afterwards, once she'd calmed down, we had a reasonable conversation. Before we got down to the day-to-day trivialities of school, though, there was something I wanted to know. "Rachael, exactly how did I die?"

"John Benzies, a year two student who lives in your street, came in on Monday after half-term and told everyone that he'd seen the ambulance services carry your corpse out of the house and said that, afterwards, your parents had fled the country with grief. As no one was home, we had no way of checking. Though *I* had my doubts all along, X, really, I couldn't imagine your mum and dad being *that* upset," Rachael said thoughtfully.

I know young Benzies, a curious lad, ginger and freckled; he once tried to sell his family's dog to me for five pounds as he had grown tired of walking it daily. Honestly, I'm unsure whether his tale impressed or angered me. Regardless, order must be maintained, so I resolved to cuff him around the ear with considerable force.

"Right; any other news worth hearing?" I asked.

"Mr Bennett's girlfriend has dumped him, and now, everywhere he goes, he's followed by year five girls keen to apply for the vacancy," Rachel informed me.

WEDNESDAY 15TH NOVEMBER

Back home, Karen received an offer of work for the first time in six months, and although she seemed sincere when she said she wasn't fussed, I persuaded her to take the job.

As I can now reach the toilet unaided, Mum has decided I'm OK to look after myself during the day and has duly returned to work.

Rachael has been over today; I don't think she liked visiting me at Karen's. "I made you chicken soup and got up early to do it, too," she proudly said.

"Wow, you did all that for me?" I asked in wonder.

"Yes, of course I did. How does Karen do it?"

I was slightly confused by the question. "Err, she opens a can."

Before she left, she said, "Other people want to see you. Is that OK?"

Rachael makes the best soup I have ever tasted.

THURSDAY 16TH NOVEMBER

"Now, I've never made soup before, so please don't be too critical," Flan said, placing a plastic container beside my computer.

"Thanks, Flan; how's school?" I asked.

"Well, everyone is talking about the Battle of the Gymnasium," Helen said.

"Sorry?" I asked.

Flan sighed. "That's what they're calling it. You know me, X, I don't like violence, but even *I* have to say that school spirit has never been stronger since we won that fight. Geoff and Matt are doing everything they can to wind up Marketon High, obviously in your name."

Pulling the duvet over my head, I said, "I'm ill; I'm not sure I want to know."

FRIDAY 17TH NOVEMBER

"You know, X, it was only when I thought you were dead that I realised how much I liked you. We should give it another go when you're better; we look good together," Helen Heaven said thoughtfully.

"Thanks, Helen, but for once in my teenage existence, girls are the furthest thing from my mind," I replied.

"Ok, well, food for thought; I put some soup in the fridge for you. Mum made it, so God knows what it tastes like."

SATURDAY 18TH NOVEMBER

Drake placed a can of soup on my desk and said kindly, "I heard you were a fan! There were two cans, I have to admit, but I got peckish this afternoon."

"Thanks!" I said.

"Say, X, as you've got nothing else to do. Would you mind helping me learn the lines for the play?" he asked expectantly.

SUNDAY 19TH NOVEMBER

"I brought you some bread. I thought you could use it to soak up all the soup," JG said, depositing a loaf on my desk when he arrived in this afternoon.

MONDAY 20TH NOVEMBER

"Another month of bed rest is the only answer, I'm afraid, X. If you push yourself too early, you'll just delay your recovery." The doctor advised.
So, if I can't go to school, the school must come to me.

TUESDAY 21ST NOVEMBER

"There you go; there's a file full of stuff there that should keep you busy," Rachael said, handing me the schoolwork I'd requested. "Also, Mr Crackett asked me to relay to you that he has never been happier in his professional life than during these past three weeks."

"Kind of him to say," I said, smiling.

"Anyway," she said, withdrawing *Much Ado about Nothing* from her bag, "nothing comes for free in this life, X."

FRIDAY 1ST DECEMBER

Dr Harris has had a heart attack. His condition is stable, but Rachael says the word around school is that he's unlikely to ever return. As the deputy head role is vacant, Ms James has been appointed acting head.

I am low.

FRIDAY 8TH DECEMBER

My recovery is almost complete. Thankfully, I've managed to get back on top of my schoolwork, as those exams next year have suddenly started to loom large.

Over the past week, I have reread *this,* which has made me think. I started this year with a grand plan to find a mate. Within less than 24 hours, I had found someone who perfectly embodied both meanings of that word, and, most critically, she *really* liked me. Yet here we are, almost a year on, and Rachael and mine's relationship is still *strictly* platonic. If *this*, through design or chance, has ended up in the public domain, you may be reading it and thinking, *This guy is an idiot!* You'd be correct, but do me one favour before you sit in on the final judgment. Truthfully, document a year of your life without editing all the bad stuff- the thoughtlessness, selfishness, humiliations, bad decisions, wasted opportunities —and see how you get on. Also, you might learn something about yourself, because I think *I* finally have.

However, the best thing about reading *this,* I've just realised, is that I can still influence the ending. So, I've set myself the target of finally winning Rachael's heart by no later than midnight on New Year's Eve.

Aside from soul-searching, my time has been spent reading, watching the collapse of communism on TV, reading *Much Ado About Nothing* countless times, and, most importantly, finally completing the Rubik's Cube without cheating; in the end, it only took three weeks to figure it out.

As I've decided, against the doctor's orders, to return to school on Monday, I am now free to leave the house. My first port of call tonight was Rachael's.

I hadn't seen Alison in nearly three months, and, as always, she made me a coffee on arrival, and we sat chatting for a quarter of an hour or so. "Don't let me keep any longer, X; I think she's in her room," she said eventually.

Rachael was soundly asleep on her bed. I was about to beat a retreat back downstairs when I realised how exhausted the walk had made me, so I lay down on the bed next to her, and within seconds, I was soundly asleep too.

When I opened my eyes, Rachael, who was still beside me, was staring at me intently. "That was weird. You just appeared," she said quietly.

"Good-weird or bad-weird?" I inquired.

"Good weird!" she said firmly. "You shouldn't be up and about, though, X."

"I'm fine," I assured her. "Anyway, I just wanted you to know that I'm sorry."

Rachael had a quizzical look on her face. "What have you done now?"

"Nothing new; that's one advantage of being ill; misbehaving is much harder. I'm sorry for any occasion on which I made you feel like you weren't the most important person on planet Earth to me because that is exactly what you are," I said honestly.

Rachael looked at me with wonder. "Wow! You should get ill more often, X."

"Right," I said, getting up, "in that case, I'm quitting while I'm ahead."

Sounding disappointed, she asked, "Where are you going?"

I got off the bed. "I'm going to see my other favourite people."

She asked, with concern, "You're not thinking about coming to school next week, are you?"

"Yes, I can't do another week at home; I really can't."

"Well, take Monday off then; break yourself in gently."

I called around at Flan's, JG's, and Drake's, who advised me to gently break myself in and not come to school on Monday.

Do they think I'm stupid?

SUNDAY 10TH DECEMBER

This evening, I visited Dr Harris in the hospital. Ms James kindly sent a request to his wife last week on my behalf, and Mrs Harris rang today to say that I was welcome to go along. Sadly, Dr Harris no longer looks good for a man his age. Instead, he is now being kept alive by tubes and enmeshed by indifferent machines' wires. Although he could not sit up, he could talk freely; at least some of his old spirit remained.

"I brought you grapes, sir," I said gently as I leaned close to my headmaster.

"What's that, 'grapes', you say, my boy? Very kind of you, but I need to stand; legs; you should have brought me legs, X," he said in a wheezy voice. "I can't run a school from here; this will never do. Tell me, has *she* ruined the place yet?"

"I don't know, sir; I've been a little under the weather myself, sir," I replied softly.

His eyes widened in realisation. "Ah, yes, X, I remember now. It came for us both at the same time. This all makes sense now. Still, my boy, you look better on it than old Dr Wilberforce H. Harris JP does, eh?"

"You look fine, sir. I'm convinced you'll be back on your feet in no time," I lied.

"What's that, 'back on your feet', you say, my boy? That's the spirit, X. I knew I could always count on you, of course. I rather like the sound of that. Another term, maybe? You and me together, the old team, one last hurrah, eh?"

"It would be my honour, sir; just say the word, and I'll be right by your side again," I said as brightly as I could, even though I could feel the tears burning to be out.

As I readied myself to leave, he asked, "Really, X, I know you have your own damn strange ideas, so tell me, what do you think is waiting for me there on the other side?"

I turned to face him for the last time and, still fighting back the emotion, replied solemnly, "A school, I would like to imagine, sir, a rather grand old school. There'll be a boy waiting for you. A year one and a rather apart sort. He's overweight, too, but put a racket in his hand, sir, and he'll soon run most of it off. He'll cause no end of trouble, too, but rest assured, he's not the malicious kind. He'll usually just be looking to get sent to your office. You see, he'll grow fond of his time there. Although he may not understand many of the things you say, sir, I know he'll love listening to your talk and hearing the rhythms of your speech. He'll opt for classics too, obviously, not because he thinks it'll look good on his application form to university, nor out of any deep love for the subject, but *purely* to gain your good grace, you understand. And don't worry if he goes completely off the rails, sir; you'll know how to set him right again. You never know; he may even get you that next win."

My headmaster sighed appreciatively. "Thank you, X. Backhand cross-court—unplayable. I'd rather like that place, you know. I think I'd be very content there, indeed. Well, farewell then, my boy."

"Farewell, sir."

Mr Bentley's right. When saying goodbye, you don't make a speech; you say what you feel. I just managed to get into the corridor before bursting into tears.

MONDAY 11TH DECEMBER

As I walked into the old school hall this morning, I heard Geoff's rather excited voice. "I knew you'd come back for this; it's just too big for you to miss?"

"What's that?" I asked curiously as I turned to face him.

"It's the big one tonight: Luther Parkinson versus Marketon High," Geoff said theatrically.

"Football?" I asked.

Geoff waved his hand in dismissal. "*No*, a fight, at least 100 on each side, brilliant, eh?"

Really, it isn't.

I sighed in dismay. "Where the *hell* do you think you're going to be able to hold a scrap like that without getting caught?"

Excitedly, Geoff replied, "On the wasteland, next to the railway line, near your place."

Even I have to admit, that's a pretty good spot.

This was the last way I wished to spend this evening. However, I asked, "What time?"

"Five—it'll be pitch black, so bring a torch," Geoff advised.

With a plan forming in my mind, I said decisively, "Right, you and Matt meet me at the end of my street at a quarter to."

"Oh, and X. This you've got to see," Geoff said, leading me to the cupboard behind the stage, where a large sign reading 'Marketon High School' had been carelessly stowed.

In English, Rachael did her best to talk me out of attending the fight. "You're not well enough for this, X; it's you they're after, you know? You're going to get yourself killed."

"Please, Rachael, just trust me for once. This is entirely my fault, and I've got to sort this out," I said.

Fortunately, the argument didn't last long, as I was soon asleep at my desk.

"Wakey, wakey, X." When I opened my eyes, the rest of the class had gone, and only Mr Bentley remained.

"Sorry, sir," I said, rubbing my eyes. "That was incredibly rude."

The English teacher laughed. "Don't worry about it, X, but I think you should head home now."

"Right, I think I might well do that. Oh, Rachael told me about your girlfriend; by the way, sorry to hear that," I said compassionately.

He smiled warmly. "Thank you, X. If you happen to know any good-looking, single, twenty-something females, then please do send them my way."

I had a lightbulb moment. "Actually, sir, now you mention it. Have you got any plans for tomorrow evening?"

I practically fell through the door when I got home. I was flat-out asleep for three hours. When I woke up, I headed over to Karen's, let myself in, and left a note on her table.

> Karen,
>
> Please buy the items below, do not ask unnecessary questions and cancel them if you have plans for tomorrow evening!

Lots of love,

Cupid

At 4.45, I met with Matt, Geoff, JG and Drake. It was a still, bitingly cold evening, and a light mist had descended. I'd assumed that second thoughts would have gotten the better of my friends as the hour of judgement loomed, but, on the contrary, they were all in the best of spirits.

Eagerly, Geoff asked, "Are we ready for this then?"

"I am!" Matt said it hungrily.

I sighed. "It's your old school, Matt; your old friends will be out there, you know?"

Intently, Matt said, "Luther Parkinson rules, Captain."

"And you, JG, are you sure this is your sort of thing?" I asked politely.

Abruptly, he replied, "Don't start, X!"

"Right, sorry… anyway, just waiting for one more," I said, looking up the street.

"Evening, all!" Pete spoke, suddenly stepping out of the gloom and rubbing his hands together. Thankfully, he'd returned to spend an early Christmas with his aunt yesterday. I was determined to bring the evening proceedings to a peaceful end, and, as such, I was employing a tactic I believe is commonly known as brinksmanship.

Geoff looked terrified at the sight of him. "Jesus Christ, X, I hope he's on our side."

"Evening, Pete," I said, shaking his hand. "I think you know everyone except Geoff." The two new acquaintances shook hands.

"OK, before we do this, just one thing: I'm doing the talking,

OK?" The others nodded in acknowledgement, and we made our way onto the wasteland.

Fortunately, Geoff's prediction of a hundred on either side was way off the mark, but there were still enough boys to make the Battle of the Gymnasium look like a minor scuffle. The wasteland is set in a little valley, so even though it is overlooked by housing, there is very little light, so all we could see was a hundred or so flashlight beams shining randomly in the darkness.

The Luther Parkinson boys had gathered on our near side. They shone their torches at us as we approached and shouted, "Friend or foe?"

"Temporarily blinded friends," I said, shielding my eyes.

Pete's presence sparked murmurs of excitement throughout the group. Rich Wilson, all-round nice guy, stepped forward and said, "Hey, School Spirit, are you OK?"

"Yes, fine, Rich," I said as I shook his hand. I noticed it was shaking violently.

"Right, what happens next, X? Do we just run over there and kick their heads in?" Geoff asked brightly.

Firmly, I said, "*No*, we call their leaders over for a talk first; that's how they do it in the movies, and that's how we'll do it too."

The six of us who'd arrived together walked further onto the wasteland, and Matt yelled, "Hey! Who's in charge over there?"

Eventually, a group of five came towards us. Rob was in the centre, flanked by the big guy who had given me the shiner in the gym and by another boy sporting a rather impressive Cochran, who looked familiar, though I couldn't put a name to his face. The other two individuals were strangers.

"Well, well, well, X, I'm surprised to see you here; I heard you were dying," Rob said mockingly.

"I'm in recovery," I replied with a smile.

Rob caught sight of Pete and frowned. "It's not exactly in the spirit of the arrangement bringing him along, X."

I stared back at him intently. "*This* is a school fight, Rob; I didn't realise there were rules. Next, you'll be saying that we shouldn't have brought weapons." I saw a flash of fear on his face and rolled my eyes. "Oh, for god's sake, *that* was a joke. I won't last long tonight, so I need someone to replace me. Pete was the best stand-in I could think of—ex-Luther Parkinson, too, so it made perfect sense. Anyway, that's the plan *if* this goes off."

"If?" Geoff asked, turning towards me.

"Shut up, Geoff; I'm talking, remember?" I snapped back.

Humbly, he said, "Sorry, School Spirit,"

"What do you mean, 'if'?" Rob asked with measured interest.

Looking around, I said, "Right, listen, before anyone does anything rash here, I've got something to say."

"Oh, yeah, what's that?" Rob enquired.

"I'm sorry, Rob, for winding you up about Rachael. You were right; I didn't have the guts to ask her out myself. You, though, had no right to tell me to stay away from her. So, if you're brave enough to apologise, we can shake hands and call the whole thing off. I reckon it's pretty stupid to get all these people hurt over our little feud," I said reasonably.

The Marketon High boys started exchanging glances, and Rob even looked surprised. "Not what I was expecting, I must say, X. What if I disagree?"

"Then throw the first punch, Rob. Please go on; take your best shot; it's what you want. I'll be honest; I'm struggling to keep standing up as it is. But, as it's my fault Luther Parkinson is here tonight, I've got to look after my boys. As I've already said, my preferred option is that we all walk safely home in opposite directions, but the backup plan is to win the fight. Your choice, though."

"And just so you know, the first one who touches a hair on his head gets his head ripped from his body," Pete snarled like some beast of the wild.

I have learned that playing your weapon of mass destruction is not the brightest of ideas. Threatening to use it, though, can pay rich dividends.

Rather hastily, Rob said, "Actually, X, we'll go with your first plan. Sorry for telling you to stay away from Rachael."

I held out my hand to him, but Rob hesitated. "Just one condition, X: some of your lot nicked the Marketon High sign from the front of our school, and we'd like it back."

Trying not to grin, I said, "I can certainly investigate its whereabouts."

"And if I ask Rachael out again?" Rob asked.

"Then the very best of luck to you!" I lied.

Rob took my hand, and we shook. "See you around, X."

"Yeah, no doubt," I replied.

The Marketon High students headed towards the old railway line, and we turned back the way we'd come.

When Geoff caught up to me, he put his arm around me and said, "You know, if it's inter-school cooperation you're after, School Spirit, then just say the word, Matt and I can do that; can't we? We honestly just thought you'd prefer a big fight."

"I appreciate the thought, Geoff; I really do," I replied sincerely.

From my other side, Matt asked, "Are we calling that one a draw then, Captain?"

"Are we hell?" I scoffed. "*We* were the bigger men back there, and that, my good friend, was Luther Parkinson's first moral victory."

Matt smiled. "Right, nice one," he replied.

Luther Parkinson 3: Marketon High 1

As we reached the wasteland's end and got back under a streetlight, we saw Flan, Helen Heaven, Lisa the Repeater, Penny Chemistry, and Rachael1989 waiting for us.

"Oh, look, it's the reserves," Geoff sneered.

Flan waved a bag petulantly. "We brought first aid. I'll have you know, you ungrateful sod."

Lisa looked between us and asked, "What happened anyway? None of you look hurt. Did they chicken out?"

Patting me on the shoulder, Matt said, "X landed us a moral victory. Not one punch was thrown."

"Right result all around. I detest violence in all its forms," Geoff said, and everyone looked at him in something approaching bemusement.

"We should celebrate," JG suggested, and there was a buzz of agreement from the others.

I clapped my hands. "You guys go ahead; I'm finished for the evening."

Pete, Flan, and Rachael all kindly offered to walk me home, but I waved their offers away. "Thanks, but I'm five minutes from my door; I'm sure I'll manage," I said politely.

As I strolled back along the street to my house, I saw a boy, walking a dog, approaching; it was young Benzies. Sixteen is too old to cuff children from the lower year groups, so I blocked his way instead.

Gravely, I said, "I heard that you told the whole school I was dead, young Benzies?"

The boy eyed me and sighed. "Sorry about that, X; I got carried away with myself, didn't I? Still, it made me the most popular boy in school for the day. I suppose you wouldn't understand something like that."

I nodded. "Actually, I'd understand it very well."

"You're not angry then?" he asked, and I shook my head. "The problem is, I've got to think of something else now. You see, I want to be school spirit one day."

"Maybe call by one day after school. Perhaps I could give you, you know, some pointers?"

Young Benzies smiled. "I'd like that," he said, then looked down at his pet. "Hey, X, you don't want to buy this dog off me, do you?"

I just shook my head, laughed, and walked on. As I got to the front gate, I heard footsteps behind me. It was Helen Heaven. "Hey, X, well done back there, by the way."

"Thanks," I said appreciatively.

"Listen, Dean and me, it's over, so I was wondering… " she started.

I smiled ruefully. "Hey, Helen, listen. You're a beautiful girl, you really are, but I'm in love with someone, and I'm just trying to build up the courage to tell her. It's not that I'm not utterly flattered,"

Helen smiled wryly. "It's Rachael, isn't it?" I nodded, "Well, I can't say I'm surprised. Still, tell her sooner rather than later; X, she's a pretty girl."

"Thanks, I intend to," I said, "Goodnight, Helen."

TUESDAY 12TH DECEMBER

At lunch, Rachael took the seat opposite me. She didn't touch her food but nervously tapped her fingers on the table.

"Why did Helen run after you last night?" she asked.

"She wanted to chat," I replied coyly.

Casually, Rachael said, "Oh yeah, Rob rang last night; he wanted to know if I'd go out with him again."

I nodded. "Oh yeah, Helen asked me out, as it happens. She's single now, you know?"

Rachael sighed deeply. "I turned him down and told him there was someone else."

My face turned serious. "*Oh*, I said yes to Helen." I allowed her face to drop before I started laughing.

"You are such a *twat*, X," she said with real venom, but eventually, a grin crossed her face.

"With the language of love spoken so poetically, it's tough to understand what's keeping you two apart." We looked up and saw Ms James standing, peering curiously down at us with her arms folded.

"Sorry for swearing, Ms James," Rachael said apologetically.

"Good god, girl, *don't* apologise. I've lost count of the times I've wanted to say that phrase to him. Professional ethics forbid, unfortunately," Ms James said, and I smiled wryly at her. "Well?" She said, looking at me expectantly. "I'm answering the note you slipped under my door."

"Oh yes, sorry, could I have a word in private?" I asked.

"Head's office, five minutes?" Ms James suggested.

"Oh, can I bring Rachael too?" I asked.

Ms James shrugged. "I suppose so, if you must."

"Ms James, have you ever watched Dr Who?" I asked after Rachael, and I sat in the head's office.

She looked somewhat unimpressed by my enquiry. "I'm not going to enjoy this conversation, am I, X?"

"It's a serious question, Ms," I said.

Ms James looked incredulously at Rachael and indicated towards me with a nod. "Is this part of his condition?"

"It does get better; trust me, Ms James," Rachael said convincingly.

Ms James turned her gaze towards me. "Yes, X, as a child, I used to watch *that* television program; why?"

"Well, in his present form, I feel it's time for school spirit to die," I said.

"Oh, that's one trigger I'm more than happy to pull, X," Ms James said enthusiastically.

"However, I still believe school spirit could be an immensely positive force within Luther Parkinson," I said passionately.

"Or, X, you could occasionally think before you act and do the job yourself," Ms James suggested.

"True, Ms, very true, and rest assured, I intend to conduct my work this week unimpeachably. However, another project is coming my way—undoubtedly the most important undertaking of my life. I sincerely doubt I'll have energy for both, and if it comes down to a choice between the school and... the other thing, the other wins hands down." Beside me, I noticed Rachael's face reddening. "As such, Ms, school spirit *must* die. Besides, the trophy you gave me clearly stated 'School Spirit:1989'. Who am I to argue with a school ruling? Also, as I know you like solutions rather than problems, I have already selected my replacement, but I suggest we surprise them on the big day."

As Rachael and I left, Ms James said, "Now, you look dreadful, X; take yourself home, please."

"What if I don't like him, X?" Karen asked in concern as I put the finishing touches on the prawn cocktail.

"I have the strangest feeling you will," I said.

When Chris Bentley and Karen saw each other, I felt the sexual sparks start to fly. I excused myself immediately and left them to *it*.

THURSDAY 14TH DECEMBER

Yesterday did not begin well. The final football match of the term had been a 4-3 thriller that Luther Parkinson had edged thanks to a glorious last-minute Geoff Travis strike. Unfortunately, Drake had gotten so carried away yelling in support on the sidelines that he'd lost his voice.

"I'm so sorry, X," he croaked when I went around to call for him first thing.

I reassured him. "Don't worry; we'll get the school nurse on the case."

The school nurse was at Marketon High, so I left a message saying that there was an urgent medical requirement at Luther Parkinson.

"This is *not* a medical emergency, young man," the school nurse said disapprovingly after I explained Drake's situation.

My eyes widened in disbelief. "Yes, it is. H*e's* our Benedick, and he's due on stage in seven hours; what *exactly* would you consider a bigger emergency?"

The school nurse pointed at me and scowled. "Listen, X, I do an important job; I can't be pulled hither-thither on the whim of one student."

"Please, School Nurse, if you still hold a grudge because of that simple misunderstanding in Eating Disorder Club... " I started.

"What's Eating Disorder Club?" Drake croaked, causing the school nurse to glare at me accusingly.

Pointing at him, I said threateningly, "You didn't hear those three words, OK?" and Drake shrugged in acknowledgement.

I asked the school nurse, "*Please*, help us; what can we do?"

She sighed. "X, the boy has lost his voice; there's no cure other than rest, I'm afraid."

Ms James then walked into the sick room, looking edgy. "Well, what's the verdict?"

The school nurse turned to her. "Headmistress, I was just saying to X that this *does not* qualify as urgent."

Ms James stared back at her in disbelief. "Yes, it does. He's our Benedick, and he's due on stage in seven hours; what *exactly* would you consider a bigger emergency?"

"I am sorry, but this boy is not going to be in that performance tonight," she said calmly.

Ms James sighed. "Right, you two, back to classes. We must fix this somehow; meet me in the drama studio at lunch. We've got 300 people coming to this school tonight, and they're expecting drama!"

"What happened to the understudy?" Ms James asked at the lunchtime meeting.

Mrs Gates cast me an accusatory stare. "He quit in protest weeks ago because he said he was a far better Benedick than Timothy was."

Ms James shrugged. "Well, can't someone just read the part?"

"Goodness gracious, *never; this* is a *performance*, not a reading!" Mrs Gates exclaimed rather dramatically, and I had to laugh when I saw the look of horror Ms James gave her in response.

Rachael was pacing behind me, making a rather tragic whimpering noise. If the show didn't go on, it would break her heart, and, unfortunately for all involved, there was only one course of action available. Quietly, I said, "I'll do it."

"Splendid!" Mrs Gates said, turning to me.

Ms James frowned. "X, you can't be serious?"

"I know it!" I said it assertively.

"X, you know some of it, not all of it," Rachael said from behind me.

"OK, I'm not exactly word for word, but I've read the bloody thing at least 50 times in the last two months, and that's the best we're going to get at such short notice," I said intently.

Ms James looked at me, concerned. "X, you shouldn't even be at school; you can barely stand, for god's sake."

"You're right. I need someone to keep me upright. I need cans of Coke—lots of them. We'll need the lines placed strategically, but most of all, I need my school spirits. Following *pro-to-col*, Ms James, may I take them from lessons this afternoon?" I asked.

Ms James looked far from convinced. "Yes. I suppose, but, X, I'm not sure we're going to pull this one off."

"Well, you did say we had 300 people arriving tonight expecting drama, Ms Really, I think that *is* my field of expertise."

After much discussion, we school spirits decided to place Penny in the centre of the stage in a large box with a hole in the top so she could hold up Benedick's lines as required.

Thankfully, Stuart Moor, school thug, was eventually located playing hooky near the local shops when Flan went to buy me some aspirin.

"Sorry, School Spirit, I didn't get the message. Shakespeare's isn't my thing, however. I'm not sure I can help," he said humbly.

I looked him up and down. "Black trousers, check! Do you have a black jumper?" The school thug nodded in the affirmative. Gloves?"

"Yes," he replied.

"And one last thing, would you, perchance, have one of those black woollen masks that the SAS wear?" I inquired.

"I do, X," he answered proudly.

Really, I just knew he was going to answer 'yes' to that one.

"So, what's my job, then?" Stuart asked with a tinge of excitement.

"You, School Spirit 13, are going to be my shadow," I said, giving him an affectionate pat on the arm.

With ten minutes till curtain up, Flan said, "Oh here, take these, by the way." She took some pills from her pocket and handed them to me.

"And the *other* thing I asked you to bring?" I asked expectantly.

Flan shook her head dismissively. "X, you shouldn't be drinking in your condition. Besides, I hardly think it will help you remember your lines."

"Flan, I'm terrified. I've only been in one production, the Christmas play, at primary school. My only line was, 'Merry Christmas, everyone', and I managed to fluff it. It is what my former psychiatrist would call a mental scar," I said confidentially.

"Well, in that case," Flan withdrew a small bottle of vodka from her bag, "bottom's up!"

I grabbed the drink and took a big swig.

"Better?" Helen enquired eagerly.

"Not yet," I said taking large gulp.

"Are we all ready?" Rachael said, coming up behind us. "Oh, what's that?" she said, looking at the bottle curiously.

In a whisper, I said, "Vodka."

"Oh, give it here; I'm having kittens," Rachael said, taking the spirit from me.

After her third swig, I said, "Right, that's enough, *you*. I've seen you drunk, and you're smutty."

"I just wanted to say the best of luck to you all," Ms James said, surprising us from behind; Rachael could not hide the bottle in time. "Oh, what's that?" the acting headmistress asked curiously.

Rachael turned scarlet. "It's vodka, Ms," she said meekly.

"Oh, I like what you're thinking, girl. Let me have a quick mouthful. I bloody hate public speaking," Ms James said, and we all looked on in astonishment as she took a lengthy swig.

"Right!" she said, handing the bottle back to Rachael. "Break a leg all," Ms James then turned to me and looked me up and down, "Oh, and X, love the tights!" With that, she headed off to make her introductory speech.

"Well!" Fran said firmly. "If she can drink, I can ruddy well drink too," she said, snatching the bottle back from Rachael.

I did manage to remember the first few lines; however, it wasn't long before I needed to read the cards Penny was holding up. Besides, it wasn't just me who was letting the side down. Firstly, Hero's skirt was far too long, and she tripped and fell several times, meaning improvised lines such as, "Oh, you poor thing, you're so upset that you've *thrown* yourself to the floor" started being improvised. Secondly, something about Don John's costume must have disagreed with him, as he couldn't stop sneezing, which made him, in my humble opinion, appear less like a bastard and rather more like a twat. Thirdly, Leonarto said, *"Fuck!"* at least three times when he forgot his lines.

Stuart Moor was a rock, though. He lifted me, sat me down, and handed me numerous cans of Coke to keep my energy levels up.

The one standout in the cast was Rachael; she nailed every line, was often able to prompt her fellow cast members, and carried the show spectacularly. Her only deviation from the text of the entire evening happened just after I'd delivered the lines, "A miracle! Here's our own hands against our hearts. Come, I will have thee, but by this light, I take thee for pity," Rachael just looked at me and started giggling.

"What's the matter?" I whispered in concern.

"Nothing," she said. "I've just had such a good time tonight, and I want to thank you for doing this, X."

The crowd seemed to like it, as they gave their first genuine applause of the evening.

"Thanks, Rachael, but 300 people are watching us, and we've put them through a lot tonight. Let's finish the play and let them go home." This comment received an even larger round of applause.

"Ok!" Rachael said it sweetly.

The audience was more than generous with their ovations after the show. Deservedly, the loudest cheer was saved for Stuart Moor, who stepped forward to receive his applause, still wearing his ski mask. Just as Rachael and I stepped forward, the world started spinning, and I passed out with no time to signal for Stuart.

I woke up in the hospital this morning attached to a drip —another 1989 first. Mum was sitting by my bedside when I awoke, looking puzzled at me. "You never mentioned you were in a play, love."

"Last-minute thing," I replied with a shrug.

She took a deep breath. "And how are you feeling?"

"OK," I said.

Rising from her chair, she said, "Right, well, I better be off to work then."

"OK."

"Your dad and I will be along later if he can get off work on time. They want to keep you in for another day."

"OK."

Mum gave me a little wave. "Bye then."

"Bye," I replied.

I'm not sure what you think, but I'd chalk that up as the most tender moment between us all year.

When she was out of sight, I started plotting my exit. It wasn't difficult; I soon had the needle out of my arm and my clothes stashed under my bed gown. I changed in the toilets and walked casually out of the building. Fortunately, the three pounds in change I had just covered the cab ride home.

Well, it's not like you can be a no-show at your regeneration.

After I got home, I went to bed. Mum woke me up when she got in from work. "The hospital rang to say you'd escaped," she said with a sigh.

FRIDAY 15TH DECEMBER

Mr Crackett looked genuinely upset when I walked into form group this morning. "Bollocks, I thought you were genuinely dead this time."

"Not yet, sir," I replied with a smile.

Sitting beside Lisa, I said, "One more for the talent contest this afternoon."

"Not a chance, X; I've spent weeks on this. I've picked 10 acts worth watching, and the whole afternoon has been timed to perfection," Lisa said resolutely.

Firmly, I said, "Tough, your school spirit commands you; add one more to the list."

"Oh yeah, who's the great discovery?"

"Me!" I replied brightly.

Pulling a notepad from her bag, she asked, "And what's the act, X?"

I sighed disappointedly. "Well, I thought you wouldn't need to ask. Isn't it obvious I'm going to sing a Frank Sinatra song? My music," I said, taking a cassette from my pocket and putting it in front of her.

When I got into English, Mr Bentley hugged me. "You, X, are a beautiful man, " he said before releasing me.

As I sat beside Rachael, she sighed and said, "And what was

that for?"

"I set him up with Karen; I think it's safe to say things are going well," I replied.

Whispering, Rachael asked, "Does he know she's half-mad?"

I smirked. "Not yet, but I'm sure he'll have fun finding out."

"Anyway, that was a nice thing to do, X," Rachael said, sounding impressed.

"What can I say? My work is almost done; I just have to get myself the right girl now," I said, taking my pad of Post-it notes from my rucksack.

"Any ideas?" Rachael asked coyly.

"Just the one," I replied as I wrote. I slapped the note before her; it read, "YOU!"

"Good afternoon, Luther Parkinson. As your acting headmistress, I welcome you to the inaugural Christmas Talent Show. Your host for the afternoon shouldn't be here. However, as he seems determined to die on the school grounds before the term finishes, he is. Please show your appreciation for someone who, after this week, even I'm happy to introduce to you as School Spirit."

Lisa had done her work well, with ten surprisingly good acts. The highlights were Fatty Jacobs' quite stunning solo on his tuba and Clare Anatomy's rendition of 'Like a Virgin', her performance so erotic that it caused Mr Crackett to fall off his chair midway through.

As the second-to-last act finished, I turned to Rachael, who stood beside me in the wings, and said, "Wish me luck?"

"Good luck! Want me to introduce you?" she asked with a smile.

"Would you?"

Rachael bounced up the stairs and walked to the microphone. "Thank you, Jenny; that was truly wonderful! Who knew a Wet Wet Wet song could be sung so hauntingly? Well, it's been left to me to introduce the final act. What can I say about this boy? Quite a lot, actually; he's made me laugh a lot this year and made me cry an almost equal number of times, too. Now that I think of it, he's also broken my heart on at least two occasions. Regardless, we'd all agree that Luther Parkinson wouldn't be the same without him. Headmistress, teachers, and fellow students, please welcome X back to the stage."

I smiled at Rachael as we passed and walked up to the microphone. "Luther Parkinson, I'm all out of speeches; I just want to say that it has been my absolute pleasure," and the music started.

Now, I'm far too much of a Frank Sinatra fan to massacre 'My Way' with my tone-deaf singing, and the track playing was the Sid Vicious version. Really, there was nothing to it, just a lot of shouting, snarling, and swearing into the microphone. I may have gotten ever so slightly carried away with myself, possibly taking my shirt off and perhaps even throwing it into the crowd, but, as Mr Bentley advised, when it comes to saying goodbye, you don't make a speech; you say what you feel. The audience seemed to enjoy it and merrily pogoed along in time with the music. I may have even seen Jimmy Crackett tapping his foot to the beat towards the back of the hall.

As per our arrangement, when the song stopped playing, Ms James took to the stage, and I slumped to the floor. Rachael then kindly came and helped me get behind the curtain.

"Luther Parkinson, it is clear that our present school spirit has *had it*," Ms James said flatly, and there were groans and jeers from the hall. "No, it's true; I'm afraid *he's kaput* and simply will not suffice anymore. However, where one falls, another will rise."

There was a buzz of excitement from the audience.

"Boys and girls, the first school spirit of 1990 is... *Helen Flannigan*," Ms James announced.

The applause was rapturous.

Really, people can be so fickle.

I was lying with my head in Rachael's lap, who was looking me up and down. "You'll miss all this," she said thoughtfully.

"I'll have other distractions."

Rachael smiled. "I like your body!"

"I like yours too—we should get them together."

Rachael ran her hands through the Cochran. "As soon as I'm back from holiday," she said.

Holiday?

Apologetically, Rachael said, "I did tell you, though I suppose you were a bit out of it at the time."

Rachael's going tonight and won't be back till the start of next term. Typical: just as things seem to be sliding into place, something happens. Something always *bloody* happens!

While we were talking, Helen named Clare as the talent show winner.

Rachael looked at me, concerned. "You're cross, aren't you?"

I sighed. "I'm not cross; I'm just disappointed. 1989 wasn't supposed to end like this."

NEW YEAR'S EVE

The 28th brought the saddest news: Dr Wilberforce H. Harris JP has passed. Kindly, Ms James came over to tell me in person. "If it's any comfort, X, apparently he died quite peacefully."

Me? I like to think he went out shouting at someone.

Flan and I will be representing the school at the funeral, and I have been asked to make a short speech, but I will not. Instead, I will say the first things that come into my head, as it seems much more appropriate. Perhaps I will tell an anecdote or two, maybe of the time in year two when he felt so guilty for keeping me out of physics for the entire lesson, discussing the Borg/McEnroe final of '81, that he took it upon himself to teach me Newton's laws of motion and accidentally caned himself in the process. Or, of the time, he, unfortunately, awarded the Academic Achievement prize to the wrong student and, upon realising his error, made her apologise to the whole assembly for taking something that didn't belong to her.

Dr Harris was an eccentric, a madman, but in the best of ways, and I shall never forget him. Everybody needs their school spirit; he was mine, just as I was his.

So, that's 1989 done. There's a party at Flan's this evening, but I can't imagine anything exciting happening.

Here's to 1990!

THE END

THE LAST BIT-NEW YEAR'S DAY

OK, OK, OK—I was a little premature there...

By the time I got to Flan's, I was already two hours late due to a detour via Karen's to see her and Chris and a chance encounter with Ms James, who was leaving the off license in The Village as I passed.

When she saw me, Catherine rolled her eyes. "Oh, *bloody typical; if* I was going to bump into a pupil whilst carrying a bag full of booze, it just had to be you, didn't it?"

I laughed. "That's not all for you, is it, Ms?"

Catherine sighed. "No, X, my old friend, Steve, is over for the night. You and he would get along rather well; you both operate an 'If it has a pulse, nail it' philosophy on life. Fortunately, he is homosexual, and our friendship has prospered.

I smiled ruefully. "You really don't have a very high opinion of me."

Ms James looked at me. "Are we off the record, X?"

"Absolutely."

"I'm *exceptionally* fond of you, X," she said with a smile.

I was so stunned that I didn't know what to say, so I threw my arms around her.

Catherine put her free arm around me and said, "Just for the record, X, please understand that my fondness is *entirely* different from Mrs Simpson's affection for you."

I smiled. "I know, Catherine; I think that's the best thing about it."

"I thought *you* weren't coming," Helen said irritably when she answered the door.

"Sorry, I was waylaid," I replied.

Flan sighed. "They'll put that on your gravestone, X. Anyway, your timing couldn't be worse as it happens."

Bemused, I asked, "Why?"

"Oh, it doesn't matter. Come in!"

This being officially the first party I have ever been invited to, I had a good time when, at about 11.30, the doorbell went, and Flan went to see who it was. When she returned, she looked at me intently and said formally, "X, can I see you in private, please?"

"Where are we going, Flan?" I asked, following her down the long corridor.

"My bedroom!" she replied abruptly.

"Listen, Fran, I'm flattered; I truly am. And pleasing as it is that you no longer view me as a 1000-piece jigsaw, it's… " I began as we ascended the staircase.

Fran had stopped outside her bedroom door. "Oh, get over yourself, you imbecile," she said with a sigh.

I was starting to feel suspicious. "What's going on then?"

Folding her arms, she said, "X, I've just got four words for you."

"And they are?" I inquired.

A broad grin crossed Fran's face. "Go get her, Romeo!"

And with that, she opened the door, thrust me inside and

slammed it firmly shut behind me. There was a shriek of horror, and someone leapt off the bed in alarm, "Rachael!"

"X!"

"When did you get back?" I asked in wonder.

"This morning, I finally put my foot down yesterday, and told Alison that 1989 wasn't meant to end in Dorset. I'd been here for two hours, and when you didn't show up, I got worried, so I went to your house. Your Mum said you might be with the nice lady whose house you painted. So, I went to Karen's, and Mr Bentley dragged me in for drinks. They are *really* drunk, by the way. How are you?"

I smiled. "So much better now that you're here."

"I'm sorry about Dr Harris, X," Rachael said condolingly, and I gave a sad little nod. "I think he was very fond of you."

"I think he liked his new girl too."

After a few moments of reflection, I noticed that Rachael was swaying ever so slightly. "So here we are then," she said dreamily.

I took a deep breath. "Here we are."

"Oh, here you go, by the way. The last one... hopefully." She withdrew a cassette from her pocket.

I took it from her. "What's this?" I asked curiously.

"Didn't you get the others?" she asked a little cautiously, but then, on spying the look of ignorance on my face, she sighed. "Oh, *please, God*, tell me you didn't just figure that one out."

I grimaced and shook my head guiltily.

"Jesus, X, you're such a loser with girls!"

"So, I'm reliably informed," I replied with a smile.

Rachael looked at me curiously. "Go on, then. Tell me, why are you called X?"

I sighed. "Oh, come off it; I've told you, it's... "

"*Really* underwhelming, I remember. If you tell me, though, you *can* have my body tonight," she said teasingly.

I clapped my hands together in delight. "*Right,* OK then." I said it brightly. "It was about four years ago. I had a crystal-clear complexion—not one single spot ever. I wake up one morning and have a monster the size of Mount Etna on my chin. So, knowing I was going to get the piss taken out of me at school about it anyway, I got a big fat marker pen and drew an 'X' over the top of it. The name stuck from there."

Rachael looked entirely unamused.

"Don't you get it?" I asked expectantly. "X marks the spot?"

Rachael rolled her eyes. "That is *really* underwhelming, X," she said flatly.

"It did the trick, though," I said, smiling at the memory. "I didn't get another spot. It could have been a miracle; now I think of it."

Rachael sighed. "*Really*, it couldn't. Put the tape on, X, before you irritate me again."

Obediently, I went over to Flan's Hi-Fi, put the cassette in the deck, and pressed play.

A lilting rhythm, the strum of an acoustic guitar.

We stared at one another in silence for what seemed like an age. Finally, I asked, "What are we listening to?"

"My favourite song, now, hit me with it, X."

A female voice I recognise, singing in French.

Unsure of what she was expecting, I moved to take hold of

her, but Rachael held up her hand to stop me. "Not so fast, Mr; I think I deserve a bit of wooing first."

Then, with the girl of my dreams standing before me and a night of unbelievable pleasure within easy reach, I, utterly predictably, said something foolish. "Rach, I'm a man without conviction. I'm a man who doesn't know... how to sell a contradiction."

X, what the fuck?

Rachael asked me curiously, "Was that Culture Club, X?"

I grimaced slightly. "Yes... *and no*," I replied after a moment's thought.

Rachael folded her arms. "It *was* Culture Club, and so the truthful answer is, in fact, *yes*, X."

I smiled. "Maybe, but I think I did very much put my spin on it."

Rachael did not look amused. "Listen, X," she said with a deep sigh. "I can't do this *again; I* just *can't* keep building myself up to these big moments with you, only for *you* to f... "

Don't make a speech, X; say what you feel. That way, you won't chalk up any more regrets.

"I love you, Rachael. I am madly in love with you." The words practically exploded from my mouth.

Rachael looked almost dumbfounded. "Good lord!" she said eventually before suspiciously asking, "When exactly did you fall in love with me?"

"The day at the lake," I replied honestly.

Rachael seemed impressed. "I've been in love with you for longer than that. That's not a problem, though; it was obvious on the day we met that *I* was quicker on the uptake than you. However, the lake is good. Why that day?"

It's a pretty tune; however, I wish I'd paid more attention in French classes.

"You were wearing a bikini," I said, and as soon as I saw her face sour, I smiled.

"You're *not* funny, X!"

Truthfully, I said, "It was when I woke up and found you asleep on me. That exact moment,"

Rachael nodded. "Excellent! I deserve more, though."

I took a deep breath. "OK, well, I now know you liked me right from the start, and when I didn't react, I wasn't being ignorant; it was just a confidence thing. I didn't exactly grow up in the house of love; whether you want it to or not, that affects you. So, I always figured that if I were going to become adorable, I'd need to change and become someone else, and that's what I've been doing all year. As a result, I almost missed out on the most beautiful, the funniest, the kindest, and, it must be said, the most wonderfully weird girl I could have ever dreamt of."

X makes an unplayable cross-court backhand to New Girl; that's my boy.

"You *almost* missed out, but not quite. Thank you, X; that was, particularly *for you*, a rather delightful thing to say. I am now yours for the taking," Rachael said, smiling.

She's singing in English now. "Well, he takes me in his arms and whispers love to me."

"OK, just before we kiss, I should warn you that glandular fever is transmitted through saliva," I said as I moved my mouth closer to hers.

Rachael sighed. "Really, X, who gives a shit?"

And then, with the last seconds of 1989 drifting away, I kissed her, and months of pent-up passion exploded. Before we knew it, we were both half-undressed. "We can't do this here," Rachael said breathlessly. "Take me home, X."

Flan, it turns out, had locked us in, and it took five minutes of banging on the door before she came to let us out. Time passed with passionate kissing. Looking at the pair of our flushed faces, School Spirit threw her arms around us and yelled, "Congratulations!"

We said our goodbyes to the others and took the short walk back to Rachael's. On the way there, I started to get nervous. Thankfully, back at hers, in the kitchen, my girlfriend turned to me and said, "Listen, I'm feeling a little scared all of a sudden. Would you like a glass of wine, X?"

Alison sneakily popped around the door as we sat drinking and talking. She was more than a little drunk. "Sorry, we're over the neighbours, and I saw you come back, and I was just wondering if... ?" she said in an appropriation of a whisper.

Rachael jumped up, shouted, "*Yes!*" and ran over and hugged her mother.

"Oh, that's wonderful. Come here, you!" Alison said, pointing to me.

After finishing the three-way hug, Alison said confidentially, "Rachael, I'd better get back, but do remember, those things I bought you are in your desk drawer."

Rachael immediately turned a rather alarming shade of scarlet. However, Alison laughed. "Really, X, *she* calls herself a modern woman, and yet *she's* scared to walk into a chemist and ask for some condoms," Alison said mockingly.

Rachael started pushing her mother out of the door.

"By the way, I chose the ribbed variety. Apparently, it'll be more stimulating for both of... " Alison didn't get a chance to finish her sentence as the door slammed shut on her.

After that, we went to bed. We stayed up all night, talking

a lot and getting to know one another even more. Suffice it to say, I discovered a fourth kind of miracle.

We got up early and came over here so I could get a change of clothes and a toothbrush.

Really, I'd tell you more about last night, but she's sitting on my bed next to me. I bet her £10 that she couldn't complete the Rubik's cube by the time I'd finished writing. Oh god, now she's trying to grab the keyboard from me.

R- WHAT DID YOU SAY ABOUT LAST NIGHT?

X- I SAID *IT* WAS SATISFACTORY.

R- YOU'RE *NOT* FUNNY! COME ON, LET'S GO BACK TO MINE; MUM AND ARTHUR ARE OUT, AND I WANT TO DO IT AGAIN!

X- YOU'VE GOT ISSUES; DO YOU KNOW THAT?

R- HAVE YOU GOT ANY YOU-KNOW-WHATS? I THINK WE USED ALL THE OTHERS.

X- YES, NOT THE RIBBED VARIETY THOUGH

R- AMATUER!

X- BETTER SAY SOMETHING TO FINISH.

R- SAY YOU'VE FOUND THE PERFECT GIRL! BY THE WAY, I DON'T OWE YOU A TENNER, DO I, X?

X- ABSOLUTELY, YOU FAILED!

R- WHAT CAN I DO TO GET OUT OF IT?

X- LIKE A PRAYER ME?

R- DREAM ON!

X- I'M SORRY, BUT WRITING AN IOU IS NOT ACCEPTABLE IN THIS CIRCUMSTANCE, RACHAEL.

R- SO, WHAT HAVE YOU DECIDED TO CALL IT?

X- I WAS THINKING OF NAMING IT *A TEENAGE ODYSSEY*.

R- YOU HAVEN'T BEEN ANYWHERE!

X- I *DID* GO TO WALES.

R- YES, BUT I HEAR IT'S A HORRIBLE PLACE. IT RAINS CONSTANTLY, AND THE PEOPLE SPIT AT ONE ANOTHER WHEN THEY TALK.

X- WHAT DO YOU THINK I SHOULD CALL IT, THEN?

R- HOW ABOUT *THE NEW GIRL*?

X- OR *SCHOOL SPIRIT '89*?

R- IT HAD TO BE ABOUT YOU.

X- WHAT DO YOU MEAN?

R- CALL IT WHAT YOU WANT. COME ON, LOVER. I'M BORED OF THIS NOW. LET'S GET BUSY!

The eighties are dead. A brave new decade has started as brightly as I could have hoped; I'm in love, and for the first time in my life, I'm 100% certain about something. I want to say something profound, to share with you the wisdom I have gained in this most eventful of years, but a beautiful girl is tugging impatiently on my arm, and desperately wants to have sex with me again. So, instead, I'll leave you with just one final thought…

Life without hair wax is not *really* living!

THE END, REALLY?

X, RACHAEL AND THE REST OF LUTHER PARKINSON WILL RETURN IN...

TAKE ON ME

Thanks for giving your time to this book. If you've enjoyed *Lessons in Love:1989*, kindly submit a review on Amazon.

Printed in Great Britain
by Amazon